Wooden Crosses

Roland Dorgeles

Must Have Books
503 Deerfield Place
Victoria, BC
V9B 6G5
Canada

ISBN 9781774640494

Copyright 2023 – Must Have Books

CONTENTS

CHAPTER I
BROTHERS IN ARMS

ALTHOUGH flowers were already scarce at this season of the year, none the less there had been found enough to bedeck all the rifles in the company, and, as rich in blossoms as a cemetery, the battalion, drums and fifes at its head, had poured helter-skelter across the town between two mute hedgerows of wide-eyed onlookers.

With songs and tears and laughing and drunkards' quarrellings and heart-rending good-byes they had gone on board their train. All night they had rolled along, had eaten their sardines and emptied their water-bottles by the wretched glimmer of a single candle; then, tired of their loud talk, they had gone to sleep, heaped up one against another, heads on shoulders, their legs intermingled with one another.

Dawn had awakened them. Hanging out their carriage doors, they scanned the villages, from which the early morning smoke was rising, for traces of the recent fighting. Man hailed man from carriage to carriage.

"Talk about a war; not as much as a spire smashed up!"

Then the houses opened their eyes, the roadways came to life, and finding voice once more to shout facetious love-makings, they flung their withered flowers at the women who were on the platform at every station, waiting the unlikely return of their vanished sailormen. At every halt they eased themselves and filled the water-bottles. And at length, about ten o'clock, they detrained at Dormans, stupefied and bruised.

A pause of an hour for soup, and they went off by the road--no drums and fifes, no flowers, no waving handkerchiefs--and reached the village where our regiment was resting, close up behind the lines.

There it was just like a great fair; their weary flock was broken up into little groups--one to a company--and the quartermasters rapidly marked off for each a section or squad, which they must hunt up from farm to farm, like shelterless tramps, reading on every door the big white numbers marked in chalk.

Bréval, the corporal, who was coming out from the grocer's shop, found the three that were for us as they were dragging along in the street, crushed under their overladen packs, in which brand-new camp utensils shone with an insolent brilliancy.

"Third company, fifth squad? I'm the corporal. Come on; we're billeted down at the end of the dear old town."

When they came into the courtyard it was Fouillard, the cook, who gave the warning.

"I say, lads, there's the new chums coming."

And flinging down in front of the blackened ashlar of his rustic fireplace the armful of paper he had just fetched up out of the cellar, he examined the new comrades.

"You've not let yourself be cheated," he said solemnly to Bréval. "They're as fine as new pins."

All of us had got up and were ringing round the three bewildered soldiers with a curious group. They stared at us and we stared at them, without a word spoken. They were arriving from behind, arriving from the towns. Yesterday they had still been walking along real streets seeing women, trains, shops; yesterday they were still living the lives of men. And we took stock of them wonderingly, enviously, as though they had been travellers disembarking from strange legendary lands.

"And so, you lads, they're not bothering themselves too much back there?"

"And dear old Panama," asked Vairon, "what are they up to there?"

They on their side eyed us hard, as though they had fallen among savages. Everything must have astonished them in this first meeting, our baked faces, our widely incongruous get-up; Papa Hamel's imitation otter-skin cap; the filthy, once white neckerchief Fouillard wore knotted about his neck; Vairon's trousers, stiff and shining with grease; the cape Lagny wore, the liaison orderly, who had stitched an astrachan collar on to a zouave's hood; some in a "rag-picker's" round jacket, some in artillery tunics--each and everyone accoutred according to his own fashion; fat Bouffioux, who wore his identification disc in his képi, as Louis XI. wore his medals; a machine gunner with his metal shoulder-pieces and his iron gauntlet that made him look like a man-at-arms from Crécy; little Bélin with his head thrust up to the ears in an old dragoon's cap; and Broucke, "the lad from oop north," who had cut puttees for himself out of green rep curtains.

Sulphart alone had remained aloof out of dignity, perched upon a cask, where he was peeling potatoes with the serious, concentrated air he always assumed to go through the simplest acts of everyday existence. Scratching in his flaming bristle beard, he turned his head with a negligent air, and gazed with affected nonchalance at one of the three newcomers, a quite young fellow with a sullen look, beardless or clean-shaven--impossible to tell which--wearing a fine fancy képi and laden with a broad satchel made of moleskin.

"He's a real dandy lad, with his little cap like a cat's-meat dish!" scoffed Sulphart first of all half to himself.

Then as the other set down his kit, he discovered the satchel. Then he broke out.

"Hi! old boy!" he exclaimed; "did you have your little game-bag made special to order for going up into the trenches? If you had a stray idea that the Boches wouldn't mark you down as much as you wanted, you might perhaps have brought along a little flag and tootled on a trumpet."

The new chum had straightened himself up, annoyed, with a frown making a bar across his obstinate little forehead. But all at once, put out of countenance by the jeering attitude of the old hand, he turned his head away and started to blush. The redhead was quite satisfied with his flattering success for his joke. He descended from his lofty throne, and, just to prove that he had no intention of savaging a comrade who was not responsible, he shifted his strictures higher up to the military powers whose every act and deed, according to him, were dictated by pure foolishness and a manifest desire to harass the soldier-man.

"I'm not saying this for you--you don't know any better yet--but those idiots that make you rub the dixies up with sabre-paste so that they may shine better. Do you fancy they don't all deserve to be shot? . . . Do they think we don't make a good enough target without that? Here, chuck us over your bag. I'll blacken it with burnt cork, and will run your bottles, your dixies, and the whole bag o' tricks through straw smoke--there's nothing better than that."

Lemoine, who was never more than a single pace away from Sulphart, shrugged his shoulders slowly.

"You're never going to drive these poor blighters daft already with your flash patter," said he reproachfully in his slow, dragging voice. "Let them alone, anyway, till they at least get well off the train."

The newcomer of the white satchel had taken his seat on a wheelbarrow. He seemed quite exhausted. Black runnels of sweat had traced bracketing lines from his temples to the lower part of his cheeks. He unrolled his puttees but did not venture to take off his boots--fine shooting-boots with extra wide welts.

"My heel is all skinned," he said to me. "My boot must be full of blood. I'm carrying such a weight."

Lemoine weighed his kit.

"That's a heavy one for sure," said he. "What on earth have you managed to bung into it? . . . Have you been putting in paving stones?"

"Just what I was told to put in."

"It's the cartridges that weigh heavy," put in the corporal. "How many did they give you?"

"Two hundred and fifty. . . . but I haven't got them in my pack."

"Where are they, then?"

"In my satchel. You see, I like it better like that. Suppose we were attacked all of a sudden."

"Attacked?"

The others stared at him in amazement. Then they all started to laugh with one accord, a huge laugh that they exaggerated still further, stifling, gesticulating, exchanging heavy slaps on the shoulder like caresses delivered with washerwomen's beetles.

"Attacked. . . . that's what he said! There's a bloke that's got them again! . . ."

"No, no. He's got the wind up . . ."

"Attacked, that's what he said. . . . He's crazy. . . . Put the dogs on him! . . ."

This vast candour made us laugh till we were like to choke. Papa Hamel laughed till he cried. Fouillard, for his part, was not laughing. He shrugged his shoulders, hostile all at once, already looking askance at this soldier who was much too clean and who spoke much too politely.

"A lad with dibs who means to come them over us," said he to Sulphart.

The redhead, bent only on talking more than anybody else, was considering the newcomer with compassion.

"But, my poor lad," said he, "you don't really suppose we are fighting that way now? That was all right for the first month. We don't fight any more now--maybe you'll never be fighting."

"Sure enough," said Lemoine, backing him up, "you won't fight; but you'll jabber about it all the same."

"You'll never fire a cartridge," prophesied Broucke, the ch'timi with the child's eyes.

The newcomer made no answer, doubtless thinking that the old hands were trying to pull his leg. But with his ear cocked, instead of listening to Sulphart's discourse, he was hearkening to the big gun shaking the very sky with its big bellow, and he would fain have been over there already, on the far side of the blue line of hills, in the unknown plain where they were playing out the game of war with its fragrance of danger.

. . . . .

The newcomer introduced himself to me. "Gilbert Demachy. . . . I was doing law. . . ."

And I made myself known.

"Jacques Larcher. I am a writer. . . ."

From his first appearance I knew that Gilbert would be my friend; I knew it at once from his voice, his speech, his ways. Before very long I was saying "vous" to him, and we talked of Paris. In short, I was finding someone with whom I could discourse of our books, our theatres, our cafés, of pretty girls breathing perfume. The very names I was pronouncing made me live over again for a moment all that lost happiness. I remember that Gilbert, as he sat on his barrow, had his shoeless feet on a newspaper by way of carpet. We talked on and on excitedly.

"You remember . . . Do you remember? . . ."

The boys gave the newcomers a hand in installing themselves in the stables where the squad had their sleeping-quarters, and piled their kits with ours in the manger. When they had finished, Gilbert held out two five-franc notes to stand drinks.

"That's that coming it over us," growled Fouillard jealous.

The others, full of gratitude, went back to the stable to make ready a place for the new comrade. They tossed up his straw in armfuls to freshen it, and made him a ledge round his feet. Broucke had taken respectful possession of Demachy's rubber pillow, and was amusing himself by inflating it, like a plaything, with a secret fear of wearing it out. Those who must needs change place in order to make room for the others were making the necessary move, and mutually stealing each other's straw.

"Here, you, big belly," said Fouillard to Bouffioux, "you're to sleep up above in the loft. Seeing that I'm sleeping just below you, take care you don't drop down on top of me in the night with your boots on my dial; I don't sleep too sound."

Sulphart never let go of the newcomer, bewildering him with useless advice and ridiculous tips, partly from natural good-nature, partly in return for his standing treat, but most of all to make himself important. Everybody was gay, as if they had already had their drink; Vairon in his shirt started to act the strong man in the fair, calling out his patter in a fat, common voice that had the true smack of the baffler. Ranged all about him, we took the place of the crowd. Jealous of the hit he was making, Sulphart took Lemoine by the sleeve.

"Come with me."

"Why the deuce should I go with you?" said Lemoine, always ready to oppose the redhead before falling in with him.

"Come along!"

Protesting the while, Lemoine followed him to the staircase. The notary's house, the stable of which we were humbly occupying, was a handsome rustic habitation with a high cap of slates, corbels of stucco, and a curiously painted sundial that showed noon precisely on the stroke of ten o'clock.

It stood to receive its guests at the top of a wide stone stair, and its newly painted shutters were of the same green as young leaves. They had remained shut since the beginning of the war. The owners had fled with the advance of the Germans, without having had time to save anything, and they had never come back. The baggage-master had at one time installed his quarters in it, but as a shell one fine morning opened a new bull's-eye window in the front, he had thought it prudent to remove himself to the other side of the district.

We had been definitely and specifically forbidden to set foot inside the house, every door of which was bolted and barred. Morache, the adjutant, who delighted in spoiling us with this kind of compromise, had forthwith announced that whoever transgressed the order would get a dozen bullets in his hide, without counting the coup de grâce to finish him. That put it in Sulphart's mind to pay a visit to the villa. Now he knew it in its every nook and corner, delicately opening the doors with great kicks when an adroit leverage with a bayonet stump proved insufficient.

He brought Lemoine to the first floor, into a large room with light-coloured hangings.

"Here's what we want," said he, opening the wardrobe.

And flinging out linen and dresses pell-mell on to the carpeted floor, rummaging in drawers, clearing the shelves, he took his choice.

"I'm going to get myself up like a girl, and you'll be a man. Do you twig, donkey-face?"

Time to tear a few bodices in unsuccessful tryings-on, and they were able to admire themselves in the long mirror, transformed to a Shrove Tuesday bridal pair. When they made their appearance in the courtyard, arm-in-arm, there was one brief moment of stupefied wonder, and then a wild clamour greeted them.

"Hurrah for the wedding!" yelled Fouillard first of all.

The others yelled and shouted louder, and the whole squad, howling with delight, surrounded the two figures of fun. Sulphart had pulled on over his red trousers a pretty pair of lady's drawers trimmed with lace, that showed his broad crimson behind through its opening. He had donned a kind of white dressing-jacket, and on his bristling collier's head he had set a bridal wreath all awry, made of slightly yellowing orange-blossom--the wreath of the lawyer's wife, that had been reposing under a glass shade. Lemoine, who was not laughing, but had rather the careworn look of a soldier on duty, had been satisfied with a Scotch kilt, a free-and-easy get-up whose regrettable lack of reticence he subdued by a frock-coat with satin lapels, and an orthodox tall hat that had been sedulously brushed the wrong way as a preliminary.

Little Broucke, in a state of happy amaze, was prancing behind them as if he was at a village festival.

"I'm off to the wedding!" he cried.

Singing and shouting, everybody started to dance, accompanied by Fouillard, who fancied he was providing music by banging on the black bottom of his pot with a bayonet hilt.

"Hurrah for the bride!" we all repeated in chorus.

Bréval's thin face was widened by a happy grin. All the same, he was trying to quiet us down.

"Not so loud! Good Lord! one of the officers will hear you."

Vairon had taken Sulphart round the waist, and was dancing a java with all the airs and graces of a village hop; while Lemoine, imagining himself at the local fête, was cutting pigeon's-wings and clapping his hobnailed heels together.

"And the feast goes on. Hurrah for the Mayor!" yelled the cook, who was vainly trying to wash his black hands by rubbing them in his perspiring forehead.

They were hopping one behind the other, like a farandole, and laughing like urchins. The new chum followed at the tail, halting and tripping, holding on to Lagny

8

by the hood. Sulphart, with his mouth dry as ashes, was the first to break away from the ring.

"Good lord, we're choking here! And that other joker who isn't coming back with the wine. So long as he doesn't let Morache grab him."

The thought of such a catastrophe halted the dancers.

"And now would be just the moment for a cherry drink," mourned Vairon.

"But someone else can go and buy more," said Demachy, producing two further notes. "I've laughed too much, I could do very well with a drink."

Respectfully or jealously, all the comrades looked on as the new chum opened his purse of fine leather, and Broucke was so overcome that he said, "Thank you," when he took the money.

Fouillard, who had forgotten all about his stew, had flung himself down on all fours before his blackened fire, and was puffing and blowing with might and main on the ashes, without raising a single spark out of them.

"Go and get some paper," he begged; "this bitch of wet wood won't catch."

Somebody made his way down into the cellar and brought up a pile of many-coloured papers, which he flung down near the fireplace. Stray leaves flew about, white and blue, mostly of the same shape and size. They were the notary's papers. The flame as it flickered up made them flutter, and for a moment it seemed as though there could be deciphered, even in the fire itself, the fine round legal script and the insertions of peasant handwriting.

"I think that's a bit thick, I do," said Lemoine in his simple voice. "Those are things that should be kept. . . . Suppose somebody was burning my old folk's bits of paper for their land; I'd have him behind bars for it."

"Shut your jaw!" coughed Fouillard out of the smoke. "It was you yourself that wouldn't let the door be burned, and made us go and hunt for this filthy rubbish of green wood that won't catch. As if it wasn't wartime!"

"For sure it's wartime," said little Bélin approvingly. He had planned to make himself a waistcoat out of a frock-coat, and was very carefully cutting away the skirts.

"That's true, we are making war," repeated the new chum, clinking glasses with Broucke.

And looking at Sulphart in his drawers of fine lawn, he began to laugh.

"Nobody would think of it," said he. "There's lots of fun up at the front. I was certain I wouldn't be nearly as bored as in barracks."

Bréval, whose hollow face had resumed his two deep lines of anguish down his cheeks, looked at him and shook his head.

"You don't suppose that it's like this every day, do you? You'd be very far out if you did, you know."

His nose buried in his cup, Fouillard was guffawing. Sulphart the sympathetic only shrugged his shoulders.

"That's not so certain," said he.

"If you had struck Charleroi like me," said Lagny to him, Lagny with his shrivelled old woman's face, "you wouldn't have been in such a hurry to get back to the front."

"And all the same you weren't in the retreat, you weren't," interrupted Vairon. "I take my oath that was no rest-camp."

"Aye, that was the stiffest of all, that was," agreed Lemoine.

"And the Marne?" asked Demachy.

"The Marne, that was nothing at all," said Sulphart decidedly. "It was during the retreat that we went through it most. That was where you learnt to know a man."

They were all the same. The retreat, that was the strategic operation they were proudest of, the one action they boasted immoderately of having shared in; it was the starting-point and foundation of all their yarns: the retreat, the terrible forced march from Charleroi to Montmirail, without halts, without food, without objective; the regiments all mixed up together, zouaves and infantry, chasseurs and engineers; wounded men, bewildered and staggering, pallid stragglers that the gendarmes bowled over; the kits and equipments flung into the ditches; one-day battles, always desperate, sometimes victorious; Guise, where the German drew back; sleep deep as a stone snatched on the bank or on the road, in spite of the waggons that thundered by, crushing the sleepers' feet; grocer's shops looted, the poultry-yards they emptied, the machine gunners without mules, dragoons without horses, blacks without chiefs; the mildewed bread that men snatched from one another; the roads blocked with covered carts and bullock-waggons, with women and children all in tears; the native troops dragging goats after them, the villages shooting up in flames, the bridges that were blown up, the comrades that must needs be abandoned all bloody and foundered; and all the time, harassing the tragic column, the Boche cannon that barked without stopping. The retreat. . . . In their mouths it took on all the air and semblance of victory.

"I take my oath that when you read on the milestones, 'Paris, 60 kilomètres,' it gave you a funny feeling."

"Especially the lads of Panama," said long Vairon.

"And then after that," wound up Sulphart carelessly, like the commonplace epilogue of a thrilling story, "after that came the Marne."

"Do you remember the little melons at Tilloy? . . . Nice lot we managed to stuff in!"

"Aye, and the buckets of wine when we came into Gueux."

"I won't forget, for my part, the sausages at Montmirail. . . . You couldn't move but the big shells were on your tracks. . . . Ah! the swine!"

Demachy had resumed his grave look, and was eyeing these men with envy.

"I should have liked well to be there," said he, "to be in a victory."

"Sure it was a victory," conceded Sulphart, who was turning his wreath round and round in his fingers like a cap. "If you had been there you'd have been bowled over like the others, and nothing more. Ask the lads what they got at Escardes. . . . Only you people shouldn't talk without knowing. . . . All the blighters that wrote their muck about it in the papers, they'd have done better to keep their mouths shut. I was there myself--yes, and I know how it all happened. Well, we went more than fifteen days without touching our pay, from the end of August. Then after the last hot time, they paid us the lot in one go: they bunged fifteen sous at every man jack of us. That's the mere truth. And so if you see any blighters that talk to you about the Marne, you've only got to tell them one thing: that the Marne was a show that brought in fifteen sous to the lads that pulled it off. . . ."

. . . . .

Night falls speedily in November. With darkness came the cold, and over there in the trenches rifle-fire had waked up at the hour of the owl's awakening. We had eaten our meal in the stable, crouched and squatting on the straw, some perched up on the mangers with their legs dangling.

The old hands were telling complicated and brutal stories with the appropriate "and so thens" and "you remember nows," essential to the due ordering of a tale. But the newcomers, whose legs they were trying to pull, whom they meant to amaze, were no longer listening: they were half asleep, with wandering eyes and drooping chins.

"Time to go to bed, lads," said Bréval, unlacing his boots. "These boys have spent last night in the train."

Everybody went to his place with the docility of horses that knew their corner. Lemoine hesitated to trample on the fine carpet of fresh straw.

"That's not bad. . . . wheat that hasn't been thrashed. . . ."

Carefully, as he did everything, little Bélin made his bed ready. First he spread out his strip of tent canvas; then by way of a pillow, he thrust his satchel under the straw. To keep his feet warm, he slipped them into the sleeves of his vest; then he rolled himself up into his wide blanket folded in two, and very neatly, like a fisherman casting his drag-net, he threw his overcoat over his legs. By that time there was nothing to be seen but a little patch of a highly satisfied face through the opening of the knitted mountain-helmet. Bélin had retired for the night.

Demachy had watched every move, but not with the same admiration as I had; rather in dismay. Then he looked at the others getting ready for the night, with stupor, a kind of culminating terror. At the third who started to take off his boots, he sat upright on his little corner of straw.

"But you surely won't keep everything shut up here!" he exclaimed. "At least you'll be leaving the door open?"

The others looked at him in astonishment.

"No, indeed; you must be hot stuff," growled Fouillard. "The door open! Do you want us to perish of cold?"

The thought of sleeping there, huddled on straw with these unwashed fellows, disgusted him, terrified him. He dared not say so, but in a panic he watched his next neighbour, Fouillard, who, having methodically and slowly unrolled his muddy puttees, was pulling off his heavy boots.

"But it's really most unwholesome, you know," he insisted; "besides, there's this fresh straw. It ferments. . . . There have been cases of suffocation, often. . . . That's been known. . . ."

"Don't worry about suffocation."

The others were ready to sleep, lying close to keep themselves warm; Sulphart was trying to reach his boot to knock over the candle that was guttering at its last gasp. Overwhelmed, the new chum said no more. On his knees before the manger, as though he were praying to the god of cattle, he fell to hunting for a flask in his satchel.

"'Ware smash!" cried Sulphart, and his big shoe neatly thrown, swept the candle off to the dark.

"Good-night, everybody."

Demachy, feeling and fumbling, rolled himself up awkwardly in his blanket, and with his face entrenched in his handkerchief well sprinkled with eau-de-Cologne, he lay without moving.

The perfume quickly spread throughout the stable. First of all Vairon uttered his astonishment.

"But there's a smell! What on earth is it?"

"It stinks like a barber."

"That's because we're going to be suffocated," jeered Fouillard, who had tumbled to what was happening.

And turning over on his left side, so as not to catch the smell, he grumbled.

"He's got all that goes to a tart, that blighter!"

The new chum made no answer. The others held their tongues, wholly indifferent. Near us sleep was about to spread his brooding wings over everything. Nevertheless, in the darkness there were voices still running on.

"That makes fifteen days now that she hasn't written to me," confided Bréval to a pal. "She's never been so long as that before. . . . That simply torments me, you know."

One of the newcomers was questioning Vairon, whose rich public-house voice I recognized.

"When you go into rest-camp you're well received, eh?"

"Oo, well, they don't prod us with pitchforks, anyway; that's about all there is to it."

Sulphart, to send himself to sleep, was softly blackguarding Lemoine, who had promised to find some rum and had come back empty-handed.

"You'll show me the way to ferret out good places, you with the face fit to crush rice," he was mumbling. "Talk about an egg. . . . a billiard-ball. . . ."

Sleep bore them away, one after another, mingling their breathing, measured or irregular, the even respiration of a child and the outcries of troubled dreaming.

Outside, the night lay in wait, hearkening to the trenches. This evening they were quiet. You could hear neither the dull, all-shaking sound of the cannon, nor the dry cracking of rifle-fire. Only a machine gun was firing, round after round, without hate; you would have said a madhouse wife beating her carpet. Round about the village lay the heavy silence that broods over a freezing countryside. But suddenly, on the roadways, a deep rumbling awoke, increased, thickened, rolled towards us, and the walls began to shake. . . . The service lorries.

They rolled on heavily, with a jolting clamour of ironmongery. How I would have liked to go to sleep with that familiar rolling roar in my ears and in my soul! Not so long ago the motorbusses passed like that under my windows and held me awake, late, late into the night. How I loathed them in those days! And now, without holding any grudge, they had nevertheless come to see me in my exile. As once upon a time, they made me start and quiver, half asleep and half awake, and I felt the walls shiver and tremble. They were coming to cradle me to sleep.

"It's queer, to-night there's no sound of their hard jolting on the pavement, nor rattling windows, nor belated passers-by calling them to stop. Their noise is no more than a snoring purr inside my drowsy head. They grind, they bump, they are gone. . . . Adieu, Paris!"

CHAPTER II
IN THE SWEAT OF THY BROW

WITH a great pile of packets in front of him like a pedlar's pack, the harassed quartermaster was calling out the post in the middle of a regular mob of soldiers, who were all plying their elbows and trampling on one another's feet. It was just at our door, between the the communal washhouse--so tiny that there would hardly have been room for three washerwomen under its sloping shelter roof--and the notary's house, which wore a red scarf of virginia creeper crosswise on its front. We had clambered up on the stone seat and were listening attentively.

"Maurice Duclou, first section."

"Killed at Courcy," cried somebody.

"Are you sure?"

"Yes, his mates saw him fall in front of the church. . . . He'd caught a bullet. Now, . . well, I wasn't there myself."

On the corner of the envelope the quartermaster wrote in pencil, "Killed."

"Edouard Marquette."

"He must be killed too," said a voice.

"You're a ninny!" protested another. "The night they said he was dropped he went on a water-party with me."

"Then," asked the quartermaster, "he would be in hospital? But we've not had his papers.

"My idea is that he was evacuated by another regiment."

"No, no, he was wounded; the Boches must have collared him."

"It's a great pity--it's always the ones that have seen nothing have most chat."

Everybody was talking at once in an uproar of opposing statements and insulting contradictions. The quartermaster, hard-pushed and in a hurry, brought them into agreement.

"I don't give a curse. I'll mark him off 'Missing.' André Brunet, thirteenth squad."

"Here for him."

The others were going on disputing in lowered tones; the men in the hindmost ranks were shouting to them to be quiet, and nobody could hear anything. Bréval listened through it all, anxiously listened, and when a name sounded like his, had it repeated.

"Isn't it for me, this time? Corporal Bréval?"

But it was never for him, and turning his poor vexed face to us, he explained.

"She writes so badly that there might be nothing queer about it, eh?"

As the heap lessened his lips tightened. When the last one was called out, he went away, heart and hands empty alike. Just as he was going indoors he turned to us.

"By the way, Demachy, your turn on fatigue. You will take a bag and go to fetch the rations."

"What? The new chum going for rations! . . . You're making game of us."

And Sulphart, all indignant, left his particular group of pals to come up to the corporal.

13

"A lad that's just come, who fancies that carrots grow at the fruiterer's, that's the best you can find to send for the rations! Ah, you're up to tricks. . . . If every fool could swim you wouldn't need a boat to cross the Seine."

"If you want to go I'm not hindering you," replied Bréval calmly.

"Sure, I'll go," shouted Sulphart. "I'll go because I don't want the squad to get the same food as wooden horses, and because that lad looks to me as if he could choose a bit of beef about as well as I could say a Mass."

Demachy, who ever since he arrived had been overwhelmed by the cries, the noisy demands, and brutal gaities of the redhead, made an attempt to rehabilitate himself.

"I beg your pardon, I assure you that I shall know what to do very well. In barracks . . ."

He was going the wrong way about it. The mere words "active service" or "barracks" was enough to send Sulphart crazy, inasmuch as he had spent his three years in stubbornly defending the cause of right against vindictive Adjutants and officers of malevolent nature, who preferably sent good soldiers to sleep in the police station the night before leave. Anger choked him.

"Barracks! . . . He fancies he's still in barracks, that lark-skull! He's just come out of the depot and he would like to put it all over us again! . . . Well then, get on with it, go to the distribution, see the rations; they'll have a good laugh. The lads of the squad are always sure to be in a nice fix and no mistake. I don't care for myself, I'll manage all right."

And to show quite clearly that he was no longer one with a squad being led to the abyss by an incapable corporal, he sauntered off towards the church, whistling a little tune to himself.

The squads were being mustered when Gilbert came into the courtyard where the quartermaster had had unloaded, a few paces from the manure tank, the quarters of frozen meat which a man was now cutting up with an axe, potatoes, bully-beef, a burst sack from which trickled a thin stream of rice, and biscuits, which the youngsters were carrying off in their aprons to make pig's-meat with.

Stooping over the cask of wine, which they were tapping to make sure that it was properly full, those who were waiting their turn were arguing as to the number of bidons that would fall to each squad, and some of them were already clamouring that that wasn't their proper figure. Lentils were given out, sweet potatoes, coffee in the berry. Taken by surprise, Demachy remarked:

"But we have no coffee-mill."

The others stared at him and laughed. Behind the group someone bellowed:

"You can go on enjoying yourselves! That's the lad they send to get the rations for a whole squad!"

It was Sulphart, who had come out of curiosity, just to look on. Heavily embarrassed, his cap full of sugar, his pockets stuffed with coffee, his bag weighed down full of lentils, Gilbert was at his wit's end, with no notion where he could put his rice. As everybody was laughing round him, and the quartermaster shouting, "Come along, here's your lot; don't you want to have it to eat?" he lost his head and emptied it anywhere he could --into his bag along with the lentils. Then Sulphart burst out:

"Here, that's a bit too much! . . . You see the cookie's phiz if he'll like sorting out his rice and his bugs! . . . Lord, what an army! And they talk. about hoofing the

14

Boches out. What a joke! . . . "

Thoroughly furious, the new chum turned round, red all over.

"Look here, you shut up. All you had to do was to come here yourself."

Sulphart, without turning a hair, waited for the remainder of the distribution. He watched the corporal on duty throwing down great chunks of meat, some of an appetizing fresh redness, others thickly veined with tallow, on a muddied piece of tent canvas.

"We're going to draw lots for them," said the corporal.

"No!" protested several squads, "there will be some faking about it. . . . Share it out according to the number of men."

"There are fourteen of us in the second squad; I want that piece."

"And what about us, in the first . . . ."

All stooping over the stall, hands stretched out, they were disputing in advance over the food, all shouting at once, under the impassive eye of the quartermaster.

"That will do with your howling," he said at last. "I'll distribute it. Third squad. . . . that piece. Fourth squad . . . Fifth squad."

He had not time to finish, nor to point out the piece intended with the end of his stick. With a roar Sulphart hurled himself into the group.

"No!" he shouted, "I'm not having any. . . . You want us all in the squad to die of hunger. They're taking advantage of its being a lad that isn't up to snuff to do us in the eye."

The others hooted him, the quartermaster would fain have driven him away, but clean beyond all restraint, wildly waving his arms, he shouted louder than them all.

"I won't have that piece at all. . . . I'll tell the Captain, and I'll tell the Colonel too, if I have to. . . . It's always the same lot that get the best. . . . I want my proper share. . . . The fifth squad is the one with the most men in it. . . ."

"There are only eleven of you."

"That's a lie! . . . We'll make a complaint. . . . That's nothing but bone!"

He was uttering cry upon cry, now shrill, now hoarse, now terrifying and now plaintive, thrusting one back and jostling others over. Those who had already been served were hugging their share to their hearts, as the mothers of Bethlehem must have held their babes on the night of Herod's slaughter. By good luck the quartermaster held out a chunk to him, taken at random, and at once he shut up completely, his calm recovered immediately, his anger all harmless and disarmed since he was served. He turned then to Demachy, while the distribution went on.

"You see," he said with a friendly air, "you've got the idea all right, but you don't give tongue enough. If you want to be better served than the others you've got to give tongue, even without knowing anything about anything: that's the only way to have your rights."

Gilbert Demachy listened without any answer, amused by this big brawler with his bristle beard; his attentive silence pleased Sulphart.

"Of course that blockhead of a Bréval never told you to fetch the bucket or the bottles for the pinard. What do you think you're going to carry it back in--in your boots? Good joy I thought something about it. There's a bucket, and I brought a can in case there might be brandy. . . . It's no matter, a corporal that doesn't go himself to the distribution; you only see that with the fifth. . . . He stayed behind once more writing to his old woman. . . . Blitherer!"

Sulphart did not deign to have any truck with the distribution of tins of bully-beef, a commodity for which he had nothing but contempt; but all the same he cried, "There's one short!" just to show that he was still on the spot.

"Now for the wine," said the quartermaster.

Sulphart dashed forward first of all, and as long as the distribution lasted he never raised his head; while a bucket was filling he groaned and moaned and uttered little cries of anguish, as if it was his heart's blood that was being run off.

"That'll do! . . . That'll do!" he cried. "It holds more than the proper measure. . . . Thief!"

But the others, who were accustomed to it all, endured the insults and kept the wine. His turn came at length, and he got his bucket filled up to the very brim, swearing that six new chums had turned up, that the corporal was going to lodge a complaint, that they had already been curtailed the day before, that the Captain. . . .

"Here, and bung off," said the exasperated quartermaster, pouring out a last quarter of a litre for him. "Lord, what a life!"

Highly pleased with himself, Sulphart went back like a conqueror, his bucket in one hand and his bag on his shoulder. They passed through the village, where the idle soldiers were roaming in quest of a pub, and on the way he tried to inculcate into the new chum the first principles of cunning and trickery essential for a soldier on campaign.

"Every man for himself, you know. I'd far rather drink other people's drink than have the others drinking mine. . . . It always is the modest folk that lose out."

Halting in a spot where nobody was passing, he dipped his drinking-cup in the bucket and offered it to Gilbert.

"Here," he said, "drink that, you've a right to it."

He had, in a word, drawn up in his own mind, and for his own sole personal guidance, a little treatise on the rights and duties of the soldier, in which it was fully and frankly conceded that the man on ration fatigue had a right to a cup of wine as a perquisite. He drank one too, since he was helping the man on duty, and started off again by so much the lighter. As they walked, he told Gilbert stories, talking in the same breath of his wife, who was a dressmaker; of the battle of Guise; the factory where he had worked in Paris, and of Morache, the Adjutant, a re-enlisted man, our special horror. When they reached cantonments he put down the bucket, taking oath that he had never so much as tasted the wine, and offering to prove it by letting anybody smell his breath; then he went to Demachy again, having taken a fancy to him.

"If I'd had the dibs like you," he said, "and had your education, I swear they wouldn't have seen me coming into the fire like this. I'd have put in for the officers' course, and I'd have gone and spent some months in camp, and then they'd have listed me sub-lieutenant in the middle of 1915. And by that the war'll be over. . . . What I say is, that you didn't know how to swim."

CHAPTER III
THE RED PENNON

FROM break of day the regiment was measuring out the road with its long blue ribbon. There was a thick sound of tramping, voices, and laughter moving forward in the midst of the dust. Untiringly the comrades, elbow to elbow, told one another those hackneyed tales of the regiment, every one like every other one, that you might imagine took place all in the same barracks. They wrangled with one another from rank to rank; head thrown back, they emptied the bidons filled at the halting-place; and as they passed, they challenged the road labourer by the roadside, the peasant in his vineyard, the woman coming back from the field. Now and then they met a gendarme.

"Hi, lad. . . . that's not the way to the trenches."

Nobody gave a thought to the war. Everything breathed devil-may-caredom and gaiety. It was not too hot, the country was bright, and they looked at things with the amused eyes of soldiers on manoeuvres. . . .

Bouffioux' shining face carried black lines, the mark of his fingers and the rills of sweat running down from his cap. He had placed himself alongside Hamel to talk about Havre. They were chumming up over the names of streets and pubs, and for the hundredth time they were astounded not to have known each other as civilians.

"And yet you have a big fat face that nobody could miss," repeated Hamel every time.

Stoutly built, he marched with wide strides; fat Bouffioux, on the contrary, went with little tripping, hurrying steps, and Fouillard, who was marching next behind him, with his dirty neckerchief knotted around his neck, never stopped grumbling.

"Will you walk straight, you fat beast! If only he'd take my mess-pot! . . . Why don't you ever carry it, anyway? . . . You don't mind a bit having a feed. . . . If it was only a scrap of wood he wouldn't carry it, no fear, that pig! . . . You'll be coming looking for soup to-night out of it. . . . We'll see about it. . . ."

The comfortable tallow of the horse-dealer was one of his special hates; Bouffioux was fat and he was thin; was well off, and he a poor man; stayed in the rear while he went up into the trenches.

"No great wonder he has a face like a behind, with all he stuffs into him. . . . The boys don't often get a taste of his parcels. He takes advantage of our being in the trenches to wire into it all by his lonesome. But that won't go on for ever; he's been playing Cuthbert long enough now, he'll have to go up to the trenches."

Bouffioux allowed the insults to pass, but he never went to the trenches. Since the war started, he had plied every trade; there was only one that really went against his grain--ours. He was ready for any mortal thing so as not to get into the trenches. He had only once been fighting, at Charleroi, and he had retained such a terror of it that now he had one idea and only one--to get out of it. He succeeded by dint of as many tricks as he used to employ in old days at the fair to sell a mangy horse. Every twist and turn, he had worn them all out. He had gone through the retreat as cyclist to the paymaster, just knowing enough to stick on the saddle, and constantly running on the flank of the column, shoving his punctured bicycle by hand. He had won the victory of the Marne as telephone operator to the brigade. Since that he had been known as wood-cutter, armourer, army service corps, cobbler. He volunteered for every sort of job, in the most barefaced way, and clung to the place he had usurped until he was hunted out of it. Did anybody want a secretary that only just knew how to read, a carpenter that had never had a plane in his hand, a tailor that couldn't sew, he was on the spot. If a chaplain for the division had been called for, he would have shouted, "Here!" He was determined not to fight, that was the whole thing, and fear taught him every kind of boldness. At the present moment he was standing drinks to all the corporals of the supply train, and sharing his parcels with the sergeant muleteer of the machine guns, who promised to get him attached to the reserve troops. But the Captain would not allow him to leave the company, and Bouffioux bowed a brooding neck beneath the threats of Fouillard.

"Why should you be any more than the others, you big lump! You're going in, I tell you. . . ."

Fouillard, very proud of having been through Montmirail on all fours in a ditch, and very uppish over his title of old soldier, equally hated Demachy, who had too much money and the ways of a toff. So when he was tired of insulting the placid back of Bouffioux, he looked at the new chum, and the thick wrinkle of grease that cut across his cheek hollowed itself in a smile.

"Twig him, if he's not in a lather all right," he grinned.

Gilbert was marching with straining neck, his thumbs passed under the straps, his feet dragging. From halt to halt his pack was getting heavier. And yet he had buckled it on gaily at the start. He had felt a kind of sporting sprightliness under this well-stowed burden. Supple and limber at the knees, he would have liked to sing, to start off at the quick step, with the fifes and drums in front.

But at the end of an hour the pack had already grown heavy. Instead of pushing him forward like at the start, it was turning into a dead weight, and seemed to be holding him, to be plucking him back by the two straps. He jerked his burden back into place with a twist of his shoulder every hundred paces or so, but it soon slipped back again, heavier than ever. His bruised foot had broken out again, his knees had dried up and seized, and now that leaden pack was playing with him, making him stagger like a drunken man. For the first time he was heard swearing, using beastly language, in a little furious voice that he didn't recognize. Chest thrust forward, labouring as if he had had to haul the road along, he panted under his slave-collar:

"I'll chuck the blasted lot in the air at the next halt, and their filthy biscuits. . . ."

At every halt he made an inventory of everything out on the bank, and lightened himself of something--bottles of drugs, a portable filter, a box of powdered beef, a pile of strange, ridiculous objects that his comrades fought for like savages without knowing very clearly what they would do with them. Sulphart meanwhile was carrying half his load for him, his water-bottle, his white satchel full to bursting, and when the day's march was nearing its end, he even took his rifle, the strap of which was sawing into his shoulder. But the little he still had to carry was still too heavy, and at every halt he felt he would go no farther. When the whistles sent them to their kits he would fain not have heard, or that they might have compassion on him and leave him there for an hour, by himself, to let his skin heal over and the fever of his throbbing temples abate. Nevertheless, he always stood up like the others and set off again, limping, more stiff and numb than ever, a pang at every step. The lightened pack was no less heavy, and the unheeding, unconscious milestones added incessantly fresh kilomètres to the already long day's march.

Little by little the noise of the marching troop died down. They were feeling fatigue. "A halt! a halt!" one or another would call out, hiding himself as he did so. Footsore men were falling out and taking off their boots, seated at the foot of the bank. On the edge of the road Barbaroux the doctor, with his four stripes, was giving a consultation, holding in with reins and knees his horse that pawed the ground. Before him, all awkward and embarrassed, a man was standing at attention.

"Hold your tongue!" yelled the doctor, the veins on his temples standing out. "You will march like the rest. . . . I'm your Commanding Officer, d'ye hear? your Commanding Officer! What is it you owe me?"

The poor stupefied foot-slogger stared at him. "You owe me respect," bellowed Barbaroux, jumping in his saddle, "Stand up straight. . . . Hold your hand out. . . . Naturally his hand shakes. . . . All alcoholics, and sons of alcoholics. . . Well, you be off now; the others are marching and you'll march too. . . . And don't let me see you straggling behind, or look out for the sawbones."

At the halt the men took their ease lying stretched at full-length behind a line of piled arms. The newcomers, less hardened of body, now didn't even unbuckle their packs; they lay on their backs, their kit pulled up under their heads like a hard pillow, and felt their weariness shivering through their tortured legs.

"Packs up!"

Off they went again, limping along. They were not laughing now, and they talked much less loudly. The regiment that just now filled the whole dusty road up to the crest of the ridge lost itself in a light steamy haze. Soon the head of the battalion could be discerned no longer; then the company itself wavered through the mist. . Nightfall was at hand, they were entering the realms of dream. The villages were at rest, their day over, and their rustic incense of burning wood rose from their steep and pointed roofs.

In September there had been fighting in this district, and all along the road stood crosses lined up at attention to see us march past.

Near a stream there was grouped a whole cemetery; from each cross flickered a little flag, those children's flags that are bought in the bazaars; and all these little flying flapping flags gave that field of the dead the gay look of a naval squadron all dressed for a fête.

Along beside the ditches ranged their line, casual poor crosses, made with two bits of board or two sticks fixed crosswise. Sometimes a whole section of dead men with never a name, and one single cross to hold them in its keeping. "French soldiers slain on the field of honour," spelled out the regiment. Round the farms, in the middle of fields, they were everywhere to be seen; a whole regiment must have fallen in that place. From the top of the still green slope they watched us pass, and one might have fancied that their crosses leaned over to choose from out our ranks those who must join them on the morrow.

And for all that they were neither sad nor gloomy, those first tombs of the war. Ranged in green, rich gardens, framed in foliage and crowned with ivy, they still assumed the air of bowers to reassure the boys that were going off to fight. Then, apart, in a naked field, a black cross, all by itself, with a grey cap atop.

"A Boche!" cried someone.

And all the newcomers jostled to have a look; it was the first they had seen.

. . . .

In a dull, confused rumbling of half-stifled voices, clinking metal, and foundered feet, the company entered the village, all drowned in darkness and shadow.

Not far away the rockets were cleaving the night with the brightness of a city street, and every now and then it was enlivened with red lights or green lights, swiftly quenched, for all the world like luminous signs.

This wartime sky made one think of a holiday night of the fourteenth of July. There was nothing tragic. Only the immense silence.

In the middle of the main street, a burning farm cast over the dismantled roofs a brutal red, like the flares of a country fair, and one was quite surprised not to hear the steam-organs going. Rabbits on fire dashed through the ranks, like little living torches. Then, between two walls on the point of crumbling in, there could be seen, running through the red haze of the conflagration, mute shadows carrying buckets.

"Hurry on! hurry on!" repeated the officers; "they will be firing again."

One fallen against the other, the wounded houses mingled their ruins, and men went stumbling over the scattered rubble. From time to time a front fallen out complete blocked up the street. They cursed their way over this mass of stonework, and the dislocated company formed up again at the double.

Where the village and the country joined, a small boy who could hardly be seen in the darkness was looking for the remains of who knows what among the ruins of his home. He raised his head, watched us pass without a word, and gravely saluted the officer, his little plaster-white paw lifted to his mop of hair.

"Young blighter!" growled Sulphart. "What are they up to out of doors just at the moment of a relief, these little lice? . . . We mustn't ask that. . . . And throw an eye on all these lights signalling. You may be sure the Boches know we're here."

An old woman passed from one yard to the other, hiding a lantern under her apron, both to cover the light and to shelter it from the wind. You might have fancied she carried a star in her bosom.

"There's another one. . . . Hi! old woman . . . that lantern!" shouted Sulphart.

Maroux, who called himself a poacher, groused with him; he saw spies everywhere, did Maroux. The smallest glimmer of a light seemed to him suspicious, and he imagined heaven knows what mysterious and complicated code of night signals between peasants lighting their candles and the enemy headquarters.

Harassed and thrusting out his neck like a horse going uphill, Demachy followed the poacher. When the file halted, he would knock up against his pack and wait in a dull stupor till they went on again. Even his fatigue had vanished; he was a thing extenuate, without will or volition, a thing to be pushed on. His eyes turned towards the front line, he was all the while trying to see the rockets through the gaps between two walls. It was a disillusion for him, this first glimpse of the war. He would fain have been deeply moved, have experienced something, and he kept his eyes stubbornly fixed in the direction of the trenches, to give himself an emotion, to win a little thrill.

But he kept repeating to himself, "This is war. . . . I am seeing war," without managing to rouse any emotion. He felt nothing at all, except perhaps a little surprise. It all seemed to him queer and out of place, that electric fairydom in the midst of the dumb and quiet fields. The few rifle shots that cracked out had an inoffensive air. Even this devastated village did not upset his calm: it was too much like a stage scene. . . . too much the kind of thing you could imagine to yourself. It would have needed cries, tumult, a burst of firing, to animate it all, to give a spirit to things; but this night, this huge silence, this was never war.

And yet, indeed, it was; a harsh and gloomy vigil rather than a battle.

The street came abruptly to an end, cut short by a barricade made of barrows and casks. This had to be traversed man by man, gliding under a plough-beam that caught up the kit on their backs.

"Silence! . . . Fall in again in the field to the left."

The motionless group of soldiers made in the darkness a kind of black vineyard with all the rifles held upright. Only there was the red top of one solitary cigarette piercing the night. It could be seen rising to the lips, glow up, then slowly sink again.

"Eh! that other filthy ruffian who's going to have us all marked down," grumbled somebody. . . . "They'd get their mates killed for a fag, those swine!"

Gilbert had unbuckled his pack and lain down. The earth in the fields was flabby and cold, still moist with the late rains, and that froze his legs through the thin overcoat. Pack under head, his hands slipped into his sleeves, he rested, filling his eyes with the sky. The pressure of the two straps was now burning his shoulders with a first-class blister, and his weariness ran down through all his relaxed limbs.

In the village, on the other side of the barricade, a company which had piled arms was jostling itself over its rations. You could hear orders, disputes, a whole uproar like a market-day. An indignant voice was crying out:

"They must be drunk! . . . In our squad we've had three lots of sugar and nothing to eat. . . ."

Others called to each other: "This way the water party. . . . Heads of squads for wine."

Next it was the machine gunners giving tongue, their mules caught in the hurly-burly. An officer was shouting to quiet things down. "Silence! less row, for the love of God!" All this clamour woke Gilbert, benumbed. He sat up on his elbows.

"Are the Boches still far from here?" he asked.

"No, the other side of the road," replied Sulphart, lying close by him in the damp grass. "You'll see that, by dint of hearing this tow-row, the Boches will start firing into the thick of it. I'd give twenty sous to see all these blankers getting themselves well hammered. . . . Just listen to them letting loose!"

He himself was not shouting now. His big, rowdy voice was prudently lowered; he had even put away his pipe, and was going forward with his back bent, and uneasy. These precautions amazed Gilbert.

"There's no danger here?" he asked.

"No, on the contrary; you listen."

Little tuneful whistling crossed the night, prolonged and dying away like a plucked guitar.

"You hear that? Those are bullets."

Gilbert listened, amused. It gave him pleasure to find that a bullet had this pretty, wasp-like sound. And it never even entered his head that that might be death. At an order sent along in low tones from mouth to mouth, the company dressed, with a long clattering of arms.

"In line at five paces. . . . Rifle in hand . . . no noise."

In the long zigzagging file, the troop dropped to the main road, whose line of trees could be seen standing out lower down. Communication trenches had not yet been dug to lead them down to it.

Beet with its tall tops, and the weeds and grass of the fallow fields, soaked our legs up to the knee, and wreathed wisps found our heavy feet. It was impossible to see anything. The world came to an end a few paces away, black earth and darkened sky melting together. Scarcely could you divine the bent profile of your nearest fellows. Now and then a man would stumble and fall full-length, with a hideous clanging of mess-tin, drinking-cup, and water-bottle. Then would stifled laughter run tittering down the line.

Suddenly Gilbert heard, as it might be, a swift sigh that came swelling up, and on the very instant he saw the long file of men go down with one single movement. He followed suit. A blaze of lightning burst forth with a dreadful shattering noise of copper and iron. The shards came lashing at the ground, shrieking viciously, and the acrid fumes subsided. Gilbert, rising on his knees, his heart dancing, drank in a big lungful of his first shell.

"That smells good," he thought.

Already the others were on their feet and starting off quicker than ever, nearly running. Tossing back the bidon that was knocking against his thighs, he followed Lemoine, who was dragging along a wretched dog at the end of a rope, propping itself back on all its four stiff legs.

"Halt!" was passed down by lowered voices.

The trench was dug just along this side of the road. Three lines of wire protected it, like the greensward of a city square. Under our very feet were murmuring, invisible soldiers, hoisting their packs on to their shoulders.

"They haven't done much bursting themselves to bring the relief," they were grousing. "For sure we'll play their dirty trick back on them."

And with this welcome, the boys went off.

A nice pallid sunshine, proper for Saint Martin. Over the soft pale blue of the sky the clouds were like wisps of shrapnel. A kestrel and a raven were pursuing one another savagely with hammering beaks. A lark was heard singing, ever in the same place, hardly moving at all. It was Sunday.

Over the sandbags the German trenches could be made out, two slender lines, one of them of brown earth, the other white marl. The devasted fields looked like mere waste land, with their ricks and ruin and their tossed and scattered sheaves. By the edge of a roadway an abandoned mowing-machine held up its long workless arms, idle and derelict.

The trench was loafing. Men sauntered about the communication trenches as in the streets of a little town, every nook and corner of which is familiar, and gossiped at the entry of the dug-outs.

Under their shelters the boys were doing odd jobs. Little Bélin was getting his fixed up to his liking, cutting one hole for his candle, a second for his drinking-cup, and another, a bigger one, to slide his feet into. Bréval was writing to his wife, and Broucke was sleeping, the only pleasure he had between grub and grub.

Fouillard was squatted down finishing a tin of bully-beef, administering it to himself in great mouthfuls between his dirty knife and his earthy thumb. Gilbert looked askance at him. He could not like that sickly, dirty creature; everything disgusted him--his voice, his pink eyes, and down to his eternal woollen scarf, with its filthy tassels hanging from it. They were both lying in the same hole, crammed together, side against side, and it was most of all for this that he execrated him.

All the same, the new chum had broken in speedily enough to our brutal life. He now knew how to wash his plate with a fistful of grass, he was beginning to drink our coarse wine with enjoyment, and was not ashamed now to relieve himself in public.

"You're coming on, you're coming on my boy!" Bréval would declare with satisfaction.

Wallowing on the rotting straw in his niche, Sulphart was drowsing away, letting only a slender shaft of light trickle into his half-shut eyes. He pulled and puffed lazily at his pipe with the well-chewed stem, and day-dreamed of Saint Romain's fair, with its balls, its circuses, its lotteries, its shooting-galleries--a whole cycle of explosive delights, all scented with frying and coarse wines.

Not having a watch to keep, they stretched themselves out one after another, wearied with the long night spent in carting corrugated iron. Vairon was growling in a doze, for Lemoine's snoring would not let him sleep. Those who had no den to doze in had lain down in the trench itself, wrapped round in their blankets. In a hole, scolding voices of card-players; all the others were deep in slumber.

Suddenly, sharply, a gust of explosions shook them awake. There was a moment of panic. They rose, came out of their holes, jostled one another to get their rifles, all at once crazed by the deafening thunder of the artillery suddenly let loose.

At the same signal, down the whole of the line our own guns set to work, and in this rending hub-bub you could no longer even hear the shells cleaving through the air. We had hurled ourselves to the loopholes, already dipping into our cartridge-pouches.

At the end of the waste ground that divided the two trench systems, precisely upon the German line, whose sinuous zigzag could still be discerned through the smoke, the shells were hammering with furious blows, making chunks of white trench fly like shavings under a carpenter's plane.

Unstrung, we were running right and left, calling out to one another, giving one another news, without knowing anything whatever.

"It's a Boche attack. . . . That's a barrage."

"No, it's to knock out their machine guns. . . ."

"It appears that the third battalion is going out to carry the wood."

Every shell sent up a long sheaf of earth in a cloud of smoke; those that fell on the wood uprooted whole trees and flung them into the undergrowth, all standing and unbroken like enormous bouquets. Our liaison orderly passed along swiftly, knocking against us as he went.

"Everybody into the dug-outs. It's a half-hour shoot; very possibly they will reply."

No one went back. The whole crowded trench was gazing at the spectacle, and as the German artillery made no answer, the most cautious became heroic. Fouillard even sat up on the parapet so as to miss nothing of the show.

When a well-aimed salvo fetched its four pickaxe blows on to the trench, ripping up a sheaf of earth, of stones and beams, a cry of admiration arose, the delighted clamour that greets a show of fireworks. In the hubbub nothing else could be heard but this happy laughter, this good sound laughter, as if we had been judging the effect of the wooden balls on an Aunt Sally in a village merry-making. Now and then a cry came through the tumult.

"Look, boys, a poilu going up in the air!" howled Vairon with wild, disjointed gestures.

"You're seeing spooks," retorted Lemoine, jealous because he had seen nothing.

"That's a stump."

"What of! I tell you it's a Boche, and more than that, he had his hoofs in the air."

Then a big Jack Johnson came along, panting like an express train coming into a railway station, and every straining eye watched for the place it was likely to come down. Then there was an enormous black geyser that belched up, striped and streaked with fire, and then the explosion was heard thundering.

"There's a beauty!" cried the trench.

The wood under the shelling was smoking like a factory. Gesticulating in the middle of the hurly-burly, Sulphart was bawling his delight.

"He that hasn't won is going to win! It's all luck and the player's own fancy. . . . Come along! hurry up, whoever hasn't got his counter! Six for a penny." In one hand he waved imaginary numbers like a cheap-jack at a fair, and his bellowings drowned the row. With a horrible cracking of splintered bones others were bursting still, ripping up the lines of wire like ribbons.

"Boom! The gentleman has won a splendid turkey-poult. Come on, next, please! Have a flutter. Try your luck. . . ."

There was a duller thunder-clap, a shell lit squarely in the trench that threw up a huge spray of earth and stumps.

"This time it is," cried Vairon, who clung to his idea. "I saw the poilu jump. He fell back on to the bank."

The others, who had not yet seen anything, anxiously watched for the next shot with fixed eyes. Demachy, strangely fevered, his fists clenched, was humming a tune to show he was not afraid. One's ears soon get accustomed to this rolling crashing. You can recognize them all by their voice: the seventy-five that cracks in fury, sets off with a whiew, and passes so quick that you can see it burst as soon as you hear it starting; the hundred-and-twenty, out of breath--you would fancy it too much a Weary Willie tofinish its journey; the hundred-and-fifty-five, that seems to go sliding along rails; and the big Jack Johnsons, that pass over high up with a tranquil sound of moving waters. The wind dissolving the thick eddying whirls brought a breath sulphur to us, a strong smell of powder. Gilbert breathed it in till he was brimful of it. Now and then you could clearly hear the shell whistle, and then five, ten seconds passed, and it didn't explode, fallen who knows where. A murmur of disappointment would go up, a growl of befooled sightseers.

"It's a dud. . ."

With his drinking-cup at his ear like a telephone-receiver, little Bélin was playing at being a gunner.

"4.800 mètres, . . . high-explosive. . . . Fire with two guns."

The firing, at first massed in front of the wood, had broadened along the whole enemy line, and the black and green plume-bursts now bordered it from end to end, like an infernal alley of trees. Suddenly it seemed as though grey caps could be seen passing.

"The Boches with a barrage!" cried Vairon.

Men jostled one another, climbed up on the sandbags.

"There, where that one has just dropped!" and many fingers pointed to the spot, under a green canopy slashed with lightnings. All the soldiers from the latest drafts were stretching their necks, tiptoeing on the square points of their big boots

"I'm going to let off a cartridge," said Vairon, loading his rifle.

He put his piece to his shoulder, barely took a snap-aim, and pulled the trigger. While still deafened by the report, he heard the infuriated yell of Morache, the Adjutant, who rushed on him gesticulating, waving his stick as though he was going to strike him.

"Who was that fired? . . . I want to know who fired! . . . It was you? You'll be punished."

His lean visage all puckered up, he was yelping into the very face of Vairon, who was clean bowled over.

"So we're forbidden to kill the Boches now," retorted the other spiritlessly. "That's the first shot I've fired for three months."

"Hold your tongue, I forbid you to argue!'

Vairon had grown pale and livid, and drooped his obstinate head, the head of a regular tough, and emptied his Lebel, clenching his teeth upon his anger.

"All right," he murmured, though he gave in, "we won't kill your Boches for you. . . . But then I'd like to know what the hell we're doing here. . . ."

"What! What's that you say?" cried Morache, fit to crack his voice. "I'll let the Captain know."

Vairon fell silent. He moved away, trailing his rifle like a useless cudgel. Then, to punish his officers, he ostentatiously dissociated himself from the bombardment, and went and lay down in his hole. He brought out his tobacco-pouch and rolled a cigarette with a hand that had not ceased to tremble. A series of coppery explosions made him lift his nose, like a connoisseur.

"Fused shrapnel," he murmured.

The outcry of admiration from the trench made him regret he hadn't seen them, but he still had his dignity as a man; he refused to get up. At that moment, crips and clear through the row, a German machine gun was heard. That was too much for him, he leaped to his loophole.

We had stopped crying out, astonished, a trifle uneasy. The machine gun was still firing without a break, exasperating, as if it was driving nails. And suddenly we saw what it was firing at.

"Polius going over the top! . . . They're attacking beyond the river."

Everybody had exclaimed together, then immediately all fell silent, anxious, nailed to the spot. A company had just left the trenches on our left. and in open skirmishing order, without their packs, with fixed bayonets, the soldiers were running over the bare fields. The regiment next to us was trying a surprise attack, and it was they that the Maxim was on to, with its regular tap-tap like a sewing-machine. Finding the range, it seemed to tear a wide gap in the line of men.

"They're mown down."

"No, they're taking cover."

The soldiers, springing up again, ran on, lay down, started off again, but in spite of the barrage pounding their line, the Germans had started firing and you could see, out in no man's land, men spin round and go down with a thud. Some of them when down still moved, dragged themselves towards the nearest shell-hole. Others, dropping heavily in a heap, never moved again. The firing crackled on, thicker and heavier, but none the less, what was left of the company thrust on, the scattered soldiers closing up as they came near the trench just as if they were afraid to tackle it alone. The machine gun concentrated its fire on this massed troop. and almost at one stroke the men went down.

One single cry of anguish broke from us. Then oaths, rage, distress.

"But no. . . . they've taken cover again!" cried Broucke.

"Yes," said Demachy, who had taken his field-glasses and was looking through them, despairing. . . . "There are some left. . . . They're in the shell-holes. The wires have held them up. . . ."

We were hustling one another behind him, stretching out our hands.

"Pass me your glasses, I say. . . . Hand them over here. . . ."

By looking closely, in spite of the smoke you could still see them, tiny, gone to ground, dotted about the shell-holes. But suddenly a cloud of smoke hid them; our own artillery was starting again and was trying--alas! too late--to hack through the wide hedge of barbed wire.

"In God's name," howled Hamel, "but they're firing on to them!"

A salvo dropped its five terrible gusts around the living wreckage, then the shrapnel broke and hailed above them. The eyeless guns were raging desperately against that poor corner.

"But they must be warned! . . . The firing must be stopped!" cried Demachy, livid with horror.

The Captain passed at the run.

"Can't they see, then! An orderly here! . . . Quick! to the telephone!"

Still it was lashing down, harrowing up the ground. Between the salvoes something could be seen moving in the shell-holes, a form rising from the earth; one of the survivors had unfastened his flannel belt, a wide red belt, and kneeling on the edge of his hole, thirty paces from the Germans, he was waving his pennon, his arms lifted as high as he could stretch.

"Red! He's asking them to lift the range," cried the trench.

Dry and tragical, Mauser shots rang out. The soldier had dropped back again, perhaps wounded. . . . Shells dug once more into the accursed spot, tearing away a whirlwind of earth in the heavy smoke. Anxiously we waited for the cloud to drift away.

No, he was not dead. The man stood up again, and stretching his arm to the utmost, he waved his belt in a sweeping red gesture. Once more again the Boches fired. The soldier fell once more.

Men were shouting: "Swine! Swine!"

"We must attack!" cried Gilbert, haggard with pity and rage.

Between every clap of thunder the soldier stood up every time, his pennon in his fist, and the bullets never sent him down for more than a second. "Red! Red!" went the waving belt. But the guns, gone crazy, fired on all the same, as if they were minded to smash them all. The shells encircled the burrowing group, came still nearer, was about to overwhelm them. . . .

Then the man stood upright, full in the open, and with a great wild gesture he brandished his pennon above his head, facing the enemy's rifles. Twenty shots were sped. They saw him stagger, and he fell, his body riddled and broken on the keen pointed wires whose strands received him.

The man had fallen, but the Boches went on firing ferociously all the same, and the murderous crackle hurt us cruelly, desperately, as if it had dealt us all a wound. A

26

cloud of shelling hid the horrible scene. But still the firing could be heard behind the moving curtain. The smoke dissipated. Nothing was moving now. . . . Yes. . . . An arm moved still, barely moved, trailing its pennon in the grass "Red! . . . Lengthen the range! . . . Lengthen the range! . . ."

. . . .

Lights were hiding under the huts. Laughter and voices were snuggling into them, shivering with cold. It was the hour before sleep. The bitter wind that swept through the branches with the sound like a weir brought from the trenches the random shots of over-anxious sentries.

Then all at once the long crackle of a salvo tore the silence, rockets abolished the night with their sinister and livid career, and the firing broke out again as you might make a fire blaze up again with a bundle of briars.

"Here, that's beginning again," the boys would say. And Vairon, his blanket about his nose, would murmur. "As long as they don't begin asking for reinforcements!"

Solicitous, perhaps uneasy, the Captain, Cruchet, walked nervously up and down in the roadway; now and then he clambered up the bank, behind the vineyards, and scanned the big black fields towards the sheepfold. That was where the firing was going on. And yet there was nothing to be seen. The night was impervious, with never a streak of lightning, never a flare from a shell, and the rockets that burst over the main road in great balls of light only disclosed stately, silent trees in the sleeping fields.

What was happening? Nobody knew. Perhaps the Germans were attacking the main road. The firing was confined to not more than a couple of hundred mètres, and was as though lost in that vast horizon of absolute quiet. Wholly ignorant of events, we listened to the war of the two opposing noises, and when silence fell again after a salvo, we thought: "That's that. . . . They have repulsed the Boches."

Sulphart was shuffling the cards over and over; and Broucke, to lull himself to sleep, was repeating his ditty.

Dors, min p'tit quinquin.
Min p'tit pouchin,
Min p'tit poujin.

The others were already sleeping. In the dark depths of the hut there was nothing now to be heard but the regular sound of the nails of one of our boys who was scratching his stomach, tormented by lice. The firing, blazing up again, failed to waken them. The Captain watched alone, a long, lean frame, all legs. He was waiting for Bourland, one of his orderlies, whom he had sent to the road to bring him news, I heard the hobnailed boots of the soldier returning.

A little later an order passed from hut to hut.

"Get up. . . . Muster. . . . ."

As the firing seemed to be extending, we tumbled out quickly, thrusting each other about, our hands disputing for our rifles in the dark. Rapidly the sections fell into line. The newly awakened men shivered, surprised by the frosty night.

"The fourth company is perhaps going to need us," said the Captain in his dry voice. "They are expecting an attack. Accordingly it is expressly forbidden to take boots off. . . . Is that clear? Kits to be kept packed, blankets on top, every man to have his rifle by him. . . . Now, I want a volunteer."

We were listening, shoulder to shoulder, the four sections forming square. A

27

desultory crackle of firing made him silent for a moment, his ear cocked; then the noise crumbled away in scattered shots, and a disturbing silence washed out everything. Were they at the road?

"A volunteer who knows the section pretty well," went on the Captain, speaking faster. "It is a matter of guiding a patrol of the fourth which is to get in touch with the territorials on the right bank of the river. Enemy details may perhaps have slipped in there. . . . I know more than one stout fellow in the company, I fancy, among my old hands."

"Here!" at once called out a voice.

It was Gilbert. Quickly he had called out, on the spur, without reflecting, merely for the vibrant delight of hearing in the silence his voice with no fear in it; merely to throw out his name proudly before three hundred dumb men.

"Demachy--first section."

And his heart thumped to hear his own voice, his proffered name. . . . Confidently he stepped out of his rank, making a way for himself with his elbows and stood at attention.

"I'd have liked an old hand better," said the Captain. "Still, since you come forward, it's well. . . . It's very well."

We were sent back to shelter, and Gilbert, having been given his orders, moved off, weapon in hand.

He climbed the bank and went by the fields. As he was skirting the vineyards he gave a jump. A man there, right in front of him. It was a sentry keeping watch on the plain.

"You're going to the road? Go down as far as the apple-tree, then you've only to follow the path. . . . But look lively, you know; it whistles a bit when they start firing."

He set off again. Partridges woke up and made away from under his feet with their heavy flight. He had again to repress a quick movement of recoil, and with freezing hands he loaded his rifle. His eyes searched the darkness; no sign of a tree there. Three hundred mètres from the dug-outs he felt himself isolated and alone, already threatened and in danger, far from everything. He was not afraid, however; it was this great silence, that void, that darkness, that troubled him.

The firing broke out again suddenly, and a few bullets sang round him. He felt no fear of them. Only he held his rifle across his body in such a way that the stock protected his belly, and he lowered his head, naively thinking that in this way nothing could touch him. Only the rockets guided him, and the invisible firing. He walked toilsomely, at every step heaving up his bootsweighted with clay. Now and then he caught a furtive sound, and dropping on his knees, finger on trigger, he peered about.

The trenches were not joined up at the river. Suppose the Germans had slipped in there! He waited a moment, then started again, bending still more. A path cut across the fields. Was this the right one? . . . He followed it at random. The brutal sound of the firing was drawing nearer. At last he could distinguish the line of trees by the road, and let himself slide down the bank. In the ditch there lay about accoutrements, kit, weapons, packs; against a heap of broken stone a dead man was lying. Gilbert turned away his eyes and quickly sped across the roadway. The fourth company was deployed in skirmishing order, the soldiers clinging to the stony side of the bank. Sitting on a milestone a man was dipping bread in a drinking-cup.

"Who are you?"

"I'm from the third company. . . . I'm looking for Captain Stanislas, for the patrol."

"That's me."

At that moment a voice came down from above:

"There's something moving close to the stack."

The Captain swelled his voice.

"Attention for a salvo! Left of the straw stack. . . . Present. . . . Fire!"

A terrible crack stunned Gilbert. He had seen all along the bank the thin edging of flames jet forth.

"Follow the road as far as the tree that lies across it, about five hundred mètres off. . . ." said the officer, sitting down again. "The patrol is waiting for you."

Gilbert hurried along. In the darkness the sheepfold could be divined, a big derelict building with its walls riddled with loopholes. Farther on the bank decreased, barely overhanging the road, and at this point a tree was down. Gilbert halted and put one knee to the ground. A voice hailed him out of the field hidden in the dark:

"Is that the man from the third company? . . . This way."

There were five of them. Sitting on his heels, the corporal was scanning the night with mistrust.

"Do you know the road well?"

"Yes," said Gilbert, "it's over there."

And with a gesture he pointed into the night.

"That's where they made a surprise attack on Sunday? . . . The lad with the red pennon?"

They fixed bayonets, and the rifles were lengthened with a slender gleam. The corporal was hoisting himself up when a rocket whistled off.

"Don't move."

They stayed motionless. The full-blown rocket fell back, shaking its dazzling head. Crouching in a ring, they looked as if they were ready to dance the capucine. On the ridge a file of men was discovered, laden with stakes and tools, then it disappeared when the rocket was quenched.

"Come along!"

The firing that had calmed down for a moment at times livened up again, to die down again as quickly.

"Hark at them," grumbled the corporal. "They don't mean to leave a beet standing."

"You've been attacked?"

"Telegraph poles, oh yes! and the straw stack. That's what they've been firing at for the last two hours. . . . Good job they don't aim this way, the b----s!"

They went on in open order, several paces apart. Gilbert went in front. On the ridge, a dull noise gave life to the darkness, the clinking of spades. Then they entered into the realm of the unknown.

They went a hundred paces, kneeled down, ransacked the fields with a piercing eye, then set off again. The corporal prodded a black shape with the point of his bayonet. . . . Gilbert's heart leaped.

"Nothing. . . . a sheaf."

They must now have been coming close up to the river when the night seemed

29

to grow brighter. There was now in front of the moon only a filmy curtain; the wind pulled it aside and the fields appeared, bare as your hand. The patrol stood still, unmasked by that huge celestial flare. They remained for one endless moment crouching, silent, without moving. Gilbert alone raised himself on his elbows, bare-headed, and tried to make out his whereabouts and the lay of the land. When the moon was hidden again, he got up the first and set off in a straight line. He had seen the first corpses lying in the grass. . . . it was the right road they were on. At the first he brushed against he made a sharp movement of terror, fear of the cold hand that was on the point of seizing him. The man had dropped in a ball, his knees doubled up, seeming to continue his dreadful praying into the infinite.

Gilbert no longer dared to go forward, fear thrilling in the pit of his stomach, his legs powerless and flabby. He pushed sharply up against the corporal.

"What, it's not there, is it?" murmured the voice.

"Yes."

He looked at the dead men, all those dead men he had seen running to their cruel, hideous fate. Their immense field frightened him, all those forgotten sheaves. . . . He guessed at them everywhere, in every shell-hole, in every furrow, and no longer dared to move. Nothing could save him, not even the comrade against whom he pressed.

"Well, then, we're going on?"

A little farther, the soldiers' overcoats were huddled in bunches. They were already so flat, the bodies so empty, that one could barely imagine that they had ever lived, had ever run. An illimitable distress weighed upon Gilbert's heart. Now they terrified him no more. Can one be afraid of those one loves? Making a powerful effort over himself, forcing his reluctant hands, he stooped over a corpse and unbuttoned its coat to take its papers. He hardly even had a little shiver of nerves when he felt the cold flesh of the neck under his timid fingers. The corporal was already stooping to take the medal from another.

The poor comrades they had come to see in their annihilation were to live again for a moment under their brotherly hands. And awakened and compassionate, it was the dead who guided the patrol, seeming to pass the living on from hand to hand.

. . . .

Gilbert came back at early dawn.

"I took the patrol right up to the Boche trench system," he recounted to the Captain.

Cruchet only replied, "Ah! . . ."

And he wore a smile so incredulous that Gilbert reddened under it. Someone present told the tale in his own version, and some of the boys looked at the volunteer with a bantering eye.

"Some blokes know how to tell the tale," said Fouillard to nobody in particular. . . . "He'll get his corporal's stripes."

And another:

"You shove yourself into shell-hole for a couple of hours, you know, and then you come and pitch it that you've visited their listening-post."

Gilbert, who was talking to us, made no retort. A little bitter smile wrinkled his mouth.

"I'm going to swaddle up my rifle like you," he said to Lemoine; "the rain has got mine all rusty."

He went off with his head down. Sitting at the entrance of his shelter, he took his rifle between his knees, and unbuttoning his coat, he brought out a wide belt of red flannel. The laughing stopped like a shot.

They looked out into the plain, in front of the German trench. The red pennon was not there now.

CHAPTER IV
GOOD DAYS

UNDER the rain we were humping ourselves like cats. This muddy black village was not expecting us, and, piled up in drenched packets along the sleeping houses, we watched out for the return of the quartermasters who were hunting for billets for us. Our own, big Lambert, had just gone into that farmhouse whose red-curtained windows crimsoned the night with a glare like a public house, and from the street we recognized, though without catching the words, his cordial tones endeavouring to convince and persuade the house-holder. The farmer, a stiff necked peasant replied noisily:

"No, no! I won't sleep any of them in my cellar, I tell you flat. They'd drink the bit of a cask I've got left on me."

The company, which was going out of the trenches, had sat down at the whistle, harassed, covered with mud, soaked. Before us, others were still passing along, with the hurrying trampling of a funeral behind time, trotting towards Bagneux. After the machine gunners with their splashed mules, half seen through a mist of rain and weariness, there passed the jolting lorries of the Army Service Corps, the butcher's cart, the ambulance with its wheels iron-shod, and at the tail of the regiment the company carts, a burlesque procession of four-wheeled waggons, old stage-coaches, and shandry-dans picked up by chance in march and countermarch, from Charleroi to Reims: old wains with creaking axles, tilt-carts overflowing with packs and rifles, covered carts under dripping awnings, family brakes and brewers' drays; then bringing up the rear of the column, the baggage-master's phaeton, dragged by a big plough-horse almost too thick to squeeze into the shafts.

The men had no eyes for anything, absolutely worn out, half-sleeping. The passing wheels brushed against them, but they didn't even shift their feet back. They had let themselves drop just where they happened to be, without looking, with no fear of the mud that could never make them dirtier than they were, and piled themselves together in soaking bundles, crouching under doorways or sitting on their packs with their backs against the wall. Some that were still standing were cramping up to the houses all along, to shelter under the eaves; their arms crossed on their rifles, they talked of fresh straw, of wine not too dear, of rest-time with no drill, a whole world of visionary happiness; and the others were listening stupidly, too done to want anything beyond the mere right to fall asleep.

Every moment an officer would pass and throw a harsh light on the squatting forms with a sudden ray of his electric torch.

"Orderlies! . . . Where are the liaison orderlies? This is simply madness!"

Running up, a quartermaster called:

"That's all right, Captain! I've found a good billet for the horses."

The rain kept on falling, falling, fine, cold, and soft. Overhead, between the high wan banks of the houses, the night swam like a black river.

. . . .

The whole house resounds from the yard to the garret. In the kitchen, where eddies the acrid smoke from green wood, men are fighting for quarts of wine. The staircase is full of comings and goings, up and down, and singing.

But out here in the garden everything is at quiet. To make a seat for myself I have taken the bucket and turned it upside down, and, installed in idleness with my back to the wall, as though deep in an armchair, I am day-dreaming. It is early morning. Day has not long finished her toilette, the grass is still dewy, and the sky is bringing out armfuls of white clouds that he hangs out to dry like linen.

Indolent eyed, still dulled with sleep, I look at the garden all lying fallow, with its bushes despoiled, its tufts of weeds, and its squeaking, creaking pump, at which the boys are cleaning themselves up. I laze on, between sleeping and waking.

We have slept sumptuously. For the first time in a fortnight we have been able to get our boots off, get rid of belt, bayonet, all that beastly equipment that cuts into your soft ribs. I woke precisely as I lay down, sausaged up in my blanket, my head in a cupboard, the plank floor for my mattress and a bag of beans for pillow. I must have had splendid dreams. When I awoke fragments were still sticking in my mind like down from an eiderdown quilt.

The corporals, all collected in the washhouse, are sharing out woollen clothing for their squads. Now that it's not so cold great bales of it arrive every week.

Down along by the hedge, Sulphart is brushing Gilbert's puttees, whistling the while. He has found a room with some good people where we are to make our mess, and already he is thinking over breakfast. To eat at a table, and off plates, . . . that seems to me something almost too rich and rare, and I don't dare quite to believe in it altogether for fear of being disappointed.

"This is a good life," repeats Sulphart. Round him are six or seven men cleaning their mud-plastered coats. First of all they scrape at the mud with their knives or a bit of broken bottle, and when it is turned into dust they beat their duds like a carpet, with lusty blows of a stick. That's what we mean by "brushing."

"Talk about your rotten mud! . . . And this does stick--it's chalk."

With the charming immodesty of soldiers two of the boys, naked to the waist, are hunting for their lice. Vairon is holding his flannel out at arm's length, as a painter might scrutinize a picture, and with nose all wrinkled up and eyes intent, he is inspecting his garment. Then, when he has discovered the beast, he brings his thumbs quickly together, and "crack!" he squashes it. Broucke, on the contrary, is going over his shirt, fold by fold, his nose almost thrust into it, and hunts quietly and methodically. When he routs out a big fat fellow he utters a cry:

"One more that'll never nibble me again!"

Vairon, whose nails are cracking, counts out loud: "Thirty-two. . . . thirty-three."

"Twenty-seven. . . . twenty-eight, . . ." responds the lad from the North quietly.

As he scrapes the puttees, Sulphart follows the hunters with the eye of a connoisseur. Already he has his favourite.

"You'll see it will be Vairon that'll bag the most. His blood's hotter. . . . Are they big 'uns?"

"Regular iron crossers," the other informs him vaingloriously.

"That's nothing, anyway, that lot isn't," says Sulphart with his important air. "Some boys have had red ones, Arab lice. They're fiercer, they wolf in your blood. And they give you diseases, too. But the other ones likely would rather draw off bad humours."

"Nothing better for the health," adds a well-informed comrade, who is pulling off his shirt to begin his own private hunt. "They suck out the evil out of you. . . ."

"There was my small brother: it was the lice and the ringworm that kept him from having a go of meningitis."

"I'm not surprised," replies the other, now beginning the inspection of his belt.

But from his very first look he finds himself discouraged. His underclothing is simply swarming with vermin; their black files can be seen crawling in every fold. For one moment he seems to hesitate, then making up his mind, he rolls everything up into a ball--his shirt, his drawers, his belt--and hurls the parcel over the wall.

"So much the worse for that. I'll get on to fresh lot. Anyway, that'll always be so much the less to wash."

Fouillard, whom I heard a moment ago shouting in his den, has just displayed himself on the threshold, his bare arms black with soot and glistening with grease; from his unlaced shoes to his dishevelled hair nobody could find, no matter how closely he searched, a spot that could be soiled. His skin, his body-linen, his trousers, everything is grey, greasy, bespotted, and when with a familiar gesture he rubs his palms on his behind to wipe them dry, you ask yourself which is going to dirty the other, the seat of his trousers or his hands. He stares at us for an instant, severely, ransacks the garden with a mistrusting look, and shouts:

"Who is the dirty dog that's pinched my bucket?"

My first impulse was to get up in order to restore him the said object. But no, I am really much too comfortable. I find myself still more comfortable seated, since somebody wants to take the thing away from me. Comfort is a kind of paralysis to me.

"Anyhow, I can't jolly well go and fetch water in my boots," yells the cook.

Oh, no! That would be very poor advice to give. Nevertheless, I keep my knees close together so as to hide my seat, and I look guilelessly at Fouillard, now thoroughly frantic and howling with impotent fury.

"Pack of pigs! So after all, I'm through with it. I'm going to drop you and your cooking; if any of you would like to take it on, he has only to go and put his name down on the roll."

. . . .

We must make a fine show, the four sections in square formation.

There aren't two rigs precisely alike. Except the latest arrivals, we have been equipped with odds and ends, in the confusion of the early months of the war, and since then we've just managed the best way we could. There are overcoats of every kind of hue, of every kind of shape, every kind of age. Tall men have too short coats, and little men too long ones. Fouillard's back strap on his coat knocked most pitiably on his backside; and on Father Hamel's wide corporation the all too narrow coat made horizontal wrinkles, all the buttons ready to fly off. For my own part, Sulphart is the one I like best.

He is clad in a top-coat of the old style, deep blue, with a big patch pocket of a pretty hussar's blue. He has stitched his first-aid packet on to his left breast, and reinforced his puttees with a band of stout leather cut out of regulation gaiters. Like every good soldier on active service, he has taken pains to distinguish himself by breaking the peak of his képi, in the fashion of the Bat' d' Af'; and he has still further adorned this headgear, now flatter than a pancake, with a plaited chin-strap of the choicest effect.

His broad crackled shoes, dried up and hard as horn, that you might fancy had been cut out of old wood with a billhook, still carry on their twisted heels something of the glorious mud of the trenches; and his red trousers show at the thigh through a wide rent in his blue cloth coat. You might fancy he had been specially drawn for l'Illustration.

Others, who have already got hold of the new overcoats of horizon blue, play the heavy swell. You might say they are off to the war in their Sunday clothes. The boys look at them with an irony a little forced.

"Don't you worry; always the same lot, that click. . . ."

"Ah, you see, the quartermaster only chucked them to the blighters that greased his paw on the quiet. . . ."

And Sulphart, looking at those dandy jacks with eyes ensnared, is already dreaming of the happy alterations he is going to transact on his own rig.

"I'll cut two big raglan pockets on the two sides, and I'll fit up a stick-up collar for myself. . . . You'll see if I won't be the complete toff."

Captain Cruchet, who has very sharp ears, turns about, his lips tight.

"Silence! Who spoke? . . . You are at attention. Look after your men, Morache."

Ricordeau, who is looking to have his sergeant's stripes, draws down his brow as he looks at us to make it appear that he is a man in authority. Sulphart doesn't turn a hair, but behind him Gilbert is on tenterhooks, afraid that someone will spot his sweater, which is too long. Everybody is silent. Satisfied, the Captain goes on with his inspection. As he draws near, backs straighten up, as if a button had been pressed; left arms hung rigid, and all eyes, a little lacking in confidence, looked intelligently into space at a distance theoretically computed at fifteen paces. Lean, long-legged, his long face framed between short black side-whiskers, Captain Cruchet has an air of natural severity that produces its effect. With eye-brows full of care, he comes forward slowly, scanning every man as if he was meeting him for the first time.

"Take off your cap."

Our comrade, very red about the gills, awkwardly removes his képi.

"Tt! Tt! Tt! Tt! It's far too long, it's simply filthy! I must have that hair cut. Take his name, Morache."

As his back is turned to us, several of our boys furtively slip their caps off, and, spitting in their hands, sleek down their restive locks as well as they can. Unluckily the Captain is not taking an interest in hair only. He notices everything: the missing button, the rust-spot on the rifle, the ill-greased boot, the spot of mud on the cartridge-pouch; and in an icy voice he enquires:

"Where did you get yourself filthy like that?"

What a fool of a question! . . .

Having properly wigged Bréval, whose cartridge-pouch holds together with string, he stops in front of Sulphart. The other stood perfectly rigid, heels clamped together, eyes right. The Captain considers him for a good minute, and then:

"He's a beauty, that fellow," he scoffs.

Sulphart has not moved a muscle, not even winked an eye. His neighbours look at him out of the corners of their eyes, with little sidelong smiles.

"You fancy yourself more seductive with the peak of your cap broken, like a vagabond. Ttt! . . . ttt! . . . Is it to give the girls a treat? They'd have queer taste!"

The delight of the neighbours breaks out in little servile laughs. Still Sulphart does not turn a hair, the left hand wide open, the head a thought thrown back.

"And that hair! My word! he's not had it cut since the very start of the. campaign. . . . Torn trousers. Ttt! . . . ttt!. . . mud on his shoes. . . . Bad turnout, shocking bad turn-out! You will take this fellow's name, Morache; four days' cells. . . . And see that his hair's cut. . . . ttt! . . . ttt! . . . as short as possible."

Sulphart has remained perfectly impassible. He has not so much as blinked, not so much as shuddered. Ah! these conquerors of the Marne!

We were fancying the review at an end, and impatience was playing pins and needles in our knees when the Captain gave the order:

"Down kits!"

I was sure it would come. It's an inspection of emergency rations this time. Kneeling before your unfastened kit, you've got to unpack everything, undo everything, bring out everything; to find the salt soup-cube crushed under your shirts, or the coffee tablet that is crumbling away among your socks and soiling your linen.

On your knees, in a fury, you empty your whole wardrobe.

"He thinks we're going to eat his blasted biscuits on him, no," growls Vairon.

You spread out all your possessions: cartridges, the little box of sugar, the tin of bully-beef. The pack that gave you so much pain and grief to put together has to be emptied to the very bottom. Some of the boys, down on all fours, are counting and recounting their cartridges with an uneasy air.

"Good Lord! I'm one packet short. . . . You've not got one to spare, have you?"

Our whole belongings are contained in this little pile of duds and tinned stuffs, which the Captain tosses over with the end of his cane to count the bunches of cartridges. He goes the round at a good pace, then planting himself face-to-face with our section, he enquires:

"Anybody got a fancy to be cook? The fifth squad's cook is relieved. Who would like to take his place?"

At once, with one accord, everybody looked at Bouffioux. Two hundred jolly, open faces are gazing on him, enjoying the joke beforehand. The horse-dealer has turned pink about the gills, but for all that he has called out:

"Here!"

"You know how to cook?" asked Cruchet.

"I was a cook in civilian life, Captain."

At that the whole company broke into laughter. Broucke was choking, bent double. Even the sergeants standing solemnly at attention could not contain themselves; and Cruchet, displeased and scandalized, had to give the order:

"Fall out! Dismiss!"

When I went down next into the kitchen, where slabs of flooring were burning with gay flames, the late cook, black as a sweep, was handing over his powers and authority to Bouffioux in front of the assembled squad. The ceremony was a very simple one. Fouillard, who was stirring the stew with a fragment of a vine-prop, held the thing out to his supplanter.

"Here, there's your ladle. You've nothing to do but dish up. This evening you'll have to make the scoff. . . . Only I'm going to feed off sausage, for it strikes me you look about as much fit to be a cook as I am to be a verger."

An uproar full of laughter greeted the cook. Bouffioux placidly took off his overcoat.

"Don't you worry about the grub," he answered mildly.

Sulphart, who was looking at him with strong fellow-feeling, dug him in the ribs.

"Hi, old bull-face, they say you've got the shivers for going up the trenches. You didn't happen to be born on a windy day, by chance?"

Bouffioux was quietly starting to stir his stew.

"Don't you worry yourself about the wind, either. . . . As long as my hair curls all right and my belly isn't flapping I'm not the boy to fash myself."

. . . .

I should fancy this must be something like the way savages do their cooking.

Down on his knees before his pot, Bouffioux, a trifle drunk, his eyes inclined to tears, his big face shining with sweat and smeared with soot, is blowing himself clean out of breath at a little fire of damp wood that is smoking, smoking, smoking, but simply refuses to break into flame. Beside him, holding the lid by way of a shield, Vairon is stirring the mess with the vine-prop, whilst Broucke, tattered and half-naked, is chopping up extremely red and raw frozen meat with a wood axe, shouting Flemish choruses the while. You might fancy he was disjointing an explorer! Then he throws the frozen gobbets very circumspectly on to a potato-sack as muddy as a straw mat.

All about the hearth-place the boys are crowding in, their hands thrust in their pockets, with airs of prodigious interest, and a slight smile hovering round the corners of their mouths. One would say that they are tightening their lips to keep their delight from bursting out: from their glistening eyes to their puffed-out cheeks you feel that they are just ripe to break into shouts of merriment.

Still down upon his knees, Bouffioux is still puffing and blowing, stopping now and then to cough and to spit out flakes of soot.

"Get on with it, my buck," Vairon exhorts encouragingly; "it's just beginning to come on the boil."

And first warning the boys with a sly wink, he adds with a perfectly serious air:

"Would you like to know what I think, my fine laddie? Well, here goes. Your mess would be better if you were to chuck a bit of rice to it. . . . That would thicken the gravy for you."

The other lifts his face with its eyes running, its lost and bewildered look.

"What. . . . rice? . . . ."

Like that, crumpled up on his knees, his eyes streaming with tears, hairy and besmeary, you could imagine he is begging forgiveness from his murderers in the hour of his being roasted alive.

"Naturally, a go of rice," perfidiously approves Fouillard, who would fain give Bouffioux all the benefit of his experience. "That will give you something smoother and more fit to serve up."

The boys dig one another in the ribs, half-choked with delight. "Come along, then, with the rice," consents Bouffioux, getting up painfully.

He goes off to get a big double handful, a porringer full, and throws it into the pot. Hidden behind the duty corporal, one of the cooks laughs into his handkerchief, unable to hold in any longer.

"Ah! This is a lark! What on earth are the lads of the fifth going to have to swallow? . . . ."

37

"More wood," orders Vairon, "the fire's catching. Don't bring any branches, they make too much smoke."

Without changing the weapon he wields, Broucke seizes the half of a door, props it up against a wall, and splits it with one stout blow.

"We'll soon have to pull up more treads out of the stair," says he, "there's no more wood left already. Anyhow, that's the stuff burns best of all."

And, in fact, over this very dry wood that is burning with a clear steady blaze, the mess begins to simmer and sing.

"That's the style! It's getting hot!" stammers the horse-dealer. "I'll be ready up to time!"

A whole ring of happy faces is contemplating him; their delight is turning to celestial happiness.

"Do you know, Bouffioux," now cunningly suggests the duty corporal; "if I was you, I'd pour a good couple of litres of wine into it and make something like a broth of it."

A laugh jerks out. Fouillard can't hold in any more. But the others approve with nodding heads, solemn as a council of state.

But this time Bouffioux protests: "There's no sense in me bunging wine into it." He is beginning to recover a slight glimmer of reason in the fumes of his rotgut brandy. . . . "You've made me stick milk into it already."

"What's that got to do with it? Milk first--you've not put in such a flood of it, and then the vegetables have soaked it all up. I tell you you're wrong."

"Sure, that would certainly improve it," is Vairon's hypocritical opinion.

"But I haven't got any pinard. And then I can't take what's for the squad."

The duty corporal, perceiving that the bewildered cook is weakening on it, has a noble notion.

"Here, I'll slip you a couple of litres on my own. . . . Broucke, fetch it out of the corner. There are six full buckets and three bottles."

Prompt at the word, the ch'timi lays hold of the nearest bucket--I recognize the canvas bucket in which I made my toilet this morning--and from it pours out four good cupfuls by guess-work.

"That will be topping!" declares Vairon, already smacking his lips with the air of an epicure.

"Do you think so?" asks Bouffioux, vaguely uneasy.

"Certain!" agree all the others in chorus. "You've put nothing bad in it. . . . Meat, sweet potatoes, milk to soften it, leeks, wine, American bacon to give it a touch of fat, rice to thicken the sauce, biscuits. That's all good stuff."

Bouffioux, careworn in spite of everything, takes off the lid and sniffs at the mixture.

"I don't know if it's only my notion, but it smells queer."

"What would it smell queer for?" protests Sulphart, who wants to take a hand.

And pushing the others aside, he comes in his turn to snuff up the bouquet of our dinner.

"That's an appetizer!" he declares with scandalous effrontery. "Aren't you going to have a taste?"

Vairon, without waiting to be pressed, digs his cup into the pot and brings up a kind of thick, mauveish mush, the very look of which turns the gorge. He tastes it slowly, with little sips like a true gourmet.

"That's topping!" says he. "Bar kid, it's first-rate, only . . . "--he seems to consider for a moment--"you might say it does want. . . ."

"What!" breaks out Bouffioux, "you're not going to say it wants something more yet!"

"I don't say that; only to my thinking, a trifle, just a wee trifle, of chocolate grated into this stew wouldn't do it any harm."

Every back bends double; they are simply strangling with mirth, they choke, they are clean bowled over. But this time the cook stands out. He shrugs his shoulders, and pulls up his trousers with both hands, with the gesture of a real dandy.

"Chocolate in stew, such a thing was never heard of. You take me for a silly ass! . . ."

"In stew, that's what he says, the blighter!" exclaims Sulphart. "To start with, is it stew, at all? And then--of course I don't care a hang, I don't--but if you were so confoundedly up to snuff as all that, it wasn't worth while to come and hunt me and Broucke out to help you to get the grub ready. Next time you won't get me again . . . ."

The whole troop approves and applauds Sulphart, and Fouillard in three crude words scarifies the black ungratefulness of his successor.

"He gives you a bit of good advice and you tell him to go to blazes. You are the last word in swine!"

"Oh no! oh no!" brays Vairon, "he knows all about everything better than anybody else."

One of the cooks shrugged his shoulders.

"They're all the same. Can't do a bally thing and don't want to listen to anybody. You ask the fellows in my squad if I don't make them chocolate and rice. . . ."

"But this isn't rice," struggles Bouffioux, but less strenuously, "it's stew."

"That's no matter," puts in the corporal. "You shouldn't be so damn obstinate. Chocolate is always a good thing. . . . To-night I'm coming to feed with your squad, so there, you've got to put my name in the pot. . . . . . ."

This time the defeated horse-dealer resigns himself once more with the docility of a drunken man. Bringing out his knife, he scrapes two bars of chocolate into his stew as it boils, whilst behind his back Broucke mimics a South Sea war-dance, flourishing his hatchet.

Pell-mell the others dash outside, choking with laughter, bending double, babbling and stuttering, and leave Bouffioux all alone before his pot.

In the garden fireplaces are sending up their smoke along the foot of the wall, all broidered over with house-leeks: the kitchen for all the squads. Here is soup, there a stew. The cook of the second squad is getting up a fry.

"We'll never have the luck to get hold of one like that," says Vairon sorrowfully.

Another, planted in perplexity before his fire, is holding in his big black paw a huge chunk of chilled beef, wrapped up in its gauze.

"More first-aid packet," he objurgated in disgust. "How do you imagine I'm to cook that kind of muck, I ask you?"

And as he looks long at his meat, with a far-away air of absorption, as Hamlet might have looked at Yorick's skull. I look round for Sulphart. There he is, whistling, planted at the foot of the garden, his thought drifting with the wind, his eyes lost out beyond the devastated woods.

"What are you thinking about, Sulphart?"

He still retains his dreamy air.

"I was thinking how, when we were mobilized, as I left the factory, I dropped my tools and my overalls at the wine-shop opposite, and said to the owner: 'Put them on one side, I'll get them from you again one of these Saturdays on my way home from Berlin.'"

CHAPTER V
VIGIL

"SIX O'CLOCK, and grub not along yet. . . . No, it's a bit too thick, anyhow!"

Sulphart can't stay in his place any longer. Having produced his mess-tin and his cup, he goes and posts himself at the entrance of the zouaves' trench, where the fatigue parties come in. Thus, propped up on his two long, lean legs, with their puttees all plastered with dried mud, you might think he was mounted on top of a pile. Leaning with his back against the trench side, he is looking, furiously looking.

"Talk about those dung-merchants of cooks! Nothing doing! And I'm as sharp set as you like."

But nobody listens, nobody pities him. Some are reading, others are sleeping in their burrow little Bélin is sewing on the buttons of his overcoat with telephone-wire, and Hamel is chewing tobacco. There is one even who, spurred on by blank laziness, is gazing from the loophole. This universal spinelessness disgusts Sulphart completely. He shrugs his shoulders, and avenges himself with a lusty kick at a casual mess-tin lying about, and, perhaps to avoid listening to his rumbling inside, he enters upon a vicious diatribe in which his comrades, the cooks, and the high command are all compared to pigs, to men of unmentionable practices, and more particularly to straw defiled by cattle! He even finds courage for a sardonic laugh.

"We'll have them! Oh yes! . . . We'll be having lentils like stones and macaroni in cold water. And all this time the cooks are chin-wagging with the other cows. . . ."

I know Sulphart and his extravagant opinions: "the other cows" can only mean to lump together all those persons who don't go into the trenches, without distinction as to sex, costume, or rank. Thereafter he loses himself in projects for army reforms in which it is expressly laid down and enacted that "every bloke is to be cook, each one in turn," and that they are to be condemned "to eat their own concoction instead of stuffing themselves with good fries, because like that they'll put a bit more zest in getting up the grub for the poor poilus." Even so are the words of a just, impartial man.

But the others, who are not hungry yet, give him not the slightest word of applause or approbation: Bréval is writing, Broucke is snoring, Vairon is whistling. So finally, disgusted for good, Sulphart holds his tongue, takes out his knife, and begins to cut into slices the hardened mud that weighs down his big boots. At that moment a familiar sound makes him lift his head.

"There they are! Soup, boys!"

With a clinkum-clankum of bottles and cans, it is, in fact, the mess party arriving. Bouffioux walks at their head, with a big chaplet of chunks of bread strung on a piece of cord slung over his shoulder, a dish of stew in one hand, and in the other a petrol-tin than now holds its five good litres of wine.

All the cooks follow him in Indian file, laden with bottles, which they carry two by two slung from a pole, potato-sacks filled out with nobody knows what, dishes into which bits of earth are dropping, canvas buckets, lumps of bread spitted on to a piece of wood, the whole rudimentary paraphernalia of a bevy of negro women bringing food to their tribesmen.

Sulphart has immediately spotted the can that Bouffioux is carrying on his hip.

"Hooray, there's a drop of brandy . . . ." Flat against the side of the trench, which crumbles away, or getting into our dug-outs, we let the fatigue go by; then we flock round our own cook and his assistant, who have put their burden down. Eagerly the dishes are uncovered.

"What have we got to eat?"

Everybody throws questions all at the same time to Bouffioux, who rubs himself down.

"Have you got the letters? Are there any for me?"

"Did you think of bringing me a waxlight and a packet of baccy?"

The two men reply quietly, with brief phrases, and with a curious air that I noticed immediately.

"It's first-aid packet," explains Bouffioux, "that was the only meat they gave out. I've made rice with chocolate, it ought to be top hole. . . . The can of wine is chock full. . . . My mate here has the letters."

But he says all this in a thoroughly unnatural voice, with a preoccupied air that Vairon in his turn tumbles to in the end.

"You've got on a very funny mug about it," he says to them politely, . . . "What's up?"

Bouffioux wags his head, and his big face, so shiny that I have long suspected him of washing himself with a piece of bacon fat, almost manages to look concerned.

"One can never be at ease," he replies, as though regretfully. "You are to attack the day after to-morrow."

A short spell of silence fell on us: just long enough for our hearts to go pit-pat. Several have turned pale all at once; there are certain almost imperceptible little nervous tricks--a nostril contracting, an eyelid fluttering. The cooks are staring at us, still shaking their heads. We look at them, willing to disbelieve. Then with one single accord we crowd round them, and questions fly thick and fast:

"Are you sure? But we were going to be relieved to-morrow. . . . Impossible! it's a buzz. . . . Who was it told you that? . . ."

Bouffioux, strong in the authentic news he brings, simply turns about to his assistant:

"Isn't it quite true?"

The other confirms it, in tones of distress.

"You can easily imagine nobody was going to stuff you up with a tale of that kind. It's as true and as certain as anything can be."

Broucke has waked up by himself and come out from his shelter. Sulphart has set down his mess-tin, in which he was just going to heat up Gilbert's tin of pork and beans, and Bréval has folded the letter he was reading. We listen with just a little pang in the chest.

"There are the niggers lying at Fismes," explains Bouffioux; "the village is stuffed with them, the whole Moroccan Division. . . . The divisional hospital orderlies have arrived at Jonchéry. They've been brought along in lorries. . . . It appears that the second corps is to come from Lorraine. . . . And then artillery as well: big guns--you ought to see those. . . ."

A whole army rises up out of their disjointed phrases: cavalry, negroes, aviators, zouaves, engineers. It seems even as if the Legion would be in it, but that Bouffioux wouldn't swear to; it was the paymaster's cyclist who has heard it on the telephone. In short, everything has been foreseen and prepared: the stretcher-bearers to pick us up, and the Chaplains to say the Mass for the dead.

For a moment I have remained nonplussed, my smile, forgotten, still on my lips like a banner of the fourteenth of July that no one has remembered to take down. "What, must still others go and play the madman in that plain? Well, then . . . ." And my smile has come down itself of its own accord.

The boys are not laughing either, now; only by turning their head they would be able to see, through the loophole, the men of the last attack still lying in the deer grass. No one brings a medallion out of a pocket to kiss it secretly; no one cries either, as in the story-books: "At last! We are going to come out of our holes." For an historic word, Sulphart says simply: "Ah! les tantes! . . ." and that without even knowing himself whom the compliment is intended for.

Dumb, we listen to the soup-fetchers, who talk in floods, one taking up the tale from the other. They are shuffling the troops, they install the artillery in position, they make arrangements for supplies, they study the coming of the reserves. . . . They talk on, talk on.

They even give so many exact details that a slight doubt begins to steal into my mind. I have heard so many of these kitchen tales which the cooks pick up behind the lines with the credulity of an aboriginal Redskin, and bring up to us in the trenches at night along with the rice and the wine.

In the mornings, when the rations are given out, they exchange their news, come from mysterious sources: what the paymaster's cyclist caught and misunderstood; what a telephone operator thought he overheard; what a brigade orderly told to the Colonel's driver. All that is brought together, commented on, chewed over, surmise follows surmise, they make their deductions and make up a little so that it may run the better. Now it's finished, and the cook's report is quite ready. So in the evening, the trenches learn that the regiment has the route for Morocco, that the Crown Prince is dead, that Joffre has killed Sarrail with one stroke of his sabre, that we are ordered to rest in Paris, that the Pope has imposed peace, or that the observer in the sausage balloon has been shot because he was found to be a Field-Marshal in the German Army. No one has any pity on that fellow: he is shot at least once every blessed month.

Nobody ever has any doubt, especially when the messenger tells you, on the eve of some big stunt, that you are to be held in reserve as artillery supports. The next day you are invariably in the thick of the barbed wire and fighting for your life like a crew of Red Indians; but you have something else to do than to blame the impostures of the cooks, and the very next time you will believe them just the same. Since the war started, Truth has been coming out of the saucepans; so much the better for her, anyway, poor thing!--she's not so chilly there as in her well.

All these tales, all this humbug, little by little come back to me, and gradually make me somewhat skeptical. I still bend an ear to Bouffioux, who is now discussing the attack from its purely strategic aspect; and most politely, careful not to vex him, I put the question to him:

"I say now, old boy, are you quite sure about it, anyhow? It's not just a kitchen yarn?"

The sweating horse-coper suddenly has stopped arguing, half a word still left on his lips, absolutely dumbfounded. . . . I must have annoyed him. For two seconds he remains gape-mouthed, too indignant to make any reply. Then he goes red about the gills, he's going to burst out. . . .

But now he recovers himself. He simply pulls a scornful face, stoops down, picks up his dish, and declares with all the dignity of a mortally insulted apostle:

"That's all right; I'm a silly ass. Everything I've been telling you is just stuff and nonsense. Only you'll see the day after to-morrow."

He tries to push the boys away and go off, but the others close up together, and so as to keep him with them, they most cowardly take sides against me.

"Don't listen to him. . . . Tell us now. . . . Is it true that the third battalion is to stay in reserve? . . . Why that one rather than any other? . . . Where are we starting from? . . . Are they going to attack the square wood too?"

They are holding him back with both hands, like the poor people clinging fast to Saint Vincent de Paul's robe. Out of sheer goodness of heart Bouffioux consents in spite of everything to ladle out the last of his yarns, and professing to forgive my insults, he instructs the boys, while expressly and frankly dropping "that other nut." That's me, the "other nut."

Without troubling myself, I move away and throw myself down on all fours, as if I was about to beg for forgiveness. But no, I will respect my uniform! I slip into my dug-out head-first, and I rummage about in my satchel looking for a box of preserved food. I fetch out my cooker with its solidified alcohol, my mess-tin full of dirty water most cherishingly kept since yesterday morning, and planting myself on a sandbag, I get ready my bain-marie.

Stooping over the blue flame, I assume an air of absorption, so as to deceive my little world; but I am slyly listening to the horse-dealer, who is still going on talking. To mortify me, he rakes up details he had forgotten, new particulars of which the least one would alone be enough to confound me. And like a chorus, he repeats:

"Maybe that's all gossiping nonsense, that too. . . ."

So much assurance begins in the long run to trouble me. Supposing it was true, all the same; . . . they don't look as if they were pulling our legs. My head down, I observe them artfully over my mess-tin, in which the water is now beginning to sing. The whole squad is grouped about them, plainly agitated. Demachy alone remains placid, and listens to their noisy talking with his habitual little smile, mocking, a trifle bitter, the smile of a spoilt child that nothing can really please now.

Seeing me begin to eat, the boys remember suddenly that their food is waiting.

"It will be getting cold," remarks Broucke sagely. And he fills his mess-tin, still greasy from the last stew with haricot beans still sticking to the bottom. After him everybody serves himself, scrupulously fair. Then in a ring, everyone holding out his tin cup, we surround Bréval, who divides the wine. While he pours it out drop by drop, Sulphart stethoscopes the can of brandy. He gives vent to a plaintive cry, a cry of grief and indignation.

"Ah, it's not even full! . . ."

And flourishing the can as an overwhelming witness to his plaint, he bellows:

"That much brandy for twelve men the night before an attack! We needn't ask who it is that's giving our poor health a knock. . . . Well, then, let them ask for volunteers another time, they can just go and . . ."

"That's the correct amount," says Bouffioux stoutly. "Not quite a full can to each squad."

"Well, then, you go up to the big house and see at the officers' mess if they haven't each got their full pint. After that we're not to give a fig for the Boches? No, let me! . . . Here, I don't want any of their brandy, they can stick it where the

44

monkey. . . ."

And he hurls the can in disgust up on to the edge of the parapet--after carefully making sure that the cork was well rammed home.

The bottles are emptied, the dishes soaked in gravy, Bouffioux and his assistant collect their utensils, carrying away also a handful of postcards scribbled off in a hurry.

"Au revoir, boys!" the big cook wishes us. . . . "Don't worry about it; come along; there will be lots of good luck in front of you yet. . . . What I wish every one of you is a nice little wound with three weeks' cosy in a hospital. . . ."

These prayers, which were delivered in a most cordial, kindly tone, have made Fouillard jump. With a particularly wicked eye he fixes the ruddy-faced horse-coper, the inheritor of his erstwhile job.

"You won't have one yourself, a nice little wound," he shoots at him in his worn, consumptive voice. "It well becomes you to chatter about the attack, you that have always managed to plant yourself down in shelter, you skulker!"

Bouffioux has turned about.

"You listen to me, you there. . . . If I had to do an attack, I wouldn't have the wind up more than you. . . . I've done the retreat, . . . now then!"

"Aye, on the back of a lorry."

"Here, you're a regular mud-walloper," retorts the other, to cut it short; "I'd rather not argue with you."

And he goes off disdainfully, with a last, "Good luck, boys!" to join up with the procession of cooks going back by the zouaves' trench. For a short while nothing further can be heard, only the sound of lapping mouths, every head bowed over the mess-tins like a cab-horse deep in his nosebag.

"That's all right, he gave you a nasty one," mocks Papa Hamel, who is gorging himself with chocolate rice.

"You shut your head!" replies Fouillard, his scanty beard fat with his soup. "I had a notion in my own head that we were going to attack."

"Well, if we do attack, we'll see," cries Gilbert. "Every bullet doesn't kill."

Squatting in his dug-out like a shopman in a booth, little Bélin applauds him:

"What, they're not such terrific fighters, the Boche aren't. Not worth while to worry about it beforehand."

The whole trench now knows the news; plate in hand, everybody is jabbering, and rumours run from squad to squad. It appears that the pioneers are to come in this very night to get ready the scaling ladders for the attack. Small thirty-seven millimetre guns have to be put in place, and bomb-throwers as well. The first company is to make one big patrol.

All this begins to shake my opinion; and yet, while sharing my cheese with Gilbert, I endeavour to convince him that we are not going to attack at all. Sulphart is giving tongue loudly, with his mouth still full. He is not now thinking about the attack at all, but only of the gross injustices that surround him on every hand. While he cleans his plate with a handful of grass, he scourges the infamy of General Headquarters, that scandalously favours "the blokes in the third battalion who never have a go at it," and doesn't even give fighting men the brandy to which they have an inalienable right. He utters his denunciations under the very nose of Bréval, the only non-commissioned officer present, and in any case quite innocent in the matter of this refusal of justice; and Berthier, the sergeant, has to disturb himself and come on the scene to make him shut up.

Men are going round and about in the trench, like a village about its main streets, after the evening meal. There is talking, arguing, and some nervousness. Somebody calls me by name.

"Jacques!"

It is Bouland, one of the Colonel's cyclists.

"Well?"

"It's quite true; we're attacking. . . . I've just been to get two thousand cigars out of the supplies department."

I raised my head sharply. What! . . . Cigars--cigars with a band round them? This time I am convinced, we are certainly going to attack.

Hamel, though his mind is barred against any subtle deduction, is not mistaken about it either.

"He was right, then, all the same, that merchant," he sighs.

Then, since the true philosopher must consider only the good side of the worst things, he adds:

"Seeing that you don't smoke, you'll give me yours, eh? I'll keep it in reserve."

Absently, with a kind of constraint in my heart, I come back to the boys.

Vairon, mounted on the firing step, is eyeing through the loophole the big desolate field, riddled with shell-holes like so many rents, in which the last attack broke up. You can count the dead men, lying scattered in the yellow grass. They have fallen as they charged, face forward; some of them, fallen on their knees, seem still ready to leap on again. Many are wearing the red trousers that belonged to the beginning of the war. One of them can be seen leaning up against a small stack, who, with his shrivelled fingers, holds his coat wide open as though to show us the hole that killed him. Vairon looks long, dreamy, pensive, without budging, and now he murmurs:

"So we have to go and reinforce the boys out in front there."

. . . .

As I am to take the second watch, I go back into the shelter to get a little rest. Bréval is there already; he is writing. At full length on his canvas, his hands under the nape of his neck, Gilbert lies pondering, dreaming. I get ready my corner, and stretch myself with my satchel for a pillow. Nothing can now be heard but our measured breathing and the shrill squeak-squeaking of the rats among the beams of the roof.

Before long the boys come in, driven by the cold that falls over the trench with the coming of the night. Another candle is lighted, with a bayonet-hilt for candlestick, and squatting in a ring about the light, they set to to play banker. But the game soon comes to an end: their hearts are not in it to-night.

"I thought we would be going to attack," said Lemoine, the first to speak.

Their momentary hot fit has subsided; they speak of the attack with resignation--almost with indifference.

"What! We'll carry it again all right, the wood," cries Broucke, who for a wonder is not sleeping yet. "We've done worse than that."

Bréval has sealed his letter. By the light of the candle I can see his lean chin quiver.

"If only after it's all over they would send us back home!" he sighs.

46

Home! Go back home! . . . Every face lights up instantaneously, their mouths part in laughter like the mouths of children when you talk to them about Christmas.

"I say, Lemoine," asks Sulphart, sitting on the white wood parapet that serves him as a stool; "here's supposing they said to you, 'You can go back home, only you'll have to go walking backwards the whole way, with a big log of wood on your back on top of your full kit, and no shoes'--would you go?"

"Indeed and surely I would," accepts Lemoine without an instant's hesitation. "And you, if they said to you, 'The war will be all over as far as you're concerned, only you're never to have the right to drink neither wine nor brandy for the rest of your natural life,' what would you say to that?"

Sulphart reflects for a moment; there must be some hidden conflict waging deep down in his soul.

"Ooh. . . . I could always drink cider, couldn't I? . . . And then on the strict q.t. that wouldn't prevent me from putting a little drop of old rum down my neck? I should say so."

And there they are, embarked upon insane suppositions, absurd hypotheses that keep them talking for hours and hours, soothed and charmed by fabulous hopes. The cage is open; the strangest most unimaginable dreams come forth and take wing. They concoct impossible bargainings, stupefying conditions that the General comes and lays before them in person--tit for tat--against their freedom. And, however formidable the conditions might be, they always say yes.

From supposition to supposition they at last come to offering a limb, sacrificing a piece of their bacon to save the rest. Everybody chooses his wound--an eye, a hand, or a leg.

"As for me," says Broucke as he scratches himself, "I'll give my left foot. . . . I don't really need it, my foot, for walking. . . . And then, far better get home dot-and-go-one than never get home at all."

"I'd rather have an eye out, I would," says Fouillard. "What's the good of it, anyway, to have two eyes? You can see just as well with one. . . . You can even see better, and the proof is that you shut one to aim better."

They argue it out soberly, reasonably, each one setting forth his own preference, and with little plain, honest phrases they cut into their live flesh, they quite placidly and coolly chop up their bodies limb by limb, choosing the spot with the utmost care.

"No, your eye, that's something that mustn't be touched," says Sulphart, who has his principles. "A good leg, that's got it just enough, that's the best of the lot. Only seeing that if you wait for the stretcher-bearers you're sure to be left in the leap, this is how I should manage."

He takes two Lebels, with their breeches swathed deep in flannel, and setting the butt under his armpits, turning them into crutches, he starts hopping through the shelter, one leg dead and hanging, moaning in a shrill voice:

"Hi, there! Hi, there! Let me pass, boys! . . ."

He has most meticulously staged the whole scene of his evacuation down to the very pitch of his cries, yelping and plaintive at the same time. But all this is not enough to convince the obstinate Broucke.

"Still and all it's the foot that would be best."

"Well, to my way of thinking," says Papa Hamel, "I don't want to leave them neither foot nor paw nor anything. . . . And the Boche that means to bag me, he'll have to make no second shots at it: if he does, I'll drive his belly in for him, like the one at Courcy."

They held their tongues, pensive. Do they catch a glimpse of themselves already, running across the plain, head down, stooping their backs under the whistling death?

Sulphart and Vairon are talking in a murmur.

"For me, I've marked down a shell-hole close by the river. . . . If I see the attack's going wrong, I'm going to plant myself down in it and wait for night."

"If they pound their trenches for them there will be pickings to be had. . . . It's a long time now that I've been wanting to have a Boche field-glass, or a revolver. . . . After Montmirail I sold one for twenty francs to a fellow in a motor."

Bréval emerges from his sour and dejected meditation.

"That's all very fine," he says as he unrolls his puttees, "we don't all come back again out of it."

Close to him Broucke is pulling off his boots.

"You know very well that there's an order not to take our boots off. Suppose there was an alarm?"

"I'll get there in my stocking soles," replies the ch'timi easily, as he lays down his tousled flaxen head upon his satchel.

Hamel and Vairon, who have dug-outs of their very own, now go out from the shelter, and under the canvas as they raise it to go there comes in a touch of the cold and darkness of the night.

"It's going to be hard and nippy again," says Fouillard as he pulls his woollen helmet well over his head. "You'll wake me up, will you? and we'll take a bite together."

I have no mind to sleep. I should barely have time just to close my eyes. I take hold of my potato-bag, and I slip my feet and legs into it to keep them from feeling too cold. Then, with my blanket pulled up to my very eyes, my hands tucked into my armpits, I drowsily eye the flame of the candle leaping and flickering at the point of death. I recognize the voice of Sulphart, whom a fit of impotent fury will not allow to get to sleep.

"What really sticks in my gizzard," he is explaining to little Bélin, "is going to have my mug split just to take three rotten fields of beet that are no good to anybody. . . . What do you suppose they're going to do with their silly little bit of wood that lies in a hollow? It's just for the pleasure of knocking folk over. What? . . ."

The redhead's monologue must be lulling the boy off to sleep like a mother's singing, and his slumbering voice replies:

"Don't you try to understand it; don't you be trying to understand."

The other voices have bumbled on for a minute, and then have dropped silent. They are asleep now. Sitting up on my elbow, I look at them; it's not easy to make them out, I guess at them rather. They are sleeping, with no nightmares, like any other night. Their respirations sound all confused together; heavy measured breathing, the sharp-sounding breath of sick men, even sighings of a child. Then it seems that I hear them no longer, that they also lose themselves in the blackness, just as though they were dead. . . . No, I can no longer bear to see them as they sleep. The crushing slumber that wafts them away is too much like the other sleep. Those

48

relaxed or contracted faces, those faces the colour of the earth, I have seen their fellows lying around the trenches, and the bodies have the same postures as those that are sleeping eternally out in the naked fields. Their brown blanket is spread over them as in the day when two comrades will carry them off stiff and stark. Dead men, all dead men. . . . And I dare not sleep, afraid to be dead like them.

Suddenly Bréval has waked up with a hoarse cry and sits upright, all scared and bewildered. For a moment he remains sitting, propped up on his stiff arms, not yet shaken loose from his bad dream. He forces a laugh.

"No humbug, I was dreaming that the Boches . . . ."

A voice growls. The others have not awaked.

"What, has nobody blown out the candle? I don't care a curse, I'll leave it. . . ."

He stretches down, curls up, goes off to sleep again. The candle, at its last gasp, suddenly lights up the shelter with a towering flame--the very last. . . . All is darkness. . . .

I am envying them now. They are so comfortable here, in shelter, feet warm, limbs relaxed. Sleep. . . . the day after to-morrow? Hang it! that's still a long way off. . . .

Someone has pulled away the canvas:

"Jacques! . . . Fouillard! . . . It's time." Already! I shake Fouillard, who grumbles; our hands fumble in the hunt for our rifles. We sally forth. How cold it is! The comrade who has waked me is chattering with his teeth under his blanket which he is wearing like a hood.

"Nothing fresh?"

"No. . . . A patrol is just going out. . . . Good-night."

There is no seeing anything; in the obscurity of the trench you can't distinguish the gabions of the sleepy lookouts. I slip my rifle into the loophole. Three hours to spend here! . . .

Nothing can be seen ten paces beyond the parapet. The eye searches the darkness up to the tangled network of wire in which the stakes lean this way and that like staggering drunken men, and then loses itself. Numb and stupid, I go on looking without seeing. I stare into the night and grow cold. The cold is running along my arms like an icy wind, and soaks into me. Then I begin to dance from one foot to the other, while I clutch my blanket tight about me.

The moment you go out from your shelter the cold starts nibbling your chin, and stings in your nose like a pinch of snuff--in fact, it rather exhilarates and pleases. Then it turns nasty, gnaws at your ears, tortures the tips of your fingers, crawls and creeps up your sleeves, down your collar, through your flesh, and becomes ice, freezing you to the very entrails. Shivering, you dance, dance. . . .

A long trampling draws near, a clatter of weapons. It is the patrol just going out. The men carry huge wire-clippers hung round their necks, as the Swiss cows wear their bells.

"Talk about a stunt!" says the first one as he clambers up. "Every man jack has to bring back a bit of Boche wire to show he's been there. Here goes for a sample!"

Heavily they scale the parapet, hunt for the gap, and move off with humping backs. Silence descends once more on our darkened ditch. Men still awake are talking in low tones. From under a tent-covering steals a thin shaft of light:

somebody must be making a jorum of hot wine.

From the shelters can be heard arise the sound of the sleepers' breathing: you might fancy that the trench is moaning like a sick child. Frozen stiff, I start dancing like a bear before my loophole, without thinking of anything but the time as it passes away. Face to face, with arms crossed, men are jumping heavily up and down as they chatter, or are stamping in a regular rhythm. The night is enlivened by this cadenced sound. In the foot-way in the communication trench the hard, cracked earth re-echoes under all these hobnailed boots. The whole line of trenches is dancing to-night. The whole regiment is dancing on this night before the attack; the whole army must be dancing; the whole of France is dancing, from the sea to the Vosges. . . . What a fine communiqué for to-morrow!

I am now fatigued, and dance no more. Leaning with my elbows on the parapet, I ponder vaguely over things. . . . Then all at once my head falls and I pull myself up again. . . . This is stupid, I'm falling asleep. I look at the watch on my wrist; . . . still two hours to go. I shall never be able to last out till midnight. Envyingly I listen to the snoring of a comrade who is doing a heavy stretch deep in his hole. If only I could slip in beside him on the warm straw, my head on his pillow of sandbags, and go to sleep! . . . My eyes close deliciously at the mere thought of it.

No, no humbug! . . . I pull myself together and force myself to look into the black opening of the loophole, where there is nothing possibly to be seen. It's much too quiet, in any case. Not a single shell; you might think the Boches had cleared out.

Tac! a single shot cracks out dry and hard, coming from the Boche lines. Then another almost on its heels. . . . The men who are day-dreaming at their loopholes have pulled themselves up sharply. We listen, filled with anxiety. A moment passes, then some shots ring out pell-mell, and the firing swells and crackles up.

They are firing on the patrol!

A Boche rocket sends up its white arrow and explodes. Another shrieks on the right, then one on the left, and their eyes of lightning, floating and sustained by the wind, peer over the awakened plain. Nothing in it is moving, our men have gone to ground.

Fronting us, the whole German line is firing: bullets are whining over the trench, very low, and several of them come smacking against the parapet, like the crack of a whip. In this noisy fusillade the regular rattling of a machine gun is the dominant note, annoying and exasperating. Look out!--a green rocket, the Germans are calling out for artillery. We wait, bent a little more, behind our loopholes.

Five shots come over, like red sheaves, five shrapnel well on the line. Their sudden glare lights up round backs and heads sedulously ducking. Out in the plain, scattering, here and there, shells are bursting, both contact shells and time fuses. A few minutes of violent row, and then with neither rhyme nor reason everything is quiet: the guns have worked off their fury. The rifle fire has also stopped.

"Let them pass, don't shoot! . . . The patrol is out there," orders a voice.

"Let them pass, don't shoot!"

The order reaches us, passes on, fades down the line. We look, we listen. . . . Crack! A few paces off a shot smashes into the silence. But is he crazy, that fellow? Crack! Yet another. . . .

"Don't fire, God Almighty!" cries Sergeant Bertheir, who has darted out of his shelter. "It's the patrol coming back."

At that very moment I hear in the darkness a voice that quavers. You would fancy that someone is singing. Indeed, yes, it is a song:

Je veux revoir ma Normandie.

Behind me Fouillard laughs. And I too laugh, in spite of myself, with a catch at my heart. It is both tragic and burlesque, this song stammered out in the darkness. The voice comes close and ceases its singing.

"Don't shoot! . . . Verneau of the fourth. . . . Patrol."

But another, farther away, has taken up the chorus in a stifled voice:

  .   .   .   ma   Normandie,
C'est le pays qui m'a donné le jour . . .

And still farther off we can hear a third of them whistling, completely lost in the fields of obscurity and gloom:

En avant la Normandie!

Everywhere in the black fields you can hear lowered voices humming and timid whistlings on the level of the ground. It is just like a homecoming from the fair, at once thrilling and droll. In order to guard against a possible rise on the part of the Germans, who might by chance have got hold of the password, orders have been given to the patrols to sing folksongs, so as to be recognized. And as they crawl among the hard beetroots, slowly dragging along, they are singing. Their half-stifled voices prowl about on the other side of the barbed thicket; they are looking out for the openings through.

"This way, you boys!"

A man jumps into the trench.

"Any of you gone under?"

"I don't know. They heard us, the cows! It couldn't be anything else, with their infernal beastly wire-cutters that anybody could hear a league away."

Others let themselves slide down into our hole, arms in hand. A dark group can be descried coming slowly towards us.

"Don't fire! A wounded man."

Hands are reached out to them up over the parapet. Painfully they lower their moaning comrade. He is bent practically double, as though broken, wounded in the flank.

"There's been another one left out there close by the river. . . . A bullet clean through the head. You might say their machine guns were firing low."

There is still another lost and wandering voice to be heard singing away outside. At last it comes up. A leap into the trench. Then nothing more. . . .

"Everyone has come back. Attention there!" Berthier has the word passed along.

"All the men are back," repeat the watchers.

In a shelter behind me there are voices arguing:

"After that patrol they'll be bound to suspect something's up. We're going to be the mugs again. . . . And the third battalion, why isn't it going to attack?"

I am barely listening; I am getting numb, developing pins and needles. Still another hour and a quarter. . . . I'm going to count up to a thousand, that will take up a quarter of an hour. After that I shall only have an hour to get through.

But it sends me off to sleep, that rosary of stupid numbers. To keep myself awake I want to think of to-morrow's attack, our wild rush through the plain, the chain of men that breaks link by link: I want to make myself feel afraid. But no, I can't do it. My heavy head refuses to obey me. My benumbed mind loses itself staggering about in a confused reverie.

The war. . . . I see ruins, mud, long files of men foundered and fordone, taverns where they fight desperately for litres of wine, gendarmes on the watch, trunks of trees splintered into matchwood, and wooden crosses, crosses, crosses. . . . All that passes through my head, mingles, melts together. The war. . . .

It seems to me that my whole life will be bespattered with these gloomy, sordid horrors, that my sullied memory will never succeed in forgetting. Never again shall I be able to look at a fine tree without subconsciously computing the weight of the stump, a hill without imagining the trench on the counter-slope, an untilled field without looking out for the corpses in it. When the red tip of a cigar will glow in the garden, I shall perhaps exclaim: "Eh! the blithering idiot that's going to get us marked down!" No, what an old bore I shall be with my tales of the war, when I am an old man!

But shall I ever be old? One never knows. . . . The day after to-morrow. How they snore, those lucky devils! A corner of straw any old where, and my blanket, that and nothing more is all my heart's wish now. To sleep. . . .

In a half-doze my wavering thoughts rough out a burlesque idyll, a kind of inconsequent, irresponsible dream that I don't altogether follow. I have met the girl at the entrance to her billet, and pointing into the landscape with a masterful gesture of authority, I fix the rendezvous for her.

"Straight in front of you, at twelve hundred mètres, a straw stack. . . . Two fingers to the left a tree like a ball."

And in proper military fashion, her feet squared, the girl replies, saluting:
"Seen."

How cold it is! . . . And black! . . . What are we here for, all of us? . . . It's stupid. . . . It's miserable. . . . My head bends forward, drops. . . . I am afraid of sleeping. . . . I am asleep.

CHAPTER VI
THE MILL WITH NO SAILS

I HAVE found the farm when we came back just the same as we had left it on Sunday, before the attack. You might think that the four companies have only just gone across the grasslands, on their way up to the trenches; and the big gambolling dog seems to be running after a belated laggard. Nothing has moved.

It was there, along that path of hard, frost-cracked mud, that we went away. How many have come back? Oh no! no! let us not count. . . .

I enter once more into the big kitchen, all fragrant with soup, and sit down close to the window on my chair. There is my bowl, there are my wooden shoes, my little bottle of ink. It seems so good, to find again these things of one's own, these friendly nothings that one might well have never seen again.

My good luck was waiting on me; life continues with fresh deferments of hope. I feel a kind of stinging, secret joy in my heart. I see the sun, I myself, I hear the song of running water; and my heart is at peace, my heart that has beaten so furiously.

How hard man is, despite his exclamations of pity! how light seems to him the anguish of others when his own is not intermingled with it! I look at things with a distracted eye. The dunghill, moist and shining, is stacked up against the wall, so that from the room you can see the little black cock on a level with the window in a thin blue mist. Strayed bullets have left upon the grey stones of the stabling a kind of white scars, as it were. In the middle of the little enclosed garden, the well with its worn curb, and its three walls stained with green. . . . What, it's not all over, down there? One would say that the guns are beginning again. Who have relieved us? The hundred-and-forty-eighth. Poor fellows! . . .

The water of the little channel runs trippingly in front of the farm. It passes through the pond without leaving any trace of its passing, and escapes from it, leaping from stone to stone, till it reaches the decayed mill-wheel, upon which there sits a great cat pretending to be asleep.

The nestling bevies of pigeons go and come, caressing the walls with their swift fleeting shadows; the geese march out their solemn troop, walking, calling out and falling silent all together. Two small calves, one with black spots, the other with red, are gambolling with the lolloping graces of young puppies; and the big spaniel amuses himself by terrifying the hens with his yap-yap-yelping. They hear nothing, take no notice. Only the donkey slowly eating his fodder, very dignified under his tunic of dried mud, is listening with one ear. Now and then he stops chewing, pausing with the straw between his teeth, raises his long, pensive head, and hearkens to the thunder of the guns.

What a row it was on Sunday in the court when the brandy was distributed--a cupful for every two men!--and the cigars given round, noble penny cigars with bands! My word! we had a feast.

"If the Boches do an autopsy on me they won't find my cupboard empty," big Vairon had said, his cheeks purple and his belt loosened.

It was over there in that barn with its bristling thatched roof that we had piled our packs. They are still there, nearly all of them. . . . the ossuary of a battalion. It is a tragic medley of rusty implements, equipment, burst haversacks, cartridge-pouches, satchels. Linen lies about, already stained with mud. A chunk of bread never touched, a bottle spilling its contents, packets of letters, coloured picture-postcards--so naive and foolish and of a kind to make one weep. . . . In spite of yourself you read the names, without, even bending: I know them all.

That is Vairon's undershirt; he left it behind, fearing he would be too hot. Everything has been gone through, the chocolate and tins of bully-beef have been shared out, and in a handkerchief have been knotted up the papers and the poor nothings that are sent on to men's families. . . . soldiers' legacies. A photograph has slipped into the rut: a mother in her Sunday dress, her big baby on her knee. Shirts still folded neatly, first-aid packets, a pipe. And, lost on this wretched pile, a silk cushion, a fine pink silk cushion, fetched there who knows how, who knows by whom!

Good Lord! how heavy that thundering is. It is like a huge convoy rolling along, a dull thunderstorm growling and coming nearer. Then rifle fire begins to rattle, a whole sharp tumult of attack.

The dog is the first to grow uneasy and come indoors, with his back down. Next arrive the fowls in a state of terror; then the two little calves, suddenly astonished to find themselves alone in the garden close. The donkey has not budged. Dreamily he stands in front of his truss. Now and then he pricks up his ears, throws back his head as if he was going to bray; then, scorning that thunder as a thing well known and familiar to him, he bends down, sagaciously tears out a jowlful of hay, and eats, his head hanging to the ground.

. . . . .

I do not like the folk belonging to this village. The shopkeepers have no regard for us, not even for the sake of the money they rob us of. They eye us with a kind of disgust or fear, and when one goes into their shops, making oneself small and pushing in, with one's notes for a hundred sous in one's hand so as to be served quicker, they squeal louder than if the Prussians were coming to loot the place.

When the Germans were in occupation, the women have told us, these people were less proud and great. They could not make up their minds to run away and become refugees on account of their goods. But when the last French troops had passed--these were chasseurs à pied, who went on firing all a whole afternoon ensconced in the cemetery--panic seized on them. They hid everything--their liqueurs, their conserves, their good-looking pennies--and the women moaned and groaned while the old men were digging holes in the garden to bury away their hoard.

The village schoolmistress--a little voluntary teacher that people disliked because she wore her hair in bands--had shut the windows of the schoolhouse and put her flag at half-mast. But big Thomas, the grocer and wine-seller of the Lion d'Or, had rushed off to her at once, followed by certain shrewish creatures, to force her to take in her flag. . . . "which would have the countryside put to fire and sword."

The little woman had stood up to him for a moment.

"You are not the mayor," she said, "you are nothing and nobody. I am not going to take any orders from you."

"Order or no order, you are going to do as everybody else does," choked the grocer, who was already in his mind's eye seeing himself shot at his own counter. "I am giving the order to do it."

"In whose name?"

"I don't care a curse whose; in the King of Prussia's name, if you like!"

Stammering, apoplectic, his eyes on the points of tumbling out of his head, the shopkeeper thumped the schoolmistress's desk furiously with his ponderous fist. She had been obliged to give in. . . .

Terrorized, some hidden away in their houses, the others in dumb groups on the side of the highway, the peasants had looked on at the passing of the first Bavarian battalions, who were braying gleefully, "Paris! Paris!" as if they were certainly bound to sack the city the very next day. It was a motor-car that arrived first of all, full of soldiers armed to the teeth. The urchins gambolled and leaped about it, pulling faces.

"Will you stop it, you little ruffians!" cried an old woman, the doyenne of the countryside. "They'll think you are making game of them."

And she made them such low bows that the long black ribbons on her Sunday bonnet trailed on the ground. The Germans laughed and flung handfuls of sweetmeats to the children--sweetmeats they had stolen in Reims. For five days the countryside had been full of Bavarians and Prussians. They had carried away three hostages that had never been seen again: the oldest it was said, had been shot a league away, on the roadside, for no reason--just to serve as an example.

"And they paid on the nail, those swine," related big Thomas admiringly. "The officers paid with chits; but the men gave us money, and French money, too."

That money--money taken from our prisoners, our wounded, our dead--the grocer had his drawers full of it, and that had been the beginning of prosperity for his shop, prosperity that continued with us.

On the day of the attack, as there was not a single soldier left in the village, he had at length been able to take a little rest. He would fain have gone fishing, but the sentries posted at the end of the Cow's Road had stopped him. He had gone home again in a fury, brandishing his fishing-pole at the risk of smashing his bottles; and then, to pass the time, he had climbed up into his garret and followed the fighting through his field-glasses, while his wife made pancakes.

When he had seen us, precisely on the stroke of noon, leap out of our trenches and dash at the charge towards the Boche line, flung into the naked fields like seeds into the wind, he had experienced something that might perhaps have been a touch of feeling.

"Come here quick and look!" he had yelled to his old woman. "Hurray! there won't be any of them left."

"I can't leave the milk," she had replied from downstairs, "it's going to boil over."

And so Thomas had seen everything by himself.

The village, however, had a thrill that day, seeing the first stretchers come in and the long file of limping, wounded men, dragging their bloody feet like injured dogs. On her doorstep, Mother Bouquet, whimpering and tearful, was trying to recognize her customers in that march past. Out in the open fields the schoolmistress had established a sort of half-way post, where she waited for the wounded with a big jug of lemonade. The curé--a gallant old man who loves us dearly --never went to bed all that night. At daybreak he was still giving absolution to dying soldiers.

There were six ditches filled with the dead, and the last had perforce to wait, laid in a heap in a corner, until the territorials had finished digging a hole for them. No flowers were found to dress their tombs, only a few frost-bitten stocks, and that was what has given Thomas the idea of opening a department for wreaths.

"There's still more profit on them than there is on jam," the big man declared.

There is a whole selection of them on a stand, arranged like brands of liqueurs.

You can find quite simple ones, of yellow immortelles, which savour of the apothecary's shop; and large ones of beads, in which are interwoven black flowers with violet-coloured stems.

"Those are for well-to-do customers, those fellows," says Demachy, as he examines them with pleased interest, like a serious gentleman considering fully before purchasing. And he adds prettily:

"That's the kind of one I shall lay at your shrine."

. . . . .

Our soup eaten, the shops fill up and the streets become animated. The village assumes a Sunday aspect. Everybody is out of doors: old grandmothers trotting with short steps, can on hip; children squalling as they play at hop-scotch with the fragments of the stone crucifix overthrown by a twelve-inch shell; peasants who no longer go to their fields; and soldiers, soldiers, soldiers. . . .

There is a regular fighting scramble about the doors of the grocer's shop, without anybody having a clear notion of what they are going to buy. As they pass along, they give one another tips.

"Hello! They've got no more pinard at the Comptoir Français."

"The schoolmistress has a batch of sausages."

"There are some at the wheelwrights' too, but you'll have to look slippy."

Everybody in this place is a shopkeeper; every house is a shop, every farm a tavern, and every window is wreathed with strings of tinder by the yard by way of sign. The pork-butcher sells combs, and the mayor vends rotgut brandy.

In front of the Comptoir Français there are thirty soldiers shoving and shouting. Nothing but empty casks.

"Pack of cows!" cries one of the men, cleaving through the group to take himself off. "How happy I'll be the day a saucepan smashes their crib in for them!"

The baker's door is bolted and the shutters are up. A dozen simple souls are none the less standing in a queue, in the insane hope of having a little new bread. An edict of the mayor's forbids selling it to anybody but civilians, and the door does not open.

And yet we have seen it in batches, in pale golden stacks, the lovely bread that civilians have, after the Marne. . . . Ah! how good it is, fresh bread! . . .

Inside the houses we can hear singing. In the village square folk are arguing, are merrymaking.

The war is over for us--over for five days. The attack, our dead, all is forgotten, only remembered just for a word or two among pals, just to say to each other with a secret joy: "Come through that all right, eh!" In five days, it is true, we shall have to go up to the trenches again, to the Redan or the left bank of the river; but nobody allows himself to think of that. Just now there is only the actual present, only to-day itself that counts--the only day one is certain to have to live. Without paying any attention, just as the ear accustoms itself to the tick-tock of a clock, even so do we hear the guns. When it is the seventy-fives at the station that are firing, you might think their whining is crossing the square.

"You'll see that by dint of playing the fool they'll get what they're after," says Lemoine who has no love for the gunners. "The Boches are leaving us alone. . . . They've got to go and annoy them. Result, they bombard the old town, and it's we that will be the mugs, as per usual."

56

The Germans bombard us frequently, and being quite new, the mayor's house, with its slate-covered bell-tower, serves them as target. There are houses smashed in down to the very cellar, displaying their poor hearts laid bare and open; and their roofs, stripped of every tile, open to the sky like a clerestory. Huge chaotic holes are dug out where once there were barns; in the bottom of the cistern the shells have piled up stones, beams of wood, and the calcined débris of Heaven knows what. Out of all this ruins the territorials are making little heaps without overmuch hustling, and the urchins come along to hunt in them for roofing-laths to make sabres with--for the children also are playing at war.

When we come away from Thomas's we go along to Mother Bouquet's, whose shop, painted black all over, casts a gloom over the square with its leafless elm-trees. We have to line up in the queue before we can get inside, and must indulge in a free fight to be served. In the grocery department with its empty bins and cases there is a mob of men who are bellowing this and that. Mother Bouquet, an enormous creature, is defending herself at her counter against a score of greedy snatching hands.

"There are no more sardines. . . . Thirty-two sous for the camembert. . . . If you don't want to have it, leave it, it will get sold. . . . Don't go tumbling everything over like that, you set of blackguards!"

Those who are crushed up against the counter become imploring, and those who are behind call over their heads.

"Madame Bouquet, that tin of beans up there, if you please. . . . I'm a good old customer of yours."

"Some pie, Madame Bouquet. . . . Hi! this way! . . . I've been waiting now for a good half-hour."

The groceress hustles and bustles about, utters cries, and serves nobody, only thinking of pushing away the hands that are thrusting forward, for fear that somebody may steal something from her.

"There's nothing left, nothing, I tell you. . . . Go away! . . . Lucie! Come and shut the door. . . . They'll be smashing everything, the dirty ruffians!"

But Lucie, the daughter of the proprietress, makes no move: she doesn't like any dirty ruffians, thank you. A silver St. Andrew's cross upon her starched bodice, her nondescript hair waved with curling-papers, she stays haughtily aloof in the little room at the back of the shop, as proud on her stool between the portrait of General Joffre and the list of bad money as a pretty lady at the beginning of her career in her taxi.

The whole regiment knows Lucie, all the men desire her, and when she goes across the crowded shop carrying the glasses, they leer at her with a greedy air, and say quite crudely what they feel. The bolder ones put out their hands secretly and stroke her as she passes by. She does not deign even to notice, and passes through their midst with the outraged air of a princess in exile condemned to do housework. They can say of her whatever they may like, she is certainly a girl that keeps her station. She smiles only on soldiers of the "right sort," and blushes for nothing less than an officer.

A soldier of the "right sort" is one that buys condensed milk, pastries, extra fine chocolate, and bottled wine. These are, in her eyes, superior wares, whose acquisition denotes a finished education and the "correct" tastes of a man of family. Demachy, having bought eau-de-Cologne and champagne, is estimated as almost on a level with a sub-lieutenant, and Lucie calls him Monsieur.

"Four petits verres, mademoiselle," orders Lemoine. "Something nice."

"Grape brandy, for instance," adds Sulphart, by way of precise hint.

The girl, bridling and affected, looks at Gilbert and says:

"How very unreasonable of you! You know quite well it's forbidden. . . . I'm going to serve you all the same, but you must make haste and drink it off quickly so that I can clear away the glasses."

Sulphart obediently empties his at one gulp, and passes into the other room, when he is to make our purchases for dinner. On the spot he starts braying:

"I had bespoken it, that sausage. Isn't that so, Madame Bouquet? . . . And the gruyère, 'my' gruyère. . . . ."

To listen to him, he had bespoken everything in the shop since yesterday, a week ago, from the beginning of time.

"That's mine, that sausage, fish-mouth. . . . You ask if it isn't."

At a table close by us there are some mates drinking red wine, litre after litre. In the old days you paid twenty-four sous for it. But an instruction from the Colonel forbade the sale of vin ordinaire at more than eighty centimes. Thereupon Mother Bouquet had her bottles sealed, and ever since we pay thirty sous for it--it's bottled wine now.

Vieublé, a soldier out of our company, is serving in his shirtsleeves. In every village where we come to rest he finds a shopkeeper to engage him. He serves in the bar, goes down to the cellar, washes the glasses, picks up his tips, puts in a little pilfering, and goes to bed every night with a skinful. With the Colonel's cook, he is the most envied man in the whole regiment.

He comes up to our table with the satisfied smug smile of a landlord whose business is prospering.

"Well, boys, so you've got out of the march too? . . . I made myself go pale; the doctor always knows me. He chucked me a purge and that's all right. . . . Of course old Morache tried to pinch me at the corner, but I dodged him. . . ."

"Yes. I saw him at his dirty tricks behind the willows. He thinks there aren't enough police as it is."

"And they've made him a sous-lieutenant!" says Vieublé indignantly, his dishcloth tucked under his arm. "Anyway, it wasn't for what he did the day of the attack."

"You can be sure that if the Colonel had seen what some of us have seen he wouldn't have been put forward. . . . You know he chucked four days' cells at Broucke and nobody has the least notion what it was all for."

"Don't be afraid," predicts Sulphart, coming back laden like a ration-party; "that'll all get paid, wholesale and retail."

"It's like minors' estates," declares Lemoine sententiously: "it goes on at compound interest."

"We'll meet again when the war's over."

It's always the same song: that'll be fixed up after the war. Settling their revenges for that uncertain date already more than by half avenges them.

During their service time, in barracks, when the adjutant put them down for fire duty or the sergeant sent them right about face as they were going out of the gates, they would go off, raging to the highest degree and growling mysterious and obscure threats.

"When the war comes, we'll settle it. . . . We'll come across them again, the blighters! . . ."

War has broken out, and they have in point of fact come across the adjutant and the sergeant, and speedily they have haled them off to the canteen, calling them "old boy." Then they have detested other ones, or even the same ones. And now that they are fighting, it is no longer the war to which they postpone their terrific plans and dark designs of vengeance, it's to the coming time of peace.

"Wait till we're civilians again, then you'll see." And Demachy, who knows perfectly well that he'll see nothing, smiles with a sceptical air, playing with the bottom of his glass in which there rolls a drop of liquid light.

Coming out of the grocery or in from the street, others sit down noisily at the tables.

"Hi! old man, a litre of red wine."

A big corporal is vainly endeavouring to soften Mademoiselle Lucie, now scornful and cross-grained.

"Just two petits verres, mamzelle: we'll drink quick. No matter what, so long as it's good and stiff, real buck-up stuff."

"Let me alone! We only sell wine here, this is no place for drunkards."

Elbows propped on the table, or sitting astride on stools, the drinkers are arguing in a turmoil and tumult of voices, of dragging heavy boots, outcries, the noise of clattering glasses.

"Appears that the ----th, that relieved us at Berry, have managed to get a trench pinched off them."

"That doesn't surprise me from those stinkers."

"Hard eaters that haven't even been up to digging decent shelters. . . . There's no kid about it, we're the only genuine ones that know the way to scratch."

A dispute bursts out all of a sudden between Vieublé and some machine gunners who want to do him for a litre. A little red-faced fellow with eyes devoid of eyelashes is defending his half-pence and his reputation in a thick and clammy voice.

"You mustn't try to bully, you know. It doesn't follow just because a fellow isn't a Parisian, that he must be a robber. Maybe less than yourself for all we know. And I've been there before you, too, at Panama, just myself that's talking to you now."

"Shut up!" replies Vieublé, without any signs of anger. "You've never had the honour of dragging your boots there, at Panama, you lump of cowdung! I know your metropolis all right: pigs in the avenue."

"What is this swanker talking about?"

"He says you never disembarked at Paris, slimy, not even in your fine Sunday clothes and a duck in your basket. For one thing you never could have, with the machine for chucking out country bumpkins. Why, you don't even know it, that machine, rawhead. It's just in front of the station, and when a lout disembarks, ping! There's a big whack of a piston and the blighter is bunged back again into his train."

His voice, pure faubourg, with its drawling words, strangely reminds me of Vairon. I fancy I hear him grousing again on the morning of the attack because he had been given a big plank to carry, a plank he was detailed to throw across the German trench to serve as a bridge. Poor lad! Broucke told us he was knocked out near him as he doubled himself up, and that he was still moving then. Now, four days after, it's certainly all over. And yet. . . .

"Come on, don't be naughty, Ferdinand," says Vieublé, holding out his hand. "Plank down your thirty bits and don't cry: you'll see your stable again."

At the table next in line with ours, there are soldiers of the company talking about the mill and the Monpoix, the farmer's family, looking sidelong at us as if they were talking for our benefit. Everything in the outfit seems suspicious to them, the pigeons that fly at set times, the chimney smoke, the white dog that jumps and plays in the meadow, in sight of the Germans; and especially the old man, who goes out every blessed evening alone by himself to smoke his pipe.

"I tell you he worked his tinder-box more than ten times."

"But some folk don't think anything about it, you know; as long as they have their little comforts," insinuates a little lean fellow with a turned-up nose."

Sulphart, who had been acting as umpire in the battle of the machine gunners, is not there to answer them, and Gilbert does not hear them at all. His chin in his palms, he is dreaming, his eyes plunged and lost in vacancy.

"What are you thinking about, Gilbert? Got the poisonous hump?"

"No. . . . memories."

And he speaks very low and from far away, as if the past was holding him.

"Last year, this very day, I was arriving at Agay. It was the morning. I can remember that near the station someone was burning a fine green pile of eucalyptus or pine, the acrid smoke of which was scenting the air with a wild odour. She told me that that made her cough. She was wearing a blue frock, periwinkle blue. . . ."

Then he forces himself a little and laughs. . . . "Now it's me that's in blue. It's the war, it's the war. . . ."

Our neighbours are talking louder, with ill-conditioned laughter and scoffings meant for us. One evening, as they were going back to their shelter with a dixie full of rice in their bellies, without as much as a cup of wine, they must have heard us laughing in the cosy house, and that has turned them sour and jealous. As they see that I am quite determined not to answer them at all, they keep on and persevere.

"I tell you they're running that girl. It can always be done, on the quiet, with a bit of money. . . . Ah! I'd jolly well like to see the war through that way."

Gilbert turns his head very slightly and looks at them. He smiles queerly, a little bitter, a little mocking, and says to me without lowering his voice:

"Do you hear them?"

Then he shrugs his shoulders, thinks for a moment and:

"After the war is gone and over," he continues, his smile of disappointment at the corner of his lips, "we shall never be able to show ourselves again, not even with wooden legs. If you look as if you might have a little money, you won't have fought. If you wear a collar and a pair of gloves, it will never be believed that you have even been in the trenches, and the waggon-driver out of the army service corps, the fellows that washed down the motor-lorries, the Colonel's cook, the mechanician whose call-up was postponed, the whole lot will insult you in the street, and will ask you in what funkhole you were hiding during the war. As far as I'm concerned myself, I don't care a pin. To make certain not to have myself torn limb from limb, as soon as I see things going to the dogs I shall buy myself canvas shoes with nice jute soles, a cap at thirty-nine sous, and wash my face with cart-grease. . . . With that and a drunken spree one is pretty sure to come through all right: the drunkards are the only folk that are spared during revolutions."

As all shops have to shut at one o'clock, we pay Lucie, who gives us back as many smiles in change as good half-pence, and we go out. Suiphart wants to drag us along to the Café Culdot, where, he assures us, absinthe is to be found, if you mention the quartermaster of the third. From mere force of habit Lemoine says that it's not true. We set out, idly loafing along. The village is now all but deserted. It is forbidden to leave billets before five o'clock, and the few laggards that are still dawdling about are shaving the walls and at every street corner sticking out their head for fear of running into the gendarmes.

"It wouldn't be the game to get pinched," says Sulphart with a watchful, mistrustful eye. "To get caught playing the giddy goat for nothing while the others are looking after their poor feet, that would be--"

"No danger," says that optimist Lemoine reassuringly--he is always an optimist when he has had his whack.

"No danger! Here, keep your mouth shut, you'll talk the better."

Prisoners in their barns, with nothing whatever to do, the men are sitting in the windows, their legs dangling. They get the full tickle out of their pleasant idleness as they watch the passing of the companies going to drill to learn how to present arms.

On the Cow's Road, where the Decauville runs, grizzle-headed territorials going to their daily work are playing at railways. One of them, a quite old fellow, sitting on a little truck, lets himself run down the slope, crying, "Pom! Pom!" and the others are running behind, shouting and squealing like children.

To get across the square we have to hug the walls, slink one by one behind piles of logs, take advantage of the ground.

"Take a squint," says Lemoine; "look at that lad Broucke giving us the time of day."

The ch'timi is shut up in the basement of the mayor's house, which has been turned into a prison. With his head thrust out through the bars of the ventilating hole, he is taking the air, and without saying a word, lest he should call attention to us, he smiles at us.

"To spend your rest-time in clink when you've done nothing at all is pretty disgusting, anyway," growls Sulphart. "There's no putting up a denial, you're just two-pennyworth less than nothing at all. If Morache were to say to us sometime, 'You're going to kiss the fat on my tail,' you couldn't say anything or do anything but just help him to let down his trousers. No mistake about it,we have got our grievances. . . . Since we've got a republic everybody ought to be equal."

Gilbert, who is by no means a democrat, shrugs up his shoulders and makes his little grimace like a disappointed monkey.

"Equality! that's nothing but a word, equality. . . . What is it, equality?"

Sulphart reflects for a moment, then he replies in all seriousness:

"Equality is to be able to say 'Go to hell' to anybody and everybody."

At the end of the village we stop for a moment to gossip with Bernadette, who is herding her cattle. Gilbert is very much taken by her, with her long slit eyes like a kid's, her cheeks dappled with freckles, and her slender neck like a Paris girl's. He says silly things to her that make her burst into wild laughing, and I fancy he is seeing her on the sly. Too simple to be corrupt, it must amuse her, all these ardent men who pursue and pester her even in her very stable. Perhaps, however, she may have singled out one from among the troop.

She thinks about us when the regiment is in the trenches. And when the guns are thundering worst, she frankly counts every shot. . . . "a little, . . . a great deal. . . . passionately," as if she was plucking the petals off a daisy.

. . . . .

"Make haste, Monsieur Sulphart, you are going to help me to pluck the duck."

A good cosy warm breath greets us as we come into the kitchen. The round table, all white and scoured under the lamp, seems to be awaiting us ready for reading. My carpet slippers are over there, near the stove, with the big ginger cat lying on top of them. You might fancy you were coming back to your own fireside on a rainy day,

Our cheeks still burning from our tramp in the keen wind of the open fields, we puff and blow and are very happy.

"We're better off here than in the trench, eh, boy?" says Mother Monpoix to us as she beats up in her salad-bowl the creamy batter for the fritters.

It's quite true, we are well off in the mill. It is now two months that we are coming to it every rest: six days in the line, three days at the farm.

At first we slept in the barns, under the cartshed, in the garret, and even on the staircase. But afterwards, without paying any heed to the Germans, who were bound from the spire of L---- to see us delving, we have made ourselves dug-outs in the paddock. From a distance all these little mounds remind you of newly made tombs awaiting their crosses. Of the frail straw shelters put up in September there remain now nothing but a few Madagascar huts, whose wood the rains have rotted, and broken in the reeds of the roof. All the same, the cantonment is always known as the "negro village." The negroes that I used to visit as a boy at twenty sous a time were not more amusing, and when I contemplate ourselves, I fancy I can once more find the same savages--not quite so black this time--preparing their couscous in their tin dixies.

We are a half-score of comrades, sergeants and privates, who live at the farm in a sort of happy family. There is Lambert the quartermaster; Bourland of the Colonel's staff; Demachy; Godin, who was a sergeant and who was broken by Barbaroux, the major, for a folly; Ricordeau; and sometimes the adjutant Berthier, when he gets bored in his own quarters.

In spite of the shelters dug out in the paddock, in spite of the smoke that shows them that the house is inhabited, the Germans never fire on this point. They saucepan everything, smash up the village roof by roof, hut never as much as a single shell on the farm. You would say that some miracle preserves it.

"It's the trees, they hide it," Monpoix explains. The farm is our house, our home. We never quite leave it, even when we are in the trenches: we leave our happiness in it when we set out from it.

The shepherds of Provence, when they take their flocks into the mountain, still see from the heights their white-walled farm, the stables, the green fields, and fancy they are still living in the house with its roof of corrugated tiles. And so we, too, in our trench, we still are living at the farm, we see rising up and falling again the white spiral of the pigeons, the light smoke unravelling, much the same blue as the colour of the poplars; and in the morning when the last watching-posts come in, we hear the cock crowing us a good-morning.

"Those are signals, all that," repeats Fouillard obstinately, knowing that it annoys us to hear it.

As for signals, they fancy they see them every night, both there and elsewhere. Sometimes a patrol dashes out and runs towards the light and beats up the countryside. They wander about for hours, lose themselves, prowl round sleeping farms, or manage to terrify some woman who was going upstairs to put her children to bed, a candle in her hand.

When we speak of this at the farm, Monpoix growls:

"They're all spies in this district, my boy. . . . Ah! the brigands!"

In the morning, very early, before he goes out to his fields, he comes to yarn with us in the dark kitchen where we are taking our chocolate. A great flaming fire licks at the fireback, with its three fleurs-de-lis half eaten away, and sticking slices of bread on the points of our bayonets, we are making toast at it.

He is delighted with our noisy, rowdy youthfulness, proper to soldiers. And then he loves to talk about our work, everything that we are digging out there is his fields.

"Good trenches, anyhow? You're not going to let those Prussian bandits through again. . . . And that listening-post, where are you putting it this time?"

He knows this section of the lines as we do, trench by trench, without ever having been there. In spite of his surly ways, he must be pretty fond of us. The cooks have told me that on the morning of the attack he was more excited and troubled than we were. I asked them:

"He knew the time fixed for the attack?"

"Yes, like everybody else. . . . He had often enquired about it from us."

Mother Monpoix, for her part, knows nothing at all "about your whole war," but the daughter takes after her father--a hard and accurate memory, a peasant woman's memory. One day, when we were talking about the German heavy batteries, masked and hidden in the black woods, she had said:

"Ah, yes, on Hill 91."

Taken by surprise, I had eyed her. Nothing clouded her look of simplicity. She must have said that quite innocently; a number that stuck in her memory.

The Monpoix hardly go out at all. They have, as a matter of fact, been given permission to stay in the farm, but they have been strictly forbidden to move about on the side of our lines. To keep his legs from rusting, the father once upon a time used to make a round of the "negro village"; but he got into a row with the soldiers over two brand-new barrows they had taken to make the frame of a door for a dug-out, and having been well cursed by them, he now does not venture to show himself in the cantonment.

Ever since that he takes his constitutional in the direction of the batteries. He whistles up Féroce his big dog, and you can see them far off as they go to and fro, the black man and the white dog, as far as the crest of the ridge--he never goes beyond. And if the Germans start firing, he makes no haste or hurry to get back indoors, he is not the least afraid.

Sometimes in the middle of the day, if the whim takes him, he goes upstairs and goes to bed, without a word to anyone. You can hear him walking about in the loft, pulling boxes here and there, opening and shutting the windows. This makes his wife laugh.

"What on earth can he be doing? He simply can't stay quiet in his place, he must be under a curse. . . ."

63

I can't tell why, but I find myself embarrassed and uneasy during these unexplained absences of his.

What we pay the Monpoix for our board helps them to live, for they have no money. They sell milk, eggs, a little poultry. But up to now they have not been willing to sell any of their pigeons, not even to the Colonel.

"You can't get hold of them as easily as all that, isn't that so, boy?" says old Monpoix to us. "You go and catch them, those creatures! And you don't want to go up to their cot by night, the Prussians would see the light. And then one gets accustomed to having one's live things about, as well."

As soon as there is a fine day, the unwearying whirligig of the pigeons makes about the mill a kind of white coronal, from out of which a few blossoms take wing. One day, from out of the trench one was shot at flying very low down above the lines. Was it terrified? It fled away in the direction of the Boches.

But we shall not see the pigeons of the farm very much longer now: the Colonel has talked of having them all killed.

The Monpoix do not display indignation at these mishaps and broils. They don't even seem to notice the distrust with which they are surrounded, and they never mention it. That is the thing that surprises me most.

If they are refused a pass for a few hours, the father grouses a bit, and that's all. The daughter occasionally makes some allusion to it in her drawling voice, but without displaying the least emotion, as she might speak of some commonplace nuisance that must be endured the same as other people, because it's the war.

A queer girl she is, droll, gentle, and quiet, not very strong, who talks in a voice as pallid as her cheeks. I can gather very well that we amuse her but she never laughs out heartily and gustily like her mother. She always has that contemplative air, and when we are talking seriously instead of our noisy chaff and chatter, she pauses in her work to listen to us, whatever the theme may be. She never forgets anything of what she hears---our lives, any of our lives, our family, our affairs--and on her part she would never get a letter from her brother, the chasseur à pied of whom she is so proud, without reading it to us.

Our military work and labours also are of deep interest to her. She knows, ever since she has been hearing us speak about them, the tortuous windings of the trenches in the woods where not so long ago she used to go gathering blackberries, and the emplacement of the batteries, that you might imagine were just in front of the farm, so furiously do the walls shake when they are firing. She never asks a question; she listens to us without ever putting in a word, and you might very well suppose that she is thinking of something else when you observe the vagueness of her eyes.

I remember how one morning, in front of Morache, who at that time used to take his chocolate at the farm, she was talking to Demachy about the fatigue we had been on the night before. We had dug an emplacement at the verge of the wood, and carted quantities of logs to make a machine-gun position. Gilbert was describing the spot to her: under the fir-trees near the river.

"Chatterbox! Dangerous chatterbox!" the Adjutant ejaculated in his squeaky voice.

Gilbert, I recollect, had turned quite pale; but the girl had only looked at Morache with an air that hardly even displayed surprise, and without saying a word in reply. And she never spoke of this incident after.

Emma is a still more thoughtful person than her mother is. Always when I come back from the trenches I find hot water to wash my chafed legs. She knows everybody's tastes, makes cabbage soup just as Gilbert likes it, and makes the coffee very black and strong, to please us, though she prefers not to drink it herself. The day the battalon goes down again to the trenches our socks are in front of the fire ever since breakfast; and when a wounded man goes by, laid out rigid on a truck, she runs out quickly as far as the road to see if it is not by chance one of her soldiers. Directly one of us begins to talk, she comes near. I observe her listening to Berthier. He is explaining to Gilbert how he would set about a fresh attack, going fully and precisely into every detail. Her bowl in her hand, she is standing close by the lamp, and you would say that her chin, all flecked with light, has dipped into the milk. Is she even listening at all?

She turns her head, catches sight of me, and immediately goes up to her mother, with lowered eyes, without a sound to be heard from her light shoes on the tiles.

Monpoix is drowsing in his corner. It is a warm and placid hour of solid, good repose. We are very comfortable. I stretch my limbs lazily, like a dog that is growing too hot, and I sit down against the bed, one arm on the head-board, one arm lying on the mattress. You feel sheltered from everything in these familiar surroundings, better than in the deepest sap. It is enough to pull the thick curtains and light the lamp to feel yourself at your own fireside and to have nothing more to fear. By way of precaution, we put a stretch of tent-canvas in front of the window as well. The night shall have none of our warmth, not a thread of our light.

We are at our own fireside, far from all danger, far from the war. The huge beams of the shelters fear the great shells, and make themselves into stiff props and buttresses; here it is a pleasant wall hung with pink paper that is our protection. We have complete confidence in it. Better than all the parapets in the world do we feel ourselves defended by this light that we find so delightful after the yellow, jumping flame of candles. We feel ourselves defended by the fire snoring and roaring, by the smoking pot, by all this happiness of low degree --and even by the stimulating smell of those onions, exactly like little white fruit, lying on a plate.

. . . . .

A regular family dinner, one of those dinners in the depth of winter, more intimate, more cordial than any other, when happiness, just feeling the cold a little, comes and nestles close up to the fire.

Are we soldiers? Hardly--at any rate, we are forgetting it. There is certainly Berthier's monkey-jacket, one or two blue coats; but the others are in sweaters, in waistcoats, with nothing about them of the soldier. Demachy has even had sent to him heavy pyjamas with silk facings, which has definitely and for good ruined him in the opinion of the "negro village," and marked him out for the persistent malevolence of Morache.

Heedless and robust, our five-and-twenty years break out in laughter. Life is a great field stretching in front of us in which we are to run our course.

To die! Come, now! He will die, maybe, and our neighbour, and others besides; but oneself--one can't possibly die, oneself. . . . It cannot be that it should be lost at one stroke, all this youth, this joy, this strength, with which one is brimful and running over. You have seen ten die, you will see a hundred fall, but that your own turn might come to be a little blue tumbled heap in the middle of the fields, that you never believe at all. In spite of death that follows on our heels and takes whenever he pleases the ones he pleases, an insensate confidence never leaves us. It is not true; there is no death! Can any one possibly die when we laugh under the lighted lamp, bending over the dish from which there rises a fresh fragrance of burnet and shallots?

Besides, we never speak about war; it is forbidden during meals. It is equally forbidden to talk slang and to let the conversation turn on service matters. For every infraction of these rules the culprit must pay a fine of two sous into the pool; this is our game every day. Ricordeau, our new sergeant, dribbles away the whole of his eighteen sous of daily pay. And yet he talks with muchcaution, for we have made him very mistrustful; but Sulphart always finds new tricks to bring the conversation round to the slippery places, and all at once the unlucky word escapes him--last night's fatigue, the attack of the sixteenth, the listening-post. . . .

"Two sous! two sous!" we all shout. If by ill-luck Ricordeau is fain to put up a defence, it only gets him deeper in the mud. "I'm not having any," he protests, wanting to get out of paying his fine.

At once everybody shouts louder still:

"That's slang! Two sous more!" . . .

What do we talk about? Everything, pell-mell, all at once. We talk about our trades, our love affairs, our concerns generally, and at all points gaily. Everyone's life is sliced up into anecdotes, and though nobody means to tell lies, everybody embroiders just a trifle: after all, there are so very few things in our past, the barely born past of the youthful.

The least merry of us never has sad recollections to recount, and there are none even to be guessed at in any of our lives. We have none the less known grief and distress. Yes, but that's all a thing of the past. . . . Of this life man retains only pleasant memories; as for the others, the lapse of time effaces them, and there is no pang whose wound oblivion does not heal, no grief for which no consolation can be found.

The past takes on beauty; seen from afar, all human beings seem better. With what love, with what tender affection, do we speak of wives, mistresses, betrothed! They are all frank and faithful and merry, and you might imagine if you heard us on these evenings that there was nothing save sheer happiness in life.

Now and then something comes whack against the wall, like the crack of a whip. Clack! It is a stray bullet.

"Come in," calls Demachy.

If any one speaks of the Fritz who has fired it, the whole table grows excited. "Two sous! two sous!" and everybody laughs.

"It has taken the war to make us learn that we were happy," says Berthier, always serious.

"Aye, we had to learn to know distress," agrees Gilbert. "Before, we knew nothing at all, we were an ungrateful lot."

Now we relish the least joy: like a dessert that is generally denied us. Happiness is found everywhere; it lies in the dug-out where the rain doesn't come through, soup that is really hot, the litter of dirty straw in which we go to bed, the comical tale related by a pal, a night with no fatigue to go out on. . . . Happiness . . . but it is held in the two pages of a letter from home, in the drop of rum at the bottom of a cup. Like poor children who build a palace with a few bits of board, the soldier makes happiness out of everything that comes his way.

A stone, a mere stone on which you can set your feet in the midst of a river of mud, even that is happiness. But you must first have gone through the mud to find it out.

I try to penetrate the future, to see beyond the time of war into that misty distance gilded like a summer dawn. Shall we ever reach as far as that? And what will it give us? Shall we ever be cleansed of this long suffering? Shall we ever forget this misery, this mud, this blood, this slavery? Oh yes, I am fully convinced of it; we shall forget, and there will remain in our memory nothing but a few images of battle that will not then be made ugly by fear, a few bits of nonsense and fun, some evenings such as this. . . . And I say to them:

"You will see. . . . Years will pass away. Then one day we shall meet each other again, we will talk about the boys, about the trenches, about the attacks, about our miseries and our bits of fun, and we will laugh and say: 'Ah, those were the good days!' . . ."

At that they all protest vehemently and noisily, even Berthier.

"Hey! that'll do!"

"If you like it, better enlist again!"

"Good days, reliefs in the mud!--you're coming it a bit strong."

"And fatigue on corrugated iron that night it was raining cats and dogs, have you forgotten that? You howled enough about it, anyway."

"Do you call it a good day, the sixteenth at two minutes to twelve noon?"

I laugh, delighted at hearing their outcry.

"You'll see!"

Mother Monpoix, who is enjoying herself as much as we are, twisting the corner of her blue apron, applauds and agrees with me through the tumult.

"Certainly you will regret the farm."

"We'll come back to see it, ma!"

Bourland has got up to go and get his violin. He has made it himself with a cigar-box and strings he got from Paris, and it is to this toy, this instrument fit for a circus, that we owe our very best evenings.

He tunes it--two notes--and immediately we are silent. Music, the friend of every one of us. . . .

It is the Adagio of the Symphonie Pathétique he is playing. Everything grows still and soothed and placid. Music as ardent and tender as our hearts. Is there anything pathetic in this long thrill? No. . . . it is like a beautiful heart-seizing dream. And then, what matter what he plays? . . . Ase's Death, an aria of Bach's. I cannot tell now. My thought has ceased to follow. .

So many stretched webs on which our dreams are busy with their delicious broidery.

We listen, our minds and our eyes gone wandering. Here are the beloved voices of old days coming to revisit us. How sweet they are, heard from how far away! We are dreaming. . . . It is a Sunday at Colonne's, the studio where the piano let fall one by one like pearls the drops of the Jardin sous la Pluie, the air a sweet friend was singing.

Berthier, his mouth a little open and his hands locked together, listens as a man prays. I see nothing of Gilbert but his smooth straight forehead, like an obstinate child's, above the interlaced fingers that cover his eyes. Sulphart has taken on a serious air, his features tense as though determined to understand. Then I shut my

67

eyelids down so as to see no more.

To be no more now than a charmed soul, and a soul that sleeps. Everything is annihilated. . . . Far, far is the present. . . . the oaths, the death rattles, the guns, all the noises that make up our poor lives of animals, all that can never harden our soul and wither its infinite tenderness. It finds new birth again, an August garden under a reviving shower. And ten soldiers are now no more than a single heart being lulled and soothed like a child to slumber, ten soldier-men. . . . "The Méditation de Thaïs,Bourland!" "No! the Valse des Ombres."

Gilbert, who has a nice voice, sings ballads, mezza voce, and all the other voices hum the chorus. And then it is an evocation of Paris, lovely autumnal Paris, whose rain-washed footwalks shimmer and gleam under the street-lamps. We sing them all, one after the other, all the successes of last winter, and from chorus to chorus the voices grow louder and louder. Thrown well back in our chairs, we are shouting now, heedless, expanded, blown out with too much joy. Bourland's violin can be heard no longer, lost in this deafening choir; we are simply yelling. . . .

"Hark!"

A sudden silence falls. Bourland has stopped, bow in air. Surprised faces are intent. . . . We are listening, uneasy. What can it be?

The same fist beats upon the door, and a voice comes from the night outside.

"A wounded man."

Quickly we open; with eyelids blinking he comes inside. He is livid and pale, with big eyes encircled with black rings that swallow up his cheeks. His left arm is in a sling made with a big dirty handkerchief, in which a red splash is seen growing bigger, and the blood, sliding down till it reaches his lifeless hand, drips as he comes along.

"No, no rum. I'd rather have wine."

Monpoix's hand shakes as he pours it out for him. Speechless, embarrassed, we press round our comrade. He has sat down heavily, all his energy simply emptied out of him. There is not a sound now but the gurgling of the wine in his dry throat.

The dog has waked up. He rises, sniffs at the newcomer's tracks, and drop by drop he licks up the still warm blood from the tiles.

. . . . .

Six days more of the trenches--six days of pouring rain--and here we are in the farm again. I am writing. Sitting huddled up close against the stove, his back humped and rounded, Monpoix has let his pipe go out. Nothing can be heard but the soup simmering and the man's labouring breathing that whistles in and out.

I find him a changed man ever since the attack. He never jokes with us now as he used to do. He remains for hours at a time without saying a word, sluggishly fastened to his low chair; and when we are talking among ourselves, he barely turns his head to listen to us, with an air of embarrassment, as though he was afraid he might meet with a snub.

His wife says he is ill. And yet he never makes any complaint. He mumbled that he didn't want to see the regimental doctor, and he is treating himself after his own fashion with bowls of home made remedies.

What can be the matter with him? I often think over it. Without any doubt his drawn features, the fever that shakes him every night, show that he is a sick man, but this reason is not enough to satisfy me. It seems to me that there must needs be something else hidden behind this prostration; it is no mere simple malady that is able to break him down like this; and pin him down for whole days on end in front of his fire without a word for anybody. He does not seem to be in pain in any way. He is reflecting, brooding, that is all.

"He is a man who digs in himself," is the diagnosis of Maroux, who once upon a time used to go out with him to tell him stories about sport and shooting.

You might say, in fact, that some secret grief is tormenting him. And yet the news from his son is always good. What can he be thinking about during these long siestas? He never goes out now, even at night, to smoke his pipe. And yet the other evening he got up, took his tobacco-pouch, and moved towards the door of the garden close with a dragging step. He opened it and stopped short on the threshold, looking out over the dark field where men were calling out to one another. Whether it was the cold wind, or whether it was the deep shadow, I saw him shiver. With a brutal movement he shut the door again, and came back to take his seat in his old place in front of the stove. He did not smoke at all that night.

What secret anxiety is working in him, then? He is not being bothered more than he was before the attack--nay, the reverse is the case. He has even been offered on several occasions passes that he has not cared to take.

Nothing interests him now, not even the jumping and antics of Féroce.

"Why don't you go off and make a little round with the dog, Monsieur Monpoix?"

"I haven't any fancy for going out, boy."

Several times Berthier has said to him:

"We are splitting your head, yelling like this. We'll eat in the kitchen."

Mother Monpoix and Emma have protested: not to hear us laughing any more, singing, chaffing one another. . . . ah no! . . . And the old man said the same as they did.

"On the contrary, do stay here. To hear you talking gives my mind a change of thoughts."

All the same, he hardly speaks to us. No longer now does he question us as in old days about the new trenches, our fatigues, our patrols, all the things that used to interest him so much. On the contrary, when we speak about them he has always some excuse to go away, or else he puts down his head and half shuts his eyes, as if he was trying to go to sleep. I am not the only one who has noticed this.

"The poor fellow!" Gilbert said to me pityingly. "You would think that it hurts him in some way when any one speaks of the attack."

It's quite true. Not once has he ever spoken to us about the affair of the sixteenth, never has he come near us to listen to the account of it. When any one mentions it, he does not even turn his eyes that way. Only you would say that his back humps itself still more, and that his head droops lower. . . . I see nothing but his back, his broad round back, but I divine in it, hidden close, I know not what sullen attentiveness. You could swear that he is sleeping, and yet he is listening--I am sure he is listening.

The other evening Berthier was telling the baggage-master sergeant about the falling back through the V-shaped trench when we had been obliged to withdraw. A few men and himself were covering the movement, firing on the grey backs that were cutting across by the fields, and flinging down across the trench broken lengths of of chevaux de frise, logs, everything that was to hand. In the straight lines he made his men run, for he feared an enfilading fire, and as they kept looking behind them, they kept catching their feet in the dead bodies and tumbling down and swearing. Happily, the wounded had already been carried off, for now it was too late for anything of that kind. As far as the first line they had only come across one wounded man. He was sitting on the parapet with his legs hanging down as though on the edge of a ditch, no longer fearing the bullets, and he was calling out in a long, persistent complaint: "I can't see clearly. . . . Don't leave me! . . . I can't see clearly." A broad red ribbon was trickling from his temple and making a stripe across his cheek.

He had heard them as they went by at full tilt, and having doubtless guessed that we were falling back, he had run behind them, at first bending low almost on hands and feet, then bolt upright, staggering, fumbling at the night with his bewildered, frightened hands. His grievous supplication had pursued them for a moment. "Don't leave me behind, boys! I swear to you I won't cry out. . . ." Then a step into the vacancy of a trench, and in one mass, with his hands thrust out in front, the blind man had fallen into his grave. As they turned the angle of the redan they had heard the dry voice of a Mauser. The coup de grâce, without a doubt.

By chance I was looking at Monpoix while Berthier was speaking. He had half raised his head to listen, and was opening strange eyes, big staring eyes whose lids never moved. But he had seen me, and at once he had dropped his head again, and again went off to his sleeping.

It was nothing, that look I caught; and yet that evening strange notions came to me. In spite of myself I keep observing the old man.

What can he be thinking about for whole days on end? I fancy now that I know. It is really nothing, not even as much as a supposition, nothing but a vague uneasiness, an irrational pang that is taking shape and crystallizing, but that is borne in on my mind, with little circumstances that all fall in together, commonplace little coincidences. I am closely watching his least movements at the moment, as if I was certain to make some discovery.

At times I stand out against this obscure suggestion. Come, now, this is ridiculous! Why should I want to lend this sick peasant a soul out of a novel? He suffers in the same way as his cattle might suffer, poor brutes that, not knowing how to tell their trouble, lie down with their masks to the wall and sleep upon their pain. There is no room for psychology in all that.

And yet, and nevertheless. . . . My hesitating doubts grow precise, it is like a presentiment that no amount of reasoning can dispel.

He must feel this persistent attention that follows him, and he does not like us to remain alone together. You might think he is afraid I might speak to him. I go and sit down on the opposite side of the stove from him, astride upon a chair, my chin set on my folded arms as if I was going to have a good yarn with him. He does not even open his eyes. None the less I am certain he knows I am there and that it embarrasses him. I could say the words that frighten him: I know what they are. Our two anguishes guess at one another. After a moment, I think I can see his big hands with their short nails, trembling and quaking on his knees covered with well-worn corduroy. Will he at length open his eyes and look at me face to face?

No. Little by little his breathing lengthens, grows more regular. He has gone to sleep. . . . Then all my scaffolding of suspicions falls to the ground at one blow, and as his hands go on still trembling, shivering with fever, I would like to awake him, ashamed of having been cruel in my own mind, and talk to him as heretofore, gaily, like a comrade.

Why have I got it into my head that he was afraid to pass close to the barn where the clothes and belongings of the dead are piled up? The other day, as he was going along in front of it, I joined him. Escaped from the bursting packs, there was underwear and linen trailing right up to the road.

"Look," I said to him, "that is long Vairon's pack. Those are his mother's letters sticking out of it. She was in the hospital. She had starved herself to send him a few sous, good knitted vests, poor old thing! . . . Two killed with one blow."

He turned to me, pale and haggard.

"You mustn't go over that to me, boy. My son is a soldier, too."

I did not know what to say, and I let him go indoors without venturing to follow him. That night I almost hesitated to push open the door of the room from which I heard his voice, out of breath. I went in with Bourland. The old man was putting a question to Gilbert:

"Is it true that that long Vairon, he was still calling out the next morning, lying wounded in the plain?"

Having caught sight of us, he stopped, quickly turning his eyes away. He never spoke again that evening, and went up to bed before we sat down to the table. I go through all that once more in memory, and I write no more. I look at the old man, breathing in pants, his shoulders shaking. He looks very ill to-night. His cheeks can be surmised grey and hollow under his week-old beard. I find him still more prostrated than in our last spell out of the trenches. Always sunk in lethargy on his low chair, he pursues his evil dreams.

And in the dying light that rubs with a frozen ray the polished backs of the chairs, it seems to me that I am about to see, bowed over him, all the shades of all our dead, for whom the clock is telling its rosary.

. . . . .

They are burying Monpoix. He died the other night, without a murmur, without any dying struggle. At daybreak his wife found him cold in his bed.

His bier, carried by hand, has just set off through the fields, two black robes behind it, a few peasants and some soldiers. As I was barely able to walk, I stayed behind at the farm alone. I feel it all vast and gloomy around me.

Nothing can be heard now except the sound of the pigeons hopping and flitting about the garret. How disquieting it is, this great silence that speaks of death! I feel myself solitary and yet threatened. The two trestle stools set close together seem still to be awaiting his coffin. It has indeed come back once already. . . .

At the moment the incident, in reality very commonplace in itself, had no effect on me: but now, as I stay here alone, a kind of vague disquiet gains upon me. I ought not to think of it any more.

Just as the funeral procession had gone across the grassland and was reaching the road, the Germans caught sight of us and began to fire. The first shell fell short, the next was fifty paces off, and the cortège was at once broken to pieces. The four bearers--I can see them yet--had stopped dead, bewildered, and then, seeing the peasants running away, they heavily put down the stretcher from which the bier had tumbled, and they jumped into the ditch behind us. It was high time: the third shell burst squarely on the slope, riddling the coffin. In single file and bending double, we passed on, pushing each other along, and the dead man remained alone in the middle of the path, his overturned bier escaped from under its black pall. The mother and the daughter, who are never afraid, had run away shrieking; and when the boys brought the bier back to the farm, Emma fainted. She had been the first to remark that the coffin was half unfastened, as if the old man had made an attempt to get out of it and run away too.

His bier lying on the two stools, he remained until twilight in his farm that he was fain not to leave. As the shadows were falling the peasants came back, and the porters once more took up their burden. They have only just gone: outside the dog is still howling, tugging at his chain.

This tragical return of the old man struck me as something significant. Never had they shelled so close to the farm. Are they going to destroy it now that he is there no longer? An inexplicable disquiet overwhelms me. I have the disagreeable impression of having someone behind me, very close.

Then, a vague fear running through my skin, I get up, and without looking round, without a glance at the old man's low chair, I go out into the garden whistling. Quick, I pull the door to behind me. . . .

Night is nearly come. The stone well has the air of a tomb. On the other side of the runnel a relief goes by, a black troop, humming as it goes; heavy confused silhouettes bristling with pickaxes and rifles, a band of navvies under arms. A few laggards follow, leaning on thick staves. Territorials, without any doubt.

Not a single shot comes from the trenches. Far away, round Berry, there is the dull sound of guns. The willows are dreaming with bowed heads about the pool; in the shadows the ducks as they lie have all the airs of swans. The whole of the night is contained in that stagnant water. The trees carve their reflection in it, exact, branch by branch, and in it you can see reduplicated the sky that seems made of tin, the big melancholy sky that gazes down at its own image.

Not a sound now of any kind. In the country a lost voice, a partridge, is drivelling. That huge silence calms me. . . . Wait, why is Féroce not barking any more?

Suddenly in the pigeon-house there stirs a slight sound of feathers, the rustling sound that can be heard when a poultry-house is wakened. One pigeon, two pigeons come out, and with one wing-beat go and take their place on a branch. . . . Why? Who has disturbed them?

An absurd notion comes to me: Emma has come back, has climbed up there in secret, and she is doing something--she is doing what the old man used to do. . . . My mind on the alert, my heart beating wildly, I keep on listening. Something cracked; was it a window someone was opening?

So much the worse! I mean to find out. I go into the farm through the dark bake-house. My hands feel and fumble in front of me. I knock up against a barrow, and my startled heart beats, beats furiously. . . .

I go up the wooden stair. Lord, how it creaks! . . . The garret. A little of the blue night comes through the dirty panes of the windows. In the shadow there are crouching shapes. . . . No, nothing, only sacks.

My legs are shaking. For all that, I am not afraid. I go forward with muffled footfall, and my cold hands ransack the blackness, recognize things. My peering eyes are growing accustomed to the dark. I recognize a soldier's coat that is drying with its sleeves hanging down.

On the other side of the wooden partition the pigeons are still excited and stirring. I come up, and slowly, so as to stifle the shrill outcry of the creaking hinges,

I push open the door. My head thrust forward, my fist clenched, I look around. Nothing, nothing. . . .

The moonlight filtering through the tiles shines clear on the pigeons sitting in round balls on their perches. One of them coos. Outside the wind whistles a shrill tune through tightly pressed lips. . . .

Then I shut the creaking door again, and alone, all alone in the dark loft, I look at the melancholy cast-off with its hanging arms, this tired, flabby coat in which a soldier will have to die.

CHAPTER VII
IN THE CAFÉ DE LA MARINE

THEY had told Demachy: "You'll find them at the Café de la Marine, near the stone bridge."

The big bridge with its broken piers was now only crossed by night. By day it was enough for a cyclist to show himself on it to let loose a salvo that thrashed the water in fury or tore a lump off the parapet. Arriving at the end of the afternoon, Demachy crossed the river farther up, by the bridge of boats.

In the greenish water, where hardly a ripple could be seen, the tall poplars were diving up to their very summits, as if they had sought to attain the sky in the quiet water as well as in the air. A big barge was sleeping up on the steep bank near the edge, lying on its side. The gaps where its planks had been torn away displayed its empty hold between its huge wooden ribs, and you asked yourself how this whale carcass had come to be stranded so far from home.

The river was rustling and whispering, breaking against the boats forming the bridge. They were those little fisherman's boats, green or black, that you sent along with a lazy oar on fine Sundays in summer. On the prow of the freshest of them, painted in white, you might read a name: "Lucienne Bremont, Roucy." A splinter from a shell had wounded it in the side.

All along the steep bank wooden crosses, slender and bare, made of boards or of branches crossed and fastened together, looked at the water as it ran. They were to be seen everywhere, and even in the flooded plain, where red képis were floating like strange waterlilies.

With the floods the crosses must needs go with the stream of grey water, to be stranded who knows where?--at the feet of a child who would spell out on the frayed wood, " . . . infantry, . . . for France. . . ." and would make a wooden sword of it. One might have said that these dead men were fleeing from their forgotten tombs, and the endless file of the other dead men watched them set forth, their crosses so close together that they seemed to be shaking hands with one another.

In the thick undergrowth the eglantines all in flower were holding up their white posies. Demachy plucked them as he went. It was coming up to the tileworks. Upon the dismantled roof the red-cross flag was no longer flying: it was a kind of grey, torn rag that hung down the whole length of the flagstaff. The brick wall, pierced with loopholes in September, had been smashed in by shells, the tower broken down, the front riddled, and at the present moment you could go into the field hospital through ten different breaches. And yet that is where the wounded had been looked after ever since the water had overwhelmed the cellars. And so no one dared to light up at night in that farm, now marked down as a target, they were dressed in the darkness, by touch, the fingers feeling for the wounds.

Those that were too badly hurt to be saved had their bed made by the door: the holes were dug, they had only to be taken outside. The cemetery also had learned to make war; it no longer allowed its dead to go as they pleased, it mustered them in company in front of the tile-works. You had to stoop down, lift up a wreath of ivy, a red, white, and blue cockade made of three rags in order to discover a regimental number and a name. A comrade's knife had indeed engraved these things on a belt-buckle, but the rust soon ate them away, as if death had meant to kill their very memory.

74

Demachy stopped at the first of the tombs. Corpses had been brought along since the previous day and were awaiting their grave, lying between the crosses. One was wrapped up in a piece of canvas, a stiff shroud that the blood made harder still. The others had remained as they had fallen, their coats foul with earth, their trousers thick with mud, and with nothing to cover their swollen or waxen faces, their poor purply faces, that you would have said might have been smeared with lees of wine. The head of a sergeant, however, was veiled. It had been thrust into a satchel, as though into a monk's cowl, and you could guess at the dreadful wound under this winding-sheet clotted with blood. He wore a wedding-ring on his finger. The arm of a little chasseur was stretched out, and seemed to lie across the path barring it, the nails driven into the soft earth. Had they dragged themselves up out of the trenches only to come there to die?

Among the white and black crosses, Demachy looked for that belonging to Nourry, who had been killed at the Springs Wood eight days earlier. Little Bélin had made the cross with a great board out of a box, split in two, and Gilbert recognized it from the back, reading on its "Champag . . ." At its foot someone had stuck in a shell-case, in which a bouquet of lily-of-the-valley was growing yellow and faded. Demachy threw it away to put his eglantine in its place.

With closed eyes, he thought of Nourry on his last day. Wounded in the stomach, he had groaned in the dug-out all night, for the stretcher-bearers never came up, and every now and then turning his thin head with its pinched-up nose to us, he would murmur:

"Eh, my poor lads, I'm keeping you from sleeping."

He was dead at daybreak. The nightly fusillade had fallen to silence, the guns were not yet begun to fire. A chaffinch was singing in the wood. And in this place we had the better felt and understood that death.

To give him a proper tomb, the squad had determined to take him to the rear. Four men had gone for rations instead of two, carrying turn about the long body rolled up in its brown blanket; and Demachy had followed them, the cross of white wood under one arm, and holding in his other hand bottles for their food.

Since Nourry's death two letters had come for him. They might have been returned with the brutal announcement of death in the corner: "The addressee cannot be found." Demachy had thought it better to take them. He took them out of his cartridge-pouch, tore them up without opening them, and over this regulation soldier's tomb, square as a barrack-bed, he scattered the petals of the letters, so that the dead man might at least sleep under words from his own folk.

This comrade of his was dearer to him now that he was no more. He regretted that he had not liked him better, that tall boy, shy and gentle; that he had not been nicer to him. He carried in the same way within him the names of several comrades left behind in the little cemeteries of Champagne or the Aisne, or even between the lines upon no man's land; and he used to talk to them, listen to them complaining, those poor fellows whom, when they were alive, he had not always liked, because they were coarse at times, and clumsy and heavy of mind and body. He forgot none of them, and loved to brood over their memory, when there was already no more left of them but a meaningless name in the short memories of their pals in the squad.

Thus staying by a tomb, he found once more, intact, his soul of old times, his soul of the days before the war, grieving and passionate, which now was asleep, worn out by fatigue, the life of misery, daily appetites, the contact and rubbing up against others. His soul would waken thus, in hours of solitude--the time of suffering.

"Hullo! old man," called a stretcher-bearer who saw him moving away. "Don't loll about in this country. They're nasty this afternoon, they keep on heaving the big stuff over."

He started again, without hurrying, following the course of the river, in no haste to arrive. He would have liked to remain alone this evening.

The first houses, whose gardens, lying fallow, were a continuation of the fields, were almost habitable, merely just had the corners, so to speak broken off by the 210-millimètre guns, their red tiles having taken flight before the shells like broods of red pigeons. But when you got to the top of the ascent it was simple massacre.

You saw the church first of all, a ruined spire without a roof, and a high dismantled wall, whose ogive windows opened on to the sky. The little door of the priest's dwelling-house, still upright, guarded those ruins, and just over the bell a little blue plate gave its innocent advice: "Tirez fort"--"Pull hard."

However artillery may rage against a countryside, there will always be something left: a piece of a wall with its flowered paper, and on it; a couple of photographs in black frames; the newly painted door of a room, looking coquettish in the midst of broken and pounded rubble; a marble chimney-piece that has remained up above, balanced in position, on three slabs of parquet.

From these ruined remains Demachy imagined the country in its lifetime. It was neither a village nor a country town, a little pleasure-place rather, a peaceful countrified retreat to which the shopkeepers from the city would retire on reaching their sixty years, to graft their roses and go a-fishing. No farms--villas, which you could recognize in spite of everything by the three freestone steps of an outside stair, by a fragment of pink façade, whose paint had been scratched by flying splinters.

He followed, tripping and stumbling along, the course of the main street bordered by devastated shops and remains of houses. Under the ruins, rising up from the stairs leading to the cellars, there could be heard voices, laughter, the neighing of a horse, the thin scraping of a violin.

Behind the fragments of wall, crouching cooks were trying to make a fire without smoke, and merely turned their heads, as though from curiosity, when a shell announced itself hurtling through the air. Something can very well be risked when one means to have a fry.

"The Café de la Marine?" Demachy called out to them.

"Lower, to the left."

He started off again, making haste a little, for a big "Jack Johnson" had just fallen quite close, wrenching up a great spout of bits of stone and plaster and smoke. He had hoped to find the sign still extant on a piece of the façade, but found the stone bridge, which the Boches were continually feeling for, there remained only a tumbled mass of stones and beams smashed and pounded up about a big red roof that the shells had not seen. All the same, through the holes of the ventilators a noise of a loud talk could be heard. He stooped down and called a query:

"The Café de la Marine?"

"Beside. . . . there's a cage at the door."

With a quick glance all round, he searched, but saw nothing at all. Shrapnel having exploded just above the church--two coppery bursts--he got irritated. "There isn't any cage, in Heaven's name!"

The splinters passed, swearing viciously, and rebounded from the tiles like big hailstones. He drew himself up again, and immediately he cocked his ears.

"Ah! they are there. . . ."

He had just recognized Sulphart's voice, who must be explaining something in a friendly fashion to Lemoine.

"What!" he was shouting, "but you poor yokel, you were going on four paws when I was already in patent leathers."

Guided by these outcries, Demachy looked for the stair and precipitated himself down it. In fact, there was a big aviary placed in the entrance, and a thin, ruffle-feathered raven was seen in one corner, his long beak buried in his feathers, observing the destruction and disaster with a round open eye.

It was the bird that was the theme of the argument down in the cellar of the Café de la Marine, where our section was waiting its relief, having only put in three days in the front line.

"You ask Demachy," shouted Sulphart, catching sight of his friend, whose eyes were feeling their way in the darkness of the subterranean chamber. "Just you ask him if ravens don't live for a good hundred years."

"I've taken more ravens from the nest than you've ever seen," replied Lemoine calmly, seated on a half-barrel cut down to a tub. "You don't know what you're talking about; there's nothing as stupid as a raven."

"That doesn't prevent it living to be old; and that fellow, he has seen more wars than you--the Revolution maybe, and 1870 . . ."

Stretched out in a corner on a hammock made of wire-netting, Vieublé protested.

"Ah, don't you keep always dishing up your 1870. You're talking about a war of walnuts. They used to fight one day a month, and thought they had done a lot. And the boys that were knocking round Panama before they went out for that little turn up at Buzenval, don't you think they were in luck? It does amuse me, it does, wars like that!"

"I'm not talking about 1870," insisted Sulphart, always obstinate. "I'm talking about the raven."

"Hou! . . . Hououu! . . . Shut your jaw!" Everybody started to shout, to make him be quiet. Somebody threw a big lump of bread at him.

"That's all right," he said in a tone of vexation. "I'm going to give it to him, anyway, to peck at."

And having taken a piece of tinned beef, a bit of cheese, and the chunk of bread that had been flung at him, he took up his raven's dinner, much more than the bird wanted.

Demachy suddenly felt himself happy. Sulphart had kept a good place for him on a mattress, and he would be able to read, to drowse, lazily outstretched at full length, as on a divan.

The big cellar looked out on the river through two long ventholes with bars in front of them. In the morning there came in at daybreak a freezing mist that smelt of the water. You could hardly see within it, and in order to write, the men had lighted a candle fixed with three drops of its own tallow on to the corner of a mahogany round table. There was something of everything in this cellar: chairs, beds, tables, bottleracks that served us as cupboards, mattresses, and even a rocking-chair, that Bouffioux had his eye on to light his fire. Never since they had been in the war had the boys of the company slept so cosily. They revelled in their good luck all day long, wallowing in their corners, marking the bedding with their dirty boots, and their heads luxuriously lying on down pillows.

In the lower cellar there was a concert going on. A corporal was playing the ocarina, and squatting all round him, the boys were taking up each song at the chorus, with sentimental voices. Perched up on an Empire writing-table, with his legs swinging down, Father Hamel was keeping time to the rhythm by kicking his heels against the rosewood panelling.

Men paid each other calls from one cellar to another. All were well supplied with furniture. There must have been nothing left in the houses, not even under the masses of stones: little by little everything had been carried off. What had not been taken down into the cellars had been lugged off into the wood, where men went down into the trenches. Every evening regular fatigue parties would arrive, shadowy bands, and go back laden with tables, armchairs, mattresses. One piece of furniture after another, the village was flitted, and you could come upon strange dug-outs in the Springs Wood with a door that had once belonged to a Renaissance cupboard, with dreadful little Bretons, excellently carved, playing on the bagpipe. In our own particular cubby-hole we had found a wicker armchair, and a red eiderdown-quilt. Sous-Lieutenant Berthier had possession of a sofa and a tall glass cracked down the middle, on which a sanguine warrior had scratched, "Three months and then out."

On the side of the road there was even a piano, which the men carrying, growing disheartened, had left derelict half-way to the wood; and at night, while waiting for the ration carts to come up, the cooks used very softly to play little tunes on it with one finger.

The front lines, in this woodland section, were not at all dreadful. A few casual shells from time to time, at long intervals--that was how Nourry had been killed--a bullet to be risked when you went to look on the hedge between two trenches; that was all. Men went freely walking about the wood, and the cooks made their stews there, a hundred mètres to the rear, sufficiently well hidden in the undergrowth. For the first time since we had been in the trenches we had eaten hot food and drunk coffee that smoked in the cups.

The Germans at the outset had fired torpedoes, huge "stove-pipes" that broke and smashed everything to atoms. Thereupon we had sent for a section of bomb-throwers to give them due and proper answer. They had dug at the earth for nearly a month, had carted logs night and day, and made a shelter with props and stays so stout that it feared nothing. Then they had brought their gun along.

It was a noble museum specimen, a kind of very tiny mortar in bronze that carried, engraved on its squat toad's belly, the date and place of its origin: "1848. République française, Toulouse." It was loaded by strict guesswork: one gramme of powder per mètre. We were a hundred and eighty mètres from the Boches, as near as might be; so in went four spoonfuls of powder, and to make good measure the bombardier-sergeant used to add a pinch extra. That made a simply terrific noise, and the mortar leaped with fright every time it fired off. We could see the projectile describe a huge parabola in the air, turning over and over, and it would fall to earth wherever it listed in the wood, cheered by the Boches, who, I verily believe, cried out "Bravo!" Now and then it exploded. After a brief sojourn, the bombardiers had got their hands on another gun--a real one this time--and had gone off to try it elsewhere, leaving us, along with their superfine dug-out, a bizarre and innocuous weapon, a sort of giant catapult or ballista constructed with pneumatic tyres for elastic and wooden levers. With this machine you could project hand-grenades: the first man who tried it met his death for his pains.

Thereafter, the various sections of the line employed it to hurl upon the Boches the most unthought-of missiles: old boots, empty bottles, trench-boots with heavy wooden soles, and, generally, any kind or sort of object that might be lying about, so long as it was of satisfactory and sufficient weight.

Sulphart was admirably skilled--had a pretty knack at this particular game. He had spent his three days in bombarding the advanced sap of the Boches, for they were about forty mètres away from our lines. He had thrown everything he possibly could: old socks stuffed out with small stones, tins of bully-beef, bricks, the bases of shells. Last night, just before we were leaving, he had let them have the farewell shot--a big mustard-jar filled with earth, which must have landed full and square in the trench, for we could hear shouting. We had cheered Sulphart, hooted the Boches, and from out of their sap one of them--possibly the wounded one---had replied in bad French, calling us unpleasant names, cows, and cuckolds.

Ever after Sulphart displayed an uppish delight. He had brayed on through the whole of the relief, recounted his brilliant feat of arms to the whole of the regiment, nagged at the officers, stampeded the cooks at the exit to the trenches, his radiant face simply exuding pride.

"He got it full in the mug, I'm telling you: I'm dead cocksure about it. The proof is he called me cuckold, and said it in French, too. . . He must have been an officer."

He had run into every single cellar to tell his story, and for a cup of wine he gave in public a detailed and cunningly heightened and embellished narration. At the entry of the cellar where he was patiently stuffing his voracious bird, he was heard recounting his tale for the hundredth time to gapers in blue, who were drinking it all in and admiring.

"Aye, my lad," he was shouting, "the General took it full in the mug, and he even called me cuckold in French."

And as, in spite of everything, he knew how to give due homage to his enemies, he added, with a tone of respect:

"There's no doubt about it, they are an educated lot, those blighters, anyhow."

CHAPTER VIII
MOUNT CALVARY

FROM the Springs Wood you could see it through the branches, on which there were now perched like swarming green bees the first buds of the year. Harrowed by shells, disembowelled by the heavy blows of torpedoes, worn, tragical, it was a tall chalky mound, bristling with a few stakes that had once been trees. On the staff maps it was certain to have a name of its own. The soldiers had called it Mount Calvary.

It was the hell of the sector. When the regiment was going up to the line, men used to ask each other anxiously: "Who is it taking over at Calvary this time? . . ." And when they had found out, the victims groused:

"Always the same! . . . One thing is certain, the Captain doesn't worry about it-- you won't often see him up above there. . . ."

Bombarded without respite, the Calvary was always smoking like a factory. They could see the torpedoes shooting up from the wood where the Boches were, and falling heavily on that dead earth whence they could wrench nothing but gobbets of men and bits of stones. By night it was there that the fireworks went off: red globes, white stars, floating green caterpillars, a vision splendid of nights of war. Lightning bursts of explosions added their uproar to the tumult. And during four whole days two sections would stay there on the watch for the unknown over a ravaged field strewn with blue coats and grey backs.

From a distance, when they looked at the yellow and green clouds from the explosions, that never cleared away, when they saw the thick plume from the torpedoes, when they heard that incessant raging storm, men said to one another:

"It's not possible. Nobody can ever hold on there. . . . There can't be a single one to come back."

They held on there all the same, and nevertheless, there were some who came back.

Our turn had come to go up there. It was not precisely a trench that led up to Calvary, but a kind of track chopped out of the chalk, a mule-path lined with narrow dug-outs, oozing and chilly. All along it there was a heartrending medley of equipment--bottles, cartridges, clothes, tools--a whole graveyard of inanimate things. And at long intervals, wooden crosses: "Brunet, 148th Infantry Regiment . . . ." "Cachin, 74th Infantry. . . ." "Here is a German soldier. . ." Barely covered with a layer of marl, you could see quite plainly the bloated swelling of the bodies. There were more than a dozen stations on this Way of the Cross.

The relief took place more quickly than usual this evening. We went forward with humped backs and uneasy, restless ears. We pushed one another on. As we made out, in the glare of the rockets, the short stumps of the trees, sous-Lieutenant Berthier, who was guiding us, sent the word along:

"We are just getting there. Silence!"

Unnecessary advice. Not a grumble, not a clink of metal, not a murmur. Lemoine, who never believed there was any danger, for all that held his bayonet because it was rattling. The same grave feelings dominated all of us. Maroux alone was satisfied. He had pretended that it was a lucky place, that up there nobody would come to see us, that we would be left in peace. But like the others, he still went along with lowered head, keeping a hand on his mess-tin that was swinging and ringing.

"Get down!"

Two shells whistled over and came and burst twenty paces off, a red lightning that dazzles us. All of us were huddled up, one pressing close upon the others. The fragments thrashed at the chalk.

"Pass the word to go on. . . ."

In the narrow trench dug in on the other slope of the hill, the men of the regiment that was being relieved were waiting for us, impatient, their packs already on their shoulders. In lowest tones, with staccato phrases, the sergeants handed on their orders.

"Their trench is in the fringe of the wood. . . . A trifle more than a hundred mètres. Don't fire farther to the left than the birches, that's a little post of our own."

Briefly the comrades wished us good-luck as they picked up their kit.

"Look out for the torpedoes, especially in the evening at soup-time. If you possibly can, bring in the lad lying out in the field there, just in front of the barbed-wire. It's one of our boys who got knocked over the other night. You'll bury him will you? Questel, his name is. . . ."

Speedily they set off, cramming the narrow gallery through which the whole trench poured itself. Their subdued murmur moved away and finally was silent. Lucky fellows! . . .

They had left nothing on Calvary: a few tins of bully-beef, some packets of cartridges, rolls of bread not touched, a pal out in the plain. . . . They had gone.

While the first sentries, leaning their elbows on the parapet, took up the watch, our section ebbed back on to the other slope of the hill in order to instal themselves.

A regiment of miners--dour and violent lads from the North--had dug at that point a kind of grotto, whose entrance gave on to our lines and its loopholes on to the Boches' wood. It comprised a fairly lofty gallery, strongly propped up, flanked right and left with narrow retreats, supplied with old straw and newspapers. The first arrivals flung themselves into them, chattering noisily, driving off the others with fists and feet; and in the half-light of a feebly flickering candle there was a sharp scrimmage, a furious uproar of cries and oaths. Berthier, before any mischief was done, re-established order.

"Come, now, no row, no arguing; that doesn't do the least bit of good! . . . Everybody will have room."

With his electric lamp he searched into the darkest corners, and quietly and sedately bestowed his men. Behind him the soldiers waited, quite well behaved, like children being arranged by the master, and nobody shouted any more, so as not to give him trouble. They each accepted the corner assigned to him and took up his lodging in it.

Bréval, as he unfolded his blanket, kept making finds in the straw. "A newspaper from my old home!" he cried out in delight. "I'm going to read that in bed, like in the dear old days. . . ."

There were four of us in our particular garret, very close-packed, our belts unfastened and our puttees undone. Broucke had even taken off his boots and was snoring already, while little Bélin was concocting out of a bit of barbed-wire a most ingenious candle-holder, whose light could not be seen from outside.

"Ah! we're well off here," sighed Bréval, stretching himself. . . . "so long as the Boches leave us alone in peace. . . ."

"At bottom, it's just what I had always said," said Maroux, who was lying on the other side of the gallery. "From a distance, with the fellows that keep coming down, you get ideas into your head; and once you're in it, it's no worse than anywhere else."

And yet at every instant a dull thick thud shook the hill, and the explosion came in with a gust into our grotto, whose candles shivered. Sometimes it fell on the other slope of Calvary, in front of the entrance to our sap, and we could see its lightning glare on the canvas.

"Too long range," Lemoine would say, reassured by the four mètres of earth that we had on top of our heads.

Broucke snored louder than usual, to keep from hearing the shells, and Bréval read his paper, far, far away from the war.

"Set of disgusting pigs!" he growled. . . . "More women arrested in the English camp. And no tarts either, you may be sure of that--married women. . . . I've been told when they catch them like that they post up their names at the Mayor's. Talk about a blow for the husband when he'll get to know about that! . . ."

He read some lines more, then angrily crumpled up his paper, flung it away from him, and turned his face to the wall of damp chalk, saying to me: "You'll blow out the candle."

With big, muffled, obstinate blows, the artillery was raging furiously against Calvary, at the very summit of Calvary, where the three crosses would have been set up. Between the explosions there was nothing at all to be heard except now and then a man's foot stumbling over the pebbles, or straggling shots, the foolishness of some sentry.

By the dancing light of the candle that was at the point of death, I looked at the squat beams on which our equipments and water-cans were hanging. Swollen satchels covered the wall, with bayonets for pegs. Under our heads our packs, in a corner our rifles--and we carry all that, for whole nights, whole days, whole long leagues. . . . We carry our houses, we carry our kitchens, and even our very shrouds-- the brown blanket in which, closely wrapped up, I am now about to fall asleep.

. . . . .

Slowly, slowly, the night seemed to melt away. You might have said the last star was hastening to go home.

In the light mist of daybreak, things were coming back from their journey into the black realms and primly taking their accustomed places: the forked tree in front of the trench, the burned stack over against the Brun wire. It was Broucke who was the first to catch sight of the dead.

"There are a rare lot of them," said he. "That's another wood that's going to come a bit dear. . . ."

Gilbert tried to discover the one who had fallen the other night, the one his comrades had asked us to bury. Daybreak at last discovered him. He had remained about twenty mètres from the barbed wire, already flattened and stale, like the others. What was the good of risking getting killed to drag that corpse nearer the trench? A place here or a hole there. . . . They had his papers, that was enough. His tomb? Somewhere, anywhere, on the front. . . .

With the day the artillery woke up. First of all thundered a salvo of shrapnel, crowning Calvary with a green halo speedily dissipated. Then it was the turn of the heavy guns.

The first ones that whistled over hurled us to earth at the bottom of the trench.

There was a rending crash, and a great spout of broken stone fell back on us like heavy hail. Bréval gave a little cry, touched on the nape by a spent splinter or a pebble. Only the skin was torn, but he was bleeding.

"No luck," said Lemoine to him as he dressed him with a little iodine. . . . "If that had just managed to break an arm for you, eh?"

"It's not me that'll ever have that kind of luck," regretted the corporal.

So the day passed, while we were bowed under the shells, scattering before the torpedoes.

Towards eleven o'clock, it all doubled in fury, and the party going for the soup hesitated a full minute before going off, more sheltered in the sap than in the trench, everywhere breached and broken. When they came back, half the wine was overturned and spilled, the macaroni full of earth, and Sulphart nearly choked insulting Lemoine, who was "not even up to carrying a bottle."

The stew eaten, we began to play cards and wait for night. Broucke had begun to snore; lying near him, Gilbert was trying to dream.

Suddenly he sat up and said to us, his voice dry and hard:

"They're digging underneath."

Everyone turned about, letting the cards drop.

"Are you sure?"

He nodded his head for yes. Brutally I shook Broucke, who was still snoring, and Maroux, Bréval, Sulphart lay down in the gallery, their ears clapped to the ground. The rest of us looked at them, dumb, our hearts seemingly gripped in a vice. We had understood completely . . . a mine. Anxiously we listened, raging at the shells that shook the hill with their battering-ram. Bréval was the first to get up again.

"There is no possibility of a mistake," said he in a half-whisper, "they are digging."

"There's only one of them at work, you can hear quite clearly," said Maroux, giving it precision. "They are not far off."

We were all clustering together, motionless, lying on the hard earth. Someone had gone to fetch Sergeant Ricordeau. He arrived, listened for a moment and said:

"Yes. . . . We must tell the lieutenant."

Each one in his turn lay down to listen, and rose up a trifle gloomier. In the trench the news had already spread like wildfire, and between each shell the watchers listened to the alarming mattock that went on digging, digging, digging. . . .

Sous-Lieutenant Berthier came along at night with the soup party. He listened for a considerable time, wagged his head, and straightway was fain to reassure us. "Pooh! . . . It may be pioneers digging a trench, and quite a long way off, too. . . . It's most deceptive, you know, a noise like that. . . . I'm going to ask somebody in the engineers. . . . But don't you be getting rattled, it's certainly a long way off still; there's no danger. . . ."

We took the watch. The shells were still falling, but they did not frighten us so much just now. We were listening to that pickaxe.

Our two hours over, we went back into the grotto. Broucke listened and said:

"He's a reasonable chap, he's not going too hard at it."

And placidly he went to sleep.

We were on the point of blowing out the candle when Lieutenant Berthier came back, accompanied by an adjutant of engineers. Everybody got up again and crowded into the gallery. The first word we caught was:

"We suspected that."

Fouillard had a spasm that puckered up his eye.

The adjutant had lain down, his ear against the earth, and was listening with closed eyes. Our very silence was intently listening with him. He rose up, brushed the chalk from his whitened coat with a slap, and went off again with Berthier without saying anything to us, not a single word.

"That means there's no danger yet," surmised Lemoine.

"It means we're going to be sent up," predicted Sulphart.

All the same, we lay down, and we went to sleep. Berthier came back at early dawn; he had an air of gloom, an air of profound concern that we did not recognize in him and which all at once made us uneasy. What did he know? He listened to the pickaxe that still went on digging, without glueing his ear to the ground, for the blows were now coming to us more distinct and clear. We felt ourselves troubled by a vague presentiment, and obscure mixed fear. Berthier came again.

"Bréval's squad, fall in."

He eyed us all, with the deep look of a brave man; then, letting his eyes rest only on Bréval, who since he had the chip knocked out of him wore a dressing about his neck like a linen collar, he said to him:

"As you had guessed, the Germans are digging a mine. The engineers perhaps will come along to open a sap, but theirs has to be very far advanced for us to be able to cut it. And so, . . . you see. . . . its unnecessary for everybody to stay here. . . . You understand that clearly of course. . . . And so. . . . it is your squad, Bréval, that is to remain; it has been drawn by lot. The two sections are to be relieved, and you are to stay here with your squad and the machine gunners. . . . It's not much, but the Colonel has every confidence in you; you are well known to be brave fellows. . . . And then there is no attack to be feared, since they are still actually digging. . . . Anyway, their mine is not yet nearly finished; you needn't be afraid. . . . There's no danger, no danger whatever at all. . . . It's just simply a measure of precaution."

He was beginning to stammer, his throat was dry and contracted. His eyes wandered once more around the whole squad, seeking all our eyes in turn. Nobody said a word; only Fouillard sputtered out:

"We can go, anyhow, to fetch the soup."

"It will be sent up to you."

The others remained silent--a little pale, that was all. Courage? No, discipline. . . . Our turn had come. . . .

"We're for it," said Vieublé simply.

"No, no, you're crazy!" broke in the Lieutenant, quickly. "Don't get that into your head. . . . . Look here--" and he dropped his eyes in embarrassment--"I would have liked very much to stay with you. It was my place. The Colonel refused. Come, good-luck to you!"

His lower lip was trembling, and under his glasses a film of moisture dimmed his eyes. With a brusque movement, he shook hands with each one of us and went off, with his teeth clenched and a pale face.

Already our comrades were going, pushing and scrambling, as if they were afraid that death might lay hold of them. They eyed us with queer looks as they passed before us, and the last of them bade us "good-luck." The light little clink of the chains on their mess-tins died away, the clatter of the empty cans, the sound of pebbles rolling under their feet, their voices. . . . We remained alone. The machine gunners sat down to their weapon. Three of the squads went down into the trench, and we went back again into the mine.

"There's nothing to be done now but wait," said Demachy, exaggerating his air of aloof indifference.

Wait for what? All of us sitting on the edge of our beds, we kept staring at the ground, as a despairing man might stare at the dark, melancholy water running by before his last leap. It seemed to us that the pickaxe was striking harder now, as hard as our beating hearts. Despite ourselves, we lay down full-length to listen yet again.

Fouillard had gone to bed in a corner, his head under the blankets so as not to go on hearing, to see nothing more. Bréval said in a hesitating voice:

"After all, it's not settled that we're going to be blown up. . . . A mine isn't made just as easy as all that."

"Especially through rock."

"You might think it's quite near, and yet there might be enough work in it to keep them at it a week."

They were all talking at once, just now, they were all making up lies to put heart in themselves, to go on hoping in spite of everything. There was a loud argument for a minute in which every one had his own story of mines to tell, and when they listened again, it seemed to them that the blows were not falling so loud. Mechanically they unrolled their blankets, and went to rest.

"Talking about waking up with a jump," grumbled Vieublé as he took off his boots.

Where was the earth going to yawn and split in two? Shutting your eyes, you could imagine you saw those horrible photographs reproduced in the illustrated papers, those gaping funnel-shaped holes with stakes and bits of old iron, and fragments of men sticking out through the surface, half buried.

Lying there with our heads resting on our packs, we no longer heard anything but the terrible pick, as regular as the ticking of a clock, that was digging our grave for us.

"That'll make something like a noise," murmured Bélin. "Talk about the sort of charge it'll need to rip up a hill like that."

"There are three days still before we get out of it."

"No, not more than two and a half: we ought to be relieved on Wednesday night."

Bréval was writing on his knees, completely absorbed, using his pack as a writing-desk.

"You're doing the emotional stunt at your old woman," chaffed Lemoine. "Are you telling her that we're going up?"

The shells were falling less thick this night. The short aurora of the rockets sprang to life and died on the tent canvas. The night was almost calm. Only that muffled sound of the mattock, lulling us to sleep. . . .

. . . . .

At midnight I took over the watch. It was cold in the trench. The wind brought icy shivers down from the wood with it, and Gilbert's teeth were chattering under his blanket.

"Can you hear?"

"Yes, the knocking is still going on."

We never looked into the plain now. What good would it do? You could never see anything there but black shadow wavering in the black dark. We listened, we pondered.

The first to speak was Gilbert, in a half-whisper, with that little mocking tone that annoyed me, and which I loved none the less.

"It was too fine, that's the truth; it was really too fine. A life free from all care or concern, a life of daily delight. One day someone knocks 'Rat-tat. It's life.' 'But I don't know you.' 'So much the worse, it's your turn now.' She has thrust a pick and a rifle into your hands, and it's 'Dig, my lad; and march, my lad; and die, my lad.'"

"Why was it you enlisted too," said Lemoine to him, "since you had been discharged? . . . And especially in the infantry."

"Duty, a fit of enthusiasm, a lot of nonsense. . ."

We had come up to the machine gunners, huddled and silent under their covered lodgment. One of them was asleep in the far corner, his head thrown back.

"Not more than two days and a half, eh?" said the chief gunner to us.

"They'll have finished long before that," said the other one.

Lemoine, who without being able to see at all, was carving away at his walking-stick that he had started the other day, squatted down in a corner.

"If they're certain it's going to be touched off" said he, "they had only to relieve us like the rest of the boys. . . . And why our squad more than any other, anyhow?"

The wind mowed the stars out of the sky with its keen scythe. The night was growing thicker. In the trench we were nothing more now than black lumps, and in the shadow of the covered gun-post there was nothing to be discerned but the reddening point of a pipe-bowl. Now and then somebody lifted the curtain from an embrasure and looked out. Nothing. . . . A shiver, a murmur: the sheep of the darkness were browsing in the fields.

After our three hours on sentry, we had gone back frozen. And lying close together under our blankets, our satchels side by side like pillows, we had gone to sleep with the good, untroubled deep sleep of animals.

. . . . .

In the morning it was a presentiment, an internal sense of distress, that woke us up. There was no longer any sound; on the contrary, a tragic silence. The squad was dumb and overwhelmed, stooping over Bréval, who was listening, lying down full length on the ground. Sitting bolt upright on our straw litter, we watched them.

"What is it?" whispered Demachy.

"They're not knocking any more. . . . They must be filling the mine."

My heart stopped dead, as if somebody had seized it in his hand. I felt a kind of cold shiver. It was true, there was no sound of digging now. It was all over.

Bréval got up, with a mechanical smile on his lips.

"There's no mistake about it, they've stopped knocking."

We looked at the ground, as dumb as itself. Fouillard, pallid and drawn, made a movement to go out. Without a word Hamel held him back by the arm. Maroux had sat down, his hands folded between his knees, and was drumming on the planking of his bed with his great heels.

"Shut up!" said Vieublé roughly to him. "Listen." . . .

We all stretched our necks, anxious, afraid to deceive ourselves. No! the pickaxe had indeed started again. It was knocking, knocking. Oh! to think that any one could feel friendly to it for even a moment, that horrible pickaxe! It was digging. That meant respite. They were not yet filling the mine, we were not yet dying. . . .

Vieublé had broken free from the feeling of agony with a single effort. Livid with fury, he leaped outside, roaring.

"He's crazy," cried Bréval. "What is he doing?"

We ran after him. He had clambered up on top of the sandbags and out of the trench to his waist, his neck at full stretch, he was yelling:

"You may dig, you lot of cows, we don't care a--damn for you! Maybe we'll all go up, but we don't care a--damn for you."

Sulphart had seized him round the middle and tugged at him.

"Will you be quiet, you big. . . !"

Bréval also was pulling him by the arm, but the other was resisting.

"I must bag one of them before I'm sent up. . . . I don't mean to die like an old rag," he bellowed. "I must have one of them!"

They succeeded, however, in getting him to come down and get back into the sap, where he grew calmer, drinking Demachy's old brandy.

"That's good stuff," he said, with the air of a connoisseur.

Tock. . . . took. . . . tock. . . . It was still digging away. Tock, tock. . . . Then it stopped. We listened then, straining, more agonized. No. Tock. . . . tock. . . . tock. . . .
. . . . .

That went on for two days more, and one night. Forty hours that we counted, that we tore off in patches of minutes. Two days and one night to listen, our mouths dried with fever. The last evening it was impossible to keep Vieublé back: he set off with four grenades in his wallet, and at the end of an hour we heard four sharp barking bursts, one after another, then cries of distress howled out in the fringes of the wood. He had well and duly distributed his "sodas."

As he was getting back into the trench, Lieutenant Berthier arrived, preceding the relief. We were already putting our packs up on our shoulders, ready to start.

"Ah," he said to us. "I am glad. . . . You see, you must never lose heart. It's all over."

"We've not got away yet," trembled Fouillard. "To be sent up now, that really would be anything but luck," remarked Lemoine, with complete gravity.

The regular strokes were still coming to us, reassuring in spite of everything. But it was no longer only the pickaxe we were watching for now, it was the relief. A dull murmur told us they were at hand.

"The relief. . . . Go into the grotto to hand over. I will look after the orders," Berthier said to us.

We looked at men of a regiment we did not know as they passed. There were ten of them only, and four machine gunners. The last man stopped, having guessed at us as we stood in the shadow of the gallery.

"So, then, they're digging a mine underneath? . . . We're certain to be sent up. What do you think?--four days of it. . . ."

All speaking at once, we endeavoured to reassure them.

"No reason why you should. . . . Look at us, we've jolly well stayed in it. . . . It takes long, that kind of stunt. You mustn't get worried."

But over his pack we were closely keeping a watch on the Lieutenant, with quaking in our knees, so hot we were to be gone. Fouillard, nobody knows how or when, had already disappeared. Berthier at last came back.

"En route! . . . Good luck, my lads!"

And turning towards Demachy, he added quite below his breath:

"Poor fellows! I am afraid for them. . . . ."

But for the Lieutenant, who was going at our head at a good round pace, we might perhaps have broken into a run. We were afraid of that sinister, wan Calvary, which every now and then the rockets showed up in all its nakedness. Fear of that danger we always felt behind us, always very near.

We slipped into the chalky road quickly; we crossed the footbridge over the river, and there only did we venture to turn ourselves about. The Calvary stood out, terrible, a dreadful thing as against the green night, with its battered stumps of trees like the uprights of a cross.

. . . . .

We had our food at the exit from the trenches. The cooks had made gravy and we ate voraciously, not feeling now in our entrails those crooked fingers that clutched and worked inside you. We drank wine in full cups: the buckets had to be emptied before we went. Bragging and boasting, Sulphart was pitching yarns to the boys of the company.

"And, I say, how we made them yelp, the Boches, with that lad Vieublé." . . .

Every man of the squad had his own group round him and was holding forth. Vieublé, whose lazy voice with its rolling r's, the typical voice of a town loafer, was notable among the others, telling about his patrol.

"You may say they did howl! I had stood up and I was holding one of the posts of their barbed wire in my left hand, and whizz, bang, in on top of them. . . . I never even got a touch of a bullet. . . . and twig the topping field-glass I took off a Boche stiff, an officer. . ."

The company was following the canal in a long, rambling disjointed file. From the gunners' dug-outs, burrowed into the steep bank, a mist was rising, and we envied their damp dens: "To see the war out in there, well, you might call that a streak of luck!"

The black water mirrored nothing but the night, and was without life except for a light lapping ripple. We crossed the river on a heaving bridge made out of boats and casks. The canal once passed, we entered into the woods, and the coolness fell on your shoulders like a damp cloak. It smelled of drenching springtime. Somewhere a bird was singing, not realizing that it was war-time.

Behind us the rockets marked out the infinite, endless line of the trenches. Soon the trees hid them out of sight, and the tall forests stifled the raging voice of the guns. We were moving away from death.

As we entered into the first village, the leading squad started to hum softly, and mechanically we all began to march in step to the rhythm.

C'est aujourd 'hui marche de nuit
Au lieu d'roupiller, on s'promène. . . .

Then suddenly, from afar, a heavy dull noise shattered and shook the night: a thundering noise of cataclysm, that the echoes repeated long and long. The mine had gone up.

The column had halted as though at the word of command. Not a voice was heard now. . . . We were still listening, our hearts contracted, as if we had been able from the bank on which we were standing to hear the cries. The guns, too, had held their tongues in order to listen.

But no, nothing more, it was all over.

"How many were there?" asked a choking voice from the ranks.

"Ten," somebody answered. "And four machine gunners."

CHAPTER IX
MOURIR POUR LA PATRIE

NO, that is horrible, the band ought not to play that tune. . . .

The man has collapsed on himself in a heap held up to the stake by his bound hands. The handkerchief tied round his head by way of a bandage makes a kind of crown for him. Pallid, livid, the Chaplain is saying a prayer, with eyes shut so that he need see no longer. . . .

Never, even in our worst hours, have we felt Death as imminent as on this day. We divine him, we scent his presence, like a dog that will break into a long howl next moment. Is it a soldier, that blue heap? He must be warm still.

Oh! To be obliged to look on that, and to keep for ever in the memory his wild cry, the cry of an animal, that dreadful, unendurable cry in which we felt both terror and horror and supplication; all that a man can utter who suddenly sees all at once Death there, in front of him--Death Himself: a little shaft of wood and eight pallid men, their rifle butts at their feet.

That long cry had driven deep into the hearts of all of us like a nail. And suddenly, in that hideous, hoarse gasping that fell upon the ears of a whole horrified regiment, words were caught, a dying prayer: "Ask for a pardon for me. . . . Ask the Colonel for a pardon. . . ."

He flung himself upon the ground, trying to thrust back the moment when he must die, and they dragged him to the stake by the arms, a dead weight, lifeless, howling. To the very end he uttered his cries. We heard them! "My little children! . . . Oh, Colonel! . . ." His sobs tore through that awe-stricken silence, and the quaking soldiers had only one idea left: "Oh! quick! . . . quick! . . . let there be an end. Let them fire, let us hear him no longer. . . ."

The tragic crackling of a volley. One other shot, one by itself: the coup de grâce. It was all over.

We had to defile in front of his corpse afterwards. The band struck up Mourir pour la Patrie, and the companies went hobbling off one after the other, their pace no better than a shamble. Berthier clenched his teeth hard so that it should not be seen how his jaw quivered. When he gave the order, En avant! Vieublé, who was weeping with his breast heaving wildly like a child's, left the ranks and flung away his rifle; then he fell down, taken with a nervous seizure.

As we passed before the stake, every head was turned away. We dared not even look one man at his fellow, haggard and hollow-eyed as if we had just been committing some crime.

There is the pig-stye in which he spent his last night, so low that he could not get up from hands and knees in it. He must have heard on the high road the rhythmic step of the companies coming down to take their arms. Will he have understood?

It was in the ballroom of the Café de la Poste that he was tried, last night. There were in it still the pineboughs from our last concert, the red, white and blue paper garlands, and on the stage the big poster painted by the musicians: "Don't worry, and let them talk!"

A little corporal, assigned to the task, defended him, embarrassed, broken with pity. All alone on that stage, his arms hanging awkwardly, you might have thought he was just going to "tip 'em a stave"; and the Government commissary laughed, discreetly, behind his neat gloved hand.

"You know what he had done?"

"The other night, after the attack, he was put forward for the patrol. As he had already been out the night before, he refused. There you are. . . ."

"Did you know him?"

"Yes, he was a fellow from Cotteville. He had two boys."

Two boys, the same height as that stake of his. . . .

CHAPTER X
OUR LADY OF THE RAG-PICKERS

[Note] Rag-picker, biffin: slang term for infantry, whose pack is like the rag-picker's basket.

THE highroad was swarming, black and noisy, like a gallery in a mine if you were suddenly to switch out all the lights at the hour of the return to the surface of the earth. A whole obscure crowd that could not be seen, but could be felt, full of life, was struggling in the heart of that inky night, each troop boring out a path for itself; and from this mob there rose a mixed noise of trampling feet, of voices, of creaking wheels, of horses neighing, of hard language, all confused and mingled, just as the fields, the road, and the men were all mingled into the same thick shadowy gloom.

And yet there was a certain order in all that mob. The Territorials making their way back to the rear, our regiments going up to the line, the carts, the waggons, each and all had their appointed road; companies met each other and passed elbow to elbow, thrust up against the bank by the motor-cyclists: "Keep to the right! Keep to the right!" the big hairy nostrils of the artillery teams blew in our faces; the huge wheels of the lorries grazed our boots; and through this turmoil of creatures and things, the army of attack slowly drove its columns with a never-ending tramp of feet.

Piled along the ditch, whole halted regiments watched us passing. The men who were on their feet were craning their necks, seeming to look for somebody in that dark stream. We could guess at others wallowing down in the grass: a white satchel, the red tip of a cigarette. From them to us, voices hailed each other back and forth.

"What regiment is that?"

"Is there another village before the trenches?"

"Where do you come from?"

The loafing Bohemian voice of a Parisian called from our ranks:

"Are there any boys from Montmartre? Good-morning to the lads of Barbès!"

These unacquainted voices sought one another and joined one another like meeting hands.

Sulphart, who had just been livened up by a draught of wine, replied with chaff.

"What company's that?"

"The gas company!"

We were going forward by jerks and starts, with an irregular pace that tired out the legs. Every now and then we came to a halt, with the road simply bottled up; we would hear in the darkness the tinkling of the curb-chains of horses rearing, and the swearing of the gunners. Men would take hold of us by the arms.

"It's you who are going to make the attack? The sidis are in position up there already. . . . And there's a swarm of guns, you know. . . ."

Then close by me, Fouillard growled out:

"And the Boches, they've got no guns, I suppose, no? Pack of old blitherers! It sticks in my gizzard to hear that kind of stuff."

When the column set off again, edging its way between two files of waggons and foaming horses, he took hold of one by the tail and tugged at it brutally. The heavy rump of the beast never so much as budged.

"So he doesn't even know how to kick, your rotten moke," he cried to the driver, huddled up on his seat. "He couldn't manage to give me a broken leg, God's truth!"

A machine-gun mule was walking in our ranks, rattling his boxes. Fouillard stuck to him like wax, in the hope that he would start plunging, and to stir him up to it he played his trick again, hauling on the mule's tail like a bell-rope. Stupefied and apathetic as any of the men, the mule never turned a hair.

"Have you gone clean crazy?" said Hamel. "And suppose he let you have a punch with his hoof in the belly?"

"I don't care a blow. . . . I'd be delighted; then I shouldn't be in the attack."

Behind him Gilbert jeered, in the tone with which he would have read a citation in Army Orders:

"Has always displayed proofs of the utmost courage and initiative, and given his comrades the example of an incomparable bravery."

Fouillard turned round about.

"You! I don't care a hang about you! You go and mind your backside!"

Weighted down under his pack, Bréval murmured;

"The courage to blackguard one another . . . more stupid than the horses. . . ."

The outlines of the trees could barely be discerned, so black was the night; and in the distance, over towards the lines where our guns were thundering in gusts, there was no gleam or light in the low sky. The invisible battle was unfolding on the other side of that wall of blackness, and the roads, filled and swollen like arteries, were driving fresh blood along up to it.

The column marked time where it stood for a minute. "Keep to the right!" was being shouted in front of us. We started again in a dislocated file. There were some black objects blocking up the road: two horses with outstretched stiff legs, an overthrown cart, and some dead bodies, whose grievous shapes could be defined under the canvas covering. A hot, insipid smell rose up from this heap. Quickly there were territorials filling up the wide hole the shell had torn out.

One of the old fellows was not working. Standing up on a milestone, he dominated our rising tide, and bending forward, straining to see, he was calling:

"Émile Bailleul, of the fifth company. . . . Isn't that the fifth company going by? Émile! Émile! . . . Don't you know Bailleul?--it's my son. Hello! Émile!"

The spent column filed on in front of him, obscure, impenetrable to the eye. No one replied. As they passed, heads would turn and look at the old man. Behind us his voice was still calling:

"Émile! . . . Don't you know young Baileul, of the fifth?"

Ah yes, indeed, we had known him. . . . Poor fellow!

. . . . . .

Out of the whole church there has been kept only this altar corner: the chapel of the Virgin and six rows of prie-dieus. All the rest has been transformed into a hospital, and from the other side of a wooden partition, that separates us from the nave, we can hear the wounded men groaning.

Two hundred men are squeezed in together to hear mass. The others are under the porch, and even in the cemetery, where, as they talk, sitting on the edges of the tombstones, they can hear the chants and canticles.

Some are arriving from the trench, covered with mud, their faces grey, their hands thick with earth; others, on the contrary, are still all ruddy and glowing from their toilette under the pump. Everyone hustles and jostles, and all are crowded on top of one another--dirty soldier's overcoats and officer's jackets. A few women in deep mourning; a few girls whom the men ogle, digging elbows in one another; and in the place of honour, a clean-shaven peasant, fifty years old, very correct and dignified in his black Sunday clothes.

At each genuflection of the priest, his blue puttees can be perceived underneath his soutane; it is one of the stretcher-bearers in our company who is taking the service. Upon the single stone step four bearded soldiers are telling the beads of their rosary: all priests as well. The wind softly stirs the white cloths that hide the broken windows.

Not a candlestick on the altar, the tabernacle even has been taken away. There is nothing left now but the Virgin in her blue robe sprinkled with stars, and with a bunch of daisies at her feet--Our Lady of the soldier-men, . . . the rag-pickers.

She reaches out both her hands, her two little pink hands of tinted plaster, two all-powerful hands that save him who prays to her. They are not all believers, these soldiers away from their labours: but all believe in her hands; they are fain to believe in them, blindly, so as to feel themselves defended, protected; they are fain to pray to her, as one presses close up against a stronger than oneself--to pray to her so as to feel fear no longer, and to keep, as a talisman, the memory of her two hands.

Some have genuinely come here to pray. The others, those whose crowded numbers are overflowing into the cemetery, are waiting to see the girls go by: the mass is a kind of soldiers' sightseeing.

On this eve of attack they have come in still greater numbers than on other Sundays. They are singing. Their masculine voices even in prayer retain a rude accent of a brutal life; they sing with no restraint, at the tops of their voices, as they would in a wine parlour, and the chant at times, drowns the guns:

Sauvez,   sauvez   la   France
Au nom du Sacré-Coeur. . . .

They sing that without a thought of the words, ingenuously, like choir boys singing themselves hoarse; and how many of us are there, with shut eyes, our foreheads bowed into our hands, that this hymn fills with emotion so that we seem to be choking!

Sauvez, sauvez la France. . . .

It is like a deep cry rising from these human organs! From the other side of the partition a wounded man is crying: "No! you are hurting me! . . . Not that way! . . ." You can imagine the hurrying hand tearing off the muddy first-aid dressing. It is these complaints, these hoarse outcries, that make the responses to the priest.

Then the bell tinkles and every head is bowed. You might say that the prayer bends them over like a field of grain before a blowing wind. We remain still, elbow against elbow, packed as though in a sap waiting the moment of attack. The guns storm and thunder, in their own way sounding the Elevation of the Host; but they are heard no longer, nor the rattling breath of the wounded. There is nothing more now in that church save the two arms of a soldier raising the Pyx towards the Virgin of the kind hands.

The bell tinkles. . . . What are we begging from you, if it is not hope, Our Lady of the Rag-Pickers?

We accept everything: the reliefs under the drenching rain, the nights in the mire, the days without bread, the superhuman weariness that turns us more brutish than the beasts--we accept all and every suffering; but let us live, only that and no more, just to live! . . . Or only to believe we are to live, up to the very end; always to have hope, to have hope in despite of everything! Now and in the hour of our death, so be it. . . .

Ranged up in two ranks, the soldiers were watching the girls coming out of church, robust, fresh, jolly girls with bright-coloured bodices, their cheeks polished as if for a regimental inspection, who were laughing and chatting loudly, to give themselves the Paris manner. Greedy eyes devoured them with desire, and compliments of the crudest greeted the handsomest.

The mayor's daughter, a miserable, anæmic-looking creature, had gone off with dropped eyes with the post-office young lady, a slender young girl in a black dress like a saleswoman in a shop, who walked with a dancing, tripping step, and would have been the better for a touch of powder on her dull cheeks. Bourland had gone quite red at sight of her, and she had smiled at him.

"Are we on?" proposed Sulphart, who, being newly shorn and groomed, fancied himself irresistible.

But Vieublé was not interested. With a long blade of grass, he was busy tickling from a distance the palm of the hand of the hostess of the wine-shop, who was playing the beauty among her women friends.

"Don't you touch it!" he replied under his breath to the redhead. "I tell you we'll be having drinks on the nod."

At the gate of the cemetery, the Chaplain whose bicycle was leaned up against the wall, was distributing scapulars and cigarette-papers.

On the other side of the street it was trench knives that were being handed out.

That was going on in the farmer's yard. In front of the house the Army Service people were unloading a covered waggon of munitions, big boxes of cartridges which they took hold of, a man at every corner, the way undertakers lower their coffins. Once through the porch, it was just like the thieves' market. On the pavement there had been dumped a heap of huge knives--stout jocta-legs with wooden handles--and Lambert, the quartermaster, squatting before his booth, was busy distributing them squad by squad. It was a noisy mob; everybody was talking loudly and using his elbows.

"It's all the same to me," shouted Lambert, his cheeks absolutely crimson. "It doesn't concern me at all. . . . I've been told to give out knives to the whole of the second section and I'm giving out the knives . . . . If they had told me to distribute umbrellas to you, I would give you umbrellas Anything else, it's not my business. . . . go and talk to the major about it."

Little by little the heap of blades grew smaller.

"Hurry on!" chaffed the quartermaster. "There won't be enough for everybody. Come along, anybody that hasn't got his knife."

And turning round to an old sergeant that I had not noticed before, and who was standing just behind him, he added, wrinkling his forehead up:

"I know some of them won't have any use for them, for knives. . . . Those are the clever ones that know the right way to go through the war, those ones. . . ."

The old man made no reply. He had a white beard, and the boys who were staring hard at him asked one another out loud what he was going to do in that place.

"What's he going to do?" explained Lambert. "Here's what he's going to do. . . . he's going to take my job, that's it plump and plain. Yes, my lads, I'm relieved, and turned over to the third as chief of section; and it's that old pilgrim who is replacing me."

"But who is he?"

"He's an old nut who has had both his sons killed," said the quartermaster angrily. "And so he enlisted. . . . Naturally, of course, when the Colonel saw that old zebra coming ashore, he didn't feel like bunging him into the trench, and he named him in my place, without making any bones about it. . . . Isn't that a pretty good shame, eh? I don't care a blow for his two blooming sons! It's not my business to avenge them. I've lathered plenty the year I put in in the trenches. If he wanted to fight about it, he had only to go and do it himself, instead of sneaking my bit of cushy and sending me to get my head broken for him. . . . All the same, it's not so dusty, eh? Enlisted at his age! The old billiard-top!"

The old man, holding aloof, said never a word, with a vacant, absent air, and with a sad and distant look that, in spite of everything, wrung my heart.

"Come along, the seventh," called Lambert "hurry up! . . . Ten beautiful brand new blades. This isn't a kind of cheapjack bargain, it's good business."

The corporals went off, their pockets full of knives. Out in the street some of the boys, just to make the girls stare, would open theirs with a dry sharp snap, and try the point on the back of the hand.

"Nice kind of business you may say," said a lad of the company to me, with a face of consternation. "What do you think I want to do with a knife? I'm a gardener, I am, in civvies. And one of my fellows even is a bookseller. What kind of trades are those to be taking to a knife?"

Berthier was strolling alone, always meditative, his hands locked behind his back and his head down. I joined him. He repeated to me everything he had been told about the attack in the morning's report. Only one order for the present: to go through. No unit would be relieved during the actual fighting; fresh waves of men would reinforce the shattered waves continuously, and we were to go forward in spite of everything. At our side the Moroccan Division, the Legion from the Twentieth Corps; behind us, the whole army. . . .

"I have complete confidence," he said to me in a resolute tone.

Stopping, he looked squarely at me.

"I believe we are going to get through."

"So do I. . . . I think so too."

This unreasoning confidence was felt by all the men, in every voice; it was in the air, even in inanimate things. Was it the guns that thundered without respite or slackening, pounding the ground we were to conquer, that drove deep into us that certainty of victory? Without reason, by mere instinct, we were full of this confidence. For the first time, we had the feeling that we were making ready for a pitched battle and not for one of those tragic clashes, one of those burlesque fittings, that was all the preceding attacks had amounted to.

At the end of the villlage, behind a small wood, the heavy artillery was firing in hurried salvos, without seeing anything more of the war than a green curtain of hazel trees. As it was hot, the gunners had taken off their vests for the sake of comfort, and glistening with sweat, they were handling their shells like bakers thrusting bread into the oven.

"Never have we fired as much as this," said a corporal of the échelon. "Every gun has not more than twenty mètres' front to pound; it's impossible anything should be left, anything at all. . . ."

In a bucket of water near a pyramid of golden shell-cases, there were bottles standing in the cool. Between two shoots, the gunners, in their shirts, came over to have a drink; then having wiped their foreheads with the back of a hand, they set to again at their infernal game of bowls.

On the road or lying all along the bank, cavalrymen were loafing about, leaving their horses to tear the bark off the trees in strips. At first we looked at them askance, jealous of their better post, their far too clean tunics, and above all, of the "good-morrows" the girls kept sending them from afar; but we didn't fire off the usual chaff at them; no one asked them with an air of making a fool of them: "Do you know whereabouts those blooming trenches are?" On the contrary, we were very soon chatting like pals. They said to us:

"We're the army of pursuit. . . . Once you'll have made your break through, we'll charge and attack their reserves for you. . . . ."

Behind us a whole army was waiting--armoured cars, bridging engineers, squadrons, batteries of seventy-fives--and we fancied already we felt the weight of that huge mass thrusting us on. We talked and argued, seized by a kind of fever. A tall gunner, somewhat soaked in wine, kept on repeating:

"I tell you that after this stroke the war is over and done. . . . It's the last attack boys. . . ."

Never had we seen before so many different uniforms, down to the great red cloaks of the spahis, behind the rusty railings of the chateau. It may perhaps have been the ardour exhaled from all these beings, like a breath, that made us live for a whole day in this warm atmosphere of hope. It intoxicated the least courageous, to have so many spectators, to be in the eyes of all those people "the boys that are going to make the attack."

To wheedle the girls, to astonish the raw conscripts, we talked loud and swaggered about; and when we met the men from a newly relieved regiment just going down to rest, we looked at them from a height, a trifle mocking.

"A lot that's only fit to lose the trenches that other people take."

"Don't be afraid, it's what you'll never win, the wooden cross!"

Through the open windows of a tavern, in a cool alley bordered with white elder-blossom that sweetened the lips, cries were heard. Chairs were being thrown about, men were pushing and jostling, and singing through the clinking of glasses knocked together, and you could feel, from the mere noise by itself, that their bellicose temper was mounting. In verity, I could hardly recognize them now.

On his feet, glass in hand, Fouillard was doing his best to shout, in a voice that kept cracking:

"Fix bayonets! . . . En avant!"

Vieublé, who happened to pass, showing off with his croix de guerre and his medal, shrugged his shoulders.

"Those are always the ones that have the most yap," he said aggressively.

"Where are you off to, that way?--for soup?"

"No; I'm feeding with you, at the wine-shop where they're making grub for you. . . . It was Gilbert who asked me to come, because I've sworn to help Sulphart to carry him back if he should happen to be wounded."

As he walked, with a yellowed fag stuck to his drooping lip, he was meditating.

"And yet. . . . Sulphart--h'm--he's one of the boys. Well, I wouldn't feel too sure myself. . . . He's another of those blighters that get punctured."

Mechanically, like horses making for their stable, we steered our way towards the enclosure where Bouffioux had established his travelling kitchen. Massed around a rustic table, a score of men were moving about.

In the midst of the group, driving the others back with a circular gesture, like a strong man of the country fairs about to go through a weight-lifting performance, Hamel with his sleeves well rolled up, was giving an exhibition. He had brought out his sailor's cutlass, which he was holding with a powerful grip in his big hairy hand; he steadied himself, and with a sudden fierce stroke and a grunt like a woodcutter, he buried the whole blade in an enormous quarter of beef already gaping with a score of wounds. Those who had got hold of trench knives were pushing and scrimmaging behind him, shouting as though they were going to fight. They flung themselves on the meat, and one after another they were hacking it to pieces with ferocious blows.

As their blade came away, they carried off with it bits of suet, shavings of tendons, and the meat, riddled with stabs, was losing its shape, was flattening down like a rag on the chipped table. Warned by Lemoine, who alone "didn't think it much of game to knock the stuffing out of a lump of beef," Bouffioux came running up, his great belly shaking and jogging above his trousers that were tumbling down.

"Pack of swabs!" he yelled. "And after all this you'll be complaining again that the stew is no good. . . . I'm through this time, and I'll tell the Lieutenant."

Hamel, as he wiped his knife, was looking at the cook with the air of a big dog who has been disturbed.

"Does it annoy you that somebody is showing them? And the boys that maybe are going to have to fight to-morrow, you're through with them, are you? . . . You'll stay where you are and peel potatoes. Shirker! Cuthbert!"

"What are you blackguarding him about?" interposed Lemoine in his soft voice. "You are quite well pleased to eat his grub."

"And you, what are you shoving your nose into, you beetroot," replied Vieublé at once.

Big Lemoine didn't turn a hair, he even still kept his hands in his pockets, towering by a head above the snarling Parisian who came up to him to provoke him to his face.

"Péquenot! He was brought up in the kitchen of a little eating-house."

"And I will as much as I like, and it isn't you that will stop me," retorted the other quietly, wrinkling up his obstinate forehead. "Nobody ought to knock meat about."

"Because they didn't have any to eat in your house, pig-belly!"

"Maybe I was better fed than you were yourself. . . . It's no good your swaggering, you can't have always had your fill to eat with that mug on you."

"Hold your tongue, baby! I'll smack you!"

Suddenly the intent circle closed in a little. Look out! . . . he had said vous. Things looked like going too far. Crimson, stammering, sweat standing out on his temples, Bouffioux was twittering all manner of confused nonsense.

"Anyway, it's not you that's going to smack me," said Lemoine, continuing the row, but with no great assurance.

"And then, after all this, when the grub . ." said Bouffioux hoarsely.

Other men were chipping in without knowing what it was all about, just for the pleasure of making a noise.

"He's not got much guts to let himself be talked to like that."

"I think he's quite right, I do. He's getting tiresome, that cook fellow. The meat is just as much ours as his."

"Those that don't belong to the company have nothing to do but shut it and keep it shut, and double quick too! . .

Summoned by this rowdy row, Sergeant Ricordeau, who was shaving, appeared at the bay-window in the loft with his face all covered with lather.

"Won't you soon have done with your row? I take my oath that if you once make me come down to you it won't be for nothing. . . . Here, there's Lieutenant Morache coming along. I hope you're all satisfied now?"

It was the one word that was necessary: the whole crowd shut up and the band crumbled away.

In the quarter of beef there remained a huge knife, planted savagely in it right up to the guard, with the mark of a bloody hand imprinted on its wooden haft.

. . . . . .

Into the shop parlour where we were breakfasting, eight of us squeezed up. about a round table, the drinkers from the large hall that was over-full were floating in and out, glass in hand. The continuous rolling thunder of the guns was making our bottles shake, and the painted plates dance on the sideboard; sometimes a more than ordinary violent outburst came in to us brutally and drowned the voices.

"How that hammers!"

"What, is it to-morrow that we're attacking?--Yes or no?"

The war, the attack, the hospital, we spoke of nothing else; and when we forgot it for a moment to talk of bygone happiness, of Paris, of our lost homes, the guns came back, knocking, battering at the door.

At the bar, in a regular tumult, the comrades were talking endlessly of the trench: it is only the soldier who listens unbored, unwearied, to soldiers' yarns. Their mouths already pursed to deliver the traditional answer, "That's just like me, just fancy! . . ." They were listening one to the other without taking anything in and thinking only of getting in their own tale.

Up till it was time for the evening soup, we loafed around, went drinking, talked, managed to tire ourselves out. The three streets of the village were absolutely chock-a-block with troops, and on the highway the dusty lorries went snoring by, bringing up infantrymen who, as they passed, shouted to us through the dust the number of their regiment.

The sky of a crude Reckitt's blue colour was dotted with shrapnel bursts, whose white flock was massed like those fleecy summer sheep-clouds that foretell fine weather. In the thick of them light and sparkling, turned and twisted and dodged an aeroplane. On the corners of tables, sitting on a wheelbarrow or a cart-shaft, squatting down under their tent or with their backs against a wall, were soldiers writing. In a meadow a game of football was going on; with loud cries some of the boys were following the game astride on polished saddles, while getting the drivers of the Army Service Corps to cut their hair for them.

On the other side of the village the little streets were deserted. Everywhere were the flowering elder-trees, whose sweet and gentle perfume smelt like a sedative to jangled nerves.

"Sure enough this is no weather to go fighting in," sighed Gilbert, nibbling at a stalk of aniseed.

Lambert, who was following us with drooping head, seemed to wake up.

"Weather for fighting in!" he said, losing his temper. "Have you been reading that in the Pêle-Mêle? . . . Ah! All the little rascals that write about the war know lots of good jokes. . . . To die in the sunshine, that's great business! . . . I'd just like to see one of them pegging out, with his mouth wide open among the barbed wire, to ask him to appreciate the landscape! . . ."

And wreaking his anger on a tall clump of cow-parsley, which he mowed down with a flick of his switch, he grumbled in a raging fury:

"Let them send the old pilgrim, since he wants to avenge his sons."

Slipping from leaf to leaf, the sunshine dripped in big drops on to the road. A stream flowed by among the mallow plants, drawing with it long dishevelled weeds-- Ophelia's hair. Among the woods some of the boys were gathering wild-flowers before fastening down their letters.

"Come, don't let us think too much," said Gilbert, shaking himself together. . . . "Let's go in here, I say, they seem to be having a jolly time."

We pushed in through the door of the café, and as soon as we had got inside, I caught sight of Bouffioux and Fouillard sitting at a table with empty litres before them. A spree had reconciled them: the cook apoplectic, with his eyes shining bright; the other pale haggard, and glassy of eye. They had tossed for round upon round, and then--a drunkard's sudden idea--Fouillard had made a proposal, coughing with laughter.

"I'll toss you for my cross, in half a jiffy. . . . I saw some dandy ones at the carpenter's, with a plate, just like an officer's. . . ."

Bouffioux had agreed: he had lost. He had then asked for his revenge, a cross for a pal in the squad. He had lost again.

"All the same, you'd need to be blind drunk, . . . some of the boys had growled. "That's not a thing to humbug about. . . . Go and play your dirty games outside."

The pair, braggarts both, had then set to work again to drink: the winners' round, then "the last one," then the "last of the last"; and now, full up to the teeth, their mouths gaping, their legs giving way, they remained stupefied, bovine, chin on table, having not even strength enough left either to drink or to jabber.

And the other nodded "yes" with a very heavy head.

"I've won off you," repeated Fouillard stupidly. "Don't let's stay here, let's get out of it," said Lambert to us sharply.

And we went out.

All day long, in spite of myself, I have been thinking of their drunkard's stake. Now, in bed, under the tent, I am still thinking about it. . . . The bombardment has slackened off, but the rising wind brings down from the trench the rolling noises of rifle fire. One side of the tent that has remained open gives towards the lines, and above and beyond the black woods, you can now and then catch sight of the fleeting dawn of the rockets.

Stretched out full length on the new straw that crackles and rustles under us, we are listening, with our hearts thrown wide open, to a confused murmur of low voices and songs. In the shadows can be caught glimpses of white patches swaying in the wind: soldiers' linen hanging out to dry. But with this clear, transparent night, these songs, this scattered tenderness and emotion, one might fancy white dresses hanging back a little; one might dream that there are women there, quite close to us, and listening to us. We shouldn't speak to them, indeed, no: only for their presence, to feel that they are there! . . .

One feels so comfortable under the caress of this soft wind. Languorous voices take up the chorus, very low, and hang upon the words of love so as to taste them more fully:

Ferme tes jolis yeux,
Car les heures sont brèves
Au pays merveilleux,
Au doux pays, du rê-ê-ve.

The voices grow more and more sentimental, the song dies away. . . . One is fain to see nothing further--the soldiers, nor the war. . . . They are not so dull, by night, our pale-hued coats. Would you not like to have a dress of that colour?

Lying in the far corner of the tent, Gilbert is repeating verses, exquisite tendernesses of Samain's, which the others are listening to without venturing to stir, their eyes sparkling with little stars.

All our minds are far, ever so far away: Paris, the village, the quiet mall, the bed with its embroidered quilts, or even the great bed of the provinces, with its big red bellying mound that you drive down with a blow of the fist. One's home! . . . The memory of bygone joys melts in the mouth like a delicious sweetmeat, and our hearts are so tender that you can make love-songs come trickling out of them if you squeeze them a little.

Ferme tes jolis yeux . . .

Suddenly on the highroad is heard the rhythmic step of a troop on the march. What is it? . . . They can be recognized at once by their white armlets. The first carry on their shoulders the stretchers rolled up; those who follow after are pushing in front of them light little carts with two wheels. One of them holds a lantern, whose yellow light dances about him like a dog wild with excitement. The regiment of the great silence is going on its way.

"Come on," breaks out an embarrassed voice, "you can let us have another one."

"No, no humbug; I don't know any more. . . ."

Silence drops down. . . . And yet there hadn't been much, only a murmur; but a murmur was enough to drown all the noises of this disturbing night. Now they all come to us: the oppressed breathing of a sleeper, the straw crackling under the bodies of men in discomfort, and over there, the agonizing, low sounds of the trench deep in its struggle. Silent, and yet the night has changed all at once--now immense and grave as a dream of thirty years.

The moon comes up unhurried and placid, behind a clump of firs that frame her face like a mantilla. Slowly she lays down upon the short grass the clean-cut shadow of the stakes and piled arms, and this paints strange black signs over that beautiful field dappled with moonlight. A carbine slung from the muzzle of a rifle outlines as it were two strange arms that I look at vacantly.

But, all at once my heart gives a sudden bound, and in that black design I can discern a cross, a prophetic cross of shadow that the moon has planted over the long body of Lambert as he lies asleep.

CHAPTER XI
VICTORY

FROM the rear the regiments for the attack were coming up to the trenches, in line, by a score of tracks full to bursting.

"Pass the word there to get on."

"Get on, you pack of swabs!" repeated furious voices.

And the dismembered column would set off again at a lumbering trot, with a clattering of mess-tins and implements. Early morning had discovered us in the communication trenches in which the company, one of the latest to start, had been tramping ever since two o'clock in the morning, incessantly cut through by stretcher-bearers, held back by reliefs; and directly it was day the German artillery had begun to fire. The shrapnel seemed to pursue us, going forward with us, and the harassed battalion was running towards the lines under a zig-zigging canopy of green smoke.

Guided by Morache, who was at his wits' end, and had now lost his way, we were going on just as the trench took us, tracked by the time-fuse shells. Between two crashes we heard the voice Cruchet, cold and precise as on drill. . . .

"Well, Morache? . . . Do you recognize where you are now?"

The shells were following us up as though they had eyes. We were going on, splitting off this way and that, retracing our way; but the pack never left us alone, baying enough to deafen us, and making us drunk and giddy with acrid smoke and fumes.

At every flaming burst we pitched one into another, heads and legs intermingled, flattened up against the wall, as though inlaid in the holes. The shrapnel was bursting low, every now and then lashing the trench with fragments, and cries sprang up from all those close-cowering bodies.

"Hub, there! I'm winged."

Dulled and stupefied, we were striding over bodies; we would go forward twenty paces, pushing one another on, then we would throw ourselves down on hands and knees, our mouths and eyes twisted by a spasm, humping our backs under the crashing turmoil.

"Well, Morache," went on the Captain, "is that the right way over there? Ttt! Ttt! . . . You're sure?"

We started off once more, dry-throated, not knowing where we were making for. And for all that there was no losing of our heads, a kind of discipline even in bewilderment: the mind wavered, a little stunned and dizzy as though coming out of some infernal forge, but lucid in spite of all; and between the salvoes orders passed along as though nothing had happened, methodically, like a foreman's orders transmitted through the din of a factory.

At length, all at once the barrage lost us. Suddenly there was a great calm, and we then perceived that the sun was up. We had just debouched on a sunk road with thick green bushes clothing the steep banks. All at once Sulphart dashed forward, ransacking among the branches.

"Hey, boys! . . . there are blackberries here."

. . . . . .

"Don't touch me! Don't touch me! . . ." repeated the wounded man, livid with pain, all the time going forward down the communication trench.

His crushed arms hung down like two red plaits of hair. Coming up to us, he said, in the same colourless voice in which there was not a thrill left even of pain.

"I want to sit down; take hold of me by the coat."

Holding him up by the collar of his coat, we settled him down on the firing-step, his trunk rigid, his two arms of bloody porridge only holding to his body by the lacerated sleeves. His nose was thin and pinched to sharpness, as if death had already tried to choke off his breath.

"You ought to make haste to the dressing-station," said Lemoine to him, seeing the two rivulets of blood running down.

"Yes, I'm going to it. . . Light me a cigarette. . . . Put it into my mouth for me."

We raised him up again; he thanked us with his head, and started off with a mechanical pace, a comrade going in front of him to ward off the massed soldiers.

"Make way!--a wounded man. . . ."

The whole company was mustered there in a mass, a great living buckler of casques crowded together, in front of four rude ladders, blanket rolled, no pack, digging-tool by each man's side--"Gala rig," Gilbert had said, ragging.

On our right, squeezed up in the same parallel, a company of a regiment of young troops had just fixed their bayonets; they were to go over with us, in the first wave. All the saps, all the trenches were full, and in feeling ourselves crowded in this way, loins pressing into loins, by hundreds, by thousands, we were conscious of a brutal confidence. Whether bold or resigned, one was nothing more than a mere grain in this human mass. The Army, on that morning, had in it the very soul of victory.

Some of the boys, eyes shining, cheeks burning red, were talking fast, seized by a kind of fever. Others remained mute, quite pale, and with a chin that quivered just a little.

Above the sandbags we gazed at the German lines, buried under a plume of smoke in which lightnings crackled and flashed; further away still, in the plain, three villages seemed to be on fire, and our artillery kept on firing continuously, in a jetting, spurting thunder in which were confounded the departure and the landing of the shells. The fields rocked under this fury, and against my elbow I could feel the trench shivering and crumbling.

At every moment Gilbert was looking at his watch. This agonizing waiting made his heart contract and thrill; he would fain have heard the signal to start at once and make an end. He thought aloud:

"They are prolonging the pleasure."

On the parapet, between the tufts of grass, two creatures were fighting; a big red-brown beetle with a thick cuirass, and blue insect with slender fine antennæ. Gilbert was eyeing them, and when the beetle was on the point of crushing the other, he turned it over on its back with the tip of one finger. From his forehead fell a drop of sweat on the little blue fellow, who shook his gaily bedizened wings.

"Attention! It is just on the hour," warned an officer on our right.

Nearer still, Cruchet gave the order:

"Fix bayonets. . . . Grenadiers at the head." A steely thrill ran down the whole length of the trench. Leaning forward, Gilbert was still observing his insects, and not listening to the beating of his heart. The beetle shook his heavy carapace, but the other had seized him between his long antennæ, and was holding on tight, did not slacken his grip.

103

Very quickly Cruchet was tightening his chin-strap. Standing on the lowest step of a sandbag staircase, he dominated all of us. He looked at us.

"Now, boys. . . . Ttt! Ttt! . . . It's for France, isn't it, eh? . . . A good attack. . . . We are going to take that. . . ."

Whether it was emotion or no, it seemed to me that his voice was not so dry, not so trenchant as usual. As a sudden revelation one understood the word--a chief. We tightened up our belts, we thrust back the tool that beat against the thigh. At the foot of a ladder, Berthier was ready to go over. Turning his head, he saw Morache with perturbed countenance.

"After you, Lieutenant," he said in true military fashion, falling back a pace.

The other, failing, saw a pretext.

"What?" he twittered. . . . "Are you afraid to be the first man over the top?"

Without saying a word, the sous-Lieutenant turned again and set his foot once more on the rung. From behind one saw merely the shrug of his shoulders.

"Morache puncturing," cried out Vieublé, in the thick of the noise.

The Lieutenant had perhaps heard, but he never stirred a muscle. Rising from out of that mass of men bristling with bayonets, the vagabondish voice went on:

"It's not enough this time to have lots of chat. . . . It's a case of having to go into it. . . . That's a harder job than chucking poor beggars into clink. . . . We're all equal at this trick."

Nothing more was to be heard but the mocking voice under the guns, and the boys laughed, with no trace of ill-feeling, as though those words had eased them.

The strong bodies ready to dash forward were swaying, already knocking on the parapet like an ebbing tide.

In shrill spurts the seventy-fives were whistling, and at the same instant the deep growling of the heavy artillery seemed to fall silent or to move away.

"Are we ready?" asked Cruchet, in a louder voice.

Our hearts leaped furiously, or one single heart for that armed crowd.

"You really have my home address?" said Sulphart once again to Gilbert, in a broken voice, his emotion running his words into one another.

Look, the gold beetle moved no more, the insect was winning the fight. . . . Oh! that powder, what a foul, acrid stench! . . . A clamour rose along by the right, cries or a song: "The Zouaves are over!" A gust of hundred-and-fives exploded, five cymbal clashes, . . .

"En avant the third!" cried the Captain. "En avant!"

Cries, a scrimmage, a man who falls back swearing, rifles catching in one another. . . . With temples humming we scramble on to the parapet, then straighten ourselves, our legs a trifle flabby. We look at the immense plain, the naked plain. "En avant!" We are over, we are running.

A machine gun, only one, had begun to cough. Reawakened to madness, the German artillery was battering everywhere.

Already the chain of men was taking shape, slender silhouettes with sloping rifles, and was going forward with a regular, even trot, faces towards the dumb trenches. On the left, bugles in front, a battalion was charging with loud cries.

Left alone, his sabre in his hand, a Commandant was driving on the last squads of the youngest soldiers, who were hesitating before the barrage.

"Come on! . . . Hurry up! Out of it! Out of it!"

A handful of lads mounted. In front of them, like a cloud of fire-damp, a timed shell exploded: a red eruption, a swarming volley of splinters, . . . A body chopped to pieces bespattered the sap. In the smoke voices groaned aloud.

"Come on! There's no danger now. . . . Out of it!"

Another section, all trembling, scaled the sandbags that rolled from under them, but a storm of fire harrowed up the field. They ebbed back again. . . .

They stormed forward again, squad by squad, knowing nothing more, haggard. But at every endeavour the fire flung them back at one stroke, beaten down into their hole. Every time a salvo plunged straight on to them.

"Out of it, God's truth!"

Their poor wave beat more and more feebly against the wall they dared no longer overpass. . . . But no, they could not now. . . .

The Commandant climbed up at a single leap.

"En avant, pack of skulkers!"

A little cadet was banging them in the back, forcing them to get over, crying and shouting in a voice like a girl. Staggering, the living holocaust appeared, driven by his fists, and in the face of death had, as it were, a supreme shudder, a last recoil.

"That's the style! . . . En avant!" cried the girl's voice.

They rushed through the passage in the wire, scattered, dashed straight into the wall of smoke. . . . It was all over, the barrage was passed.

Dotted all about the fields, the battalions were running, and somebody out beyond the first lines was waving a pennon: the village was taken.

. . . . . .

Walls tumbled down, gaping façades, heaps of tiles and rubble, roofs fallen in all in one piece, rigid stiff legs sticking up out of the ruins. . . . The street could just be divined by twisted railings here and there to be seen under the lumps of broken stone. We were running from ruin to ruin, sidling along by pieces of walls, firing in front of us, riddling empty cellars with hand-grenades. Everybody was shouting. . . .

The guns were thundering less heavily but through the ventholes machine guns were simply sweeping the village like scythes. Men were going down, doubled up as though borne down by the weight of their heads. Others were spinning round like a teetotum, their arms straight out like a cross, and falling face to the sky, their legs bent in two. We hardly noticed them even: we were running on.

Someone all white with plaster called out to Gilbert:

"Lambert is killed!"

Around a well, men were fighting with rifle butts, with fists, or with knives: a brawl in the midst of the battle. Vieublé with one stroke butted a German clean over the curb of the well, and we could see his cap fly off, a grey cap with a crimson band. All that was engraved on the mind with accurate detail, brutally, without rousing any feeling: shouts of men being killed, explosions, the bark of hand-grenades, comrades going down. Without knowing where we were making for, one following another blindly, we charged straight before us. . . .

Flattening themselves out, there were some laggards hiding behind a wall: "With us, you dirty dogs!" Gilbert yelled to them.

Some Boches passed by us, running, shorn of their equipment, their hands high in the air, scampering towards our lines. Sitting at the entrance of a cellar, another was sponging away with a filthy handkerchief the blood that was trickling from his forehead; with his left hand he made us a salutation.

In spite of the crackling of the firing, we could hear the long panting rattle of the saucepans shattering into fragments in the middle of the village, tearing up a thick cloud of dust and smoke, and hunching our backs, we would throw ourselves against the walls.

In the flying dust and the debris of plaster, we had assumed the neutral colour of this cemetery of all things. Nothing there was alive, shapely, fashioned; a whirl of pounded debris, a great work-yard of catastrophe where everything was confounded in confusion: dead bodies emerging from the fallen rubbish, stones ground to powder, tatters of cloth, the smashed bits of household furnishings, soldiers' packs--all that brought to one common denominator, annihilated, the dead men not more tragic than the pebbles.

Exhausted, panting, out of breath, we were running no longer. A road cut through the ruins, and an invisible machine gun was riddling it with bullets, raising a little cloud of dust in the surface of the ground. "All into the trench!" cried an adjutant.

Without looking, we all leaped in, as we touched this flabby flooring with our feet. human disgust threw me backwards, appalled. It was a dreadful squalid mass, a monstrous disinterring of waxy Bavarians on top of others already black, whose wrenched and twisted mouths exhaled a breath of corruption, a whole accumulation of slashed and mangled flesh, with corpses that you might have fancied unscrewed, knocked awry, the feet and knees twisted completely round; and to watch over them all, one single dead body remaining on his feet, propped up with his back against the face of the trench, and buttressed by a monster with no head. The first of our file did not dare to go forward over this charnel-heap, we felt a kind of almost religious fear to walk over those dead bodies, to crunch under our feet these faces of what had been men. For all that, hunted by the machine guns, the last ranks leaped in, and that common burying ditch seemed to over-flow.

"Go on, God's truth!"

Still we hesitated to trample upon that pavement that squelched at every step; then thrust forward by the others, we went on without looking, splashing, paddling in Death. . . . By some demoniac caprice he had spared nothing save inanimate things: along ten mètres of trench, untouched in their little niches, there were ranged spiked helmets, each clad in a cloth cover. Some of the boys took possession of them; others got hold of satchels, water-bottles.

"Look, a gorgeous pair of pumps!" bellowed Sulphart, brandishing two yellow boots.

At the exit of the trench a squatting sergeant was shouting, "To the left, in skirmishing order! To the left!" and our file set off again, running along a little road with a ditch flanking it. Further out, in the fields, we saw nothing but a wire system half hidden by weeds. . . . And not a trench, not a German, not a single shot.

Soon, as there was no firing, our trot slowed up, and we fell into little groups; but a salvo of shrapnel thundered out, planting all along the road its line of vaporous trees, and when we looked again the road was empty. Everybody had gone to ground in the ditch or behind pieces of wall. All in a bunch, we had crowded together in a narrow channel dug at the foot of a mud wall. Nervously we pulled round the nape of our neck the padding of our tightly rolled blankets, and we waited. . . . The shells raged for a moment, eighty-eights that passed so low, so close, that we were astonished not to see the grass mown away in front of us, and we buried our heads in our two hands. Then the rambling firing lengthened the range, continuing its hide-and-seek in the village. All along the road the file of men stood upright, but without quitting their individual shelters.

"Are we to stay where we are?" asked a soldier who seemed well buried in a huge burrow.

"No, we're going on still," shouted Ricordeau to us, passing by at a run.

"It's not worth while; the other village over there has been taken."

"What's it called, that village? "--Nobody knew.

"The stunt has slipped up," wheezed Fouillard, squeezed up against me. "We'll be having to go back."

Some were crying out, "You can see the Legion still advancing"; and others: "Look out! there are the Boches attacking."

"We'll be taken in flank!"

"You're drunk! That's our own trenches." The bombardment made them quiet for a moment. Shrivelled and parched, we emptied the water-bottles between two gusts of fire.

"Captain! Here they are, Captain . . ." Cruchet had just let himself slide down from the top of the bank, bringing down bits of mortar and pebbles with him. Berthier was running at his heels, and they were going from hole to hole, throwing themselves flat on their faces when a shell roared over. The Captain called out:

"You are brave old pigs! We're just going to take their third line. . . ."

"Look out for the signal on the right. . . ." He wore a new visage, ruddy and sweaty, his mouth split in a great soundless laugh. Still as he ran he repeated:

"Mind the signal on the right. . . . The right. . ."

A crash, and I heard nothing more. . . . It was like the stroke of a club that knocked us all over, a shock that overwhelms you, a blast that flings you down. . . . And the thick, thick cloud, the blackness of night. . . . Ten different thoughts tumbling together: We are killed! I am blinded! We are buried! Then cries . . . .

"Help! quick! quick . . ."

In the smoke there are wounded men bolting. Fouillard was lying before me, his head in a red puddle, and his back working convulsively as if he was sobbing. It was his blood he was shedding like tears.

Again a blast darted on us. . . .

I had picked myself up, my head between my knees, my body rolled into a ball, my teeth clenched. My face screwed up, my eyes wrinkled so as to be half shut, I was waiting. . . . The shells followed one another; precipitate, hurried: but you couldn't hear them come, it was too near, it was too much. At every detonation your heart, torn from its place, makes a tremendous leap; your head, your entrails jump. You long to be tiny, more tiny still; every separate bit of you is afraid, your limbs shrink on themselves; your head, buzzing and completely empty, is fain to bury itself anywhere--you are afraid, in short, desperately, cruelly afraid. . . . Under this thundering death you are no more than a quivering heap, a waiting ear, a heart that fears. . . .

Between each salvo ten seconds would go by--ten seconds to live, ten enormous seconds that held the whole of happiness; and I looked at Fouillard, who now moved no longer. Lying on his side, his face turned purple, his neck was gaping, his throat cut as the throats of cattle are cut.

The slinking smoke masked the road, but one had no wish to see anything, one simply listened, wild with horror. Thudding all round like a pickaxe, the shells pelted us with bits of stone, and we remained piled on one another in our rut, two living men and one dead.

Suddenly, without rhyme or reason, the firing came to a stop. Huge shells were still falling on the ruins, sending up black geysers; but that was further off, they were for others. In our shaken heads that moment of peace was imperial luxury. I turned round, and at the foot of the bank I saw Berthier stooping above a body lying stretched out. Who?

All along the road the boys were picking themselves up. "Grenadiers!" called a voice.

Then coming right from the right, an order reached us, called out from hole to hole.

"The Colonel asks who is in command on the left."

"Pass the word. . . . The Colonel asks who is commanding on the left."

I saw Berthier gently lay back the head of the dead man on the grass. He stood up, pale and haggard, and he called:

"Sous-Lieutenant Berthier, of the third. . . . Pass the word. . . ."

. . . . . .

Dragging it by the coat, Gilbert pulled the dead body up to the lip of the big funnel-hole into which we had thrown ourselves. For a long time now dead men no longer touched him with fear. Even so, he did not dare to take it by the hand, that poor shrivelled hand, yellow and muddy, and he avoided the quenched look of its yellow eyes.

"We need still three--four more like that," said Lemoine. "That would make a decent parapet for us with a little earth over all."

Only a moment ago the poor lad was running side by side with us, his eyes riveted, fixed with agony of stress, full on the German trench from which were spurting the short, straight, stabbing flames of the Mausers. Then gusts of shells had torn gaps in the company, the machine guns had mown down men in whole lines, and of the palpitating band that charged, tragic and silent, there remained now only these twenty cowering men, these wounded dragging themselves along, groaning and moaning, and all these dead. . . .

Gilbert between two explosions had heard the comrade exclaim: "Ah! that's the end!" The wounded man had still dragged himself on for a few mètres, like a creature that has been run over and he died there, in a sob. Was it sad? Hardly. . . . In that poor field that had all the appearance of waste ground, he made just one corpse more, one more blue sleeper that would be buried after the attack, if it was possible. A few paces away under a chalky mound there were Boches interred: their cross would do for our dead, a grey cap on one arm, a blue cap on the other.

"Now then, what are we going to do?" asked Hamel, whose torn sleeve was dropping a little blood. "Don't you see they're leaving us in the lurch?"

"But no," said Gilbert. "The second battalion is certainly coming over, but we must wait till the artillery prepares the way."

"And if they fire short, that will still be for our mugs."

Hidden in the long grass and weeds, the German trench was hardly to be distinguished behind the barbed cobweb of iron. The Germans were no longer firing, and even their big guns were silent. Only a few two-hundred-and-tens were going over out of breath at a great height, with the gurgle of an emptying bottle, and would fall on the village, wreathing the ruins with a heavy cloud of smoke like a factory.

Lying on the edge of our funnel, a few soldiers were watching, their eyes on a level with the grass; the others were arguing, piled up in the hole.

"Do you think they'll patch up again to take their third line?"

"Very likely. Unless they dig a trench through here."

"No mistake, it's not with all the poilus that are left that they can hope to attack."

"I'm perishing of thirst. Haven't you got a drop left in your bottle?"

"No. . . . Look how many of the boys have gone down since we left the village."

There were dead men everywhere: hanging in the iron brambles, knocked over in the grass, piled up in the shell-holes. Here blue overcoats, there grey-backs. Some were horrible to see, their swollen faces already as though covered with a thick mask of grey felt. Others were black as coals, their eye-sockets already empty: those were the fruits of the early attacks. You looked on them without emotion, without disgust, and when you read an unfamiliar number on the collar of a coat, you merely said to your neighbours: "I say, I never knew their regiment had done its bit."

A few paces from the funnel an officer was lying on his side, his coat open, and in his long fingers he held his first-aid dressing that he had never been able to unroll.

"We ought to try and haul him up to here," said Lemoine, who still clung to his idea, "that would make one more for the parapet. And with that Boche out there a bit further on. . . ."

"You're off your head," growled Hamel. "You want to get us taped off, piling them all up in front."

"The fellows in the other holes have managed to put up parapets for themselves with them."

As a matter of fact, at intervals all along the ridge there were men down and dodging that you might have taken for bunches of dead. Lying flat behind the smallest pimple of earth, cowered down in the smallest holes, they were toiling almost without a movement, scratching at the earth with their little entrenching tool, and patiently, with infinite pains, they were erecting in front of them little hillocks, mole-heaps that a breath would have flung to the winds.

"Our hole is deeper, we are in less danger," observed Gilbert.

"Aye, but when they have once got ranged on to the ridge, what are we going to have handed to us?"

At that moment the Boche artillery awoke. We heard a few shells arrive, time-fused shrapnel, that burst far too high up in a black fleecy cloud; then when they had got the range the bombardment started. The first shells fell comfortably far off, on the left; then the storm came nearer, following the ridge; and suddenly, all at once, four quick reports, four spurts of steamy smoke, four explosions. . . . The salvo had landed squarely in front of our funnel, and a thick cloud, stinking of powder, filled the hole. . . . Our bodies curled into a ball, we had thrown ourselves one against the other, everyone trying to burrow underneath the mingled mass of legs. Gilbert instinctively hid his head under his bended arm, like a frightened child. A rain of earth fell down. .

. . Already the second salvo was arriving, thudding all round us, with furious blows to the right, to the left. Then suddenly there was something absolutely brutish, one knew not what, terrific, that one might imagine had burst out from oneself.

The shell must have burst full on the edge of the funnel. Two men moved no more, sliding to the bottom of the hole. Wounded men, driven crazy, were running away, their faces bloody, their hands red. Those who remained hardly even looked at them, inlaid into the earth, head pulled down into shoulders, waiting the supreme stroke. But suddenly the range lengthened: they were sweeping on the right. Every head was raised. Oh! that unique moment of happiness, when death has passed farther on.

Gilbert threw an eye into the plain. Were not the Boches coming over? No. . . . there was nothing to be seen. Not till after did he look at the two comrades whose half-opened mouths seemed to be speaking to heaven.

"We can't leave them there to be tramped over," proposed Lemoine, "let us put them on the edge."

Two comrades took hold of the first one, making their hands thick and sticky with coagulated blood, and hoisted him up on to the edge of the funnel. Gilbert turned the face towards the enemy so that he would not see it. The other body was heavier, and he had to give them a hand, holding up the dead man's head that hung down and refused to stay in place.

"Like that," said Lemoine with satisfaction, "one has a decent parapet already. . . . Poor beggars! if they had thought of such a thing just now. . . . And that's just a fellow that I've got the home address of. . . . Look out!"

It was all beginning over again, eighty-eights this time, under which we flattened ourselves down, our faces crushed into the dry earth. They were coming over in batches of five, so quickly that the report of their starting and the explosion shocked together.

In the field the wounded were running, and the shell splinters mowed down those who had not gone out of reach. But on the other side of the network of wire there was nothing to be seen, always the same nothing. It was a battle without enemies, death without combat. From early morning when we had started fighting, we had not seen twenty Germans. Dead men, nothing but dead men.

With our faces screwed up, our fists clenched, and our jaws tight set, we were counting the shells. Little by little the head empties, though all the while seeming to grow heavier. But why do we remain so calm despite it all? We are watching, we are being wary, but our hearts beat no quicker, and we look about us without fever, with no astonishment. Nothing now can be heard but these hellish explosions that tear your breast asunder. They fire, fire, fire. . . . We feel our legs powerless, our hands cold, our foreheads burning. Is that it? Is this fear?

Another body was lying in the bottom of the hole. That one had not died on the spot. He had writhed and twisted for an interminable moment, breathing hoarse and loud, livid. Now he stirred no longer.

"Are we going to put him up on top too?" asked Lemoine, his head sheltered behind his bent arm.

"Waiting till it's our own turn," replied Hamel. We looked at one another in a sort of vague, confused agony. Which of us would presently be hoisted up there aloft, in a moment, to enlarge the wall of the dead?

Painfully we fetched up the last one from the common grave, and his mutilated body marked the flank of the funnel with a brown furrow.

As a thunderstorm dies away, so the cannonade had slackened off, and from every hole uneasy heads were peering out. Were they going to attack? An officer showed himself behind a hillock.

"Stick it, boys!" he shouted. "Stick it! . . ."

At the same instant, a few paces away, a voice warned us.

"Look out! there they are!"

They had just sprung up, barely a round hundred of them, out of a little scrap of wood about two hundred mètres from the ridge. Immediately another group showed itself, come from nobody knew where; then another still, that hurled itself forward shouting--and the lines of skirmishers deployed.

"The Boches! Fire! Fire! . . . Aim low. . . "

Everybody was shouting, orders came up from every hole, and all along the whole line of the ridge the fusillade crackled up and increased. Suddenly we saw nothing more. Had they lain down? Had we brought them down?

A minute after, the bombardment resumed, more brutal, more delicately accurate than ever. Between the gusts of fire we could see the wounded clearing out. Running or dragging themselves along, they were trying to get to a little leafy bank that bordered the great field.

"They're taking cover in the Boche trench," cried a boy of the 1915 class. "Nobody can get through it now there are such lots of them. And the shells falling plump into it--talk about a hash!"

Our artillery was replying--seventy-fives whining, hundred-and-twenties brutal, and the revolver canon swearing like a cat. Salvoes were answering salvoes. And in our hole, cowering down against the dead that the fellows who were most frightened pulled down upon themselves, like bloody bucklers, the survivors were waiting. Nothing now could be seen but a stray soldier here and there, a blue object huddled up in a hole. You might have said that the chain of men stretched out in front of the conquered village was being broken link by link. Every ten paces there were soldiers lying at full length, forehead upturned to the sky, thighs apart and knees up; or indeed flat on their bellies, their heads on their arms. One of them was lying so snugly that you would have said he was asleep; and having taken one look at him, Gilbert envied him.

Sharp and sudden a fresh salvo thundered. When Gilbert raised his head again he saw in the vanishing smoke the little soldier-boy turned over on his side. On his new coat a big red splash was shaping itself to a ghastly round. He crawled to him, lifted him, then, having let him drop back heavily, he came back to his place at one bound.

"Not worth while," he said, "he's got a lump of shell . . . he's in the death-rattle already. . . ."

The explosions were now all jumbled up together, the smoke no longer had time to unwind itself, and the splinters were sailing over us in furious volleys. Suddenly a yellow and red flame-burst blinded us. With one single movement we had crammed ourselves down one into the other, stunned, our very hearts torn from their places. And Gilbert must have fallen without seeing anything or feeling anything but a great blow like a fisticuff on his head, a blast of hell-breath full in the face. . . .

When he recovered his wits, with a heavy head, he timidly moved his legs. They obeyed, they changed position. . . . No, there was nothing wrong there. He then

111

passed his hand over his face. See, it was red. It was in the forehead, near the temple. Leaning over him, I said.

"It's nothing at all. Just a bit of a cut."

He made no answer, still giddy and stayed without moving for a good minute. Full up against him, Hamel was still on his knees, his face on the ground. He neither stirred nor breathed, but Gilbert did not dare to speak to him, not even to touch him, simply to keep for a moment longer the illusion that he was not dead. Then he put the question to Lemoine, but avoiding the actual word:

"He's got it, eh?"

Simply the other showed him, between the helmet and the overcoat, a thin trickle of blood making a stripe across his neck. At the bottom of the funnel at least ten dead bodies were piled together in a heap. Between two bloody coats, under the corpses, a wan face showed itself, its eyes open wide, haggard--dead or alive?

Gilbert opened up his first-aid packet and bandaged up his forehead. With his handkerchief he wiped away the blood that ran all down his cheek like a warm caress, then, to soothe his burning head, he laid it against the cold iron barrel of his rifle. During a brief time of quietude, he heard to the right rifle fire crackling and the barking of the hand-grenades. He thought vaguely: "They are going to attack again." But he had not the courage to lift his head to look over into the plain.

A frantic salvo landed, searching the dead ground, and then a hundred-and-five shrapnel shell burst straight over our hole. Gilbert remained dazed for a moment, his heart stopped. Then with a twist of the loins he sprang up, leaped on the edge of the funnel and bolted. He was going to tuck himself away into another hole never mind where, but he was not going to stay any longer in that ditch, in that yawning, gaping grave. Another salvo hurled across, he flung himself flat. Then he got up again, crazed, ran to the right, then to the left, tripping and stumbling over the bodies. All the holes were taken; everywhere there were squashed dead bodies, haggard wounded men, soldiers sternly on the alert, watching.

"Is there any room in with you?"

"No. I've got a wounded pal here."

He still turned about for a moment, then he threw himself down flat on his stomach behind a little mound. His heart was beating wildly, like some wild creature he had crushed underneath him. Panting and gasping he was listening to the guns, without a single idea in his fevered head. Suddenly he thought:

"But I've run away."

He repeated it several times to himself, not clearly understanding at first go off. Then, having lifted his head, he saw Lemoine making signals to him. And then, running, in one single breath, he got back to the funnel again.

It was for all the world like a wine-press, that tragic hole with its purpling sides, and in order to avoid trampling on the bodies of the comrades that filled the vat, you had to maintain yourself on the flank of the ditch, with your fingers thrusting into the breaking, crumbling soil. Gilbert thought he was going to faint. No suffering and no emotion, rather a dreadful listlessness. The officer, still on his knees behind his hummock, caught sight of him and hailed him.

"Hey, you over there, going strong?"

Gilbert looked at him, he looked at the dead. With the back of a hand he wiped away the blood that was prickling and tickling his cheek then he called back his answer.

"Going strong. . . ."

Day is departing, trailing its skirts of mist over the plain. On the left, the fusillade is still sparkling and glinting, but like a fire that is on the point of extinction.

What has happened since noon? We have fired, burned by the sun, our heads heavy, our throats parched. At last it rained, and that thunder-shower washed away the fever that was burning us all up. In gusts the artillery was sweeping the ridge, raging wildly to find men on it still persisting in being alive. Then we fancied we saw the Boche dash forward. And we fired, we fired, we kept on firing----

Quite close, in their own wire, there are Germans lying, their bodies curled up like a ball, and you might call them the beads of a funereal rosary. I noticed one of them with his bag of hand grenades on his stomach, who now and then lifts his arm with a dying effort and beats the air for a moment.

In the deepening shadows the little young recruit is still in the death-rattle. It is a terrifying thing that lad who will not die.

Is that the relief? Men are arriving, at the run and going from hole to hole stooping with rounded backs.

"Hi, lads, how's things. Are we coming out? What regiment?"

No, these are our own orderlies.

"Well! Are we coming out?"

"No.... We must get through the night here still. The reinforcing companies are coming up with the tools. We've got to dig ourselves in on the ridge."

Coming up out of all the holes, men are coming together, going on all fours.

"What? stay here? No, kid. . . . There aren't thirty left out of the company."

"So it's the same old thing as usual then. . . . I don't give a blow. . . . I'm wounded. They can all go to. . . ."

"That's the orders," repeat the orderlies. "We've got to stick it. We'll be relieved to-morrow."

There, we can't hear the little wounded recruit any more. Gilbert feels weak, his head absolutely empty. He would like never to move again, and to sleep to sleep. His underlinen is sticking to his back. Is it the rain? or sweat?

The artillery is silent, exhausted, its voice broken. The complaints and cries of the wounded can be heard better now-- "Wait, children, wait, don't cry out any more, the stretcher-bearers will be coming."

Night draws on. . . .

And softly the silent evening weaves its misty web one single wide winding sheet of grey linen, for all those dead men who will have no other.

. . . . .

It is a great flock of emaciated men, a regiment of dried mud, that leaves the trenches and makes off across the fields, helter-skelter at its own sweet will. We carry wan and filthy faces innocent of any washing but what the rain may have given us. We march with lifeless, dragging pace, our backs humped, our necks thrust forward.

Once arrived on the height, I stop and turn around, to see for a last time, to carry away in my very soul, the picture of that great plain, gashed with trenches, harrowed by shells, with the three villages we captured, three heaps of grey, grisly ruins.

What a sad and gloomy thing is a panorama of victory. The mist still hides corners of it under its shroud, and I can recognize nothing now on that vast map of upturned earth. The Three Ways, the Farm, the White Trench, all that is confused, it is the same plain, worn away down to its woof of white marl, a flat moor, annihilated, without a tree, without a roof, without any live thing, and everywhere fly specked with tiny spots, dead men, dead men, dead men. . . .

"There are twenty thousand Boche corpses here," cried the Colonel, proud of us.

How many French?

We have had to hold on for ten days in that hellish work-yard, be cut to pieces by whole battalions, just to add a patch of field to our victory, a broken-down trench, a paltry hamlet in ruins. But however I may strive and search, I can recognize nothing now. The places where we have suffered so terribly are just like any others; lost in the greyness, as if there could be but one and the same outward aspect for one and the same martyrdom. It is down there. . . . some where. . . . The dull, sickly smell of the corpses is obliterated; nothing now can be smelt but chloride of lime exhaled all about from the water-casks. But for me it is in my head, in my very flesh, that I . carry the horrible breath of the dead. It is in me for evermore: I know now the odour of pity.

As we got farther and farther from the lines, the shattered fragments of the section knitted together again, the companies once more took a certain shape. We looked one at another, and we frightened each other.

Soldiers lying stretched out on the leprous grass got up and came towards us. That very evening they were to go up into the line.

"It's stiff, mates?"

"The sector of death."

And pointing out our harassed band with a motion of his chin, Bréval said simply:

"One company. . . ."

With heads drooping we passed through a most woebegone country, with windows devoid of panes, and with roofs like sieves; then we were halted in a field on the edge of the highroad where the lorries were waiting. There we had food: hot rice that filled up your stomach, and that we simply couldn't tire of devouring, greedily, with full cups of boiling hot coffee, less for true hunger than for the bestial delight of eating, to overtake those days of abject distress, to stodge ourselves, to feel ourselves stuffed full.

The old white bearded quartermaster was giving out brandy as you pour out wine, by brimming cupfuls.

"It's got to be finished," he cried cordially to us.

As for wine, you had only to go and ladle it up. As they drank, the boys, absolutely full to the teeth, followed the old fellow about with an unfriendly eye.

"It's his fault that big Lambert is killed."

"Poor beggar! . . . He hadn't been in the trenches since Berry."

Silent, I thought of his cross, his prophetic cross of shadow in the moon.

"It seems he got up three times," narrated Gilbert in a loud voice, so that the quartermaster should hear him, "and all three times he was hit by machine guns. After that he still dragged himself along, crying out. . . . I had promised him to write to his mother."

Those of us who were most done up had fallen asleep. The others, mixed up in little groups with the lorry-drivers, were arguing and discussing: they were all talking at once, feverishly, throwing out pell-mell their still palpitating impressions, seeming to want to unburthen themselves of these too crushing memories. Far more moved and excited than ourselves, the drivers were listening, and as they were the only ones who had been able to read the newspapers, they expounded to us the battle of which we knew nothing whatever.

The comrades were proudly displaying all their trophies and enemy spoils, helmets hung to their belts, like scalps.

"I'll buy it off you," proposed one of the chauffeurs to one of the boys.

Tempted by the price, another offered his own booty, and there on the edge of the road a regular market came into being. Every kind of souvenir was on sale, every sort of thing that an attack can throw up by way of wreckage: shoulder-straps, grey caps, shell-fuses--"They make topping ink-stands, my boy "--Boche cartridge-clips that were going for twenty sous, little cups made of aluminium that are very light but burn your fingers, water-bottles covered in khaki cloth, postcards covered with unintelligible loving messages. Over certain helmets carrying eagles with outstretched wings men leaned curiously, to see the murderous hole through which the life had taken flight. Sulphart was flourishing his pair of yellow boots, as a rare specimen of merchandise.

"A Boche's shoes, blokes!" cried he. . . . "Ripping officer's booties! Who's going to have them? A nice present for a little chicken. . . . Who would like to go clumping about Panama with Boche boots on him!"

He shut up sharply and picked up his wares, like a pedlar surprised in the act.

"Oh, sugar! there's Morache. . . ." We hadn't set eyes on him for ten days, since the morning of the attack. Not for one single instant had he left the stinking cellar-- the first he came to--that he had seized on as command post, and he had come out of it with a face like mildew, discoloured lips, and his eyes all blinking. Squeaking, he was making the company fall in--his company now that Cruchet was killed--and brutally awakening the sleepers by prodding them with the end of his cane.

"Come on, I've given orders for packs up, you lazy beggar!" he cried into the face of little Broucke, who was getting up, swaying dizzily, his eyes still vague with sleep.

Sore against our will, we got under our equipment.

"All the same, it's not him they'll stick on to us for Captain, after the way he's played up. . . . It was Berthier that did all the work. . . ."

"Yes, but he's got only one string."

"It's a good job for Vieublé that he got himself sent down; it would have knocked him endways."

"He's the lad with the sure enough luck, I say. . . . If you had seen him streaking off with his leg chipped, I swear he was funny!"

We went all aboard. In a moment everybody was settled in his corner, packs piled up in the bottom of the lorries, and we could once more sit down, lie down, take our ease.

"They might have foreseen that," said the driver, shrugging his shoulders. He was kneeling on his seat, and looking us over. "They ordered up just the same number of carts as fetched you, and there's not the same number of you now, is there?"

Then, and not till then, did we notice the empty places. What a lot were missing! I still saw in fancy big Lambert, forcing himself to laugh: Father Hamel smoking his pipe in the corner: and Fouillard, who had sat right at the back with his legs dangling down. At every jolt we would say:

"If only, if only I could tumble out and break my head!"

The convoy set itself in motion, disappearing in a thick cloud of dust that clung like a fringe round the chauffeurs' eyes and gave them white beards. Dizzy and stunned, and lulled at the same time, prostrated with heat, weariness, and bad wine, men were half dozing, and yet too much shaken to sleep. Broucke alone at once started again to snore, lying on his back, his yellow straw head quivering and jolting on his pack.

Maroux, leaning forward, would chaff the girls, triumphantly flourishing a spiked helmet as if he had won it himself in single combat? Between the villages and the lorries signals were exchanged, shoutings, even kisses, that were sent back to us by girls all bathed in sweat, their shirts open and tucked in over their bosoms.

We were moving away from the war: the windows now had their glazed panes, the roofs had their tiles. All of a sudden the lorries danced over cobbled pavements, and straightway we could hear shouts from the foremost waggons. Every head was slipped under the awnings, every body was leaning towards the rear; and then, all along the convoy there was a burst of wild cheering. Fabulous apparition, double miracle, a railway was in full view, a real civilian railway, with real carriages and on the station square a woman in a hat.

The level crossing once passed, it was a regular little town, with shops, footpaths, women, cafés, all of which we eyed with the dazzled stupidity of savages, without ever growing tired of shouting our delight. Those who had dressings on their foreheads pushed back their helmets so as to be seen the better, and Bélin was proudly blowing kisses with his wounded hand just like a bundle of fresh white linen.

At a flower-adorned window a pretty fair head showed itself--every face is always pretty when it is only seen in a glimpse for a moment--greeted as we passed by with a long whoop, and the whirlwind was already far past while she still listened, leaning out over that wake of dust and cries.

The convoy was still rumbling on, and nobody complained of the length of the way. We would fain have put still more villages, still more fields, still more leagues between us and the war. So much the better: we should have the guns in our ears no longer. Among the stubble the thrashing-machines were snoring and eating up the fair-haired sheaves, the little woods and thickets bathed our scorched eyes in their verdurous fresh coolth; we envied the peace and snug happiness of the villages we caught glimpses of under the trees, of those farms with the red roofs, farms that to us were now only so many billets.

It was too hot under the awnings, on which the sun was beating straight down. We were torpid we shouted no more, we would fain have slept. . . . At last the lorries slowed down and then halted.

Our legs were hurting us, our heads were heavy, our bodies filled with aches and discomforts. Growling, we buckled on our packs, which had never seemed so heavy.

"Why didn't they set us down properly in the village itself? It's easily seen they're not tired those Johnnies----"

Hardly had we alighted when certain of us slipped down on to the grass. Others went forward limping, their feet swollen in the stiff leather of the boots we had not taken off for two weeks. They propped themselves up on their rifles, leaned up against the trees, a mud-covered troop of foot-sore cripples that no will power held up any longer. Bourland arrived on his low bicycle and called to me:

"Jacques!--We are to march past in the village, the band at our head. The General is in the village square."

Upon the bank, the heads of the lads lying down rose up in indignation, the cripples flocked together.

"What? A parade now? Don't they care a curse about us? Aren't we broken up enough already?"

"No, the General wants to count the ones he hasn't got killed. . . ."

"Well, then, I won't march, I won't! Morache can yelp as much as he likes."

Sulphart shouted louder than all the rest, waving his still unsold boots.

"They're only good for turning out in processions on horseback. It's only in the trenches you never set eyes on them. They didn't join in the carnival up at the Three Ways."

"To hold a review after all we've just had shoved on us, they must be a set of criminals!" assented Lemoine soberly. "We ought to refuse."

As they were arguing a motor-car came to a halt, and Berthier got out of it. His mud soaked coat fell stiffly down like a cylinder of hardened clay: his eyes were sunken behind his glasses, he came forward with a dragging step. Plainly he was absolutely all in.

"We're fed up, Lieutenant," declared Sulphart to him with the firm and solid dignity of a free man. "We simply don't feel like marching past in front of any bally little civilians."

"Very likely not, indeed; but there's the General," replied Berthier quietly. "Come, my lads, packs up! There's a battalion of young recruits quartered there, it's up to us to let them see we're not a regiment of little girls."

They got into their equipment in spite of everything, grumbling the while. They lined up.

"By the right, form fours!"

On the road, we could see the band forming up, the regimental colour brought out of its case and take its place in the ranks. "En avant! --March!"

The regiment shook itself into motion. At the head the band was playing the regimental march, and at the victorious repetition of the bugles, it seemed to me that the weary backs were stiffening up. The start had been sluggish, had hung fire, but already the cadence was becoming crisper, and the feet were pounding the earth with a regular rhythmic beat. They were lay figures of mud, that marched along, boots of mud, thigh breeches of mud, coats of mud, and water-bottles for all the world like big lumps of clay.

Not one of the slightly wounded had quitted the ranks, but they were not a whit more pallid, not more exhausted now than the rest. All had underneath their helmets the self-same features of late dismay and horror: a march past of ghosts.

117

The country folk at the front have toughened hearts, and are now little to be touched with emotion after so many horrors, but when they saw debouching the foremost company of this regiment from the other world, their faces changed.

"Oh! the poor lads! . . ."

A woman fell aweeping, then others, then all the women. It was a homage of tears all along the houses, and it was only by seeing them weep that we understood how much we had suffered and endured. A sad pride came to the dullest of us. Every head went up, a new, strange, honourable arrogance in their eyes. The band drew us along, with all its brass sounding, the drums rolling, the most foundered seemed to revive, and one could feel them ready to shout, "It is we that made the attack! It is we that are back from up there!"

On the square, the battalion of young recruits was drawn up in new coats, and with bayonets fixed. A few paces to the front, the General, on horseback, with his staff in all their war paint. Not a voice in all our ranks, not a murmur to the front. Under the music, like fever in the blood, there was nothing heard but the mechanical cadence of the regiment on the march. The volunteer look of the men defiling by seemed fain to dominate all those silent boys who were presenting arms.

The General had stood up in his stirrups, and with a great dramatic gesture of his naked sword, he saluted our riddled colours, he saluted US. And all at once the regiment was no more than one single being. One single pride to be those that are saluted! Proud of our mud, proud of our toil and distress, proud of our dead! . . .

The bugles burst forth once more, and we entered into the main street, superb, glorious stiffened up, between a moving hedge of young soldiers keeping step with us. The girl of the post office, red-eyed, her head thrown well back, greeted us with her damp handkerchief, crying out something that was stifled in a sob.

Then Sulphart, pale as chalk, could hold in no longer.

"We're the fellows that made the attack!" he shouted to her in a mighty voice. "It was us!"

And from all the turning heads, from all the gleaming eyes, from every lip, the same cry of pride seemed to jet forth: "It is we! It is we!"

The sonorous music went to our heads like strong drink, seeming to bear us off in a kind of Sunday festival; we went forward, our loins filled with ardour, opposing to those tears our virile pride of conquerors.

Come, come! There will always be wars, always, always. . . .

THE company was going forward by fits and starts, stopped here by the rockets, farther on by the wounded men that were being carried down.

The broadening trench now and then came up out on to the surface, filled in by a shell, and before one might be seen emerging from the shadow comrades, with humping backs, running full-tilt through the fields, rifle in hand, and then jumping quickly down again into the shattered ditch. No one spoke, no one hardly even so much as grumbled: we filed on, quick, as if happiness had been waiting for us at the end of the journey.

"Look out!"--the word was passed down in a low voice by the orderly guide who was leading us up to the front lines--"there are two men on fatigue lying across the trench. We haven't had time yet to take them away."

Gilbert, who was walking next in front of me, warned me:

"Step out!"

I knocked into something: two swollen objects, two flabby hummocks. Trodden on by a whole relief, the flattened corpses were already covered over with a thin, filmy shroud of mud.

"Between this and to-morrow you won't be able to see them any more," said a voice.

The Boche heavy stuff was still coming over, regular, ferocious. But in that continuous rumbling we gave ear only to the shells that crashed close to us: the others were of no account whatever. At every salvo we went to ground, huddled up under our packs, watching for the red torch of the explosion. Then we would go on at a jolting trot.

Close up behind the back of the orderly, who now and then hesitated between two trenches, the men would grouse and grumble out of mere habit.

"It's most unfortunate. . . . Always the silliest bounders are the ones chosen to guide the others. You'll see he'll manage to lose our way for us."

At the double we crossed a road covered with chunks of stone, and leaving the trench, we turned round the ruins of the village, defiling behind the stumps of walls that came up to our waists. Where were we making for? To relieve whom? We had no notion.

"Quicker! quicker!" squeaked Morache.

The rockets were now seen very close, behind a steep bank, and their fantastic curve seemed to dive down on top of us. We no longer heard around us the half-stifled rumour of the reliefs, the wrangling buzzing of the fatigues; each and every noise was hushed, and under the mad thundering of the guns we felt close at hand the great uneasy silence of the trenches.

"Pass the word down for silence," murmured our guide.

"Don't be afraid," answered Sulphart, "nobody wants to sing."

A big wall ran right aross the plain, shattered, dismantled, with big patches almost untouched. It stood up black and tragic against this war time sky of a harsh whiteness. At long intervals a stump of a tree. Was that the sugar factory, since they were talking about it? Or the park of the château?

"There you are," said the orderly under his breath.

In the wall was a wider breach than usual, we passed through. . Bayonets caught in things, a water-bottle clinked, and, each man following another's silhouette, we advanced stumbling and knocking into the stones. With a long whistle two rockets went up along the same path.

"Don't budge!"

The blinding light lit up the whole brutally. Immobile, without so much as stirring the head, the men looked out. In one single glance they saw the crosses, the tombstones, the cypress-trees: we were in the cemetery. It was a huge yard of smashed-up stones, trees slashed to tatters, and dominating these ruins was a great austere Saint, holding on his folded arms a marble book, in which night by night flying, whispering shell-splinters engraved strange matters.

"This way, leading section," ordered Sergeant Ricordeau.

Our file followed him. A torpedo burst twenty paces off in a big red fountain. Everybody went down like a shot. In the dark a wounded man cried out.

"Come on, quick, now!" urged the Sergeant. . . . "Bréval's squad here."

In front of me, flattened up against a parapet of sandbags, a sentry growled.

"Pack up fools! If you bellow like that you will never get back, not a one of you. The Boches aren't twenty mètres away."

Ricordeau, who was sticking out his head, peering to recognize his people, was placing his men in position.

"Lemoine, to the parapet; you will take the first watch. You will have your orders passed up to you. Bréval, you have these three dug-outs for your squad. Look lively!"

Bréval and others went into a little narrow chapel without a roof, and I saw them thrust themselves under the earth, lying flat on their stomachs. Demachy, who was just in front of me, threw his satchel into a black hole at the foot of a slab of stone, and jumped down. I followed him. At the same moment a terrific explosion made the earth quiver, and there was a beating of hail on our stone roof.

"That was just in time," said Gilbert.

Groping and fumbling, we tried to discover the objects around us, and our hands glided on the cold walls. Above our heads the entrance opened, like a blue window.

"Let's stop that up and make a light."

We hung up a breadth of canvas folded in two, and Gilbert struck a light with his patent lighter. The candle with its squashed wick hesitated, vacillating, and then the light showed up our hole. The four walls were gleaming with damp. On the pavement of the cavern there was nothing but a dirty mattress of old newspapers, on which we could read the headlines in German.

"The old occupiers have left us something to read, you see. . . . I say, one of them has cut his name."

On the bare chalk, as a matter of fact, a German with vast patience had begun to engrave "Siegf. . . ." Why had he wanted to leave his name in this grave? . . . And the other one, the first who had been laid to rest there, he whose name must have been engraved on the cross, what had they done with him?

"You don't mind being down there? As far as that goes you know, with a blanket underneath and one on top, we won't be too badly off."

"And then those tombstones up there, they're pretty thick, and it would have to

120

drop clean on top of them to come through. I'm taking the second watch, from three to five; and what about you?"

We stretched ourselves out. The space was no wider than in a child's bed; in spite of our great coats, the blanket, and the thin layer of newspaper for bedding, we could feel under our loins the chill of the stone. I had put my head on Gilbert's shoulder, and with my hands slipped into my armpits and my coat-collar about my ears, I endeavoured to sleep. There was nothing to be seen, absolutely nothing.

Up above, in a frightened kind of growling, the bombardment was continuing, preparing their counter-attack, and now and then the battering-ram blow of a torpedo made the whole cemetery quake. A kind of lucid nightmare haunted my mind. Against my back I could feel the damp breath of the tomb that sent cold shivers over me.

"Are you cold?"

The bones? Where have they flung out their bones? A ridiculous notion pursues me. I should like to go outside to decipher the name, to find out in whose bed I happen to be lying. Then if a torpedo came slamming down there, it would be all over? Not even the trouble to bury us, no need even of a cross; that has been already erected for the other. Isn't it in a way tempting death, isn't it very like cheeking him, to make your bed in a grave? However, it is not our fault. . . .

Yes, I would really dearly like to know the name of that other fellow. In spite of myself I am thinking of him. I imagine him lying there, very straight and stiff. And superstitious, afraid, being straight and stiff like him, of being taken for a dead man, I curl myself up, I pull up my knees.

"How you thrash about!"

A heavy shadowy darkness presses us down. The two walls, coming together, squeeze us one up against the other, like two children in their mother's lap. Gilbert is not sleeping any more than myself, and against my cheek I can feel his quick breathing.

Siegfried. . . . Why didn't he stay here, seeing that he had carved his name? It was the other dead man that must have driven him away, who would not have him there; and he went to die outside, no matter where, among those broken stones chopped to pieces by the iron storm. Perhaps his even were the stiffened feet that a little while ago made me stumble.

I have seen a carbine hanging from the arm of a cross, satchels fastened on to it where the wreaths used to be; the shells have wrenched and twisted the railings. . . . Not so long ago I have gone through some of those country churchyards where the honeysuckles knotted their tendrils over forgotten tombs! A girl in a red bodice hoed and scraped the pathway. It was summer. No, they could never be as cold as we are, under their hillock of rich grass; we are more dead than they, under these stone slabs where we are shivering. A thrill of cold and distress sliding down by way of my sleeves has just frozen me down to the stomach. It is no lie, then, no fiction, the cold of the tomb that the poets talk of? Oh, how cold I am!

Up above the groping shells go on, always hunting for men in the blackness. For all that, we are going to sleep. Under the crosses there are fifty of us, a hundred of us, dead men sleeping. Resurrected, the sentries are on the watch, with hard eyes, above the breaking parapet. How many dreams, how many visions, to-night, in these eternal alcoves?

Certe,   ils   doivent   trouver   les   vivants   bien   ingrats

De dormir, comme ils font chaudement, dans leurs draps. . . .

. . . . . .

Three days--this makes three days we have been holding the cemetery, all smashed and pounded by the shells. Nothing to be done, nothing but wait. When everything will have been overturned and shattered, when there should be nothing left but a churned-up mixture of stones and men, they will attack. Then it is necessary that there should be live men remaining for that.

Between these four walls that are being loop-holed and bitten away, the company is a prisoner, isolated from the rest of the regiment by the sauce-pans that are digging into the ruins, the machine guns that sweep the communicating paths.

At nightfall some men on fatigue set off, and a few stretcher-bearers risk it. And quickly, working in the utmost concealment, they exhume a man from a great family vault where wounded men have been groaning for days, and no help possible for them. They steal a dead man from the cemetery.

There are still six more of them, in the vault that has been enlarged by the Boches. When you bend over their hole, you breathe in the hideous odour of their fever, and the imploring plaint of their indistinguishable, raucous breathing. One of them has been there for a week, abandoned by his regiment. He speaks no longer. He is a thing of tragic leanness, emaciated, with enormous eyes, hollow cheeks defiled with a sprouting beard, and fleshless hands, whose claws rake at the stone. He does not even move any more, so as to feel no more the deadened wound of his mangled thighs; but a dreadful thirst forces him to groan.

By night we take water to him, coffee when any comes up. But from mid-day all the water-bottles are empty. Then, parched with fever, he stretches out his lean neck and greedily licks the stone of the tomb, on which the water sweats and trickles down.

One lad, in a corner, scrapes at his white tongue with a knife. Another now lives only in the imperceptible panting of his breast, with eyes shut, teeth tight clenched, all his poor strength pulled together and concentrated to defend him against death, to save his little remnant of life that quivers and is about to slip away.

All the same he hopes, they all hope, even the one at the point of death. All of them are fain to live, and the lad keeps repeating persistently:

"To-night the stretcher-bearers are sure to come, they promised us yesterday."

Life. . . . how it defends itself up to the last shiver, up to the last gasp! Verily, if they had no hope of the stretcher-bearers, if the hospital bed did not gleam out like a point of happiness in their fever-dream, they would come forth from their tomb, in spite of their shattered limbs or gaping belly; they would drag themselves on through the stones with their claws, with their very teeth. It needs a terrific force to kill a man; it needs a tremendous amount of suffering to overthrow a man. . . .

And yet it happens. Hope flees away, resignation, all in black, settles heavily upon the soul. Then the man, resigned to his destiny, pulls up his blanket over him, says never a word more, and like that poor fellow dying in a corner of the tomb, he merely turns his feverish head and licks the weeping stone.

. . . . . .

You would say that nothing is alive in that stone yard of broken fragments baking in the sun. Last night we were shivering with cold in our holes, now we are suffocating. Nothing is stirring. Crammed up against the sandbag parapet, his silhouette of the same colour, the watcher is waiting, without a movement, fixed, immobile, like him whom you see lying before the chapel, his arms stretched out in the form of a cross, the back of his neck gaping wide, his skull swallowed up in the wound.

The shells are falling without ceasing, but we hear them no longer. Stupefied, feverish, we have gone to pay a visit in Sulphart's tomb. We recognize it by its sign:

MATHIEU, SOMETIME MAYOR OF THIS PLACE.

From morning to night he plays cards with Lemoine, and as he is a steady loser he cries out, swears at the other, and accuses him of robbing him. Lemoine remains quite placid.

"Don't you yell so much," he merely says, "you'll be waking the Mayor."

Heaped up, all four of us, in the narrow tomb, we pant and puff. It is only three o'clock; all the water-bottles have long been empty, and the ration party that starts at dusk will not be back before midnight. I am not talking any more so as not to be so thirsty. This dust of pounded stone and powder burns and parches our throats, and with dried lips and humming temples we think of drinking--of drinking as beasts drink, with our heads plunged in a bucket.

"You'll buy us a bucket of wine, eh, Gilbert?" repeats Sulphart. . . . "We'll get down on our knees all round it, and we'll drink like that, fit to burst."

Since he first said that to us the idea pursues us and sticks to us. That delight, impossible of fulfilment, fascinates us to the point of driving us crazy: to drink, to drink with the whole face, your chin, your cheeks--to drink out of a regular trough.

Every now and then Demachy bursts out in a fury. "Drink!" he cries, "I want a drink!"

Nobody has any left now, not a drop. Yesterday I bought a cup of coffee for forty sous, but to-day the seller preferred to keep it all for himself. There is a well, nevertheless, in the village: round it are lying some fifteen men. The Boche snipers are on the watch, perched up on top of a wall; they wait till the comrade who has devoted himself to the task arrives with all his water-bottles slung over his shoulder, and they bring him down, taking careful aim, like a head of game. Now a sous-lieutenant has been posted at the entrance to the trench, and he prevents any one from passing. No one now goes for water except by night.

"I tell you I'm going, I am!" bellows Sulphart. . . . "I'd rather take the chance of being brought down than peg out like this. I feel I'm going dotty. . . ."

"You're not going there; you'll get killed," says Lemoine to him.

Then it is on him that Sulphart turns his fury. "Naturally you don't care a hang, you hump of cow-dung! You're not thirsty. It's not the custom to drink in the fields; you are broken in to not drinking, at the tail of a plough, you Parisian in wooden shoes! You pig-stuffer! . . ."

"If you were as thirsty as all that," says Lemoine logically, "you wouldn't shout so much. . . ."

Then we all sit down again with our backs against the wall, and wait. Making war is nothing more than that: to wait. Wait for the relief, wait for letters, wait for the soup, wait for the dawn, wait for death. . . . And all that arrives, at its appointed hour: it suffices simply to wait. . . .

. . . . . .

Somebody sharply jerked up our canvas covering, flinging a handful of daylight into the vault.

"Come quick, Bréval is wounded."

Demachy got on his feet. He was sleeping with a veil tied over his face, on account of the flies.

"Eh, what! Bréval?"

And without taking off his flowered veil, that still exhaled the perfume of rice-powder, he ran towards the chapel where the rockets are stored, into which the corporal has been dragged.

He is wounded in the breast: a shrapnel bullet. Lying down, with his head on the altar step, he looks at the boys with eyes of uneasy distress, with wide eyes full of fear. Catching sight of Gilbert, he made a motion of his head, like a greeting.

"I am glad to see you, you know."

Demachy, with quivering hands, untied his veil.

"That's handy, that business of yours," said Bréval. "With these bitches of flies nobody can sleep. The boys were wrong to make game of you."

Suddenly full of weariness he shut his eyes. In spite of the first-aid dressing, a brown spot is widening on his overcoat. He has it, and soundly too. All at once his lip has fallen, and he has begun to cry like a child, to weep and to sob, with a dolorous plaint under his convulsive tears.

Gilbert lifted his head to take it on his arm, and leaning over him spoke to him in a choking voice.

"What's the matter. . . . You've not gone off your head. You mustn't weep, don't get notions into your mind; come now. You're wounded, that's nothing. On the contrary it's a bit of luck. They'll take you off to-night to the dressing station and to-morrow you'll be lying in a bed."

Without reply, without opening his eyes, Bréval went on steadily weeping. Then it was assuaged, and he said:

"It is my poor little girl that I am weeping for." He looked at Gilbert for a good minute still without speaking, then--seeming to make up his mind he said to him in a half whisper:

"Listen, I am going to tell you something, something for you alone; it is a commission. . . ."

Gilbert would have stopped him, talked to him about the pleasant consolation of being sent down from the line, would have deceived him. But he shook his head.

"No, I'm done for. I would like you to do a commission for me. You'll swear to me, eh? You will go to Rouen; you will see my wife. . . . You will tell her that it's ill done, what she has done. That I have suffered too much. I can't tell you everything, but she has played the fool with an assistant she took on. You will tell her that she mustn't, won't you, for the sake of our little girl. . . . And that I forgave her everything before I died. You'll tell her, won't you? . . . ."

And he began afresh to weep, silently. Nobody said a word. We all of us looked at him, leaning over him as we might over an opening tomb. At last he ceased to weep, with only a faint moan, and was silent for a moment. Then his teeth clenched, and sitting up on his elbows, with a fierce eye, he snarled:

"And after all no! I won't. . . . Listen, Gilbert, in the name of the good God, I ask of you to go to Rouen. You must go to Rouen! . . . You swear to me you will go. And you will tell her she is a bitch, do you hear, you will tell her that it was through her that I have been killed. . . . You must tell her that. . . . And you will tell it to everybody, that she's a filthy trollop, that she was leading the gay life while I was at the front. . . . I curse her, do you hear, and I wish she may die like me, with her Johnny. . . . You will tell her that I spat in her face before I died, you will tell her . . . ."

He pushed out his thin face, terrible, with a little red froth at the corner of his lips. Pale and drawn, Gilbert tried to soothe him. He had taken him round the neck very gently and wanted to lay him down. . . . The other, quite done and powerless, did not resist. He remained for a minute or so inert and lifeless, with his eyes shut, then big tears rolled from his closed lids.

Leaning over him, Gilbert touched his forehead lightly and close with his breath, just so that he felt against his lips the last sweat already forming in little pearls on his temples.

"Come, old boy, don't weep," he repeated in a voice hoarse with the tears he kept back. . . . "Don't cry, you are only wounded."

And he caressed with almost filial tenderness the poor thin head that went on weeping. Bréval murmured still lower:

"No . . . for the sake of the little girl . . . better not say all that to her. . . . You will tell her she must be wise and straight, mustn't she, for the sake of the child . . . that she must give her happiness, not a bad example. You will tell her she must sacrifice herself to the child. You will tell her that I asked this of her before I died, and that it is a hard thing to die like that. . . ."

The words rolled from his mouth, very gently, as his tears rolled. In the corner, his head in his bended arm Sulphart was sobbing. Lieutenant Morache, who had been informed, was livid. He did his best to control himself, but we could see his lips and his chin quivering.

Bréval moved no longer: nothing could be heard but his short hissing breathing. But suddenly he sat up with a jerk in Gilbert's arms, as if he was trying to get up, and wringing his hand hard he groaned chokingly.

"No . . . no. . . . I want her to know . . . I have had too much distress. . . . You will tell her she's a bitch, you will tell her. . . ."

He could hardly speak now, he had to stop exhausted. His head fell back a clumsy load on Gilbert's arm, whose coat was now being soiled with blood. Paler than the dying man, he was cradling him in his arms and gently wiped his mouth, on which the froth came up to burst in little pinkish bubbles. Bréval still tried to open his eyes, his too heavy lidded eyes, and was fain to speak still:

"Little girl happy . . . mustn't. . . . You will tell her, eh . . . you. . . ."

His prayer died out unsaid, as the last conscious look flickered and wavered in his piteous eyes. And as if he had fancied he could still save a moment of life for him by hiding him from Him that carries away the dead. Gilbert clasped him close to his breast, his own cheek against his cheek, his own hands under his shoulders, and his own tears falling on his forehead.

. . . . .

"They are attacking!"

Gilbert and myself have leaped up with one accord, deafened. Our blind hands hunt for the rifles and pluck away the spread of canvas that covers the entrance.

"They are in the sunk road!"

The cemetery is bellowing with grenades, it flames, it crackles. It is like a

125

madness of fire and uproar suddenly bursting out upon the night. Everybody is shouting. Nobody knows anything; no one has any orders: they are attacking, they are in the sunk road, that is all. . . .

A man runs past in front of our hole, and down he goes as if he had tripped on something. Other shadow figures pass, run, advance, give back. From a ruined chapel red rockets shoot up, calling for the barrage. Their day seems to be on us all at once; great wan stars burst above us, and as though in the glare of a lighthouse you can see spring up phantoms that rush about among the crosses. Hand grenades are bursting, flung on all sides. A machine gun slips under a tombstone like a snake and begins to shoot, with rapid fire, sweeping the ruins like a scythe.

"They are in the road," repeat various voices.

And clinging flat against the sloping bank, men keep on hurling grenades, without ever stopping for a moment, from the other side of the wall. Men are firing over the parapet, without ever dreaming of taking aim. All the tombs are open, all the dead have risen, and still blind they are slaying in the dark, without seeing anything, they are slaying either the night itself or else men.

Everything stinks of powder. The white rockets as they fall send fantastic shadows scampering over the bewitched cemetery. Close by me Maroux is hiding his head and firing between two sandbags from which the earth is trickling away. A man is walking among the stones, like a worm that has been cut in two by a stroke of the spade. And other red rockets still go up, seeming to cry out: "Barrage! barrage!"

The torpedoes are falling in volleys, smashing everything in, crumbling everything. They come in salvoes, and it is just like a peal of thunder that reverberates five times.

"Fire! fire!" yells Ricordeau, who is not to be seen.

Stupefied, dazed, we reload the Lebel that burns our fingers. Demachy, his own satchel already emptied, has gathered up the grenades from a fallen comrade and is flinging them, with the large sweeping gesture of a slinger. In the uproar you can hear cries, groanings, without giving heed to them. There are certainly some poor fellows who have been buried under. For a moment two rockets disclose a long dead man, lying out on a tombstone, at full length, like a man of stone.

In a storm our own barrage at length arrives, and a red hedge of time-fused shells splits the night with a noise of thunder. The shells follow one another, mingling their paths in the air and forge an iron hedge above us. Percussion shells and timed shells plant themselves in a fury before our lines, barring the road, and covered with plumes of rockets, clattering with shells, the cemetery seems to belch with flames. From one parapet to another the men run without knowing what they are doing, stumbling, pushing one another. Many go down, heavy of head, bent double, and always the tombs vomit up others, whose silhouettes are always discovered by the shrapnel and the rockets that hem them in.

In the centre, before the impassive saint, the torpedoes fall like pickaxe blows, slashing to pieces the soldiers under the tombstones, smashing the wounded at the foot of the crosses. In the tombs, upon the broken stones they groan, they drag themselves about. Someone is knocked over beside me and seizes my leg in a furious grip while he breathes in a hoarse death rattle.

The hurried slamming blows hammer up on the nape of the neck. It is falling so close that you go all anyhow, blinded with the bursts. Our shells and their shells join and do yelling battle together. You can no longer see, can know nothing now. It is red, and smoke, and uproar. . . .

What, is it from the Boche, or from the seventy-five firing short? . . . The pack of fire surrounds us, tears at us. The smashed crosses riddle us with whistling splinters. . . . The torpedoes, the grenades, the shells, even the tombs are bursting, everything is blown up; it is a volcano in full burst. The night in eruption will crush us all to nothingness.

Help! Help! Men are being murdered!

CHAPTER XIII
THE HOUSE WITH THE WHITE BOUQUET

DINNER has just come to an end. How cosy and comfortable we should be if only they were holding their tongues. The yellow light of the candle is dancing in an empty bottle. There is a little wine still in the bottom of the cups, a pale gold wine, a little cloudy, that makes the fingers sticky, and goes caressingly down the throat. In the fire-place great thick beams are burning and crackling themselves away.

Leaning over a smoking basin, red of face, and glistening with sweat, Sulphart is absorbed in preparing our mulled wine. He has rolled up his sleeves up to his elbows and opened his shirt wide over his hairy chest. At his left side are hanging six safety pins stuck in like brooches, the only badge that was never stolen from the soldiers. Lemoine is setting in front of the fire, on a billet of wood, his huge useless hanging hands placidly joined between his knees, and he is watching his pal, carrying on with a little whistling noise that sounds perfectly meaningless, but in which Sulphart being a very touchy fellow, divines criticism.

"Don't imagine you can teach me how to mull wine, no, you herring skin!" he jeers with a touch of sourness. "I say and I hold that to sweeten it you must add two cups of water to the litre of wine and stick in five proper lumps of sugar to the cupful."

"That's too much," replies Lemoine quietly. "You don't taste the wine then."

"Don't taste the wine then!" he says.

But instead of flying into a rage, Sulphart simply shrugs his shoulders, as if he was benevolently allowing himself to be insulted with impunity.

"I prefer not to argue, here; you start turning nasty at once."

Lemoine makes no answer. He spits into the fire and ponders over things. The wine begins to sing in the basin.

The walls of the farm are very old, dumpy, and blackened. The window is filled with small panes covered with dust which the moonlight passed through in a hesitating way. Wonderful great cobwebs, that you might fancy are grey velvet, hang down from the roof in which an enormous beam of chestnut wood is warping. All the war and all the life of the fields, all that is held in this darkroom, expressed by certain incongruous objects lying about casually in it, earthenware on a bandy-legged chest, cartridges in a jar, sacks of nobody knows what, rifles in a row, helmets, a great winnowing fan.

Huddled up on a little milking stool Broucke is roasting his legs, watching the steam rising out of his blue trousers, which he has put to dry over the fire-place with Maroux' linen.

"I'll be able to sleep better," he explains to our new corporal. "The lice won't chew my stomach any more."

At the big table--an old carpenter's bench all hacked about, with a plank across two baskets by way of a chair--the squad was finishing its meal, in a clatter of noise. One comrade was eating as he stood, lapping off his tin plate. Down on his knees another was splitting up some wet wood, rainy autumnal branches that burned with big volumes of smoke.

Brutally thrust in, the door opened, letting the cold night enter like an intruder.

"The distributions, my lads!" cried fat Bouffioux. "Who is coming with me?"

"I'm going," replied Maroux.

"I'm with you," said little Bélin getting up. "Don't forget to come back, I say," cried Sulphart to the cook, "if you don't, look out for your skin. You--promised to stand the drinks."

The door shut again, and our intimate snugness seemed suddenly better, the warmth more agreeable.

"You might think you were at your own fireside," murmured one fellow happily.

Rare moments when happiness comes to pay us a visit, like a friend that we had never hoped to see again. Rare moments when you remember you had once been a man, had once been a master, the most powerful of all: your own master. A fire flaming nobly, a table, a lamp--there is the whole past returning.

One of the last comers having wiped his hands on his corduroy trousers, delicately slipped a photograph out of his dog's-eared little book of military papers.

"She's a little darling, eh? That's my wife--she wasn't eighteen when I married her."

"You have better taste than she had," said Sulphart to him.

"Who has been taking your place while she's been a grass widow?"

Broucke began to laugh. But a little spasm made the comrade's mouth twitch, and almost stuttering he replied:

"Don't talk rot. I'm all off any humbugging about that kind of thing. If you were a married man you'd understand."

"I am married," said Sulphart with a swaggering air. "Only I'm not jealous; mine shows what she feels by sending me parcels."

The others had each and all brought out a photo, from a well-worn pocketbook or a soldier's little portfolio, greasy with sweat. They passed them round from hand to hand, awkward portraits of nice looking girls all in their Sunday finery, and housewives in black dresses, clasping to them the small boy with the carefully tied necktie.

At the big table they were squabbling noisily over the dessert--tasteless, dusty biscuits that were a contribution from Gilbert. They were drinking somewhat copiously. In front of the fire little Bélin was spinning a yarn.

"It was a lot of fellows that had died in the field hospital. Didn't you see the coffin of the fourth? The blood had run out through and had stained the flag. That was the sergeant, that one was."

They drained cupful after cupful, their faces lighted up.

"You remember the day they knocked old father Hundred's face in. Thirty litres among eight! Pretty well full everybody was."

"And the new adjutant, a Corsican. . . ."

Sulphart and Lemoine, who had divided the mulled wine, were exchanging reminiscences at the very top of their voices as if they had been confessing to the whole farm.

"They were all howling, 'Don't shoot! English comrades!' And then all at once, pif!--ping! ping! It was the Boches--Ah, the dirty dogs!'"

"And I was going forward. I was holding my satchel in front of me as if that could stop a bullet. What silly asses you are at those moments?"

Demachy was listening to them as he drank in the hot breath from his mulled wine. At that moment we could hear the noise of heavy feet galloping in the yard, and Bouffioux came in puffing and blowing.

"Eh, boys," he said, throwing down his bag full of lentils on the big table, "we're going to have some fun. I'm going to stand treat in a shanty where there are girls."

Everybody had turned towards him, allured but--mistrustful.

"What? You're having us on. . . . No, honest injun', you're trying to stuff us up."

But the brightened face of the fat fellow from Normandy, and with his skin stretched tight and radiant, his shining eyes, all proved that he was telling the truth.

"Chickens that are on, rather," he affirmed, "chickens that are asking for it."

"They'll have it!" shouted Sulphart.

They all rose up tumbling over one another, and crowded round Bouffioux.

"It was big Chambosse at the baggage-master's that gave me the tip. It's a crib at the end of the old town, a big house with all its shutters closed, as you might expect. And so that you can't make any mistake, the fillies have stuck a white bouquet at the door."

An uproar of laughter and cries broke out. Their flesh kindled, they got ready to go out hurriedly and dug each other in the ribs with chaffing and fooling. Feverishly Broucke pulled his trousers on again, rolling his flannel belt like a rope round them all wet as they were, without smoothing it out of its folds.

"Don't go without me," he implored.

"On patrol lads," bellowed Sulphart, already certain he was going to captivate all the girls.

Gilbert alone remained calm. He deemed to mistrust the whole affair.

"I know that fellow, Chambosse," he said to me, "a rogue, a leg puller. He probably wanted to make a hare of that big, fat idiot."

But the others were already fixed up to go.

"Aren't we going to wait for Maroux?"

All of them protested, in a hurry to get there.

"Ah, no, let's get along there quick, often they have too many people there. He'll come along after us."

We set off. The earth frozen hard in that November night rang under our feet like a hollow box. The sky itself seemed to be frozen, a great wide sky of dull tin, speckled with gold. In the neighbouring barns men were singing in chorus. Through a window with broken panes I caught sight of some faces lit up with brutal clearness by a lantern, and in the dark background of the room, shadow shapes dancing to the strains of an accordeon. In front of the mayor's house, squatting round a bonfire, there were machine gunners cooking a hot mess in a dixie.

"Where are you off to?"

"On a reconnaissance," replied Sulphart, who was hurrying, well on in front.

We were strung out in Indian file, like a relief going through the communication trenches. We were playing at war, knowing nothing else.

"Not so fast up there in front," cried Bélin.

"Pass down the word, the third company is not following."

"Look out for the wire!"

Sulphart was imitating the harsh crow's voice of the commandant.

"You do get lost here, in this confounded sector, you do get lost. Orderly here. . . ."

The moonlight fell like fine dust on the fields, and laid the shadows of the trees down on the white highway. The night had unmoored the trees anchored to the soil, and we could see them take the ocean, on the infinite mist. Over yonder the weary guns were barking no longer. We began to sing. Broucke was our guide without knowing where to. Gilbert and I both came behind, linked arm in arm.

En revenant de Montmartre,
De Montmartre à Paris.
J'recontre un grand prunier qu' était couvert de prunes
Voilà l'beau temps.

We were singing at the top of our voices as though we had it in mind to spend our brutal, animal joy in mere noise.

Voilà l'beau temps
Ture-lure-lure,
Voilà l'beau temps
Pourvu que ça dure.
Voilà l'beau temps pour les amants.

"Don't shout like that," Maroux said to us--he had just come up with us, running, "we'll all get pinched."

"That's right," approved Lemoine, who was following, dragging his great lazy feet, "and if the chickens hear that kind of bellowing, it'll be midday before we get in."

Obediently we choked down our joy into big bursts of subdued laughter.

"I'm in form," confessed Sulphart. "Appears the mistress of the place is a ripping dark girl," explained Bouffioux, "a real fine woman.

"I've seen her, I have," cried Broucke, "she's got a pair of eyes as big as a plate. . . ."

"Ah, well, if it's that one we'll have lots of fun. . . ."

We were arriving at the edge of the country, where the farmhouses were spaced out. Some dark object took shape crouched up on the side of the road.

"A sentry," exclaimed Maroux.

The soldier, an old Territorial, eyed us as we advanced, without moving a muscle, propped up on his rifle. A comforter that was wrapped round him up to the eyes muffled his voice.

"You haven't got the password," he asked us. "It's Clermont."

We went by quickly, all but running, and presently through the thin night we could perceive a big white building, painted by the moon, with all its shutters closed.

"Th306 it is."

We approached with soundless feet. Yes, there it was indeed, and a white bouquet was fixed over the doorway. Everybody saw it at the same moment and a murmur of delight gave thanks to Bouffioux.

"I'm going to hammer," said Sulphart all of a twitter.

He knocked. We listened, hardly venturing to breathe, crowding close, elbow against elbow. Broucke gave a little laugh like a hen clucking. Sulphart with his ear glued to the panel of the door signed to us to be quiet. We heard someone walking inside, then a key turned in the lock and the door opened a little showing as it were a strip of light. For a second we caught a glimpse of a handsome woman's face, very pale, with hair in smooth black bands. Then straightway the door was closed again brutally.

"That's her," Broucke had cried, having seen nothing at all of her but her eyes, her beautiful big eyes.

"What's going on?" asked Bouffioux in amazement.

And we stayed there dumbfounded, disappointed in front of the fast shut door. Nobody could understand.

"She's crazy, the wench," growled Sulphart ready to fly in a rage.

"Hi, inside there. . . ."

And he banged on the door.

"They're not going to leave us out in the yard . . . no."

Lemoine, who kept in the background, his hand stuck in his pockets, silently wagged his head.

"She guessed there were a lot too many of us," he judged. "Some of us ought to have taken cover."

"That's no reason for not opening," raged Sulphart.

And brutally he banged harder still on the door with his clenched fist. There was no answer of any kind.

"No, now I'd train that one with a stick if I was in civilians again," he muttered through his clenched teeth.

Lemoine was still hoping. He could not believe that this warm happiness he had so much desired had so quickly fled away.

"No, kid," he murmured, "she's coming back."

"We've got plenty of stuff," cried Bouffioux, who understood the heart of woman.

Lemoine, at all risks, shouted out the word for the night, "Clermont! Clermont!" thinking that perhaps no one was admitted into the house except soldiers in due form.

Everybody according to his own notion started to shout something, thinking to persuade the women to open.

"Hi, little girls, we've come to give you a song! Open the door for us, come on, we've got our pennies. We'll buy champagne."

Plucking the strings of an imaginary mandolin, Sulphart began to sing a serenade under the lighted windows.

Si je chante sous ta fenêtre
Ainsi qu 'un galant troubadour. . . .

Another was drumming louder against the door in a regular rhythm to the cry of "Let-us-IN . . . let-- us -- IN," while Broucke was covering himself with scratches, trying to clamber up walls as far as the closed venetian blinds. Still no one was opening. So then we all began to sing in chorus:

Si tu veux faire mon bonheur,
Marguerite. Marguerite.
Si tu veux faire. . . .

Women should love music. The door opened again, this time it stood wide open.

132

"Ah," cried our band.

It was like a long cry at a gala of fireworks when the first rocket goes up. And we rushed forward. . . .

The dark beauty was standing back holding up her lamp so as to throw the light on us. They wanted to go in all at once, and bumped and squashed each other, laughing. Having been the first to break his way in, Sulphart was already thrusting out his hands greedily. The woman pushed him back.

"You are coming to have a good time," said she in a hard voice that amazed me; "do you want to look? . . . Here, it's a pretty sight, well worth looking at. . . ."

And with a hard brutal gesture she pushed open a door.

In the great room, cold and bare a single wax light kept vigil near a little iron bed. A child was lying on it, all in white, its frail hands clasping on its tiny breast a big black crucifix. A sprig of boxwood was steeped in a saucer. Without even a cry, stricken with fright, the squad swirled back and away. . . .

It is the custom, in this countryside, to place a bouquet at the door of a house where a child has died.

CHAPTER XIV
LOVE'S OWN WORDS

THE rain was lashing both the mud and the men. You did not see it, but you could hear it hailing down its gusts on the sodden earth and drenched soaking overcoats.

The black night hid everything, a thick night, with no sky visible, no horizon, and the last mess parties leaving the trench had nothing to guide them but the stifled buzzing and humming of voices. The men were going on, their eyelids screwed up, their cheeks frozen cold. The wind whistled in their ears, a lost wind that could find nothing to shake, neither branches, nor things of any kind.

Around the travelling kitchens the squads came flocking and pressing. Soldiers were cowering underneath the carts like beggars in doorways and porches. The first to be served were bumping each other, holding out their plate or their bottle. The rain was getting in solid lumps into the open boiler, and the man from the last squad, who was trampling in a regular pool, grumbled as he pushed at the others.

"It soon won't be a stew we'll be getting, it will be just soup."

Standing on his cart like a wretched booth owner of a country fair who insists on going through his parade, a cook was brandishing a great cross made of white wood, and brand new.

"Isn't the seventh here?" he was shouting. "Who was it ordered a cross?"

He was growing excited, seemed to be offering it like a token for a lottery. The men asked one another questions.

"They've got somebody killed in the seventh?"

"Yes, Audibert, a torpedo. They buried him in the sunken road."

Rain streaming from them, their trousers glued to their thighs, they splashed about as they chatted. Several were leaning over the gurgling cask and watching the distribution of the wine. Sulphart kept watch for a good minute over the distribution of his rolls of bread, sodden and sticky, spitted on to his cane, then he left the group.

"You take the letters, Demachy. I'm going to get the drink."

The letters. That was all that Gilbert had come for. He had asked to be allowed to go on the mess fatigue--four hours to go and return in the sticky glue of the mud in the communication trenches--to make sure of getting Suzy's letter, to hunt for it himself in the quartermaster's pile; it was now five days since he had last had anything from her, five nights that he had been raging at his loophole against the baggage-master, the quartermaster, the cooks, all the people that must of course have stolen his letters. This evening unable to contain himself any longer, he had volunteered to go on the ration fatigue.

Several times he stopped the old re-enlisted soldier who was hurrying from the cask to the cooking carts, supervising the cooks.

"Are there any letters for me?"

But the quartermaster had no time.

At length, the wine having been distributed, he came and took shelter under a cart and brought out his letters from a sack, tied up in bundles according to the squads. At once all the scattered shadows loomed up through the night and fell into groups.

The letters! The letters!

The circle buzzed and drew closer round the cart, the first ranks down on their hams, the others between the wheels. Everybody wanted to be as near as possible so as to hear the better. This was the best of all rations that was now about to be given out, all the happiness to be got for twenty-four hours. Lighted by a pocket electric torch, whose beam was muffled under a cap, the quartermaster read none too well. All listened with hands and heart outstretched towards him.

"Here! . . . Here! . . ."

Every man as soon as he had his packet in his hands, quickly looked for his own letter with his wet fingers, and in spite of the thick darkness, in spite of the blinding rain he recognized it immediately, by its mere shape, only by the feel of it. The bag was rapidly emptied. A murmur of disappointment rose up.

"Well, and what about us then? . . . Aren't there some for me? Are you sure, have you looked carefully?"

Those who had got nothing went away out of heart, and to ease themselves of their impotent anger they were eyeing the quartermaster with a nasty look as if they had really suspected him of throwing their letters away.

"Don't you worry, he gets his own alright, he does."

Gilbert was happy. As he took his bundle he had at once recognized Suzy's big envelope sticking out beyond all the others. A little wave of happiness went up to his head.

Now that he had his letter in his pocket he was no longer in any hurry to read it, he did not wish to expend all his delight at one go. He would taste it phrase by phrase, slowly, when he was in bed in his hole, and he would go to sleep with their sweetness in his heart.

In the field of shadows, among the carts sunk deep in the mud that the cooks were trundling along by the wheels, swearing the while, men were hailing one another. Heavy silhouettes hooded under bits of canvas, sheepskins rudely fastened with coarse string, strange shadowy forms laden with bags, with dishes, and with water cans. To keep the stew safe they were covering the bottles as well as they could with a lappet of an overcoat, the corner of a hood, a newspaper turned into a lid. Driven by gusts of wind, the rain was falling thicker than ever, thicker and fiercer. It drummed on the helmets and slipped down necks, in spite of the handkerchief tied round by way of scarf. Everybody was shivering.

"Off we go, the third. . . ."

The fatigues were starting back again, company by company, in long staggering files. In a hum and murmur the black plain emptied itself of its shadowy forms.

The mud reached up to mid-leg in the communication trench. Water ran out of everything--out of the sodden sticky walls, out of the very night. They splashed heavily in this river of black bird-lime, and to avoid being wholly stuck in the mud, it was necessary to put one's feet exactly in the print of one's predecessors, and walk from hole to hole. Nothing could be heard but the sucking clack of feet wrenched out of the mire and the growlings of the men who were forced to walk sideways on account of their burdens. The softened wall stuck to their elbows, and lumps of mud fell into the buckets of wine or the stew with a disheartening "plop."

The farther they went the deeper became the river. Hesitating feet would search for a solid patch to plant themselves on, then one false step and the man would slip into a drainage pit up to the knees. Then, as he couldn't possibly get any wetter now he would jerk out a resolute . . . "b----" and set off again straight forward through thick and thin deliberately going into the mire. Chaff now began to mingle with the swearing.

"I'm going to ask the Colonel to fetch my wife here, I am."

"I say, have you seen in the papers that they can't get a cab now in Paris coming out of theatres at night?"

"Don't lose your wool, the barometer is at 'set fair.'"

Every step was a fresh effort, as the mud kept sucking down the clumsy boots, and in spite of the rain they had to stop and take a breather. Their backs humped, their hands seeking warmth in their pockets, the men would puff and pant. The foreseeing ones never forgot their cup, it passed from hand to hand and everyone dipped up a draught of wine from the canvas bucket, or indeed by way of a treat they would drink a little hot coffee out of the can.

There was no firing going on in the trenches, they were too much benumbed under the rain. Not a single shell. There was nothing to be heard but the dull striving onward of the fatigue party. At long intervals the weary troop would knock up against another coming in the opposite direction or against a relief. The two files would then struggle front to front, obstinate, neither willing to give way to the other. An officer in a lowered hood kept launching orders that nobody listened to. Insults flew busily from one band to the other.

"You move back there . . . talk about a set of blighted idiots . . . we're loaded up . . . ."

"We can't. There are stretcher-bearers behind."

A wan rocket whose light was thinned and diluted in the rain disclosed for a moment a fatigue party laden with tools. Then it all melted together. Inlaid in the wall, legs and back well into the mud, the men passed each other in opposite directions, with a confused tumult of curses. We set off again with growls in the rear.

"Not so fast, in front there. . . . Send the word along that we're not keeping up. . . ."

At the next turn, the blinded column suddenly came to a halt in front of a fresh obstacle. Only the foremost knew, the others could see nothing but the line of bent backs, losing themselves in the blackness. Frozen hands laid down their burdens.

"Well, then, what now? Are we going on again?"

From the front came back the order:

"Back there . . . make way for a wounded man."

The ditch choked with mire was barely wide enough for a stretcher, and it was necessary to leave the way clear for the bearers. The tail end of the fatigue party ebbed back with a great fat splashing of violently churned mud, as far as the last parallel. Others on hands and knees tucked themselves away into niches, and those who had no holes to flatten themselves into, placing their bread or their vessels up on the edge of the communication trench, hoisted themselves up out of it, clutching and clambering up the viscid parapet, the mud of which gave way under the palms.

Exclamations were heard:

"My wine's all bunged over the ground."

Kneeling on the edge of the sloping wall, the men watched the wounded man go by. Something stiff under the dark brown blanket, the clumsy boots sticking out from under. Haggard and pale of face, his eyes enormous, his lips shut tight, he did not speak a word, nothing but a hoarse moaning when the bearers knocked the stretcher against something. He seemed not to see any one, as though he was looking within himself at life ebbing away. His hand was hanging down like a dead thing.

Almost crushed under their burden, the stretcher-bearers toiled and strained on, skating and slipping in the mud, and as the dull buzzing murmuring noise of another fatigue was coming nearer, the foremost carrier called out a warning in a spent voice:

"Make way. . . . A wounded man."

It was necessary to wait until the file was formed up again in order to make a fresh start. The squads were hunting for one another, mere voices lost in the blackness and the rain. The water had burst all the paper lids and the wet streaming down from the walls was dropping into the dishes. From the tail voices were constantly calling:

"Not so fast . . . we're not keeping up. . . ." But the rain was hunting them on before it, slashing at the frozen cheeks and they went on splashing in the mud, hearing nothing at all, seeing nothing at all, spent and worn out links in the long benunbed file.

At the Nancy parallel where our section was in reserve the fatigue split off into two portions, Sulphart having put down his skewerful of rolls and his dish of stew went from hole to hole.

"Grub, boys," he cried.

At the same time as his voice they could hear the raging rain. Sleepy growls answered him.

"You can stick it where the monkey. . . ! You and your grub. Good Lord, how it's coming down. You'd want to be hungry!"

For all that a few came out. In a narrow shelter, level with the earth, a candle sprang to life. Squatting down they filled their mess-tins, and you could hear them eating.

"I'm going to take my cupful of wine," said Broucke.

But from out of his hole Maroux cries out, waking up:

"Pass me the bucket of wine and the brandy. I don't mean any one to touch them. I'll share it out to-morrow at dawn."

Gilbert took them to him with the bundle of letters, and then scampered off to his own hole. He bent low to pass under the sandbags and went leaping. It splashed just as if he had put his foot in a river. In spite of the plank he had set up edgewise to make a barrier, the rain had penetrated into his shelter, and as it was dug with a slope, it had made a regular little pool towards the entrance. To kneel in the mud once again in order to scoop a drainage hole with a trenching tool, to bail it out once more with his bully-beef tin, to struggle against the water that slips in all the same. . . . He hadn't courage for it. So much the worse, he would stay lazy instead of lying down full length.

He pulled off his waterproof coat and was quite happy at finding his great-coat dry. But in the night the rain was drumming and pattering and he smiled as he listened to it. He was in a shelter; he was at home; nothing to do but read his letter, then read it again, then go to sleep with it.

Having unrolled his puttees--one mass of mud--and having scraped his boots, he slid his soakin feet into two little sandbags that would keep them warm for him. Then he rolled himself up in his blanket, threw his glistening rubber coat over his knees and snuffed his damp candle. Then, with nothing more to be desired, just for the moment. . . .

He read:

"I am extremely pleased with this place; the hotel is very gay and jolly. From a distance you can't see anything but its red roof; the mimosas hide all the rest.

"By the way, in the hotel I've come across a friend of mine I've told you about before, Marcel Bizot. He is a charming boy that I shall be awfully pleased to introduce to you, after the war.

"We often go out together. You don't mind that, do you, my own big boy? I like better to tell you about it myself, because there are idiots that have met us, and I think they're quite up to writing nasty things to you. I've been to Le Mal Infernet with him. Le Mal Infernet, you remember. . . ."

Outside a relief was passing by, a slow rumble of dull noises. The water was always streaming at the entrance to the dug-out, and drop by drop it dripped weeping into the pool.

A fresh sweet perfume rose up from the letter--verbena. Once upon a time she used to pursue him with her scent spray held under his nose, to frighten him. So far away now, the time of perfumes. And yet, so near to his heart. . . . with, aye, a thought vague and wandering he listened to the rain singing its dirge.

Sulphart lifted the canvas and, simply spouting with water, jumped down into the hole.

"Ouf! That's that. . . . You had a letter?"

"Yes," replied Gilbert in a far away voice.

Was he thinking? Motionless, his smile as of a disappointed child hovering at the corner of his lips he was looking into space, far, far off, with an absent-minded air.

"Your news is good?"

The rain . . . You might have thought a drop of rain in his look also.

"Yes, good. . . ."

CHAPTER XV
EN REVENANT DE MONTMARTRE

WE were gazing at the countryside with a very heedless eye: in Artois or in Champagne, in Lorraine or in Flanders, whether they are fringed with elm trees or with pale gold fields, with bogs or with vines, the roads are all the same to the rag-picker: dust or maybe mud that leads, by hard stages, from rest to the trenches.

Leaning out of the back of the lorries, soldiers with whitened eyelashes amused themselves crying "Baa! baa!" and the convoy went clanging and clattering on carrying their sheep calls along with the clamour. Others were singing.

This roadway, carrying men, always men seemed to me alive with an infernal life, and I fancied I could see, afar off, all these tributaries of dust that inexhaustibly feed the dried up bed of the great nameless river, the broad Styx of stone and smoke where seem to rest all the world's drowned on a silt of wreckage and tangled, blighted creepers.

Behind us rose up the black buildings of a field hospital, and by way of appendage, a whole orchard of wooden crosses. They stood up straight and stiff on their little chalky mounds, correctly in line. Eternally ready for the great Review, and a little farther off had been laid to rest the "tirailleurs,' the colonials, with their heads towards Mecca, watched over by the narrow board shaped to a pointed arch.

At the far end of the cemetery, the territorials were at work. We went up to them, without thinking of anything, simply to look on. It was graves they were digging, a whole alley of graves. Catching sight of us the old things had stopped their digging, as though they were ashamed. One of them, leaning, on his shovel, gave us an explanation with an embarrassed air.

"It is orders, you see. . . . Before a hot bit of work it's better to take precautions and be ready. . . . The last time, there were some that had to wait for three days; luckily it was the winter time."

We made no answer. We were looking at our destined holes. . . . First of all of us Sulphart burst into indignation:

"Ah, no!" he exclaimed, "this trick, it's too much. . . . To let us have this for a movie show before going up again to the butcher's, that's simply putting it across a fellow."

And like a shot he was off to tell the commandant who happened to be passing by on horseback. We had just time to see him come to attention and say two words: with one bound the horse was up the bank. Crimson, choking with wrath, the commandant was shouting to the frightened oldsters:

"Will you get to hell out of this? . . . Clear out, I tell you, or I'll get my poilus to chuck you out with their toe in your rump. . . Who gave you that order? I order you to tell me that!"

All the territorials had filed off, abandoning their implements; there was nobody left now but one tall old man, who was listening with his head down, contemplating his feet turned into big clods of clay.

"Are you deaf? . . . I want to know who set you on to that work?"

"There was no harm meant, Commandant," stammered the old man in a voice like an old nanny-goat, "it doesn't distress me at all, that job, it's my special line. I am a sexton, a grave digger in civilian life, at Prieuré-sur-Claise, by Mézières, Indre."

All the while he was speaking he was pulling at his blue coat with his earthy fingers, as though he had meant to make it come down below his stomach. Disarmed from his anger, the commandant looked at him with a kind of surly pity.

"Come, clear out of it," he said with a shrug of his shoulders. "I'll see about this myself."

And leaving his horse there, he went over and disappeared into the hospital, from which the attendants were following the little scene while rolling up bandages.

With no chaff or fooling, our hearts gnawed with discomfort, we rejoined our comrades in the field where they were having a simple meal. We used to eat in little groups, always the same men together: those who were always having big parcels shared with the chaps that had as big, the little parcels ate with the little parcels, and those who got none at all used to eat by themselves, pooling their poverty to buy themselves a litre of wine. The cutest of them used to flatter and pay court to Gilbert, knowing that he was never particularly stingy, and readily gave a share of his tinned stuff to comrades stuffed and fed up with macaroni.

Standing behind him a little lean fellow with his cheeks peppered with freckles said to him with a sly air.

"Ah! that was playing the game the other day, when you wouldn't let them take you off to a nice cushy job, when you wouldn't leave the rest of the boys. . . ."

Demachy, lying on his side, was nibbling at a straw. Roughly, without even turning round, he made answer:

"No, cut that out, my lad. . . . It wasn't playing the game at all: it was idiotic. But it pleases me now and then, it does, to do idiotic things."

A week before, while we were having long rest, one of his cousins had come to see him, an officer with an embroidered armlet, who had offered to have him transferred into the motor transport.

"Thanks," Gilbert had replied, "but as far as motors go I only drive my own."

We had all been astonished, and Sulphart himself, who nevertheless would have been a heavy loser if Gilbert had gone, had sworn at him for a whole evening, shouting like a deaf man that water always went to the river and strokes of luck to "chaps too silly to know how to work them."

To me Gilbert had made his confession:

"The pleasure of swanking, you may know, of landing somebody a nasty one by way of a retort. . . . It was most of all for that. . . . I didn't even take time to reflect, it just slipped out of me like a curse. And afterwards I couldn't go back on it, it was too late. . . . Isn't it stupid, eh, to stake your life for a word? . . . But really and truly he disgusted me with his nice laced boots and his straw-coloured gloves."

I had never seen him drink as much as he did that night, and he had filled fat Bouffioux, who that same day had been sent back into the ranks, his place at the kitchen being taken by a mason who had three children.

Our walk in the cemetery and the discovery of the empty graves had completely and finally overwhelmed the sometime cook, whose morale was already very low. Nothing more than his way of wagging his head and repeating, "I'm afraid they're too much for us. . . ." would have taken the heart out of a crack regiment. He recounted the incident to Gilbert, exaggerating the number of the holes, and Sulphart could find nothing to add except this comforting assurance:

"I swear to you there won't be any jostling, everybody will be able to find room to settle down comfortably. . . . Ah! les tantes!"

As he ate Bouffioux said little, and from time to time put uneasy queries which gave away the grounds of his meditation.

"In your opinion, is it really as bad as that, as sectors go? Do the stretcher-bearers do their duty properly where there's tough work going on? . . . Is it certain, anyway that we've got to attack? . . . In your opinion how many fellows can get bowled over in a business of that kind?"

To reassure him, Maroux made answer:

"Perhaps a bit more than half; one never knows." Bouffioux, now instructed, asked nothing further. He drank his coffee--the mason's coffee--as clear as small beer and the same colour, and lying on his back, he gave himself up to meditation. I heard him sigh.

"If only we knew for certain that prisoners would be well treated. . . ."

. . . . . .

Groping and silently the battalion left the Adrian barracks, where we had been sleeping for half a night, and the companies of shadows lined up along the road.

"No one missing . . . no one missing," answered the corporals to the roll-call of their squads.

When his turn came Maroux answered:

"Bouffioux missing. . . . He went to wake the adjutant at the farm opposite there. I'll go and fetch him."

He went into the big dark yard, bogged himself in the dung-heap, cursed as he knocked into a forgotten harrow, and called blindly into the darkness.

"Hi! Bouffioux! . . . Where are you?" He heard a sort of cracking at his back, from the level of the roof, and a falling mass just grazed his shoulder and fell sprawling on to the dung-heap with a soft thud, dragging down the ladder from the loft, which fell flat on to the stone pavement.

Maroux had made a startled leap to one side, then he sprang upon the man who was getting up half-stunned and dizzy.

"Have you broken anything?"

"No, nothing . . ." chattered a frightened voice.

"What! . . . That's you, Bouffioux?"

"Yes," stammered the other, still trembling violently; "I missed my step; I missed the rung of the ladder."

"But what were you messing about up there for?"

"Well . . . I thought the adjutant sometimes . . ."

The corporal shrugged his shoulders. He had understood.

"That's all right. . . . Pick up your rifle and your pack. . . Come on. But don't you ever try this game again, do you follow me, I'm not going to have any scandals in my squad. . . ."

They rejoined the column, which was now forming up, and Maroux called out: "Nobody missing."

We got into a wet road the stiff clay of which clogged our feet. In the darkness we could divine from the clinking of weapons the other troops going forward or coming back. The guns were growling, indefatigably, without any single salient outburst, with a continuous rumble, and from invisible slopes, red lightnings answered one another. The road jolted along, more and more hummockey at every step; then every trace of it disappeared; it lost itself in a wilderness of rough stones. Not as much as a communication trench even in this smash-up; winding tracks with dead men for landmarks.

The relief snaked its way along in complete silence. Companies met us, going the other way through the gloom, with such gaps in their half-seen files that we were appalled. A smell of powder, of acid and of dead bodies steamed up from this ground that seemed gnawed by some horrible animal. At long intervals there could be discerned the stooping silhouettes of stretcher-bearers in harness, striking across the plain.

We marched for a full hour, we passed through ruins from underneath which we could hear talking, we clambered up a road filled with pebbles on which our heavy hobnailed boots kept skidding; and then, harassed and worn, we had a breather. Quite close to us, scantily protected by a bank hastily thrown up, there was a battery of seventy-fives. Their vicinity strongly displeased Sulphart.

"To make us halt just beside a pack of guns, that's just one of Morache's bright ideas. Like that, if Fritz takes it in his head to start firing it will be for our mugs."

As we got under way again the snoring of a shell coming to the end of its breath bent us all double: it burst right in front of the guns with a nasty soft noise.

"Gas shells!"

Our hands fumbled feverishly at our gas masks. Our lips tight shut, our whole breast walled up against the foul thing, we quickly slipped on our cowls. Noisily the helmets rolled clattering down. Other shells were bursting, and their red torch lit up for a moment that terrifying troop of divers out of their element seeking a thicker night to plunge into.

We marched quickly. By the light of the bursting shells I divined upon the slope a melancholy smash-up of human bodies, of stones, of tatters of every sort, of broken weapons. Then the mask was misted over and hid everything from me. I was suffocating under my gag, my lungs burning, and feeling at my temples the irritating trickling of sweat. The relief filed on in spite of everything, blinded, groping, and got into a wide communication trench. Men were squatting down and eating in it. We took our masks off.

"Don't be afraid," ragged the boys, pulling their legs up to leave us room to get past, "they're stink-balls! . . . If you put your veils on for everything you won't have time even to eat a bite, they're letting us have them all day long."

Fatigues were passing, parties laden with stakes, corrugated iron, tools, cobwebs of barbed wire that grappled our packs and refused to let go.

Bowed to the ground under their load, jostled, panting, the men would growl curses at us just to relieve their feelings, as they would have sworn at their boxes of rockets, their bags of grenades, or the drums of wire netting, that made them like circus riders. Sometimes the roadway would widen, coming up almost to the level of the fields, then timidly it would bury itself again between two walls of disembowelled sandbags. Farther on, it overflowed afresh, making a kind of extensive cross-roads, and all the time could be guessed, in these dark places, a strange moving to and fro of silent, shadowy shapes. Soldiers were coming out from their communication trenches, others arriving down the tracks, all leaning forward like men tugging barges, and at first it was impossible to understand what were those long bundles they were dragging along at the end of their tautened ropes. They were dead men.

Stretchers? . . . There were barely enough for the wounded, and then dressing-stations were highly reluctant to lend theirs. And so they used to drag along by the feet all the bodies gleaned through the fields; they used to drag them along by a rope, like the disembowelled horses at a bull fight, and then they were piled up in a long sap, one on top of another, face to the stars, feeling upon their piteous faces the eternal earth trickling down, flowing from burst sandbags as though from so many hour glasses.

The ditch was already full, and two men on their knees were pressing down the corpses, heaping them closer together, to make room for others.

Captain Morache had halted the column and the order came down to us, murmured hardly above a whisper.

"Fix bayonets."

The company lined up, facing the enormous tomb. A distant rocket made a fugitive lightning run gleaming along the hedge of bayonets.

"To the soldiers dead on the field of honour. . . . Present . . . arms!"

Every rifle-butt clattered with one single movement, then nothing more. Bodies rigid, heads up, we looked on, dumb, with our teeth clenched: soldiers have no other offering to make but their silence.

"Ground . . . arms!"

The company set off again and left the road which now came up out of the earth, seeming to continue in a track. A man was jumping up and down clumsily, wearing his blanket by way of a hood and cloak.

"No one is to pass that way," he warned us in a sleepy voice, "it's strictly forbidden. You must take the other track; that one is registered on."

The new sous-lieutenant to whom he addressed himself looked at the huge forge of gloom in which lightnings sprang out here and there, under the blows of the sledge-hammer.

"But it doesn't look as if it was dropping along there more than anywhere else," he observed.

The man continued to beat the ground with his heavy dance, his hands deep in his armpits and his face shrouded.

"I don't say no," he replied, his voice lost under his blanket. "I'm only here to tell you it's forbidden, I am . . . Now let anybody that wants to go that way go that way. Naturally as you may well think I don't give a blow, not me."

. . . . . .

This brand-new trench was lined with fresh earth like a common grave. Maybe it was just to save a little time that we had been sent into it alive.

The men we were relieving had dug it in two nights, disinterring heaped up bodies with every stroke of the pickaxe, and in places fragments of human frames were sticking out of the wall. On a hobnailed foot that came boldly out Sulphart had hung his satchels, and the machine gunners had planted their weapon on the swollen belly of a German, one of whose arms was hanging down, and with only a thin envelope of friable earth hiding him. In that hole there lay heavy on the air the acrid and sweetish smell of a dangerous marsh. The entrance to two German dug-outs had been laid open. The stair of one had been smashed up, its props pulped by a torpedo. On a board at the entrance somebody had written by way of epitaph:

"HERE ARE GERMAN SOLDIERS"

In the other dug-out one half of the section could sleep while their comrades took the watch.

It had begun to rain again, a thick driving rain that slashed down in gusts, sticking your soaked coat on to your back. With his handkerchief knotted about his neck to stop the water, Gilbert was coughing. As the general had forbidden the wearing of waterproofs on pain of prison, he had had to abandon his and had caught cold. To keep themselves from the rain, some of the men had cut out of their oilskin sleeping-bags canary yellow chasubles, which they tied on with strings. Others made themselves hoods of their tent canvas, soaked through in an instant. Lemoine who had no fears except for his broken boots, had pulled on by way of a sort of snow-boots, two brand-new sand-bags that came up to mid-leg; and standing up on those big wide elephant feet he remained standing on a board with the resigned back of an old heron, both hands in his pockets. As for little Broucke, insensible to everything, with his ill-buttoned coat letting the water stream in on his thin chest, he was sleeping bolt upright as he stood, alongside the sticky wall of the trench, his elbow held up by the boot of the Prussian coming out through.

The explosions were not so loud, muffled by the rain, the light of the rockets was thinned and diluted in that moving pond, and the shell-bursts were seen as through a veil. Not a single shot was fired: the two lines, face to face, watched each other, rancorous and resigned.

As we had taken over the watch, Ricordeau, who since he had been made adjutant no longer dared to sleep, for fear of Morache, came to choose men for the listening post. This was a hole in front of ours, with no less water and a few more bombs, rifle "turtledoves" which could be recognized by their dull sounding start, etc., and which landed with a whistle.

Taking the first comers at random, avoiding finding himself caught up among the complication of the "turns" in which watchers and fatigues were confounded without cancelling one another, the first to go for soup being the last to go on patrol, so that is was impossible to tell anybody off for a duty without drawing a protesting outcry from everybody. Ricordeau recruited his watchers. We saw them push their way into an embryo sap, then move off crawling, on hands and knees, trailing their rifles in the mud.

"Hi! old man," said Gilbert to the one who was last to go out, "try to bring in the wounded man they've left out in front there. . . . You can hear him crying still, the poor devil."

"We'll have a shot at it."

This wounded man was lying out no one knew exactly where, lost in that great funereal field. At regular intervals, as if he had each time had to steel himself up for a fresh effort, he would call out:

"Sergeant Brunet, of the seventh. . . . To me, mates. . . . Don't leave me! . . ."

Then his voice would be silent, exhausted. Our ears would be strained, but we could hear nothing more, only the wavering noise of rain and wind, now swelling, now dying away.

Under my arms laid flat along the parapet the very earth was shivering, pounded without respite. But just in front of us they were not actually "saucepanning" now. On our left we could catch a muffled hurly-burly of a relief going on: a company of ours was just arrived and the others who had their packs on their backs for a long time were hurriedly making off. The newcomers were growling.

"Just one dug-out and it's the third that have collared it. . . . Always the same lot that manage to get what's going. . . . The other chaps can always go and burst themselves."

Shelterless, without a hole to cower down into, those of them that weren't on watch squatted down, their backs humped under the tent canvas, and chin on knee they tried to sleep.

A little flame spurted up from a lighter; the rain quenched it at once. It broke out again, and was blown out on the instant.

"Light there!" growled an irritated voice. In no way intimidated, the man obstinately persisted, no doubt wanting to light his pipe. Three times, four times the little will-o'-the-wisp sprang up. Then I saw a shape get up and push against the others to get up to the smoker.

"You're not crazy, are you? . . . Don't you know it's against orders to show a light? . . ."

"You've got the wind up for fear they'll spot you?" replied the man in a voice that took me by surprise.

"Hold your tongue! . . . I tell you. . . ."

"Ah! cut it out, my lad, cut it out," returned the other placidly, with the same lazy good-for-nothing voice I thought I knew.

"Do you know who you're talking to? . . . First of all stand up when you answer me."

"I say, you try it on somebody else, you're making me sick."

"I am your adjutant."

"Nothing shocking in that. . . ."

"Adjutant Rouget. . . ."

"And I'm Vieublé, a soldier of the second-class, by favour, military medal and Croix de guerre. . . . If the Boches don't like the light, I don't give a . . ."

"Ah! Vieublé come back again," cried Lemoine in delight.

We slipped quickly along to his corner, where still down on his hams he was listening, without moving, to the adjutant, a real good fellow, who was addressing to him by way of punishment a few disjointed remarks on the proper prudence that should be observed in the front line, and the respect due to superior officers, without which "everybody would be in command, everybody would do just as he pleased, and we would be about as fit to carry on the war as a herd of pigs."

"Hi! Vieublé, aren't you going to say 'how do you do' to your pals?"

The Parisian lifted his head and recognized us all at once.

"Ah, the old slackers! . . . Ah! aren't I pleased to find you again. . . . I thought you were all dead or evacuated, the boys in the company hadn't the wits to tell me anything. . . . We turned up by way of reinforcements this morning; we're being chucked into the trenches in the evening. You might say they're not losing much time. . . . Ah! I am pleased. And Sulphart?"

Some of our neighbours growled out:

"Not so loud, son of a . . . ."

Vieublé slipped along behind us as far as our corner of the sap. Staring into every face in the darkness, he looked for the old crew.

"What about it, ch'timi, eh? Here we are again. . . . Ah, Bouffioux, you bad

145

big girl, what are you up to there? . . . and Bélin?"

"Evacuated. . . . He got gassed. . . . You knew Bréval got killed, and it's Maroux that is our corporal now. . . . Berthier was marked missing in Argonne."

"A good lad; that's a pity. And so it's Morache that's gone up captain. Lord, what we've got to put up with. . . . No matter, there aren't so many of your old lot left now."

We were all crowded together at the entrance of the dug-out, sitting on the muddy steps. Sulphart, down at the back was getting up a hot brew, having brought nothing in his pack, neither cartridges, nor linen, nor biscuits, so that he could carry along two bottles of rum, which he had carefully packed in among knitted socks.

"Well, and down in the rear there, they're taking things easy?"

"You may say so. Three months in hospital, in a mansion that was a regular palatial palace. Nothing to do but let them wash your feet for you; as much jam as ever you want, the real proper good life, what! . . . And us, too, that was nothing at all, it's the English you ought to see. If you saw that: officers always on the lookout; nice new soldiers that buy themselves everything that takes their fancy, blokes in petticoats that go to drill playing the fife. The girls are all sweet on them, I'll only say that much: You can be sure that those boys aren't clamouring to change their sector. And their wounded, if you could see them! A topping blue coat, very tasty, a white shirt and a red tie. Very tasty, you know, and clean, you couldn't imagine they've been through it."

"And ours? Are there a lot of them?"

"A handful. At the hospital where I was, it was never anything but crammed; . . . only us fellows, we were got up with any old cast-off duds, jackets too big, coats too short, old overcoats: I swear you had to be a real handsome boy to wipe the Tommy's eye. . . . The only thing we had on our side was that we could talk. . . . We got herded together according to the kind of wound we'd got--it would make you split! The fellows that had lost an arm or had their heads chipped, they go about in bands, because their wound doesn't stop them walking, they can get along quick enough. But us ones, with game legs, they make us a crew by ourselves. I had only to go on two sticks, I had, but the rest--one had a foot missing, or a bit of a leg, and that makes you melancholy, that sound of a crutch knocking on the pavement, you can't imagine. . . . The civilians don't notice it any more now they say that now they've got used to it. The boys have'nt got used to it, you can be sure of that. . . . I had a companion who had the lower part of his phiz carried away, he didn't dare to show himself, he was ashamed to. . . . By the way, he was a fellow out of the 269th, the ones that went in with us at Carency."

Having swallowed a good mouthful of the hot rum, he gave his thanks:

"That warms you up. Good old Demachy still looks well after his little Mary, I can see that."

Sulphart was stooping over and trying to read the future in the bottom of his cup.

"And the war," he asked, "when is that going to finish off?"

Vieublé, before he answered, was taken with a fit of loud laughter.

"Ah! this delay. . . . You don't fancy they ever talk about it? No! In Panama they simply don't know any longer now that there is a war. Nobody thinks about it except the old women that have their kids at the front. . . . The pretty ladies have never been so just so. . . . I found old friends making twenty francs a day. . . . I say, a

146

fellow that had a wretched little den where he mended bicycles, he's a millionaire now; he smokes cigars with bands on them, that I wouldn't dare to touch. And that crowd in the cinemas, in the bars, everywhere, . . . You can go and walk in the Champs Elysées to see the rich folk, they're still all there, don't you worry. For that lot it's all the same as if the war was in Madagascar or in China. I'll swear they don't fash themselves for any winter campaign. It's high living, I tell you, high living all the time. . . ."

"Aye I saw that, too, when I was on leave," assented one of the newcomers.

The narrator shot a look at the interrupter.

"You've seen nothing at all," said he. "You don't get time to take note of everything in a single week. Now I stayed for twenty days in a convalescent hospital, I did, and then two leaves of forty-eight hours besides, and a Sunday I took on the strict q.t. . . . For you can ask if one is bored stiff at the depot. . . . Non-com. that are simply breaking their necks to escape being sent back again, and who make you gasp to get back, marches by day, marches by night, fatigues, drill. One day they wanted to shove me on to a week's duty with prisoners of war. I said to the sergeant-major, 'If you stick me along with the Fritzes I'll do one of them in, . . . I don't ever want to see one of their mugs again. . . .' After that he never said a word to me again about it. On account of my medal they always pushed me into doing orderly to officers because that looks well. . . . One Saturday I was well on and I told them all off properly when I got back: I said I was fed up with the shirkers in the rear and asked to get back. . . . I was kept three weeks at divisional depot and so here I am. . . ."

"Pity they haven't put you back again with us," regretted Maroux.

"With my old pal Morache? . . . You've got a nice notion of a joke, you have. I'll take you to St. Cloud some Sunday, and you can carry the basket."

The rain had stopped. Sitting on the first step, his eyes boring into the thick night with its clouds so low that the bursting rockets lit up their mud-coloured bulk, Gilbert was listening to the grievous plaint of the wounded man. Oppressed at heart he could think now of nothing else, divining the moment when the poor dying fellow would call out again, counting up the seconds. . . .

"Come and fetch me, mates. . . . Sergeant Brunet of the Seventh. . . ."

Then the exhausted voice would die away again in the night.

"If they don't go and hunt for him I shall go," Gilbert thought, deeply troubled. "So much the worse if I get knocked over."

As he scraped out the bottom of his mess-tin, "Lot's of extra grub, boys!" Vieublé was still speaking.

"On the whole, out here, we've a good job. In the rear they're always being messed about, they're always talking about relieving them, the doctors have their clothes off once a fortnight, the women cross-question them. . . . While up here, there's none of all that to be afraid of. You've never seen a commission coming to inspect the front line, to relieve the blighters that aren't in their places. No use talking, you're well off, they leave you in peace. . . . We've got a good place, and we only have to keep off playing the fool to hold it."

A rifle grenade burst just in front of the parapet. In the deeper silence after the detonation we could hear a broken sob.

"Mates, Louis! Little Louis! Come quick, boys," cried the voice, completely done, "quick. . . ."

Another grenade burst, and its red flame lit up with a brutal light the watchers with their curving backs; then a third. . . . In the German trench a little fusillade was crackling up, with the object of hiding the starting of the grenades in its own noise.

"Alarm there! They're attacking," cried a voice.

A wave ran through the men from the end of the sap to the black depths of the dug-out. In the trench bent backs straightened up. A rocket whistled aloft, imperiously. You could hear the dry click of rifles being cocked, and without any further waiting, at random, with a violent gesture of their bodies putting every ounce of force into it, the bombers hurled their lemons. That crash of explosives covered the whole general uproar.

"Alarm there! Up and out! . . ." they were shouting in the dug-out.

Hands were groping and feverishly hunting for rifles, every man recognizing his own with his fingers, by its vest of flannel or oilcloth. Feet trampled on one another. It was a low tumult of swearing, of unhooked mess-tins, of rifles falling clumsily with their necklace of equipment hung on the muzzle.

"Outside! God's truth! . . ."

Going out, the brutal glare of the rockets was simply blinding. Firing began at random. Everyone flung himself at the parapet, no matter where, and brought his rifle to the shoulder. Elbow to elbow, we were suddenly like so many machines at work: brutal blow of the recoil when the bullet goes on its way, automatic movement of the breech opened and shut, a hand burning itself on the overheated barrel. In gulps we breathed in wafts of powder. One idea only: to fire and go on firing. The bursting of the shells nosing after the trench made us rock and stagger without our ever thinking of it, we reload, present, fire. . . .

"Cease firing!" cried a voice behind us.

Ricordeau, mounted on a pile of sandbags, was looking out into the plain torn with glaring lights. When the rifle fire was stopped the thundering explosions of the barrage were heard better. All heads went into hiding.

"It was just to get us out," said the Adjutant. "Now they'll 'saucepan' us like blazes. . . . Come on, everybody into shelter."

In a confused rout we all piled up in the staircase leading into the dug-out. The two-hundred-and-tens that were coming over puffing seemed to thrust the last ones on with a brutal grip. We tumbled in, blind. . . .

"Make a light, good Lord! . . . who has got a lighter?"

A candle lit up the dug-out, vast in extent, low, seeming to stiffen and buttress itself to hold up that huge load on its squat props. Overhead the guns were thundering harder than ever, and at every battering thud the tree trunk pillars shook.

"Did any one stay on watch up above?" asked Ricordeau whose plump and rosy face was glistening in the light of the candle.

Nobody answered.

"There are the fellows in the listening-post."

"That's not enough, we must tell off a man for it. It's for your squad, Maroux."

The corporal, on principle, growled under his breath. "Naturally," and he asked us: "Whose turn is it to go out?"

A newcomer said at once:

"It's not my turn. . . . There's Bouffioux who has never taken it over yet."

The quondam cook was buried away in a corner between two piles of

148

sandbags.

"And why should it fall on me?" he protested in a tearful voice turning his pitiful big head towards us. 'But you're never going to put me out as sentry all by myself? . . . I can hardly see at all, especially at night, one eye as good as gone. . . ."

"That's enough, Bouffioux," interrupted Ricordeau, "the tear office is shut."

"All the same," twittered the other, "I think I'd be more useful by and by for digging."

Little Broucke looked at the fat lump of a fellow with an air of complete disgust.

"Here, I'll go out," he declared, "I'll go in your place. . . . I know well enough what you've got in your stomach, but it's not up to much anyway."

He clambered up the stair. As he was going outside, a stroke more violent than ever shook the dug-out and hurled into it a lurid glare.

"Broucke!" called Maroux, uneasy. From overhead a calm voice answered:

"Don't you fash yourself. . . ."

It was a rhythmic pounding, regular, inexorable, the shells following one upon another without respite, churning up the ravaged earth mètre by mètre. Standing at the foot of the stair Ricordeau counted the strokes.

"That one fell not far away. . . . That one was a hundred-and-fifty. . . . They're giving us a fair treat!"

Their faces turned up to the low roof constructed of closely laid trunks of trees, the comrades were arguing.

"I'm just asking myself suppose a two-hundred-and-ten was to come along here."

"What do you think? . . . There's more than four mètres of earth above us."

"That proves nothing. Their big stuff with delayed percussion fuse. . ."

"Have you got any baccy? My pouch is empty."

"You won't have time to roll yourself one."

"Oh well, they've been bombarding us for a whole hour."

"It would have to drop just clean on top."

"And then . . . I saw once, myself, at Vanquois. . . ."

There was nothing to be heard but a dull low growling, and now and then a crash nearer at hand that resounded right down through the dug-out. Maroux would spring out, climb a few steps, and call:

"Broucke!"

The lowered voice would reply:

"Going strong. Going strong. . . ."

Under the infernal bombardment one had a moment of mere stupefaction. One remained knocked out, hands between knees, head absolutely empty. We eased ourselves in a bully-beef-tin passed from hand to hand. Then, nervously, we began again to talk quick, quicker. We let fly all kinds of chaff, with dry mouths: "He awakened too soon. . . . What a packet he's been getting from old Krupp's! . . . When do you fancy the war's going to start? If only I'd known I'd have gone to sleep at the hotel."

But the terrible ram seemed to draw nearer still, in a fury of thunder, and the chatterers held their tongues. I fancied I could feel against my shoulder the beating of

Gilbert's heart. Bouffioux had rolled himself up in his blanket, hiding his head so as to see nothing further. With resignation in our backs we were waiting.

A big shell burst, a clattering crash of iron-mongery, and the wind in furious eddies blew out our candle. With the dark, anguish gripped us hard. Maroux, at first stunned, climbed quickly out.

"Broucke! Broucke! . . ." he called.

We heard his voice going outside, then go farther away. . . . He came back just as someone was lighting the candle again. It lit up his pallid face in full under the bar of shadow thrown by his helmet.

"Someone must go," he said simply, in a choked voice. . . . "It's your turn, Demachy."

Gilbert said, "Right." He put on his helmet, which he had laid down, took up his rifle, made me a little au revoir with a movement of his head, and went up.

He had barely got outside, when two explosions bent him double, and something lashed his coat, stone or splinter. The trench in front of him was smashed down, he strode over the sacks, trampling in the loose, sticky earth.

Broucke had not so much as budged. Half sitting on a jutting bit of the trench wall, his arm extended on the parapet he seemed to be continuing his sleep, his head drooping, his collar buttoned awry, letting the rain drip through on to his thin chest. There was nothing much to remark: two little red threads trickling from his nostrils-- that was all.

The shells now were thudding down on the left, less regularly, with a kind of fatigued rage. The reports came at intervals. . . . And then on the level of the ground. Gilbert heard the voice, the almost imperceptible voice of the unknown wounded man who was still imploring.

"Fetch me. . . . I've got a maman, mates, I've got a maman."

And he pronounced it, "moman" as Paris children do.

. . . . . .

It was going to rain again, the day showed a livid blinding whiteness. On the earth there lay about fragments and tatters of rain in yellowy shallow puddles, which the wind ruffled, and in which a few stray drops made circles. And yet the rain could not surely be hoping to wash all that mud, to wash those rags, to wash those dead bodies? Though it were to rain all the tears of heaven, rain a whole deluge, it would blot nothing out. No, an age to rain would never avail to wash all that away.

There was no defence in front of us, not a stake, not a strand of wire. Humps, holes, a lacerated earth sprouting with débris, and some twelve hundred mètres off, the wood we were to carry, a melancholy nursery of slashed and despoiled tree trunks.

They said the attack was to be at eight o'clock, but nobody knew anything definitely about it. All night long the liaison orderlies had brought us orders, and then counter orders; a note sent to the commandant had advised him that the plan of the sector that had been sent to him when we came away was not up to date, and Ricordean had been asking ever since daybreak whether the sandbag works that could be seen on the left belonged to the Germans or were really ours. Only once had our artillery been in action, but the shells had fallen short and killed the watchers in the advance post, and we had quickly sent up a rocket asking them to lengthen the range. After that the artillery had not fired again.

150

Some of the soldiers were still sleeping and dozing, curled up under their blankets, and the liaison orderlies strode over them in their hurry to and fro, without knowing whether they were alive or dead.

"He is killed, that one, is he?"

"Not yet, wait till to-night," muttered the man drawing in his feet.

Cowering away in a corner, Bouffioux would not part for a moment from his mask, terrified at the least whiff of powder the wind brought down on us. For an hour he had been heard stuttering: "That smells of apples. . . . That smells of mustard. . . . That smells of garlic. . . ." and every time he put on his hood again in a fright. Now he no longer took it off, and crouched in his hole, one might have thought him a carnival monster, with that wild beast head waggling and swaying about.

"It's always the funkiest ones that cop it," cried a pal to him, to restore his courage.

They were not talking to each other. Some were eating, moistening their bread with the rain that dripped from their helmets, the others were waiting, with humped-up backs, looking at nothing, saying nothing.

Between two explosions a heavy silence weighed upon the trench, and when one looked at the comrades full in the face, one fancied in their tired eyes one same idea, like a reflection from the livid sky. Suddenly an order was repeated:

"Pass along there, the colonel's watch. . . ."

They passed it along from hand to hand, and without a word, the chiefs of sections took the time.

It was a little silver watch case, thickly convex and chased like a gift for a girl's first communion, with its garlands of roses. And it was that watch, that watch alone, that knew the hour. The dreadful moment when we must leave, our holes, dash through and into the smoke. Straight to meet the bullets.

"I bought its twin for my little girl," said a comrade to me.

Gilbert, who was always a little feverish on days of a stiff affair, was strangely calm this morning. There was in his voice, in his resigned manner, something fateful that made one uneasy, and he himself felt in his heart a fear he had never known before. Silent and taciturn he looked at the wood, the tragic forest of gnawed stakes where the shells tore their smoke to rags. How far away it was. . . . "How many machine guns could they have?"

He was so cold, that he did not feel the wet barrel of his rifle in his right hand. It was strange, he was always cold on these days. But these nerveless legs, this empty head, this fear at heart, it was the first time. . . .

"Come and sit down, Gilbert," said Sulphart to him, "we're comfortable here in the dry. . . ."

We were huddied together, three of us, under a kind of penthouse, made of a barn-door held up by the sandbags of the parapet, and to pass the time, without an appetite we were broaching a tin of bully beef. Gilbert did not turn round. He suddenly lifted his head and cried:

"Ah!"

At the same moment we heard the lashing out of rifle fire, the explosion of bombs. A whole tumult of battle suddenly let loose.

Ricordeau, who had been sitting at the entrance to the dug-out, rushed out, and without paying any heed to the bullets whining about him he leaped on a pile of sandbags and looked out over the parapet: it was the attack. Little flaky bombs were bursting in the fields, and already shells were arriving, exploding in thick clouds. Going to earth under the salvoes, then starting off again, our men were charging. Dispersed, scattered, like crumbs, they were so tiny that they appeared lost in that immense plain.

Mechanically Ricordeau had tightened his chin-strap, and he was crying in a broken voice:

"It's not possible, they are mistaken. . . . It's only in an hour's time. . . . Fix bayonets! No, no, don't move, it's not time. . . . It's a mistake. . . . Quick, pass it down to the Captain: What are we to do?"

He was running about the trench, out of his wits, jostling all of us, then showing himself completely, standing up on the broken down sandbags, he tried to see what the other companies were doing. Some sections were going out, as if hesitating, one here, then another farther on. Two hundred mètres away, an officer was making signs that we could not understand, and behind him we could see in the trench a compact troop, bristling with bayonets.

"So much the worse, we're going into it," cried Ricordeau, his voice suddenly lightened of all its distress.

Without giving any order, he jumped on the parapet, ran a few yards, then turning round as though he was just recollecting us, he cried without halting:

"En avant!"

A movement eddied along the trench. Down its whole length the parapet went down, the sandbags torn away. One man pushing another forward, we clambered up. One moment's hesitation before the earth all in uproar, before the naked plain: a moment's waiting to see a few comrades come up, and to feel them side by side, then a last look behind. . . . And without a cry, tragic, silent, the dislocated company dashed forward. . . .

More than a hundred mètres in front of us Ricordeau was running bolt upright, still farther away, under the smoke, we could see sections disappearing in the wood. Concealed among the broken ruins of trees the machine guns were tap, tap, tapping; a trench gun was also firing, as hard as it could, furiously. Men were being bowled over. . . . We were running straight before us, dourly, without a cry: we would have been afraid, if we only opened our mouths, of letting escape all the courage we were holding back, behind our clenched teeth.

Bodies and spirits were all straining onwards towards that single aim: the wood, to reach the wood. It appeared horribly far away, with all those spouting shells that separated us from it. An unending thunder echoed and re-echoed in our heads, and the shaken earth was quaking beneath our feet. We ran panting on. We threw ourselves flat on our faces when a shell exploded, then, stunned, we set off once more, drowned in the smoke. The bunches of men seemed to melt away under the lightnings.

In front of me a wounded man dropped his rifle. I saw him swaying for a moment as he stood, then heavy and awkward he set off again with his arms dangling, and ran like us, without knowing that he was dead already. . . . He went a few yards staggering, and then rolled over. . . .

. . . . .

As they were going out last of all from the trench, a shrapnel shell had brutally flung them back with its burning breath--a detonation so terrific that they had heard

152

nothing, completely overwhelmed. Sulphart let himself slip down back into the trench. Voices were crying out:

"Houla! I'm wounded."

The smoke dispersing disclosed men trying to pick themselves up from the ground. Stretched out, his face buried in the earth, Bouffioux shivered for one moment, then moved no more, his flank torn open. The wounded men, once they had stood up again, flung away their rifle, their equipment, their satchel, and set off at a run.

Others less seriously hit, waited until the bombardment slackened off and then quietly they tore open their first-aid packet with their teeth. Sulphart remained bent double, for he could hardly breathe.

"I've got it," he breathed in a whisper, looking at a comrade, with a bewildered air.

"It's not much," the other said to him, "it's only your hand."

"No. In the back."

Under the shoulder his overcoat was holed and the blood was scarcely to be seen, making merely a spot of deep dark red.

"Is it bleeding a lot?" he asked.

"No. Go along quick to the dressing-station. I'm just going to dress your hand."

Then, and not till then, did Sulphart look at his hand. His fingers were as though crushed and mangled, all caked together with blood, and when he had actually seen his wound he at once felt the pain of it.

"Go gently with it, it's hurting me a lot. I've got some iodine in my yellow cartridge pouch, take it out. . . ."

The comrade poured over the mangled hand a half of the contents of the flask, and that cruel smarting made him cry out. Coarsely, without daring to tie it close, the other carried out the dressing for him, the bandage reddening as it was rolled round.

"And you? Where are you wounded?" asked Sulphart

"Nowhere. . . . I'm going to join the others." There were three of them, who had been spared by the shell.

They looked at their section, which, brought to a halt for a moment by a burst of machine-gun fire, was starting off again in skirmishing order, and then they looked at the wounded.

"You're taking your skin out of it, you fellows," said one with an air of envy. . . . "Haven't any of you got a scrap of tobacco?"

"Yes. I've got a packet left, wait."

"I've got some chocolate," said Sulphart in a clipped voice. "Who wants it?"

The wounded men emptied their packs, and their satchels, and the other three chose what they pleased. When the booty was divided:

"So then, are we going up?" said one of the three, a corporal whose pallor could be discovered under the trails of sweat and mud. . . . "Au revoir, mates, and good luck to you!"

They got out of the trench and bending under the noise, they ran at a clumsy trot towards the wood, all alone-three pygmies charging down on giants of smoke.

Sitting on the sandbags, leaning up against the soft trench wall, Sulphart felt himself almost comfortable as he was, though his flesh was racked with pain and his head was burning. But he was without strength, without will: a comrade less sorely wounded than himself had to help him to get up.

"Come along, hurry up," repeated those men that were going down in front of him.

He could not walk quickly, with that piercing point that kept him from breathing.

"Hi!" he wanted to call. . . . "Wait for me!" But his choked voice could not carry far, and the others were hurrying on. He saw the last man's coat disappear round the angle of the trench. Halting for a moment he recovered his breath, and then having picked up a stick he started again, bending like an old man.

There were wounded men making their way all along the trenches. There were some of them terrifying, grey of hue, who continually halted to gasp, crouching down in recesses, and who gazed at the others as they passed with haggard eyes that saw nothing. Sulphart barely noticed them, as he went on steadfastly with the same unvarying pace.

At this point the trench wound its way among the ruins of a tiny village. As he was passing at the back of a wall he heard the whistling of a shell and crouched down. The explosion was so close that he fancied he could see its red lightning behind his shut eyelids. With fear in the pit of his stomach he set off quicker than ever. Other shells followed, a whole pack let loose upon these smashed fragments of houses. Sulphart then started to run, seeking for a place to shelter. He caught sight of a cellar stair, at the top of which a stretcher-bearer was standing.

"There's no more room here," the man said to him as he pushed him away. "You go farther along."

In the darkness of the stair you could divine the shapes of soldiers crowded together and the white patches of their dressings. Sulphart, shrinking himself together, nevertheless thought he would take shelter a little, as another time-shell exploded. The splinters lashed the wall. He ran a few yards farther, but the other cellar was full too. Lips and eyes twisting with a nervous spasm, he went on humping up his back under the explosions, seeking a hole into which he could dive. At every burst of flame he flattened himself against the wall, hiding his head behind his bended arm.

There were territorials laden with tools cramming themselves into the smallest nooks and crannies; he flung himself upon one of them whose legs were the only part of him still sticking outside, and with a furious effort made his way also into the hole. Crammed together, face to face, their breath mingling, the two men stared at one another, neither able to see anything of the other beyond his fixed eyes, and the old man's hard moustache pricked Sulphart's lips. They said not a word to one another, they were simply stupefied, and their intermingled legs timidly tried to find their way in farther, seeking to hide themselves still better.

The guns followed one another in infernal salvoes, and the shells were falling so close that at every one they felt the earth struggling beneath them. A detonation more dreadful than the rest belched up, and the smoke suddenly filled the hole. . . . Sulphart thought he was engulfed, entombed. He made a violent movement to free himself, but his arm was caught under the other man's bust, their two bodies were wedging each other in and he could not move at all. Frightened he struggled violently, fancying he felt himself stifling under the giving way of the earth above them: already suffocating, when the smoke as it cleared off showed him the light of day. And then right in front of his face, up against his very eyes, Sulphart saw Death in the look of the old man. For one moment it was terrible, that human look, it had one second of tremendous resistance, and then a light seemed to be quenched in it, it became dull, troubled, glassy. . . . And Sulphart took upon his own lips the last breath of the dying man, a horrible moan, as if he had actually given up his life in that last convulsive hiccough. For a moment Sulphart remained still closely pressed against the dead man, whose eyes were now rolling backwards; he freed himself brutally and came out from the hole, holding up his left hand, which gave him torture at the least knock. When he was standing up, he saw that the territorial had his abdomen torn open, and a big patch of blood stained his faded blue tunic with deep red. He was calling to the others who were getting up from the ground and gathering their tools together when he felt a strange taste in his mouth. He spat--it was quite pink. . . . Frightened, he drank off at one draught the little amount of rum he had left in his bottle, and he set off quicker than before, fearing lest he should fall down on the way.

He did not know these twisting communication ditches hacked out of the mud. But at intervals there were liaison orderlies or stretcher-bearers who told him: "Go straight on," and he went straight on, without caring to take any rest.

At length he saw a notice board marked "Dressing Station," and went down into the dug-out. To get to the bottom, it was necessary to step over the wounded men huddled up on the stairs. The room was also filled with them--badly wounded men lying upon stretchers and gasping hoarsely, their eyes closed upon their pain.

The doctor said to Sulphart:

"I can do nothing for you here. . . . Stay there and rest, and at night when there is less firing going on you will all go together to the hospital."

He was looking for room to sit down when a little sergeant whose arm was hung in a sling by a big check handkerchief got up and said:

"I won't wait here any longer. . . . I won't have any blood left in me by to-night."

And all tottering and staggering he went out, bumping into the others, and Sulphart sat down on the stair step he had left.

The rainy sky hurried on the coming of night, and at the close of the day several of the wounded set off. Sulphart followed them. Before him there walked a chasseur-à-pied holding his smashed jaw in his two hands. On the way they came up with others and their swollen band arrived near the place where the batteries were installed. The gunners came out to look at them.

"You're on the right track, boys. . . . The village is not far from here. . . ."

They went on again. At long intervals a soldier was found lying, wounded and emptied of all his blood, a man with whom Death was now in company. Death must needs have known their track and be watching for them as they passed, to finish them. In such guise they found and recognized the sergeant by his big check handkerchief. And why too had he insisted on going off alone. Two by two, He can be stood up to, can be resisted. . . .

The little remnant of the day was trickling away as though from the cracked basin of a fountain. In the thin twilight haze they could catch veiled glimpses of the companies going up as reinforcements, bent under their packs and implements. The evening became alive for a moment with a chinking sound of arms and mess-tins. Then the road was deserted again.

One wounded man, and then a second, halted unable to hold out any farther.

One of them let himself drop on the edge of the ditch and began to weep.

"We'll send the stretcher-bearers," his comrades promised as they went away with their spent and weary pace.

At length they perceived in the darkness a farm with low roof, whose blinded windows allowed a thin blade of light to escape. They went in. At the far end of a dark passage a great glass window poured its cheery light: that drew them on like moths. They followed the passage, groping, and flattening their pallid faces against the window panes they looked through. The table was modestly laid--more drinking-cups than glasses--but those white plates, that lamp, that smoking dish wore to their eyes a look of unheard-of luxury and daintiness. Greedily they gazed and contemplated it. . . . . One of the officers sitting at the table, having raised his eyes saw in the shadow their row of fever-stricken eyes, all those dead men in the helmets, and fastened to the glass the dreadful face of the chasseur, whose pulped chin was nothing but a black lump of clotted blood. He started convulsively and stood up on his feet, very pale. The others, amazed, turned around and in their turn they saw the ghosts. All at once their voices ceased as though broken off short. . . .

"You must have a drink here, eh?" said an artillery commandant opening the door to them at length. "You have earned it indeed, my poor lads."

They hesitated at going in, for the over bright light made their eyes blink. For all that they crowded in close by the door with a noise of dragging shuffling boots, and passing the cups from one to another they drank eagerly. At every mouthful the chasseur took, the wine passing through his holed chin fell down on to his coat in a thin stream.

"I say, let's both drink one another's health," the commandant said to him.
. . . . . .
As they went away from the lighted room the thick night dazed them. Bands of men could be discerned, making dark patches on the road with their confused masses and their confused uproar; they followed them towards the village. The obscure streets and dark courtyards swarmed with invisible soldiers and hidden voices. Now and then the strong brutal flare of a motor lit up a silhouetted group of shadows.

There were battalions of reinforcements waiting, clogging up the street, and the soldiers were continually getting up to question the wounded.

"We don't know a thing more than you do. It's a bad corner. . . . Where is the field hospital?"

They caught sight of the red lantern a long way off in the depths of the night, and hurried on. Upon the pillar of the door a placard was nailed up:

THIS WAY FOR MEN SLIGHTLY WOUNDED AND ABLE TO WALK

The sign inspired no confidence in them with its somewhat mocking air.

"Not here," said one of them: "they can't be evacuating men from this place."

The divisional hospital was on the opposite side of the square. It was a large house, black and deserted, without a single piece of furniture, not even a pallet bed.

In shirt and trousers, with his forehead glistening with sweat, the doctor was carrying out a hasty examination of the wounded, whose hurts a hospital orderly illuminated with his lantern. On the ground were everywhere lying soiled dressings, pads of cotton wool. Standing on a stool was a big basin overflowing with reddened water.

"Now another," the doctor would say, wiping his forehead with his bare arm.

And the next man would take his seat, holding out his bandaged arm or taking off his tunic. On a deal table a very busy soldier was filling up papers, which the wounded men themselves attached to their coats, like a badge.

In a neighbouring room, where there was no light, a grievously wounded man was heard crying out:

"Aren't they going to put me in a bed, doctor? . . . Oh! how I wish I was in one. . . . A bed with sheets, eh, doctor? . . . Will the ambulance waggon be coming soon? . . . Quick, fetch it here."

The doctor tore Sulphart's shirt to look at his wound.

"The bleeding has stopped now. . . . They'll wash it down there. . . . Give me your hand now."

Sulphart could not keep from crying out when his dressing, all stuck together, was unrolled.

"That's nothing; a nice little wound," said the doctor. . . . "Only we'll have to cut off two of your fingers."

"So much the worse," replied the redhead. . . . "Oh well, I'm not a pianist."

. . . . . .

"That hurts. . . . Oh! how that's hurting me. . . ."

Gilbert was repeating the words under his breath, as if he had fancied he would soften his pain by complaining. He had remained lying on his side just as he had fallen, and when with a great effort he would manage to raise his heavy head, a tearless sob rose up from his heart.

The agony had dazed and stupefied him, and he was no longer conscious of his limbs or his head; he felt nothing now but his wound, the deep hurt that was ransacking his belly.

Not for one moment had he lost consciousness, and yet the hours passed quicker than if he had been wholly awake. Now that his thought was freeing itself from his anæsthesia he was beginning to feel that he was suffering. The first notion that came to him struck him roughly like a wound: "Will the stretcher-bearers ever come to me at all?"

Anguish laid hold of him, and he half pulled himself up to look round. But the agony of the movement flung him brutally down again. Were the stretcher-bearers ever going to come? . . . Yes, certainly when night would have come completely. And if they did not come at all, ever? A black horror drew a veil over his brain, and he remained for a moment immobile, as though he had been poleaxed, and almost free from pain. Then he opened his eyes again.

Twilight was now saddening that tragic wood whose trees were all as stripped and bare as the uprights of so many crosses. A few yards away a soldier had fallen, his body crumpled together like a ball, and under his open overcoat could be seen the white of his shirt, as if he had tried to get at his wound before he died. Another, still farther off, seemed to be taking a siesta, his back set against a tree trunk all scarred and bitten by shelling, his head falling over on to his shoulder. And that piece of blue stuff, was that yet another one? Yes, still another. . . .

Fear took hold of him again. Why should he be the only living man left in that haunted forest? To remain lying there must not one be dumb like them, cold like them? It was inevitable, there was no help for it, one must die. . . .

But that one word--die--revolted him and roused him instead of overwhelming him. Well then, no! . . . He was determined not to die, he was absolutely determined not to. His spirit straining, his fists contracted, he tried to make out where he was. There was no sign or indication, none at all. . . . Shells were crossing one another's tracks, above the wood or exploding quite near him, flinging up the earth under the dead men's sleeping. Were they German shells, or were they shells from our own side? . . . He could hear many a short burst of rifle fire in the outskirts of the wood, but without being able to fix his position or direction. Had we advanced? Had the Boches retaken the forest? . . . There was nothing that could give him the answer. Nothing save his anguish was alive within that mutilated wood, among those quiet insensitive sleeping ones whom all fear had left.

With the fall of evening, however, the gun fire slackened away. A cold wind was prowling about smelling of rain, and the moist sticky earth was freezing his legs. Fear was drawing up to him, coloured like the night.

Suddenly he seemed to hear a crackling of twigs. Making a sharp effort he sat up on his elbow and called:

"This way. . . . I'm wounded. . . ."

Nothing replied, nothing even stirred. Broken up by his effort he fell back again on his side, moaning. His aggravated wound was torturing his breast, his entrails, his flanks, his whole body as though with red hot pincers. In the vertigo of his bitter pain he was stammering to himself:

"I won't move again. . . . I swear I won't move again, but don't hurt me so much. . . ."

And to inspire pity in the dark Master who was forcing him to suffer, he remained inert, unmoving, his eyes fast sealed, burying his crooked fingers in the cold earth.

Slowly the agony became less cruel and a thought awoke in his buzzing head.

"I mustn't stay any longer without moving. . . . If I faint no one will ever see me, and I shall be left here to die. I must manage to pull myself up again, I must call out."

And then with all his tenacity of will-power, he decided, "I shall go and get my back up against a tree and dress my wound. . . . Then when any soldiers pass by I shall shout to them. . . . I must do it. . . . It's my life at stake. . . ."

As yet he had not dared to touch his wound, it frightened him to think of it, and his hand even kept strictly away from his belly, so that he need not feel, need not know.

"The hæmorrhage must have stopped," he thought, "it's not bleeding any longer. I'll do my dressing now."

With his teeth clenched upon the cries that came through his throat he pulled himself up with great difficulty, and dragged himself along and then let himself drop with his back against a tree. His wound awakened throbbed in his sides, with a fever pulse. He granted himself a moment's respite, with eyes shut; it seemed to him he had just achieved a little towards saving himself.

He took his packet of dressings out of his pouch and tore the covering. Now, he must needs get at his wound, must touch it. Many a time his hands moved towards his belly, but they hesitated, did not dare. At length he mastered himself, and, bandage ready, he resolutely touched the wound. It was on the left just above the groin. Slowly, to avoid the pain, he unbuckled his belt, opened his great coat, and trousers, and then he tried to pull up his shirt. It was horrible, he felt as though he

158

was tearing out his entrails, carrying his live flesh with it. . . . Tortured, he stopped, his hand laid on his naked flesh. He felt something warm gently dripping all along his fingers. Then terrified, to stop the loss of his blood, he took his dressing, and without unrolling it, he applied it as a pad to his wound. Over this he put the covering of heavy linen, then his handkerchief, and to keep it all well pressed home over the bloody sore, he fastened his trousers again, a gruesome torture that was death to his loins.

At last at the very end of his strength, he let his arms drop down again, and with head lying back he descended into the very gulf of pain. He was breathing with jerky convulsive respirations, a hoarse panting. The shadows were falling in his eyes as thought to fill them. Upon his frozen body his head seemed to burn, buzzing with fever, and the cold wind that blew against the gloom brought no refreshing coolness to his forehead. A few drops of rain, big and slow and heavy, gave him a feeling of infinite comfort, splashing down on to his face. He would fain have remained so for ever, until the stretcher-bearers should come.

Under his temples his thought ran to and fro like a fever. No, they would never come to fetch him. . . . It was a punishment for him. Why had not he gone to look for that wounded man last night? . . . Yet he had called the whole night through. It was to punish him: he too would be left, abandoned, to die. . . .

He still kept thinking of that poor man who had cried out the whole night through, in the black desert. That was an obsession. . . . In his delirium he said to himself, "If I can manage not to think of him any more, I am saved. . . . It is he that is keeping me from being healed. . . . I mustn't . . . ."

And he kept on repeating to himself: "I will . . . I will . . ." but in a voice with no strength in it, like a child in tears whose grief is about to send it to sleep.

In the gloom tragic voices were awakening. He heard a German who was imploring with a thick accent: "This way . . . French wounded. . . . Come, Frenchmen."

Then suddenly it was a dreadful laugh, a crazy laugh that made the night shudder.

"Hi, boys!" another was shouting, . . . "I'll never be a soldier any more. . . . Come and look, boys, I can't be a soldier any more, I've got no legs now. . . ."

The dying men roused up one after another, answered one another. . . . Then the silence fell again, frozen, stony.

Gilbert felt his head grow heavier, his whole body crushed, giving way. Once more he stiffened himself up. Now that it was dark, it was certain that stretcher-bearers must come, or drafts of reinforcements, or someone. . . . He must not sleep, he must take pains not to sleep.

In his darkening brain the two mamans became confused: his own and the one the dying man had called on through a whole night. . . . Which one was his? . . . No, one mustn't think of that any longer. His hands lying flat on the cold soft earth, his face offered to the gracious rain, he looked into the heavy night, where nothing stirred at all. . . .

One must stay like this a long time, as long as necessary, until somebody comes. One must not think of anything any more, must force oneself not to think any more. And so in a strangling voice that frightened itself he began to sing:

En revenant de Montmartre,
De Montmartre à Paris,

J' rencontre un grand prunier qu' était couvert de prunes.
Voilà l' beau temps. . . .

Still was Sulphart before him, uttering his ditty at the top of his voice. Little Broucke was dancing behind him, for he was dead no longer:

Voilà l' beau temps,
Ture-lure-lure,
Voilà l' beau temps
Pourvu que ça dure
Voilà l' beau temps pour les amants.

The rain was falling thicker now, in cold gusts, making a duller sound on the coats of the dead men. . . . All along his cheeks it was gliding in chilly shivering threads that were quenching his fever. . . . Without understanding, in mere delirium, he was still singing, with breaks in his voice:

J' rencontre un grand prunier
Qu' était couvert de prunes.
Je jette mon baton dedans, j'en fais toinber quelque-z-unes.
Voilà l' beau temps. . . .

The night seemed to be setting itself in motion, on its thousand little feet of rain that went trampling. Against the wet tree that held him up, a huddled corpse slipped and fell heavily, clumsily, without coming out of its dreaming. Gilbert was singing no longer now. His exhausted breath was dying away in a murmur drowned by the soft sound of the rain. But his lips seemed still to be moving:

Voilà l' beau temps,
Ture-lure-lure,
. . . l' beau temps, pourvu que ça dure. . . .

The rain was streaming like tears down his cheeks all sunken and fallen away. Then two heavy tears rolled from out his hollowed eyes, the last two. . . .

CHAPTER XVI
THE HERO'S RETURN

IT was Springtime. Behind the long curtains of the hospital she could be divined rose pink and blonde, and the light air dropping from the casement windows was cool and soft as caressing hands.

Never had Sulphart been so happy as during the few months he spent in the City Hospital of Bourg. It was only the first weeks that were painful, and whenever he woke up in the morning the bitter thought clutched at his heart directly.

"Blast! . . . the billiard table!"

His coffee seemed not so good--he found it had a tang--and he read without interest or enjoyment the Lyons papers that the paper-woman brought from ward to ward. He could think of nothing but the "billiard table," and those ten minutes of suffering used to spoil his morning for him, those good hours of idleness when the sun rises in the spirits as well as in the sky. When the first wheeled stretchers on to which they slid the wounded came along, in spite of himself he would pull a wry face, and look quickly the other way. Apprehensively he used to count up how many there remained to be gone through before his turn came, his stomach contracted as his time drew nearer, he hoped vaguely that something or other would happen, that they would perhaps forget him, and when the little carriage would none the less draw up alongside his bed, he would let his impotent anger burst out, just to relieve his feelings. He eyed the porter with a nasty look--a tall fellow with cheeks bristling with stiff hairs.

"Blighters that get through the war carting about the fellows that get smashed up in their place," he would growl. "There are some blokes know how to get indoors when it rains. . . . Houla! Houla! Couldn't you go a bit gentler? No? Do you think you're bringing home your hay? Peasant!"

"You're not pleased to be going for your game," the other would say banteringly, without getting angry.

From the operating ward there could be heard cries, shrill complainings, and now and then hoarse shuddering moans when the pain was too severe. Those who had already had their turn or were not going down to be dressed used to have a thoroughly good time as they lay in their beds.

"That's the little chasseur. . . . Listen to him singing out. . . . A real nice light tenor, I tell you."

When they brought up a patient just operated on, inert and waxen on his carrier, still under chloroform, it was a whole hour's entertainment; everybody would remain sedulously silent to listen to him rambling. The day Sulphart had been operated on, the nuns, although they were accustomed to hear every kind of thing, had been forced to go away for decency's sake. He had shouted out all kinds of horrors, and the boys of the youngest classes of recruits, who had never known a barrack before the war, nor enjoyed the profitable instruction of their seniors in arms, had an opportunity of learning by heart Mother Blaise and le Navet,which he sang through without omitting a single couplet.

Once his operation had been got through, and sure of not having to go back to the front for a long time, Sulphart now alleviated of two sources of torment, felt himself revive, and if only it had not been for the daily ceremony of dressing his wound he would have been completely happy. His hand, still all swathed about in white, with its two amputated fingers gave him a certain amount of discomfort, and he could not talk without tiring, for the surgeons had twice opened up his chest to take out shell splinters, but that classed him amongst the seriously wounded, and over and above the specially favourable treatment it ensured for him--café au lait, jams, beefsteaks--he derived from it also certain moral advantages of which he was very sensible. Everybody had a certain consideration for him, the doctors spoke more gently to him than to the others, the "mandoline" was forthcoming for him at the first time of asking. And never had a nurse halted anywhere near his bed without arranging his pillow for him according to her ideas of his comfort, even if he had taken ever so much pains to settle them otherwise. They said of him, always with a shade of sympathy appearing in their voices:

"That's the one who has had a rib sawed away." And he would bend his head with a pallid smile as if he meant to say "thank you."

In the whole ward he had practically only one serious rival, a poor devil who had had one of his legs cut off, and he was just a trifle jealous when he saw this other gravely wounded case receiving something of the fuss and kindness that used to come to him by right and due. To begin with, the other fellow was an artilleryman, and according to Sulphart, the only soldiers who went through the war were the "rag-pickers," the rest were there for nothing else but just to "keep the score"; and so, when anybody talked to him about the lofty feats of an aviator, an artilleryman, or cavalryman he would say simply: "Up a stick," which signified that he didn't believe a word of all these alleged heroisms. To tease the fellow who had lost his leg, he used to tell the nurses that the gunners were "boys that spent all their days breeding rabbits and running after the girls," and that it was a matter of the most complete notoriety that they couldn't set to work with their guns without firing short and killing three fourths of the poor poilus in the trench.

Like all the wounded men, Sulphart was stuffed with reminiscences of the war that he was very fain to narrate, he had his cheeks, so to say, bulging with them, and they dribbled quite as a matter of course from his lips like the milk out of the mouth of a baby that has sucked too much. Directly he spoke, it was the trenches, barbed wire, sentry-go, macaroni, the barrage, gas, all that nightmare he could never manage to forget.

And yet at the outset he had been strangely reserved. He had read in the newspapers accounts that had made him ashamed: the gallant corporal who all by himself alone exterminated a whole company with his automatic rifle and finished off the rest with bombs; the Zouave who spitted fifty Boches on the point of his bayonet; a boy soldier who brought back from patrol a whole string of prisoners, including one officer that he led along on a leash; the convalescent chasseur-à-pied who ran away from hospital as soon as he heard that the offensive had begun, and had gone to a glorious death with his regiment. . . . When he had read a tale of this kind, he no longer dared to put out one of his own, calculating within himself that his little anecdotes could have but little or no effect in the midst of those feats of arms.

But it was quite impossible for him to remain silent for very long. One day he risked it, and told in his own way, with no attempt at glorification, rather with a touch of mockery, an entirely fabricated story in which he played with modest bravery the exposed part of a volunteer patrol. One night he had left the trench to go and gather a clump of mistletoe he had marked down between the lines, and astride on a branch he had found a big Bavarian equally a collector and connoisseur of mistletoe. He had made him come down, forced him to give him a back to climb into the tree, and then, with his bunch of mistletoe in his hand, he had brought back his Boche to his own trench showing him the way with hearty kicks behind.

His neighbour in the next bed, a little chasseur, hadn't believed a single word, and had nearly died with wrath: but the good sister for whom the tale was meant had laughed over it the whole of the day.

That had decided Sulphart to tell other yarns of the same kind; and soon he was the hero of the whole establishment and civilians came in specially and expressly to hear him.

The hospital staff--the doctors, the nurses, the nuns, the chaplain, the ladies who came in at eleven o'clock all out of breath, and quickly donned their white blouses to serve the wounded men their luncheon--each and all had heard so many soldiers' tales that no stories of the war were capable of surprising them any more, but with Sulphart it was a complete change and novelty of style and fashion.

In his mouth the war became a sort of gigantic, humbugging joke, a marvellous succession of vigils, of patrols, attacks, stunning adventures. Listening to him, the most backward fellow of the auxiliary services would have begged to be allowed to go to the front.

But the other wounded men who were coming back from that front were less credulous listeners, and Sulphart's stories made them ill with fury. As long as the nurses were thronging round the bed, listening in attentive enthralment to the narrator, they dared say nothing--at the most to grin surreptitiously--but the moment the nurses had gone, even the most feeble of them, could be seen to rouse themselves to life again, the most recently operated on coming out of their semi-comatose condition, the convalescents abandoning their macramé lace, and, sitting up in their beds, they would begin to curse and swear at Sulphart with faces convulsed with wrath.

"Was it at the cinema you saw all that played?"

"We'll make you shut your big jaw, you crammer! you and your yarns!"

"One thing certain, he can't have done much of anything up at the front to tell all that stuff about it. . . ."

"That sort of fellow would do anything to suck up to the women just to be better served than the rest of the boys."

The artilleryman was the only one who never got angry over it. Whenever Sulphart had been talking at great length and was squaring himself up against his pillows, his cheeks full of colour and proud of his success, he would merely say to him in a friendly affectionate little way:

"You're looking well. . . . It's a great pleasure to see it. . . . The doctor is looking pleased and satisfied, did you notice? . . . Come, don't you worry, at the next inspection everything will be settled nicely, fifteen days in a convalescent home, and you'll be going back to the firing----"

That sort of promise shut up Sulphart's joy like a knife, and when he was telling his tales, nothing annoyed him more than the perfidious voice of the amputated one repeating softly with the persistency of a parrot:

"Fit! . . . Fit!"

The others, for that matter, never held any ill will to him for long: he used to distribute among them the packets of cigarettes the ladies gave him, and share round the litres of wine he used to have brought up to him by night on the sly. That always ended in making them lenient.

Sulphart remained for more than a month with no news from the regiment; and then one morning a letter from Lemoine told him everything at once: Gilbert's death, and that Bouffioux was dead too, Vieublé severely wounded, Ricordeau missing . . . a regular massacre.

His sorrow was far from dumb. He re-read the letter twice with exclamations of grief and despair. All day long he talked of nothing but Gilbert, his generosity, his intelligence, the hard fighting they had been through together, and the good life they lived when the regiment was resting, and he diluted his distress with wordy gossiping, repeating to all and sundry that he had lost his best pal, nothing short of a brother to him, and then when night had come, and his agitation had calmed down, lying the only one left awake in the ward with its white beds, he had dreamed to himself and then only did he really feel that his friend was dead.

With a strange clearness and preciseness he had recalled Gilbert, the day of his arrival at the front, and their first sleeping in the cramped stable where the squad was crowded together. With his eyes fixed on the bare ceiling, upon which the night-lights threw their melancholy shadows of their screens, he saw once again all the comrades in the exact positions they occupied that night, this one all curled up under his blanket, and that one stiff and straight, with his socks full of holes sticking out from his sleeping place. They were all born again in his memory, their faces all cleared up with their precise features, their aspect, their voices, little details of uniform that he had fancied forgotten. And resuscitating one after another, he fancied they all seemed to rise up for one last roll-call: Bréval, Vairon, Fouillard, Noury, Bouffioux, Broucke, Demachy, . . . And their own voices made answer: "Dead, dead, dead. . . ."

Sulphart took his first outings in the little garden belonging to the hospital, in which the handsome trees let the sunlight come sifting delicately through. Sitting on a bench he used to watch the comrades playing at bowls, giving them advice they had not asked for, or else he chatted with the young women who used to go there to do sewing.

Then he was given leave to go out into the town, and now he was leading the life of a gentleman of restricted but independent means. Taking his constitutional as far as the railway station, through the Avenue d'Alsace-Lorraine, loafing along the shop-windows, going to look at the communiques to see whether there was any mention of the sectors in which he had fought, taking an apéritif when any one offered him one, and going back to hospital only just for meals.

They found a change in him. He was less noisy, not so gay now. At times one of the nurses, a lady belonging to the town, robust and cheery, who was a great favourite with the wounded men, would question him.

"Things aren't very bright, my boy? . . . Are you in trouble?"

But he would reply quickly:

"Oh, no, Madame. . . . There's nothing to complain about."

He confided his cares to no one. Posing as a breaker of hearts in all the little bars, the gay lad who was a regular "chicken trainer," he could not very well confess that it was on his wife's account that he was so often melancholy. She now wrote to him only at long intervals, and then letters ten lines long in which she said very politely: "I hope you are going on well," but without troubling over much. Never had she asked whether he was expecting to come home soon, nor for how long. She had

164

indeed gone so far as to write that she was no longer in the same workrooms, but without informing him where she was working since, and to all the questions he put to her, she never made any answer at all. He was seen sweating over long, long letters in which he piled up reproaches and outpourings of affection all mixed up together, but she never so much as referred to them in her reply.

And then he would think as he suddenly clutched his fists:

"Just let me once get there convalescent! . . . Won't I give her what for!"

But on reflection his anger never held out.

"If I start playing the husband and she lets me down with a thud," he calculated, "it will still be me that'll be in trouble."

Ever since he was healed, the thought of his medical inspection was also troubling him. Suppose they were going to keep him on active service, to send him back to the front? He followed with breathless interest the discussions of the discharge boards and the leave committee. Interminably he used to question those who had just been through; he followed with anxiety the barometer of the boards, to-day lenient, to-morrow severe, and was intriguing with the secretaries. Already he knew the names of all the doctors, knew their fads, their preferences, and he had a very decided opinion on every one, finding them clever or the reverse in accordance with whether they gave discharges more or less rapidly.

He was beginning to cough again, and putting some constraint on himself, he refused to eat as much as his appetite prompted, and learned to walk round-backed and leaning heavily on a stick. The artilleryman even accused him of smoking sulphur on inspection mornings, to make his lungs wheeze.

When he was out on his walks he recovered his voice to talk loudly and confidently.

"They'll never have me. . . . A fellow chipped about like me can't be sent back to the slaughter. . . . They'll have to drag me along by the feet first."

The artilleryman who was following them on his crutches would growl in his back.

"He's punctured! . . . I was sure he would."

"I've done my fair share," Sulphart would retort. "Now I'm fed up. . . . Anybody that feels on for it, it's not me that's going to take his place."

The day he went before his board, his comrades were having a bite in a little café whose proprietress was famous for her frying. He arrived transfigured without his stick, his cheeks rosy.

"Discharged, category one," he shouted. . . . "With a pension, boys. . . . Hurrah for the end of my service."

The artilleryman held out a letter to him.

"Here," he said, "here's a screed that's come for you. . . ."

It was from his concierge: it told him that his wife had gone off with a Belgian, taking all the furniture with her.

The others noticed nothing: not even his dreadful pallor. He stood two bottles, he ragged and chaffed with them, and glass in hand, sang Le Rêve Passe. Only, as he went out--perhaps a touch of chill--he began to spit blood.

. . . . .

"Yes, Madame Quignon, I tell you she's a filthy bitch, that woman is."

"Bah!" replied the concierge, stirring away at her ragout, "it's always not till they've left you that you men discover that kind of thing."

Vexed, Sulphart had climbed once more up to his home, where his wife had left nothing but a bedstead, a cane bottomed chair, and a handsome calendar that had been a wedding present to them. For a whole week since he had come back he had been idly kicking his heels about Rouen with nothing to do. Going to see old friends of his family life, killing time in wine shops, waiting for comrades at the door of the factory, and everywhere and at all times he spoke of nothing but his wife, even to those who had never known her.

"To clear out with all the sticks, the trollop! . . . And not as much as a letter, nothing. . . ."

By dint of everlastingly repeating the same old story he had very speedily tired everybody out. The women, for the most part, took sides against him, saying that Mathilde couldn't very well be expected to remain alone always and bore herself with her own company, that "that" had been going on a great deal too long now, and that the men would perhaps have done much worse if they had been in the same boat as the women.

Sulphart was turning sour. He had had nothing but disappointments since his arrival. In the barracks, where he looked to recover his civilian effects that he had left there on the second of August, 1914, the sergeant-major had simply shrugged his shoulders: "His duds? they were far enough. . . ." They had, as a matter of fact, made up bundles of clothes, carefully labelled and packed away in well-ordered piles according to regulations, but unhappily some fellows had left a bit of cheese in a pocket, others a sandwich or the butt end of a sausage, all had gone rotten, the rats and vermin had got into them, and it had been necessary to burn the lot. . . .

It was an association that was obliged to fit him out with clothes, and for footgear they left him by way of keepsake his old laced-up-trench boots, all hardened and stiff with mud. In his workshop he had not found his job again, as the proprietor had sub-let it to a munition facotry, and at the railway they had found him not strong enough. Besides, in any case, he was looking for work with no great wish to find it, leaving it to chance to feed him when he should have eaten his last francs, and too much used now to find his stew ready at the kitchen cart to take any other view than that grub was the inalienable right of men even as the light of the sun. Everything appeared to him to be going crooked, and he used to say:

"If there had been anything like the mess and dirty tricks at the front like what there is in the rear, the Boches would have been in Bordeaux since pay-day."

When he was going home at night--often with a glass too much inside him--he used to stop with his concierge, and before going up into his bare room, he would relieve himself of all the rage and fury he had in his heart and only half concealed. This unjust stroke of ill fate-his wife's running away--raised about him four prison walls against which he beat and bruised his head.

"No, after I've been through . . . it's a bit too much. . . . We've really had some bad times and suffering, us fellows, Madame Quignon. . . . Look here, at Craonne, just fancy. . . ."

But the concierge straightway threw up her arms, as though to beg for mercy.

"Ah! Monsieur Sulphart," she implored, "don't go on telling me any more of these tales about trenches; we've had our ears burst in with them."

Discouraged, he went up to go to bed. He had stuck a bayonet in the floor, at the head of his bed, and that served him as a candlestick, just as it had done at the front. Out of a cupboard he brought dusty illustrated papers, old newspapers, and read at them to put himself to sleep. That was how he came upon the forgotten article of a member of the Academy.

"We have contracted a debt of gratitude to our poilus that we shall never forget," said the writer. . . . "We are their debtors for all the sufferings that we have not gone through. . . ."

Sulphart cut out the article and carefully laid it away in his notebook.

. . . . . .

He reached Paris with only seven francs in his pocket, but the very same morning he was engaged to start work next day in a firm at Lévallois. For the first time since he had resumed civilian attire he felt himself happy. Fifteen francs a day! He kept reckoning up all the comfort, all the ease, all the happiness he was going to have for his fifteen francs a day.

It was his turn now to take life easy. He would make a few good pals--boys who had been to the front like himself--he would ferret out a little wine-shop handy to eat his midday meal in; he would find a room not too far away, so that he would be able to rise late in the mornings. Already as he went through the workrooms, he had noticed the girls, and one especially who was laughing as she pushed back her hair with a work-blackened hand. It made him smile to think of her.

"They're a nice steady kind, these chickens are. . . . They know how to look after a house."

He was following his little dream, with heedless eyes, when a motor-car full of ultra smart women and smart uniforms all but knocked him over. With a sharp leap backwards he dodged the bonnet.

"Slacker!" shouted the man who held the steering wheel.

Sulphart made a movement, as though to fling himself on him, but he contented himself with showing his fist to the car, shouting curses from which only the passers-by could have any benefit.

The insult he had received weighed upon his heart all through his luncheon, and to wash it down he had three separate goes of old brandy with his coffee. Bucked up by this he then went for a turn on the boulevards. At the door of a newspaper office where the communiqué was posted up there were people discussing it.

"They ought to make a big offensive," said a fat gentleman with round staring eyes, in a short curt voice.

"With your beef," shouted Sulphart into his face. All these civilians who had the impertinence to speak about the war drove him beside himself with rage, but he had no less detestation for those who never mentioned it at all, and whom he charged with egoism.

As he went loafing along the shops he caught sight in a tobacconist's window of a superb picture all in colours which brought him to a standstill in wonder and delight. Formed of a dozen post-cards arranged together, this masterpiece represented a woman of giant stature in a silver cuirass, holding a palm in one hand and a torch in the other, and seeming to be leading a farandole in which could be recognized soldiers in grey, soldiers in green, soldiers in khaki. The French soldier, he fancied, resembled him like a brother, and that flattered him infinitely. He went inside and asked the woman behind the counter:

"How much is your thingummy?"

"Three francs," said the proprietress drily.

Sulphart pulled a face as he remembered that he had no more than thirty-eight sous left.

"I would like just one single one out of the bottom," he persisted. "Where there is a poilu that looks like me."

The shopkeeper shrugged her shoulders.

"We can't chop it about," she replied still in the same dry fashion.

Sulphart felt he was going very red. And striking the counter a furious blow with his mutilated hand, he growled:

"And my hand, haven't I chopped it about for you? Haven't I?"

The shopkeeper simply blinked her eyes, as if those outcries hurt her, but without raising her head, and she continued to weigh out snuff.

"At all events," said Sulphart addressing himself to a gentleman who was choosing cigars, "any body who has come back from the front would know how sick that makes me."

The customer made a vague sign with his head, turned and took a light, with big slow puffs. The drinkers at the side were staring into the bottom of their glasses, and the waiter had opened a newspaper so as to hear nothing. Sulphart, having eyed them all, understood and shrugged his shoulders, resigned already.

"That's all right," he said, tossing thirty sous on the counter. "Here, give me a packet of English cigarettes; it's a long time now that I've been smoking nothing but rough stuff."

That afternoon, having hesitated a long time, passed and repassed in front of the door without daring to enter, he paid a visit to Demachy's parents. The luxury of their flat made a deep impression on him, the mother's grief and distress tore at his heart, and he felt embarrassed, afraid to seem ill-bred by shuffling his feet or talking too loud. As he went away the mother kissed him and gave him a hundred francs. Sulphart felt his tears at the point of flowing, and could not even say "Thank you," and hurried away. The concierge alone saw him weep.

"He was my pal, Gilbert," he said to her. "A brave lad. . . ."

With pockets full, he went off to Lévallois to pay his "say when" to the boys of the works. In the warm atmosphere of the café--the smoke, the cordial friendly voices, the chinking glasses--he felt his grief dissolve away.

Lying well back and all relaxed on the seat covered with moleskin, he drank his apéritif in little sips as he watched the light puffs of blue smoke waft away. The other drinkers were talking about the war with the evening papers open in front of them, and that annoyed him. The armies were just now going forward ten kilomètres in a day, while in his time they had to toil and moil for weeks on end to wrench away a few hundred mètres, and cover them with dead men in doing it. When he pronounced the names of his battles, tragic names that had been deemed immortal, nobody knew them now: the egoism of the rear had forgotten them all. And he felt a kind of jealousy over it.

And yet that evening he was happy. The speaker's words came to him through a mist, like a meaningless prattle.

"We've only got to wait," the proprietor was declaring noisily, as he juggled his bottles about on the counter. "Now we're sure to have them. We'll do in their country

168

what they've been doing in ours."

"Oh, do hold your tongue anyhow," protested a workman who was gambling his day's pay at zanzibar. "What's wanted is peace. It's disgraceful to keep this filthy business going on."

Astride of a chair, with a completely used-up look, livid cheeks, and crimson ears, a drinker, pretty well full, was mumbling his considered opinion.

"Peace or no peace, it's too late now, it's a defeat. There's nothing to be done, I tell you, the game is played out. For us it's a defeat."

Sulphart raised his head and stared purposefully at the one who talked in that way.

"For my part," said he, "I say and I maintain that it is a victory."

The drinker looked at him and shrugged his shoulders.

"Why so, why is it a victory?"

Disconcerted, Sulphart cast about for a moment, not finding immediately the words he needed to express his saturnine happiness. Then without even understanding the terrible grandeur of his declaration and avowal, he replied crudely:

"I call it a victory, because I have come out of it with my life."

CHAPTER XVII
AND NOW IT IS OVER

AND now it's over.

There is the white sheet on the table, and the quiet steady lamp, and the books. . . . Could one ever have believed one would see them again, when one was out there, so far from one's lost penates?

One used to speak of one's life as of something dead and gone; the certainty of never returning drove between us and it like a sea without a shore, and even hope itself seemed to shrink and be dwarfed, limiting its whole desire to living until the relief was due. There were too many shells, too many dead, too many crosses; sooner or later our turn was bound to come.

And yet it's all over now.

Life will take up its smooth course once more. The cruel memories that torment us still will be assuaged, will be healed; we shall forget, and mayhap the time will come when confounding the war and our past and vanished youth, we shall breathe a sigh of regret when we think of those years.

I recall one of our noisy evenings in the mill without sails. I said to the lads: "A day will come when we will all run across one another, when we will talk about our pals, about the trenches, about our hardships and our sprees. . . . And we will say with a smile: 'Those were the days!'"

How you shouted at me that night, my comrades. I even half felt indeed that it was not over true, when I spoke to you in this way. And yet . . . and yet. . . .

It is most true, we will forget. Oh! I know perfectly it is hateful, it is cruel, but why be indignant and rebel? It is human. . . . Yes, there will be happiness, there will be joy without you, for even as those transparent pools whose limpid water sleeps over a bed of slime, man's heart filters out its memories and keeps none but those of the good days. Griefs, hates, everlasting regrets, all these are too heavy, they fall to the bottom. . . .

We shall forget. The veils of mourning will fall, even as the dead leaves fall. The image of the soldier who is disappeared for ever will slowly fade in the consoled hearts of those he loved so much. And all the dead men will die for the second time.

No, your martyrdom is not over, my comrades, and iron will deal you another wound on the day when the peasant's spade will break into your graves.

The houses will spring up again, reborn under their red roofs, the ruins will become towns once more, and the trenches will be fields again; the soldiers full of victory and weariness will go back to their own homes. But you . . . you will never go home.

Those were the good days. . . .

I think of your myriads of wooden crosses, lined up all along the dusty highways where they seem to watch over the relief of the living, that will never come tp bring the dead to life. Crosses of 1914, adorned with children's flags, that looked like ships dressed for a festival; crosses crowned with képis; crosses helmeted, crosses of the Argonne forests that were wreathed in leafy green; crosses of Artois whose upright rigid army followed on the heels of ours, progressing with us from trench to trench; crosses that the swollen Aisne swept away, far away from the guns, and you, brotherly, kindly crosses of the rear, that gave yourselves, nestling in the undergrowth, the air of verdant bowers, to reassure the men starting for the front. How many are there still standing, of all the crosses that I have planted?

O my dead, my dear dead, my poor dead, it is now that you are to suffer, with no crosses to watch over you, no hearts in which you can nestle down. I think I see you wandering forlornly with groping gestures, seeking in the everlasting night all those ungrateful living folk that are forgetting you already.

On evenings such as this when, weary with all I have written, I let my head fall into my two hands, I feel you all beside me, my comrades. You have all risen up from out of the insecure tenancy of your graves, and you are round about me, and in a strange confusion, I can no longer distinguish between those whom in the flesh and blood and bone I knew out there, and those I have created to be the humble heroes of a book. These have taken up the sufferings of those, as though to ease and relieve them, they have taken on their face, their voice, and they are so much alike, with their mingled pains and woes that my memories stray, and now and then I strive in my disconsolate heart to recognize a missing comrade whom a shadow in his very semblance has hidden from me.

You are so young, so confident, so strong, my comrades: ah, no! you should not have died. . . . Such a power of life and joy was in you that it was lord over the blackest trials. In the mud of the relief, under the overwhelming crushing toil of fatigue, in the face of Death himself I have heard your laughter, never seen your tears. Was it your soul, poor lads, that divine bright nonsense that made you ever strong and stronger?

To tell of your long ordeal I have been fain to laugh, to laugh with your own laughter. All alone, in silent dreaming, I have hoisted pack on back again, and with no companion for the way, I have followed, adream, your regiment of ghosts. Will you recognize our villages, our trenches, the communication ditches we dug together, the crosses we planted? Will you recognize your own gaiety, my comrades?

Those were the good days. . . . Aye, in spite of all, those were the good days, since they saw you in your life. . . . It was a good laughter when we were resting between two murderous marches; it was a good laughter for a find of a handful of straw, or a hot meal; it was a good laughter for one night's respite; good laughter for a dug-out that was deep and solid, a winged piece of fun, a stave of a song. . . . A comrade the less, that was quickly forgotten, and we laughed all the same; and yet their memory is etched deeper and deeper with time, like an acid that goes on biting. . . .

And now, when I have come to the last halt, there steals upon me a feeling of remorse that I should have dared to laugh over your hardships, as if I had carved a penny whistle out of the wood of your crosses.

171